The Devil's Queen

A NOVEL OF CATHERINE DE MEDICI

JEANNE KALOGRIDIS

St. Martin's Press
New York

This is a work of fiction. All of the characters, organizations, and events portrayed in this novel are either products of the author's imagination or are used fictitiously.

Printed in the United States of America. For information, address St. Martin's Press, 175 Fifth Avenue, New York, N.Y. 10010.

www.stmartins.com

Library of Congress Cataloging-in-Publication Data

Kalogridis, Jeanne.

The devil's queen: a novel of Catherine de Medici / Jeanne Kalogridis.—1st ed.

p. cm.

ISBN-13: 978-0-312-36843-2

ISBN-10: 0-312-36843-7

1. Catherine de Medicis, Queen, consort of Henry II, King of France, 1519–1589—Fiction. 2. Courts and courtiers—Fiction. 3. France—History—Francis II, 1559–1560—Fiction. I. Title.

PS3561.A41675D48 2009

813'.54—dc22 2008046318

First Edition: July 2009

10 9 8 7 6 5 4 3 2 1

For Russell Galen

ACKNOWLEDGMENTS

My thanks go to the following hardy souls:
My amazing agents, Russell Galen and Danny Baror
My wise and patient editors, Charles Spicer of St. Martin's Press and Emma Coode of HarperCollins UK
My friend, reader, and editor extraordinaire, Sherry Gottlieb
My best friend for life, Helen King Knight
Tom Jacobs, evolutionary astrologer
Christopher Warnock, Renaissance astrologer
Nina Toumanoff, who helped me rediscover the joy of writing

Those who are interested in learning more about my books and writing process can visit my web site, www.jeannekalogridis.com or my blog, www.historyisabitch.com.

PART I

Blois, France

August 1556

Prologue

At first glance he was an unremarkable man, short and stout with graying hair and the drab clothes of a commoner. I could not see his face from my vantage two floors above, but I watched him recoil as he emerged from the carriage and his foot first met the cobblestone; he signaled for his cane and reached for the coachman's arm. Even with these aids, he moved gingerly, haltingly through the sultry morning, and I thought, aghast, *He is a sick, aging man—nothing more.*

Behind him, clouds had gathered early over the river, promising an afternoon storm, but for now the sun was not entirely occluded. Its rays slipped through gaps and reflected blindingly off the waters of the Loire.

I receded from the window to settle in my chair. I had wanted to dazzle my summoned guest, to charm him so he would not detect my nervousness, but I had no heart in those days for pretense. I sported mourning, black and plain, and looked anything but grand. I was a thick, unlovely creature, very worn and very sad.

Thank God they are only children, the midwife had muttered.

She had thought I was sleeping. But I had heard, and understood: A queen's life was valued more than those of her daughters. And they had left behind siblings; the royal bloodline was safe. But had I not been drained of blood and hope, I would have slapped her. My heart was no less broken.

I had approached my final attempt at childbirth without trepidation; the process had always gone smoothly for me. I am strong and determined and have never feared pain. I had even chosen names—Victoire and Jeanne—for Ruggieri had predicted I would have girl twins. But he had not told me they would die.

The first infant was long in coming, so long that I and even the midwife grew anxious. I became too tired to sit in the birthing chair.

After a day and half a night, Victoire arrived. She was the smallest infant I had ever seen, too weak to let go a proper wail. Her birth brought me no respite; Jeanne refused to appear. Hours of agony passed, until night became day again, and morning led to afternoon. The child's body was so stubbornly situated that she would not pass; the decision was made to break her legs so that she could be pulled out without killing me.

There followed the midwife's hand inside me and the dreadful muffled snap of tiny bones. I cried out at the sound, not at the pain. When Jeanne emerged dead, I would not look at her.

Her sickly twin lived three weeks. On the day Victoire, too, succumbed, a cold, prickling conviction settled over me: After all these years, Ruggieri's spell was failing; my husband and surviving children were in mortal danger.

There was, as well, the quatrain in the great tome written by the prophet, the quatrain I feared predicted my darling Henri's fate. I am dogged in the pursuit of answers, and I would not rest until I had learned the truth from the lips of the famed seer himself.

A knock came at the door, and the guard's low voice, both of which drew me back to the present. At my reply, the door swung open and the guard and his limping charge entered. The former's expression grew quizzical at finding me entirely alone, without my ladies to attend me; I had busied Diane elsewhere, and had dismissed even Madame Gondi. My conversation with my visitor was to be strictly private.

"Madame la Reine." The seer's accent betrayed his southern origins. He had a soft moon of a face and the gentlest of eyes. "Your Majesty."

Madame Gondi said that he had been born a Jew, but I saw no evidence of it in his features. Unsteady even with his cane, he nonetheless managed to doff his cap and execute a passable genuflection. His hair, long and tangled and thinning at the crown, hung forward to obscure his face.

"I am honored and humbled that you would receive me," he said. "My greatest desire is to be of service to you and to His Majesty in whatever manner most pleases you. Ask for my life, and it is yours." His voice shook, and the hand that gripped the cap trembled. "If there is any question of impropriety, of heresy, I can only say that I am a good Catholic who has endeavored all my life to serve God. At his bidding, I wrote down the visions. They are sent by Him alone, and not some unclean spirit."

I had heard that he had often been accused of consorting with devils, and had moved from village to village over the past several years to avoid arrest. Frail, vulnerable, he regarded me with hesitation. He had read my letter, yet he had no doubt heard of my husband the King's hatred for the occult and for Protestants; perhaps he feared that he was walking into an inquisitional trap.

I hurried to put him at ease.

"I have no doubt of that, Monsieur de Nostredame," I said warmly, smiling, and extended my hand. "That is why I have asked for your help. Thank you for traveling such a distance, in your discomfort, to see us. We are deeply grateful."

His body shuddered as fear unclenched it. He tottered forward and kissed my hand; his hair fell soft against my knuckles. His breath smelled of garlic.

I looked up at the guard. "That will be all," I said, and when he lifted a brow—why would I be so eager to forsake propriety by dismissing him?—I subtly hardened my gaze until he nodded, bowed, and departed.

I was alone with the unlikely prophet.

Monsieur de Nostredame straightened and stepped back. As he did, his gaze fell upon the window, and the scene beyond; his nervousness vanished, replaced by a calm intensity.

"Ah," he said, as if to himself. "The children."

I turned to see Edouard running after Margot and little Navarre on the grassy swath of courtyard, altogether ignoring the cries of the governess to slow down.

"His Highness Prince Edouard," I said by way of explanation, "likes to chase his little sister." At five, Edouard was already unusually tall for his age.

"The two younger ones—the little boy and girl—they appear to be twins, but I know that is not the case."

"They are my daughter Margot and her cousin Henri of Navarre. Little Henri, we call him, or sometimes Navarre, so as not to confuse him with the King."

"The resemblance is remarkable," he murmured.

"They are both three years old, Monsieur; Margot was born on the thirteenth of May, Navarre on the thirteenth of December."

"Tied by fate," he said, thoughtlessly, then glanced back at me.

His eyes were too large for his face, like mine, but a clear, light grey. They possessed a child's openness, and beneath their scrutiny, I felt uncharacteristic discomfort.

"I had a son," he said wistfully, "and a daughter."

I opened my mouth to offer sympathy and say I had already heard of this. The most talented physician in all France, he had earned fame by saving many sick with plague—only to watch helplessly as his children and wife died of it.

But I had no chance to speak, for he continued. "I do not wish to seem an ogre, Madame, mentioning my own sorrow with you here dressed in mourning; I do so only to explain that I understand the nature of your grief. I recently learned that you mourn the loss of two little girls. There is no greater tragedy than the death of a child. I pray that God will ease your grief, and the King's."

"Thank you, Monsieur de Nostredame." I changed the subject quickly, for his sympathy was so genuine, I feared I might cry if he said more. "Please." I gestured at the chair set across from mine, and the footstool that had been placed there expressly for him. "You have suffered enough on my behalf already. Sit down, and I will tell you when the children were born."

"You are too gracious, Your Majesty."

He eased himself into the chair and settled his affected foot onto the little stool with a faint groan. He propped the cane next to him so that it remained within reach.

"Do you require paper and pen, Monsieur?"

He tapped his brow with a finger. "No, I shall remember. Let us start with the eldest, then. The Dauphin, born the nineteenth of January, in the year 1544. To cast a proper chart, I need—"

"The hour and place," I interrupted. Having a talent for calculation, I had already taught myself to cast charts, though I did not entirely trust my own interpretations—and I all too often hoped they were wrong. "No mother could ever forget such a thing, of course. François was born at the Château at Fontainebleau, a few minutes after four o'clock in the afternoon."

"A few minutes after . . . ," he echoed, and the finger that had thumped his brow began instead to massage it, as if he were pressing the fact into his memory. "Do you know how many minutes? Three, perhaps, or ten?"

I frowned, trying to remember. "Fewer than ten. Unfortunately, I was exhausted at the time; I cannot be more precise."

We did not speak of the girls, Elisabeth and Margot; under Salic law, a woman could not ascend the throne of France. For now, it was time to focus on the heirs—on Charles-Maximilien, born the twenty-seventh of June at Saint-Germain-en-Laye, in the year 1550, and on my darling Edouard-Alexandre. He was born the year after Charles, on the nineteenth of September, twenty minutes past midnight.

"Thank you, *Madame la Reine,*" Nostredame said, when I had finished. "I will give you my full report within two days. I have already done some preparations, since the dates of the boys' births are widely known."

He did not move to rise, as would be expected. He sat gazing on me with those clear, calm eyes, and in the silence that followed, I found my courage and my voice.

"I have evil dreams," I said.

He seemed not at all surprised by this strange outburst.

"May I speak candidly, Madame?" he asked politely. Before I could answer, he continued, "You have astrologers. I am not the first to chart the children's nativities. I will construct them, surely, but you did not call me here to do only that."

"No," I admitted. "I have read your book of prophecy." I cleared my throat and recited the thirty-fifth quatrain, the one that had brought me to my knees when I first read it:

The young lion will overcome the old, in
A field of combat in a single fight. He will
Pierce his eyes in a golden cage, two
Wounds in one, he then dies a cruel death.

"I write down what I must." Monsieur de Nostredame's gaze had grown guarded. "I do not presume to understand its meaning."

"But I do." I leaned forward, no longer able to hide my agitation. "My husband the King—he is the lion. The older one. I dreamt . . ." I faltered, unwilling to put into words the horrifying vision in my head.

"Madame," he said gently. "You and I understand each other well, I think—better than the rest of the world understands us. You and I see things others do not. Too much for our comfort."

I turned my face from him and stared out the window at the garden, where Edouard and Margot and little Navarre chased one another round green hedges beneath a bright sun. In my mind's eye, skulls were split and bodies pierced; men thrashed, drowning, in a swelling tide of blood.

"I don't want to see anymore," I said.

I don't know how he knew. Perhaps he read it in my face, the way a sorcerer reads the lines of a palm; perhaps he had already consulted my natal stars, and read it in my ill-placed Mars. Perhaps he read it in my eyes, in the flash of knowing fear there when I uttered the thirty-fifth quatrain.

"The King will die," I told him. "My Henri will die too young, a terrible death, unless something is done to stop it. You know this; you have written of it, in this poem. Tell me that I am right, Monsieur, and that you will help me to do whatever is necessary to prevent it. My husband is my life, my soul. If he dies, I will not want to live."

I believed, those many years ago, that my dream had to do only with Henri. I had thought that his violent end would be the worst that could possibly happen to me, to his heirs, to France.

It is easy now to see how wrong I was. And foolish, to have been angered by the prophet's calm words.

I write what God bids me, Madame la Reine. His will must be accomplished; I do not presume to understand its meaning.

If God has sent you these visions, you must strive to discover why He has done so. You have the responsibility.

I had a responsibility to keep the King safe, I told him. I had a responsibility to our children.

"Your heart misleads you," he said and shuddered as if gripped by invisible talons. When he spoke again, it was with the voice of another . . . another who was not altogether human.

"These children," he murmured, and I knew then that even the darkest secret could not be hidden from him. I pressed a palm against the bloodied pearl at my heart, as if the act could conceal the truth.

"These children, their stars are marred. Madame la Reine, these children should not be."

PART II

Florence, Italy

May 1527

One

The day I met the magician Cosimo Ruggieri—the eleventh of May—was an evil one.

I sensed it at daybreak, in the drum of hoofbeats on the cobblestone street in front of the house. I had already risen and dressed and was about to make my way downstairs when I heard the commotion. I stood on tiptoe and peered down through my unshuttered bedroom window.

Out on the broad Via Larga, Passerini reined in his lathered mount, accompanied by a dozen men at arms. He wore his red cardinal's robes but had forgotten his hat—or perhaps it had fallen off during the wild ride—and his white hair stood up in wisps like a coxcomb. He shouted frantically for the stablehand to open the gate.

I hurried to the stairs, arriving at the landing at the same moment as my aunt Clarice.

She was a beautiful woman in that year before her untimely death, delicate as one of Botticelli's Graces. That morning found her dressed in a gown of rose velvet and a diaphanous veil over her chestnut hair.

But there was nothing delicate about Aunt Clarice's disposition. My cousin Piero often referred to his mother as "the toughest man in the family." She deferred to no one—least of all to her four sons or to her husband,

Filippo Strozzi, a powerful banker. She had a sharp tongue and a swift hand, and did not hesitate to lash out with either.

And she was scowling that morning. When she caught sight of me, I ducked my head and dropped my gaze, for there was no winning with Aunt Clarice.

At the age of eight, I was an inconvenient child. My mother had died nine days after I was born, followed six days later by my father. Happily, my mother left me enormous wealth, my father, the title of Duchess and the right to rule Florence.

Those things prompted Aunt Clarice to bring me to the Palazzo Medici to groom me for my destiny, but she made it clear that I was a burden. In addition to her own sons, she was obliged to raise two other Medici orphans—my half brother Alessandro and my cousin Ippolito, the bastard of my great-uncle Giuliano de' Medici.

As Clarice stepped alongside me on the landing, a voice drifted up from the downstairs entry: Cardinal Passerini, acting regent of Florence, was speaking to a servant. Though I could not make out his words, the timbre of his voice conveyed their message clearly: disaster. The safe and comfortable life I had shared with my cousins in our ancestors' house was about to disappear.

As Clarice listened, fear rippled over her features, only to be replaced by her customary hardness. She narrowed her eyes at me, searching to see if I had detected her instant of weakness, threatening me in case I had.

"Straight down to the kitchen with you. No stopping, no speaking to anyone," she ordered.

I obeyed and headed downstairs, but soon realized I was too nervous to eat. I wandered instead toward the great hall, where Aunt Clarice and Cardinal Passerini were engaged in strenuous conversation. His Eminence's voice was muffled, but I caught an impassioned word or two uttered by Aunt Clarice:

*You **fool**.*

*What did Clement **expect**, the idiot?*

Their conversation centered on the Pope—born Giulio de' Medici—whose influence helped keep our family in power. Even as a child, I understood enough of politics to know that my distant cousin Pope Clement was at odds with the Holy Roman Emperor Charles, whose troops had invaded Italy; Rome was in especial danger.

Abruptly, the door swung open, and Passerini's head appeared as he called for Leda, Aunt Clarice's slave. The cardinal was grey-faced, his breath coming hard, the corners of his mouth pulled down by agitation. He waited in the doorway with an air of desolate urgency until Leda appeared, at which point he ordered her to bring Uncle Filippo, Ippolito, and Alessandro.

Within moments, Ippolito and Sandro were ushered inside. Clarice must have come to stand near the doorway, for I could hear her say, quite clearly, to someone waiting in the hall:

We need men, as many as will fight. Until we know their number, we must tread carefully. Assemble as many as you can by nightfall, then come to me. A strange hesitancy crept into her tone. *And send Agostino to fetch the astrologer's son*—now.

I heard my uncle Filippo's low assent and departure, then the door closed again. I remained a few minutes, trying vainly to interpret the sounds emanating from the chamber; defeated, I wandered toward the staircase leading to the children's rooms.

Six-year-old Roberto, Clarice's youngest, came running in my direction, wailing and wringing his hands. His eyes were squeezed tightly shut; I barely caught him in time to stop him from knocking me down.

I was small, but Roberto was smaller still. He smelled of heat and slightly sour sweat; his cheeks were flushed and tear-streaked, and his girlishly long hair clung to his damp neck.

At that instant the boys' nursemaid appeared behind him. Ginevra was a simple, uneducated woman, dressed in worn cotton skirts covered by a white apron, her hair always wrapped in a scarf. On that morning, however, Ginevra's scarf and nerves were undone; a lock of golden hair had fallen across her face.

Roberto stamped his foot at me and emitted a scream. "Let me *go!*" He struck out with little fists, but I averted my face and held him fast.

"What is it? Why is he frightened?" I called to Ginevra as she neared.

"They're coming after us!" Robert howled, spewing tears and spittle. "They're coming to hurt us!"

Ginevra, dull with fright, answered, "There are men at the gate."

"What sort of men?" I asked.

When Ginevra would not answer, I ran upstairs to the chambermaids' quarters, which overlooked the stables and the gate that opened onto the busy Via Larga. I dragged a stool to the window, stepped onto it, and flung open the shutters.

The stables stood west of the house; to the north lay the massive iron gate that kept out trespassers. It was closed and bolted; just inside it stood three of our armed guards.

On the other side of its spiked bars, the street hosted lively traffic: a flock of Dominican monks on foot from nearby San Marco, a cardinal in his gilded carriage, merchants on horseback. And Roberto's men—perhaps twenty in those early hours, before Passerini's news had permeated Florence. Some stood along the edges of the Via Larga, others in front of the iron gate near the stables. They gazed on our house with hawkeyed intensity, waiting for prey to emerge.

One of them shouted exuberantly at the passing crowd. "Did you hear? The Pope has fallen! Rome lies in the Emperor's hands!"

At the palazzo's front entrance, a banner bore the Medici coat of arms so proudly displayed throughout the city: six red balls, six *palle,* arranged in rows upon a golden shield. *Palle, palle!* was our rallying cry, the words on our supporters' lips as they raised their swords in our defense.

As I watched, a wool dyer, his hands and tattered tunic stained dark blue, climbed onto his fellow's shoulders and pulled down the banner to shouts of approval. A third man touched a torch to the banner and set it ablaze. Passersby slowed and gawked.

"Abaso le palle!" the wool dyer cried, and those surrounding him picked up the chant. "Down with the balls! Death to the Medici!"

In the midst of the tumult, the iron gates opened a crack, and Agostino—Aunt Clarice's errand boy—slipped out unobserved. But as the gate clanged shut behind him, a few of the men hurled pebbles at him. He shielded his head and dashed away, disappearing into the traffic.

I leaned farther out of the open window. Behind the thin streams of smoke rising from the burning banner, the wool dyer spied me; his face lit up with hatred. Had he been able to reach up into the window, he would have seized me—an eight-year-old girl, an innocent—and dashed my brains against the pavement.

"Abaso le palle!" he roared. At me.

I withdrew. I could not run to Clarice for comfort—she would not have provided it even had she been available. I wanted my cousin Piero; nothing cowed him, not even his formidable mother . . . and he was the one person I trusted. Since he was not in the boys' classroom receiving his lessons, I hurried to the library.

As I suspected, Piero was there. Like me, he was an insatiable student, often demanding more of his tutors than they knew, with the result that we frequently encountered each other huddled behind book. Unlike me, he was, at a rather immature sixteen, still cherub-cheeked, with close-cropped ringlets and a sweet, ingenuous temperament. I trusted him more than anyone, and adored him as a brother.

Piero sat cross-legged on the floor, squinting down at the heavy tome open in his lap, utterly captivated and utterly calm. He glanced up at me, and just as quickly returned to his reading.

"I told you this morning about Passerini coming," I said. "The news is very bad. Pope Clement has fallen."

Piero sighed calmly and told me the story of Clement's predicament, which he had learned from the cook. In Rome, a secret passageway leads from the Vatican to the fortress known as the Castel Sant'Angelo. Emperor Charles's mutinous soldiers had joined with anti-Medici fighters and attacked the Papal Palace. Caught unawares, Pope Clement had run for his life—robes flapping like the wings of a startled dove—across the passage to the fortress. There he remained, trapped in his stronghold by jeering troops.

Piero was totally unfazed by it all.

"We've always had enemies," he said. "They want to form their own government. The Pope has always known about them, but Mother says he grew careless and missed clear signs of trouble. She warned him, but Clement didn't listen."

"But what will happen to *us*?" I said, annoyed that my voice shook. "Piero, there are men outside burning our banner! They're calling for our deaths!"

"Cat," he said softly and reached for my hand. I let him draw me down to sit beside him on the cool marble.

"We always knew the rebels would try to take advantage of something like this," Piero said soothingly, "but they aren't that organized. It will take them a few days to react. By then, we'll have gone to one of the country villas, and Mother and Passerini will have decided what to do."

I pulled away from him. "How will we get to the country? The crowd won't even let us out of the house!"

"Cat," he chided gently, "they're just troublemakers. Come nightfall, they'll get bored and go away."

Before he could say anything further, I asked, "Who is the astrologer's son? Your mother sent Agostino to fetch him."

He digested this with dawning surprise. "That would be Ser Benozzo's eldest, Cosimo."

I shook my head, indicating my ignorance.

"The Ruggieri family has always served as the Medicis' astrologers," Piero explained. "Ser Benozzo advised Lorenzo *il Magnifico.* They say his son Cosimo is a prodigy of sorts, and a very powerful magician. Others say such talk is nothing more than a rumor circulated by Ser Benozzo to help the family business."

I interrupted. "But Aunt Clarice doesn't put a lot of faith in such things."

"No," he said thoughtfully. "Cosimo wrote Mother a letter well over a week ago. He offered his services; he said that serious trouble was coming, and that she would need his help."

I was intrigued. "What did she do?"

"You know Mother. She refused to reply, because she felt insulted that such a young man—a boy, she called him—should presume that she would need help from the likes of him."

"Father Domenico says it's the work of the Devil."

Piero clicked his tongue scornfully. "Magic isn't evil—unless you mean for it to hurt someone—and it's not superstition, it's science. It can be used to make medicines, not poisons. Here." He proudly lifted the large volume in his lap so that I could see its cover. "I'm reading Ficino."

"Who?"

"Marsilio Ficino. He was Lorenzo *il Magnifico*'s tutor. Old Cosimo hired him to translate the *Corpus Hermeticum,* an ancient text on magic. Ficino was brilliant, and this is one of his finest works." He pointed at the title: *De Vita Coelitus Comparanda.*

"Gaining Life from the Heavens," he translated. "Ficino was an excellent astrologer, and he understood that magic is a natural power." He grew animated. "Listen to this. . . ." He translated haltingly from the Latin. " 'Using this power of the stars, the Magi were first to worship the infant Christ. Therefore, why fear the name Magus, a name which is pleasing to the Gospel?' "

"So this astrologer's son is coming to bring us help," I said. "Help from God's stars."

"Yes." Piero gave a reassuring nod. "Even if he weren't, we would still be all right. Mother might complain, but we'll just go to the country until it's safe again."

I let myself be convinced—temporarily. On the library floor, I nestled against my cousin and listened to him read in Latin. This continued until Aunt Clarice's slave Leda—pale, frowning, and heavily pregnant—appeared in the doorway.

"There you are." She motioned impatiently. "Come at once, Caterina. Madonna Clarice is waiting."

The horoscopist was a tall, skinny youth of eighteen, if one estimated generously, yet he wore the grey tunic and somber attitude of a city elder. His pitted skin was sickly white, his hair so black it gleamed blue; he brushed it straight back to reveal a sharp widow's peak. His eyes seemed even blacker and held something old and shrewd, something that fascinated and frightened me. He was ugly: His long nose was crooked, his lips uneven, his ears too large. Yet I did not want to look away. I stared, a rude, stupid child.

Aunt Clarice said, "Stand there, Caterina, in the light. No, save your little curtsy and just hold still. Leda, close the door behind you and wait in the hall until I call you. I'll have no interruptions." Her tone was distracted and oddly soft.

After a worried glance at her mistress, Leda stole out and quietly shut the door. I stepped into a pane of sunlight and stood dutifully a few paces from Clarice, who sat beside the cold fireplace. My aunt was arguably the most influential woman in Italy and old enough to be this young man's mother, but his presence—calm and focused as a viper's before the strike—was the more powerful, and even Clarice, long inured to the company of pontiffs and kings, was afraid of him.

"This is the girl," she said. "She is plain, but generally obedient."

"Donna Caterina, it is an honor to meet you," the visitor said. "I am Cosimo Ruggieri, son of Ser Benozzo the astrologer."

His appearance was forbidding, but his voice was beautiful and deep. I could have closed my eyes and listened to it as if it were music.

"Think of me as a physician," Ser Cosimo said. "I wish to conduct a brief examination of your person."

"Will it hurt?" I asked.

Ser Cosimo smiled a bit more broadly, revealing crooked upper teeth.

"Not in the least. I have already completed a portion; I see that you are quite short for your age, and your aunt reports that you are rarely sick. Is that true?"

"Yes," I answered.

"She is always running in the garden," Clarice offered palely. "She rides as well as the boys do. By the time she was four, we could not keep her from the horses."

"May I . . . ?" Ser Cosimo paused delicately. "Could you lift your skirts a bit so that I can examine your legs, Caterina?"

I dropped my gaze, embarrassed and perplexed, but raised the hem of my dress first above my ankles and then—at his gentle urging—to my knee.

Ser Cosimo nodded approvingly. "Very strong legs, just as one would expect."

"And thighs," I said, dropping my skirts. "Jupiter's influence."

Intrigued, he smiled faintly and brought his face closer to mine. "You have studied such things?"

"Only a little," I said. I did not tell him that I had just been listening to Piero reading Ficino's attributions for Jupiter.

Aunt Clarice interrupted, her tone detached. "But her Jupiter is in detriment."

Ser Cosimo kept his penetrating gaze focused on me. "In Libra, in the Third House. But there are ways to strengthen it."

I braved a question. "You know about my stars, then, Ser Cosimo?"

"I have taken an interest in them for some time," he replied. "They present a great many challenges and a great many opportunities. May I ask what moles you have?"

"There are two on my face."

Ser Cosimo lowered himself onto his haunches, bringing us eye to eye. "Show me, Caterina."

I smoothed my dull, mousy hair away from my right cheek. "Here and here." I pointed at my temple, near the hairline, and at a spot between my jaw and ear.

He drew in a sharp breath and turned to Aunt Clarice, his manner grave.

"Is it bad?" she asked.

"Not so bad that we cannot repair it," he said. "I will return tomorrow at this very hour, with talismans and herbs for her protection. You must employ them according to my precise directions."

"For me," Clarice said swiftly, "and for my sons, not just for her."

The astrologer's son cast a sharp glance at her. "Certainly. For everyone who has need." A threat crept into his tone. "But such things bring no benefit unless they are used exactly as prescribed—and exactly for whom they are created."

Clarice dropped her gaze, intimidated—and furious at herself for being so. "Of course, Ser Cosimo."

"Good," he said and bowed his farewell.

"God be with you, Donna Clarice," he said graciously. "And with you, Donna Caterina."

I murmured a good-bye as he walked out the door. It was odd watching a youth move like an elderly man. Many years later, he would confess to having been fifteen years old at the time. He had used the aid of a glamour, he claimed, to make himself appear older, knowing Clarice would never have listened to him otherwise.

As soon as the astrologer was out of earshot, Aunt Clarice said, "I've heard rumors of this one, the eldest boy. Smart, true—smart at conjuring devils and making poisons. I've heard that his father despairs."

"He isn't a good man?" I asked timidly.

"He is evil. A necessary evil, now." She lowered her face into her hand and began to massage her temple. "It's all falling apart. Rome, the papacy,

Florence herself. It's only a matter of time before the news spreads all over the city. And then . . . everything will go to Hell. I need to figure out what to do before . . ." I thought I heard tears, but she gathered herself and snapped open her eyes. "Go to your chambers and study your texts. There will be no lessons today, but you'd best comport yourself quietly. I won't tolerate any distractions."

I left the great hall. Rather than follow my aunt's instructions to go upstairs, I dashed out to the courtyard. The astrologer's son was there, moving swiftly for the gardens.

I cried out, "Ser Cosimo! Wait!"

He stopped and faced me. His expression was knowing and amused, as if he had completely expected to find a breathless eight-year-old girl tearing after him.

"Caterina," he said, with odd familiarity.

"You can't leave," I said. "There are men outside calling for our deaths. Even if you got out safely, you would never be able to come back again."

He bent forward and faced me at my level. "But I *will* get out safely," he said. "And I will come back again tomorrow. When I do, you must find me alone in the courtyard or the garden. There are things we must discuss, unhappy secrets. But not today. The hour is not propitious."

As he spoke, his eyes hardened, as if he was watching a distant but approaching evil. He straightened and said, "But nothing bad will happen. I will see to it. We will speak again tomorrow. God keep you, Caterina."

He turned and strode off.

I hurried after him, but he walked faster than I could run. In seconds he was at the entrance to the stables, in view of the large gate leading to the Via Larga. I hung back, afraid.

The palazzo was a fortress of thick stone; its main entry was an impenetrable brass door positioned in the building's center. To the west lay the gardens and the stables, viewable from the street behind a north-facing iron gate that began where the citadel proper ended.

Just inside that gate were seven armed guards, warily eyeing the crowd on the other side of the thick iron bars. When I had last peered through the upstairs window, only six men had lingered by the western gate. Now more than two dozen peasants and merchants stood staring back at the guards.

A groom handed Ser Cosimo the reins to a glossy black mare. At the sight of the astrologer, a few in the mob hissed. One hurled a stone, which banked off an iron bar and struck the earth several paces from its target.

Ser Cosimo calmly led his mount to the gate. The mare stamped her feet and turned her face from the waiting men as one of them cried out: "*Abaso le palle!* Down with the balls!"

"What," called another, "did they bring you here to suck the cardinal's cock?"

"And his Medici-loving balls! *Abaso le palle!*"

The commotion alerted others who had been standing watch across the street, who hurried to join those at the gate. The chant grew louder.

"Abaso le palle.

Abaso le palle."

Men shook their fists in the air and pushed their hands between the bars to claw at those on the other side. The mare whinnied and showed them the whites of her eyes.

Ser Cosimo's composure never wavered. Serene and unflinching, he walked toward the metal bars amid a hail of pebbles. He was not struck, but our guards were not as fortunate; they yelped curses as they tried to shield their faces. One hurried to the bolt and slid the heavy iron bar back while the others drew their swords and formed a shoulder-to-shoulder barricade in front of Ser Cosimo.

The guard at the bolt glanced over his shoulder at the departing guest. "You're mad, sir," he said. "They'll tear you to pieces."

I broke out from my hiding place and ran to Ser Cosimo.

"Don't hurt him!" I shouted at the crowd. "He's not one of us!"

Ser Cosimo dropped the reins of his nervous mount and knelt down to catch my shoulders.

"Go inside, Catherine," he said. *Catherine,* my name in a foreign tongue. "I know what I am doing. I will be safe."

As he finished speaking, a pebble grazed my shoulder. I flinched; Ser Cosimo saw it strike. And his eyes—

The look of the Devil, I was going to say, but perhaps it is better called the look of God. For the Devil can trick and test, but God alone metes out death, and only He can will a man to suffer for eternity.

That was that look I saw in Cosimo's eye. He was capable, I decided, of undying spite, of murder without the slightest regret. Yet it was not that look that unsettled me. It was the fact that I recognized it and was still drawn to him; it was the fact that I knew it and did not want to look away.

He whirled on the crowd with that infinitely evil look. At once, the rain of stones ceased. When every man had grown silent, he called out, strong and clear:

"I am Cosimo Ruggieri, the astrologer's son. Strike her again, if you dare."

Nothing more was said. Darkly radiant, Ser Cosimo mounted his horse, and the guard pushed open the singing gate. The magician rode out, and the crowd parted for him.

The gate swung shut with a clang, and the guard slid the bolt into place. It was as though a signal had been given: The crowd came alive and again hurled pebbles and curses at the guards.

But the astrologer's son passed unharmed, his head high, his shoulders square and sure. While the rest of the world fixed its unruly attention on the palazzo gates, he rode away, and soon disappeared from my sight.

Two

My memories of Florence are blurred by terror, affection, distance, and time, but some impressions from that long-ago past remain sharp. The peals of church bells, for one: I woke and ate and prayed to the songs of the cathedral of San Lorenzo, which holds my ancestors' bones; of Santa Maria del Fiore, with its vast impossible dome; of San Marco, where the mad monk Savonarola once dwelled. I can still hear the low "mooing" of the bell called the Cow, which hung in the great Palazzo della Signoria, seat of Florence's government.

I remember, too, the rooms of my childhood, especially the family chapel. On the walls above the wooden choir stalls, my ancestors rode on grandly caparisoned horses in Gozzoli's masterpiece, *The Procession of the Magi.* The mural spanned three walls. The eastern one captured my imagination, for it was the wall of the Magus Gaspar, he who led the way after Bethlehem's star. My forefathers rode just behind him, in dazzling shades of crimson, blue, and gold.

The mural had been commissioned in Piero the Gouty's time. He rode just behind Gaspar; my great-great-grandfather was a serious, tight-lipped man in his fifth decade, riding immediately in front of his own father, the aged but still wily Cosimo. His son Lorenzo *il Magnifico* followed them both.

He was only eleven then, a homely boy with a jutting lower lip and wildly crooked nose. Yet there was something beautiful in his upward-slanting eyes, in their clear, focused intelligence that made me yearn to touch his cheek. But he had been painted high upon the wall, beyond my reach. Many times I had climbed onto a choir stall when the chapel was empty, but I could touch only the fresco's lower edge. I had often been told that I possessed Lorenzo's quick wit, and felt a kinship with him. His father had died when he was young, leaving him a city to rule; not long after, his adored brother was assassinated, leaving him truly alone.

But Lorenzo was wise. His child's gaze was sober and steady. And it was fastened not on his father, Piero, or his grandfather Cosimo—but directly on golden-haired Gaspar, the Magus who followed the star.

Young Lorenzo gazed down at me that evening at vespers. Uncle Filippo was absent, but Clarice was there, her tense features softened beneath a gossamer black veil. She murmured prayers with one eye open, her monocular gaze darting behind her, at the open door. She had seemed chastened during her encounter with Ser Cosimo, but the intervening hours had restored her nerve.

To her immediate right was my cousin Ippolito, straight and tall, having recently sprouted a man's broad chest and back. Tanned from hunting, he had grown a goatee and mustache, which enhanced his dark eyes and made him dizzyingly handsome. He was kind to me—we were after all, to be married someday and rule Florence together—but now he was eighteen and had come to notice women. And I was just a homely little girl.

Alessandro, his junior by two years, stood beside him, murmuring prayers with his eyes wide open. My half brother, Sandro, son of an African slave, had thick black brows, full lips, and a taciturn demeanor. No matter how long I studied his heavy, pouting features, I never glimpsed a hint of our common ancestry. Sandro was well aware that he lacked his elder cousin Ippolito's physical beauty and charm. Their relationship had become marked by competitiveness, yet the two were inseparable, bound by their special status.

In the chapel, Ginevra prayed on Clarice's immediate left, flanked by little Roberto, then Leone and Tommaso, then my beloved Piero. Even he, who had earlier been so dismissive of my fears, had grown quiet and pensive as the crowd outside our gates swelled.

I remember little of the actual ritual that evening—just Aunt Clarice's strong alto as we sang the psalms, and the priest's wavering tenor as he led the *Kyrie eleison.*

He had just begun to chant the benediction when Aunt Clarice's head turned sharply. Outside, in the corridor, Uncle Filippo held his cap in his hands.

He was a grim man with sunken cheeks and grey hair cut short in the style of a Roman senator; when he caught Clarice's eye, his expression grew even grimmer. She motioned quickly at Ginevra: *Go, go. Take the children with you.* She inclined her head at Ippolito and Alessandro. *And take them, too.*

The priest's hand sliced horizontally through the air to complete the invisible cross. He, too, had seen the crowds at the gate and departed quickly through the exit near the altar.

Clarice moved aside, allowing Ginevra to herd the cousins toward the door. At the same time, Uncle Filippo advanced into the chapel. Last of the children, I lagged behind.

Sandro followed the others meekly, but Ippolito broke away from the group to face Clarice. "I will stay," he said. "Filippo bears important news, doesn't he?"

Clarice's expression hardened, a sight that made Ginevra redouble her efforts to shoo the children outside. I ducked behind a choir stall, itching to hear Uncle Filippo's news.

"Here now," Filippo said gently as he came to stand beside his wife. "Ippolito, I need a moment alone with her." He waited until Ginevra cleared the other boys out of the chapel. "You'll hear everything in good time."

Ippolito looked sharply from his aunt to his uncle. "*Now* is good time. I've been watching quietly while Passerini alienated the people. I can't be patient any longer." He drew in a breath. "You've been summoning military support, I take it. How do we stand?"

"We stand in a complicated situation," Filippo said. "And I will tell you everything I have learned this evening. But first, I *will* have a private word with my wife."

For a long moment, he and Ippolito stared at each other; Uncle Filippo was solid as stone. At last, Ippolito let go a sound of disgust, then turned away and strode out after the others.

Filippo drew Clarice to a pew. As he sat down beside her, she raised her veil and said, stricken: "So. We are lost then."

Filippo nodded.

Flaring, Clarice jumped to her feet. *"They've forsaken us already?"* There was fury as well as disappointment in her tone. She had already known what news Filippo would bring, yet she had hoped wildly, secretly, that it would not be the news she expected.

Filippo remained seated. "They're afraid. Without Clement's support—"

"*Damn* them!" When Filippo reached for her arm, she shook him off. "Cowards! Damn the Emperor, damn Passerini—and damn the Pope!"

"Clarice," Filippo said forcefully. This time when he caught her arm, she did not pull away but instead sat down hard.

Her features contorted in a spasm of grief, and sudden tears—diamonds caught in candlelight—rained onto her cheeks and bosom. The impossible had occurred: Aunt Clarice was crying.

"Damn them *all*," she said. "They're idiots, every one. Just like my father, who lost this city through sheer stupidity. And now I'll lose it, too."

Filippo put a hand upon her shoulder and waited patiently for her to calm herself. Once she had, he brushed away her tears and asked softly, "You will talk to them, then?"

She gave a helpless little wave. "What else can I do?" She let go a deep sigh, then reached out and stroked Filippo's cheek with a bitter, fleeting smile. He caught her hand and kissed it with genuine tenderness.

Clarice's smile vanished abruptly. "I'll negotiate with no one but Capponi himself," she said. "You'll have to find him tonight—tomorrow morning will be too late. By then, there will be bloodshed."

"Tonight," Filippo echoed. "I'll see to it."

"We meet on *my* terms," Clarice said. "I'll write it down; I'll have no misunderstanding." She gave Filippo a meaningful look. "You already know my condition."

"Clarice," he said, but she put a finger to his lips.

"They won't hurt me, Lippo. It's not me they want. When it's all over, I'll join you."

"I won't leave you without protection," Filippo said.

"I'll have it," she countered. "The best kind—better than soldiers. Tomorrow, the astrologer's son is coming—the magician, Cosimo. I'll meet with him before I see Capponi."

Filippo recoiled. "Cosimo Ruggieri? Benozzo's black-hearted boy?"

"He *knew,* Lippo. He knew the hour and the day that Clement would fall. He tried to warn me weeks ago, but I wouldn't listen. Well, I'm listening now."

"Clarice, they say he conjures demons, that he—"

"He knew the hour and the day," she interrupted. "I cannot dismiss such an ally."

Filippo remained troubled. "I will still make sure you have the best men and arms."

Clarice graced him with a cold, sly smile. "I have the best insurance of all, Lippo. I have the heirs." She rose and took her husband's hand. "Come. I need quill and paper. Capponi must have my letter tonight."

Uncle Filippo followed her out. I crawled out from my hiding place, but lingered in the chapel.

He knew. He knew the hour and the day.

If Ser Cosimo had been able to convince Clarice of his knowledge weeks earlier, could Pope Clement have been warned? Even more: Had my mother been warned that mine would be a difficult birth, would she not have consulted a physician earlier? Might my father have been warned to see to his health? Might both their lives have been spared?

Surely God would have wanted to spare the Pope and my parents. Surely He would not condemn a frightened child for seeking safety, even if it lay in the arms of a man who spoke to devils.

There are things we must discuss, unhappy secrets.

I stared up at Gaspar, the King of the East, young and glorious astride his white mount. He did not hold my attention long; it was the boy Lorenzo who captivated me—an ugly, lonely, brilliant child, forced by fate to grow shrewd before his time. Lorenzo, who ignored all others and kept his gaze intently focused on the Magus.

The next morning I woke to the sounds of a household unbearably alert but subdued. The usual lilts of servants' voices had become terse whispers; their steps were muted. I could not even hear the cook and scullery maid banging pots and dishes in the kitchen.

Ginevra dressed me hurriedly and left. I should have gone directly down to breakfast—but I knew that the chambermaids would already be busy at their tasks, so I headed to their empty bedroom. I dragged a stool to the window, stepped up, and looked down.

The composition of the crowd had changed. The day before had brought unarmed merchants and peasants. Today the men were highborn and armed with short swords at their hips; they stood in disciplined ranks, forming a barricade around the compound. Traffic in the Via Larga had stalled, thanks to sentries who questioned each passerby.

Troubled, I quit the window and went down to seek Piero. I found him in the boys' apartment, where Ginevra was lifting a stack of folded items from an open wardrobe. She had turned to set them down into a half-packed trunk when she caught sight of me standing in the doorway.

I stared at the bundle of boys' clothing in her arms. Beside Ginevra, Leda sat on a low stool folding bed linens, which she set in a second trunk. I could not imagine why Leda, who always tended Aunt Clarice, should be fussing with the boys' linens.

Ginevra flushed brilliantly. "You shouldn't be here, Caterina," she said. "Did you get your breakfast?"

I shook my head. "What are you doing?"

Piero heard and came out of the bedroom. "Packing," he said, smiling. "Don't look so frightened, Cat. We're going to the country, just like I said. Mother's going to speak to the rebels tonight, after we're gone."

In a small voice, I said, "No one is packing *my* things."

"Well, they *will*." Piero turned to Ginevra, whose gaze was carefully fixed on the trunk in front of her. "Who's going to take care of her things?"

Ginevra's reply was so long in coming that Leda, the braver of the two, said sternly, "Her aunt will speak to her about it when the time is right. In the meantime, she should get her breakfast and stay out of trouble."

My lower lip twitched despite my best efforts to control it, and I said, tearfully, to Piero, "They're not going to let me go with you."

"Don't be silly!" he said and turned his gaze on Leda. "She is going with us, *isn't* she?"

Leda tried to meet his stare brazenly, but in the end, she looked away. "Madonna Clarice will speak to her later."

Piero's voice rose in protest, but I bolted before I heard what he had to say. I raced breakneck down the stairs, out into the courtyard, and past the formal garden to the far end of the stables. A large sycamore grew beside the stone wall that enclosed the rear of the property. I hurled myself beneath its shade and wept. The world had betrayed me; my only hope, my only happiness, was Piero, but now he was to be taken from me. I cried undisturbed for what seemed an eternity, then lay with my back against the damp ground and stared up at green leaves punctuated by bits of sky.

I have the best insurance of all; I have the heirs. Piero and his brothers would be taken to safety, and I, an heir, would remain. I was currency Clarice could use in her negotiations with the rebels.

In my reverie, I almost failed to notice the songs of church bells—San Marco, San Lorenzo, Santa Maria del Fiore—tumbling over each other in melodic cascades. They had nearly stilled when I sat up and reconstructed the number of tolls from memory. It was terce, the third hour of the morning.

I rose, brushed the twigs from my skirts, and hurried along the side of the stables until I was able to peer around the corner toward the gates that opened onto the Via Larga.

Our two dozen guards were focused on the silent rebels on the other side of the iron bars, while a boy was leading a gleaming black mare to the stalls. She was spirited and tossed her head, obedient enough but letting him know, with a disdainful glare, that she did not trust him.

Ser Cosimo could not be far away. I went to the deserted garden and waited there for half an hour—an agonizing length of time for a restless child.

At last the magician appeared, in a farsetto of black and red striped silk. He spotted me and silently led me to an alcove sheltered from view by a tall hedge.

Once there, he said sternly, "You must promise me, Donna Caterina, that you will tell no one of our meeting—for many reasons, not the least of which is the unseemliness of my meeting privately with a young girl. You must repeat what I tell you to no one—especially your aunt Clarice."

"I promise."

"Good." He leaned down so that his face was at the level of mine. "Your natal stars are remarkable. I would like to help you, Caterina, to mitigate their evil and strengthen the good." He paused. "You *will* rule. But not for many years. Saturn in Capricorn assures that."

"We will lose Florence—for a while?" I asked. "And then come back, as we did before?"

"You will never rule Florence," he said, and when my features began to crumple, he snapped, "Listen to me! The chart of your nativity shows Leo ascending and Aries in your Tenth House. That is the marker of a king, Caterina. You will rule far more than a single city. *If*—" He stopped himself. "Your horoscope holds many terrible challenges, and now is the first. I intend to see you survive it. Do you understand?"

I nodded, intrigued and terrified. "Is that what you saw yesterday, when you looked at the moles near my ear? You saw something that frightened you."

He frowned, trying to remember, then broke into an amused smile. "I wasn't frightened. I was . . . impressed."

"Impressed?"

"By the king," he said. "The one you are to marry."

I gaped, dumbstruck.

"I do not know how far we can rely on Madonna Clarice," he continued. "A betrayal is coming, one that threatens your life, but I am not sure whence it arises. I have been honest with your aunt about your singular importance, and I have given her talismans of protection for you and your cousins. But I did not know whether I could trust her to give you this."

His fingers dug into the pouch on his belt and found a small item; he opened them to reveal a polished black stone accompanied by a bit of greenery.

"This is the Wing of Corvus Rising, from Agrippa, created under the aegis of Mars and Saturn. It holds the power of the raven's star. Its wing will shelter you from harm until we meet again. Wear it hidden, with the stone on top and the comfrey touching your skin. Make absolutely certain that no one sees it or takes it from you."

"I'll make certain," I said. "I'm not stupid."

"I can see that," he answered, with a glimmer of humor. He held out his hand, and I took the dark gift. I had expected the gem's touch to be cold, but his flesh had warmed it.

"Why do you do this for me?" I asked.

Something sly flashed in his smile. "We are tied, Caterina Maria Romula de' Medici. You appeared in *my* stars long before you were born. It serves my interests to keep you safe, if I can." He paused. "Let me see you hide the talisman on your person."

I insinuated my fingers beneath my tightly laced bodice and placed the gem between my undeveloped breasts. The bit of crushed comfrey took some maneuvering before it rested properly under the stone.

"Good," Ser Cosimo said. "Now I must take my leave." But as he turned to go, a thought occurred to him, and he asked quickly, "Do you dream, Caterina? Memorable dreams, remarkable ones?"

"I try not to remember them," I said. "They frighten me."

"You will recall them clearly now, under Corvus's wing," he said. "Mars dwells in your Twelfth House, the House of Hidden Enemies and Dreams. Heaven itself reveals what you must know of your fate. It is your gift and your burden." He executed a shallow bow. "I take my leave of you for a time, Donna Caterina. May God permit us to meet again soon."

He did not intend for his voice to betray any doubt regarding that future meeting—but it did, and I heard that doubt all too well. I turned away without answer and ran back across the courtyard, the raven's stone hard against my chest.

Three

I ran to the library and threw open the shutters to let in the sun and any sounds from the street or the stables near the gate. Then I found *De Vita Coelitus Comparanda,* written in the author's script on yellowing parchment. Piero had left it on the bottom shelf so he could easily retrieve it, which allowed me to slide it off and guide it clumsily down to the floor.

I sat cross-legged, pulled the volume onto my lap, and opened it. I was far too agitated to read, but pressed my palms against the cool pages and stared at the words. I calmed myself by lifting a page, turning it, and smoothing it down with my hand. I turned another page, and another, until my breathing slowed, until my eyes relaxed and began to recognize a word here, a phrase there.

I had finally settled down enough to read when my eyes caught a flash of movement. Piero stood in the doorway, his cheeks flushed, his chest heaving. His face betrayed such misery and guilt I could not bear to look at him but lowered my gaze back to the book in my lap.

"I told them I couldn't leave you," he said. "If you can't go, then I won't."

"It doesn't matter what we want," I said flatly. If I was in grave danger, then Piero was better off abandoning my company; the kindest thing I could do for him now was to be cruel. "I'm an heir and must remain. You're not, so you must respect your mother's bargain and leave."

"They want Ippolito and Sandro, not you," he persisted. "I'll talk to Mother. They'll see reason. . . ."

I ran my finger down a page and said coldly, "It's already decided, Piero. There's no point in talking about it."

"Cat," he said, with such anguish that my resolve wavered—but I kept my gaze fixed on the page.

He stood in the doorway a bit longer, but I would not look up, not until the sound of his footsteps had faded.

I sat alone in the library until the sun passed midheaven and did not stir until a sound drew me to the window.

The coach bearing Piero, his brothers, and Uncle Filippo had rolled up to the gate and paused there while our soldiers moved aside to let the gate swing inward. As they did, two men walked through the opening onto our estate. Both were of noble birth; one wore a self-important air and an embroidered blue tunic. The other was dark and muscular, with a military commander's bearing. Once they made their way past our guards, the man in blue signaled the carriage driver.

I stared, stricken, as the carriage rumbled through the gate and onto the street outside. There was no chance Piero could see me: The low sun created a blinding glare, and I could not see the windows of the carriage. Even so I waved, and watched as it headed north down the Via de' Gori and disappeared.

At suppertime, Paola found me and shooed me to my room, where a plate of food awaited me. She also brought a talisman on a leather thong and hung it round my neck. I agreed to remain in my room in exchange for Ficino's book, but before Paola could deliver it and leave, I pelted her with questions: What were the names of the two men at the gate? How long were they expected to stay?

She was overworked and exasperated, but I managed to tease from her the phrase "Niccolò Capponi, leader of the rebels, and his general, Bernardo Rinuccini."

I obeyed her and kept to my room. After many hours of anxious reading, I fell asleep.

I woke to the sound of shouting and hurried to the main landing. In the foyer at the foot of the stairs, Passerini—in his scarlet cardinal's gown trimmed with ermine, his ample jowls spilling over the too-tight neck—stood shouting, flanked by Ippolito and Sandro. The Cardinal had apparently drunk a good portion of wine.

"It's an outrage!" he shrieked. "*I* am the regent, I alone possess the authority to make such decisions. And I denounce this one!" He stood inches from Aunt Clarice, who, accompanied by two men at arms, barred entry to the dining hall. "You insult us!"

He seized Clarice's right wrist, wrenching it so violently that she cried out in surprise and pain.

"Worthless bastard!" she shouted. "Let go of me!"

On either side of her, the guards unsheathed their swords. Passerini dropped hold of her at once. The younger of the guards was ready to strike, but Clarice signaled for peace and caught Ippolito's gaze.

"Get them from my sight," she hissed.

Cradling her injured wrist, she turned and swept imperiously back into the dining hall. The door closed behind her, and the guards positioned themselves in front of it. The Cardinal lurched slightly, as if considering whether to charge the door, but Ippolito caught his arm.

"They've made the decision to deal with her," he said. "There's nothing we can do here. Come." Still gripping Passerini's arm, he moved for the stairs; Sandro followed.

I held my ground on the landing as they ascended toward me and looked questioningly at Ippolito.

"Our aunt has chosen to humiliate us, Caterina," Ippolito said tautly, "by barring us from the negotiations at the request of the rebels. I'm sure they'll find her more accommodating." His voice grew very low and soft. "She has humiliated us. And she *will* pay."

I watched as they made their way to their apartments, then I returned to my bed and stared at the window and the darkness beyond it, broken by the wavering glow from the rebels' torches.

I slept fitfully, with dreams of men and swords and shouting. At dawn, sounds pulled me from sleep: the ring of bootheels on marble, the murmur of men's voices. I called for Paola, who came and dressed me with a far rougher hand than Ginevra ever had. On her orders, I ran down toward the kitchen but stopped in the ground-floor corridor. The door to the dining hall was open; curiosity compelled me to peer past the threshold.

Clarice was inside. She sat alone at the long table littered with empty goblets; hers was full, untouched. She was dressed gorgeously in deep green brocade, and the train of her gown spilled over the side of the chair and pooled artfully at her feet. Her arm rested on the table, and her face, nestled in the crook, was turned from me. Her chestnut hair hung upon her shoulder, restrained by a gold net studded with tiny diamonds.

She heard me and languidly lifted her head. She was full awake, but her expression was lifeless; I was too young to interpret it then, but over the years I have come to recognize the dull look of undigested grief.

"Caterina," she said, without inflection; her eyes were heavy-lidded with exhaustion. She leaned over and patted the seat of the chair beside her. "Come, sit with me. The men will be down soon, and you might as well hear."

I sat. Her wrist, propped upon the table, was badly swollen, with dark marks left by Passerini's fingers. Within a few minutes, Leda led Passerini and the cousins to the table. Ippolito's manner was reserved; Passerini's and Sandro's, angry and challenging.

When they had taken their seats, Aunt Clarice waved Leda out of the room. Capponi had guaranteed us all safe passage, she said. We would go to Naples, where her mother's people, the Orsini, would take us in. With their help, we would raise an army. The Duke of Milan would support us, and the d'Estes of Ferrara, and every other dynasty in Italy with sense enough to see that the formation of another Venice-style republic was an outright threat to them.

Passerini interrupted. "You gave Capponi *everything* he wanted, didn't you? No wonder they preferred to deal with a woman!"

Clarice looked wearily at him. "Their men surround this house, Silvio. They have soldiers and weapons, and we have neither. With what did you intend me to bargain?"

"They came to us!" Passerini snarled. "They wanted something."

"They wanted our *heads*," Clarice said, with a faint trace of spirit. "Instead they will grant us safe passage. And in exchange, we must give them this."

She spoke tonelessly and at length: The rebels would let us live, if, in four days, on the seventeenth of May at midday, Ippolito, Alessandro, and I went to the great public square, the Piazza della Signoria, and announced our abdication. We would then swear oaths of allegiance to the new Third Republic of Florence. We would also swear never to return. Afterward, rebel soldiers would lead us to the city gates and waiting carriages.

The cardinal swore and sputtered. "Betrayal," Sandro said. The magician's face rose in my imagination and whispered: *One that threatens your life.* They both fell silent the instant Ippolito rose.

"I knew Florence was lost," he told Clarice, his voice unsteady. "But there are other things we could have purchased our safety with—properties, hidden family treasure, promises of alliances. For you to agree to *humiliate* us publicly—"

Clarice raised a brow. "Would you prefer the bite of the executioner's blade?"

"I will not bow to them, Aunt," Ippolito said.

"I kept our dignity," Clarice countered; the tiny diamonds in her hairnet sparkled as she lifted her chin. "They could have taken our heads. They could have stripped us and hung us in the Piazza della Signoria. Instead, they wait outside. They give us a bit of freedom. They give us time."

Ippolito drew in a long breath, and when he let it go, he shuddered. "I will not bow to them," he said, and the words held a threat.

Four miserable days passed; the men spent them closeted in Ippolito's chambers. Aunt Clarice wandered empty halls, as all of the house servants—except the most loyal, which included Leda, Paola, the stablehands, and the cook—had left. Beyond the iron gate, the rebels kept watch; the soldiers who had guarded our palazzo abandoned us.

By the afternoon of the sixteenth—one day before we were all to humble ourselves in the Piazza della Signoria—my room was stripped. I begged Paola to pack the volume of Ficino, but she murmured that it was a very big book for such a little girl.

That evening, Aunt Clarice prevailed upon us to have supper in one of the smaller dining rooms. Ippolito had little to say to anyone; Sandro, however, seemed surprisingly lighthearted, as did Passerini—who, when Clarice voiced her regret over leaving the family home in hostile hands, patted her hand, pointedly ignoring her bandaged right wrist.

The dinner ended quietly—at least, for Clarice, Ippolito, and me. The three of us retired, leaving Sandro and Passerini to their wine and jokes. I could hear them laughing as I headed back toward the children's apartments.

That night, I dreamt.

I stood in the center of a vast open field and spied in the distance a man, his body backlit by the rays of the dying sun. I could not see his face, but he knew me and called out to me in a foreign tongue.

Catherine . . .

Not Caterina, as I was christened at birth, but *Catherine.* I recognized it as my name, just as I had when the magician had once uttered it so.

Catherine, he cried again, anguished.

The setting changed abruptly, as happens in dreams. He lay on the ground at my feet and I stood over him, wanting to help. Blood welled up from his shadowed face like water from a spring and soaked the earth beneath him. I knew that I was responsible for this blood, that he would die if I did not do something. Yet I could not fathom what I was to do.

Catherine, he whispered, and died, and I woke to the sound of Leda screaming.

Four

The sound came from across the landing, from Ippolito and Alessandro's shared apartments. I ran toward the source.

Leda had fallen in front of the wide-open door onto all fours. Her screams were now moans, which merged with the song of bells from the nearby cathedral of San Lorenzo, announcing the dawn.

I ran up to her. "Is it the baby?"

Gritting her teeth, Leda shook her head. Her stricken gaze was on Clarice, who had also come running in her chemise, a shawl thrown around her shoulders. She knelt beside the fallen woman. "The child is coming, then?"

Again, Leda shook her head and gestured at the heirs' room. "I went to wake them," she gasped.

Clarice's face went slack. Wordlessly, she rose and hurried on bare feet into the men's antechamber. I followed.

The outer room looked as it always had—with chairs, table, writing desks, a cold hearth for summer. Without announcing herself, Clarice sailed through the open door into Ippolito's bedroom.

In its center—as if the perpetrators had intended to draw attention to their dramatic display—a pile of clothes lay on the floor: the farsettos Alessandro and Ippolito had worn the previous night, atop a tangle of black leggings and Passerini's scarlet gown.

I stood behind my aunt as she bent down to check the abandoned fabric for warmth. As she straightened, she let go a whispered roar, filled with infinite rage.

"Traitors! Traitors! Sons of whores, all of you!"

She whirled about and saw me standing, terrified, in front of her. Her eyes were wild, her features contorted.

"I pledged on my honor," she said, but not to me. "On my honor, on my family name, and Capponi trusted me."

She fell silent until her anger transformed into ruthless determination. She took my hand firmly and led me ungently back into the corridor, where Leda was still moaning on the floor.

She seized the pregnant woman's arm. "Get up. Quick, go to the stables and see if the carriages have gone."

Leda arched her back and went rigid; liquid splashed softly against marble. Clarice took a step back from the clear puddle around Leda's knees and shouted for Paola—who was, of course, horrified by the revelation of the men's departure and needed severe chastising before she calmed.

Clarice ordered Paola to go to the stables to see if all the carriages were gone. "Calmly," Clarice urged, "as if you had forgotten to pack something. Remember—the rebels are watching just beyond the gate."

Once Paola had gone on her mission, Clarice glanced down at Leda and turned to me. "Help me get her to my room," she said.

We lifted the laboring woman to her feet and helped her up the stairs to my aunt's chambers. The spasm that had earlier seized her eased, and she sat, panting, in a chair near Clarice's bed.

In due time, Paola returned, hysterical: Passerini and the heirs were nowhere to be found, yet the carriages that had been packed with their belongings still waited. The master of the horses and all the grooms were gone—and the bodies of three stablehands lay bloodied in the straw. Only a boy remained. He had been asleep, he said, and woke terrified to discover his fellows murdered and the master gone.

In Clarice's eyes, I saw the flash of Lorenzo's brilliant mind at work.

"My quill," she said to Paola, "and paper."

When Paola had delivered them both, Clarice sat at her desk and wrote two letters. The effort exasperated her, as her bandaged hand pained her; many times, she dropped the quill. She bade Paola fold one letter several times into a small square, the other, into thirds. With the smaller letter in hand, Aunt Clarice knelt at the foot of Leda's chair and took the servant's cheeks in her hands. A look passed between them that I, a child, did not understand. Then Clarice leaned forward and pressed her lips to Leda's as a man might kiss a woman; Leda wound her arms about Clarice and held her fast. After a long moment, Clarice pulled away and touched her forehead to Leda's in the tenderest of gestures.

Finally Clarice straightened. "You must be brave for me, Leda, or we are all dead. I will arrange with Capponi for you to go to my physician. You must give the doctor this"—she held up the little square of paper—"without anyone seeing or knowing."

"But the rebels . . . ," Leda breathed, owl-eyed.

"They'll have pity on you," Clarice said firmly. "Doctor Cattani will make sure that your child arrives safely in this world. We will meet again, and soon. Only trust me."

When Leda, tight-lipped, finally nodded, Clarice gestured for Paola to take the other letter, folded in thirds.

"Tell the rebels at the gate to deliver this to Capponi immediately. Wait for his answer, then come to me."

Paola hesitated—only an instant, as Aunt Clarice's gaze was far more frightening than the prospect of facing the rebels—and disappeared with the letter.

After a long, anxious hour—during which I managed to dress myself, with Clarice's help—Paola reappeared with news that Capponi would let Leda leave provided she was judged sincerely pregnant and about to give birth. This led to an urgent consultation between the women as to where the letter should be concealed, and how Leda should pass it to the doctor without detection.

Then, per Capponi's instruction, Clarice and Paola helped the pregnant woman down the stairs to the large brass door that opened directly onto the Via Larga. I shadowed them at a distance.

Just outside the door, two respectful nobles waited; beyond them, rebel soldiers held back the crowd that had gathered in the street. The nobles helped Leda into a waiting wagon. Aunt Clarice stood in the doorway, her palm pressed against the jamb, and watched as they drove Leda away. When she turned to face me, she was bereft. She did not expect to see Leda again—a ghastly thought, since the latter had served Clarice since both were children.

We headed back upstairs. In my aunt's carriage, I read the truth: The world we knew was dissolving to make room for something new and terrible. I had been sad, thinking I would be separated from Piero for a few weeks; now, looking at Clarice's face, I realized I might never set eyes on him again.

Once in her room, Clarice went to a cupboard and retrieved a gold florin.

"Take this to the stableboy," she told Paola. "Tell him to remain at his post until the fifth hour of the morning, when he must saddle the largest stallion and lead it out through the back of the stables, to the rear walls of the estate. If he waits there for us, I will bring him another florin." She paused. "If you tell him the heirs have gone—if you so much as hint at the truth—I will throw you over the gate myself and let them tear you to shreds, because he just might realize he can tell the rebels our secret to save his skin."

Paola accepted the coin but hesitated, troubled. "There is no chance—even on the largest horse—that we could make it past the gate—"

Clarice's gaze silenced her; Paola gave a quick little curtsy, then disappeared. Her expression, when she returned, was one of relief: The boy was still there, happy to obey. "He swears on his life that he will tell the rebels nothing," she said.

I puzzled over Clarice's scheme. I had been told several times that I was to go to the dining hall no later than the fifth hour of the morning, because Capponi's general and his men would be on our doorstep half an hour later to escort us to the Piazza. Whatever her plan, she intended to execute it before their arrival.

I watched as Paola arranged Clarice's hair and dressed her in the black-and-gold brocade gown she had chosen to wear for our family's public humiliation. Paola was lacing on the first heavy, velvet-edged sleeve when the church bells signaled terce, the third hour of the morning. Three hours had passed since daybreak, when I had discovered Leda huddled on the floor; three more would pass until the bells chimed sext, the sixth hour, midday, when we were to arrive at the Piazza della Signoria.

Paola continued her task, although her fingers were clumsy and shaking. In the end, Clarice was dressed and achingly beautiful. She glanced into the mirror Paola held for her and scowled, sighing. Some new worry, some problem, had occurred to her, one she did not yet know how to resolve. But she turned to me with forced, hollow cheer.

"Now," she asked, "how shall we amuse ourselves for the next two hours? We must find a way to busy ourselves, you and I."

"I would like to go to the chapel," I said.

Clarice entered the chapel slowly, reverently, and I reluctantly followed suit, genuflecting and crossing myself when she did, then settling beside her on the pew.

Clarice closed her eyes, but I could still see her mind struggling with some fresh challenge. I left her to it while I wriggled, straining my neck to get a better view of the mural.

Clarice sighed and opened her eyes again. "Didn't you come to pray, child?"

I expected irritation but heard only curiosity, so I answered honestly. "No. I wanted to see Lorenzo again."

Her face softened. "Then go and see him."

I went over to the wooden choir stall just beneath the painting of the crowd following the youthful magus Gaspar and tilted my head back.

"Do you know them all, then?" Clarice asked behind me, her tone low and faintly sad.

I pointed to the first horse behind Gaspar's. "Here is Piero the Gouty, Lorenzo's father," I said. "And beside him, *his* father, Cosimo the Old." They had been shrewdest, most powerful men Florence had known, until Lorenzo *il Magnifico* supplanted them both.

Clarice stepped forward to gesture at a small face near Lorenzo's, almost lost in the crowd. "And here is Giuliano, his brother. He was murdered in the cathedral, you know. They tried to murder Lorenzo, too. He was wounded and bleeding, but he wouldn't leave his brother. His friends dragged him away as he shouted Giuliano's name. No one was more loyal to those he loved.

"There are those who aren't there beside him but should have been," she continued. "Ghosts, of whom you have not heard enough. My mother should be there—your grandmother Alfonsina. She married Lorenzo's eldest son, an idiot who promptly alienated the people and was banished. But she had a son—your father—and educated him in the subject of politics, so that when we Medici returned to Florence, he ruled it well enough. When your father went away to war, Alfonsina governed quite capably. And now . . . we have lost the city again." She sighed. "No matter how brightly we shine, we Medici women are doomed to be eclipsed by our men."

"I won't let it happen to me," I said.

She turned her head sharply to look down at me. "Won't you?" she asked slowly. In her eyes I saw an idea being birthed, one that caused the recent worry there to vanish.

"I can be strong," I said, "like Lorenzo. Please, I would like to touch him. Just once, before we go."

She was not a large woman, but I was not a large child. She lifted me with effort, trying to spare her injured wrist, just high enough so that I could touch Lorenzo's cheek. Silly child, I had expected the contours and warmth of flesh, and was surprised to find the surface beneath my fingertips flat and cold.

"He was no fool," she said, when she had lowered me. "He knew when to love, and when to hate.

"When his brother was murdered—when he saw the House of Medici was in danger—he struck out." She looked pointedly at me.

"Do you understand that it is possible to be good yet destroy one's enemies, Caterina? That sometimes, to protect one's own blood, it is necessary to let the blood of others?"

I shook my head, shocked.

"If a man came to our door," Clarice persisted, "and wanted to murder me, to murder Piero and you, could you do what was necessary to stop him?"

I looked away for an instant, summoning the scene in my imagination. "Yes," I answered. "I could."

"You are like me," Clarice said approvingly, "and Lorenzo: sensitive, yet able to do what needs to be done. The House of Medici must survive, and you, Caterina, are its only hope."

She smiled darkly at me and, with her bandaged hand, reached into the folds of her skirt to draw out something slender and shining and very, very sharp.

We returned to Clarice's quarters, where Paola waited, and spent the next hour twisting silk scarves around jewels and gold florins. With Paola's help, my aunt tied four heavy makeshift belts around her waist, beneath her gown. A pair of emerald earrings and a large diamond went into her bodice. Clarice helped Paola secure two of the belts on her person, then set aside one gold florin.

Then we sat for half an hour, with only Clarice knowing what awaited us. Prompted by a signal known only to her, Clarice picked up the gold florin and handed it to Paola.

"Take this to the boy," she said. "Tell him to ready a horse and lead it through the stables and out the back, then wait there. Then you come to us at the main entry."

Paola left. Aunt Clarice took my hand and led me downstairs to stand with her by the front door. When the servant returned, Clarice caught her shoulders.

"Be calm," she said, "and listen carefully to me. Caterina and I are going to the stables. Stay here. The instant we leave, count to twenty—then open this door."

Paola's arms thrashed to free herself from Clarice's grasp; she began to cry out, but my aunt silenced her with a harsh shake.

"Listen," Clarice snarled. "You must scream loudly to get everyone's attention. Say that the heirs are upstairs, that they are escaping. Repeat it until everyone rushes into the house. Then you can run out and lose yourself in the crowd." She paused. "The jewels are yours. If I don't see you again, I wish you well." She drew back and gave the servant a piercing look. "Before God Almighty, will you do it?"

Paola trembled mightily but whispered: "I'll do it."

"May He keep you, then."

Clarice gripped my hand. Together we ran the length of the palazzo, through the corridors and courtyard and garden until we were in sight of the stables. She stopped abruptly in the shelter of a tall hedge and peered past it at the now-unlocked iron gate.

I peered with her. On the other side of the black bars, bored rebel soldiers kept watch in front of a milling crowd.

Then I heard them, high and shrill: Paola's screams. Clarice stooped down and pulled off her slippers; I did the same. She waited while all the men turned toward the source of the noise—then, when they all surged to the east, away from the gate, she drew in a long breath and ran west, dragging me with her.

We kicked up clouds of dust as we dashed past the heirs' waiting carriage, past our own; the harnessed horses whinnied in protest. We came alongside the stables, then veered behind them, past the spot where I had lain after I learned Piero would leave me. There, next to the high stone wall, stood a saddled mount and an astonished boy—a wiry Ethiopian not much older than I, with a cloud of feather-light hair. Bits of straw clung to his hair and clothes. Like the horse's, his eyes were wide and worried and white. The massive roan shied, but the boy reined it in with ease.

"Help me up!" Clarice demanded; the shouting out in the street had grown so loud he could barely hear her.

My aunt wasted no time with modesty. She hiked up her skirts, exposing white legs, and placed her bare foot in the stirrup. The horse was tall and she could not bring her leg over its withers; the boy gave her rump a mighty shove, which allowed her to scramble up into the saddle. She sat astride it, taking the reins in her good hand, and maneuvered the horse sidelong to the wall until her leg was pressed between the animal's barrel and the stone. Then she pierced our young rescuer with her gaze.

"You swore on your life that you would tell the rebels nothing," she said. It was an accusation.

"Yes, yes," he responded anxiously. "I will say nothing, Madonna."

"Only those who know a secret promise to keep it," she said. "And there is only one secret the rebels would want to hear today. What might it be? They would not care about an absent stable master and his murdered grooms."

His mouth fell open; he looked as though he wanted to cry.

"Look at you, covered in straw," Clarice told him. "You hid because, like the others, you had heard too much, and they were going to kill you, too. You know where the heirs have gone, don't you?"

Owl-eyed, he dropped his head and stared hard at the grass. "No, Madonna, no . . ."

"You lie," Clarice said. "And I don't blame you. I would be frightened, too."

His face contorted as he began to weep. "Please, Donna Clarice, don't be angry, please. . . . Before God, I swear I will not tell anyone. . . . I could have gone to the rebels, run to the gate and told them everything, but I stayed. I have always been loyal, I will be loyal still. Only do not be angry."

"I'm not angry," she soothed. "We'll take you with us. Lord knows, if we don't, the rebels will torture you until you speak. I'll give you another florin if you tell me where Ser Ippolito and the others have gone. But first, hand me the girl." She leaned down and held her arms out to me.

He was bony but strong; he seized me below the ribs and swung me like a bale of hay up into Clarice's fierce clutches.

A wave of fear slammed against me. I endured it until it crested and faded, leaving everything still and silent its wake. I had a choice: to quail, or to harden.

I hardened.

At the instant the boy handed me to my aunt, I slipped the stiletto from its sheath, hidden in my skirt pocket. It sliced easily through the skin beneath the boy's jaw, in the same grinning arc Clarice had drawn for me on her own throat, with her finger.

But I was a child and not very strong. The wound was shallow; he flinched and drew back before I could finish. With all my might, I plunged the weapon deeper into the side of his neck. He clawed at the protruding dagger and let go a gurgling shriek, his eyes bulging with furious reproach.

Clutching me, Clarice kicked the boy's shoulder. He fell backward, still screaming while Clarice set me on the saddle in front of her.

I stared down at him, horrified and intrigued by what I had just done.

He's going to die in any case, my aunt had said. *But the rebels would torture him hor-*

ribly, until he confessed, and then they would hand him over to the crowd. You can spare him that.

Even we must not know where Ippolito and the others have gone. Can you understand that, Caterina?

It did not seem like a kindness now, watching him flail in the new grass, the blood from his throat collecting in a pool on the grass near his shoulder, crimson against spring green.

Suddenly, ominously, he stilled and fell silent.

He will break, Clarice had said, *and tell them where the heirs have gone, and the House of Medici will be no more. But he will not be suspicious of a child. You will be able to get very close to him.*

Clarice shouted in my ear. "Stand up in the saddle, Caterina! Stand up, I won't let you fall."

Miraculously, I struggled to my feet, swaying. I was now almost the height of the wall next to me.

"Crawl up, child!"

I pulled myself up while Clarice pushed. In an instant, I was kneeling on the wide ledge.

"What do you see?" my aunt demanded. "Is there a carriage?"

I looked out onto the narrow Via de' Ginori—deserted save for a peasant woman dragging two small children with her, and a motionless one-horse carriage sitting next to the curb.

"Yes," I called to her, then shouted and waved a hand at the carriage. Slowly, the horse lifted its hooves, and the wheels began to turn. When it finally arrived, the driver pulled so close to the wall that the wheels screeched against the stone.

I looked over the roof of the stables as the gate squealed; it swung wide open as a small crowd swarmed onto the estate. A man pointed up at me and let go a shout; the crowd headed directly toward us.

The driver, dressed in rumpled, oil-stained linen, stood up in his seat and stretched out his dirty hands to me. "Jump! I'll catch you."

Behind me, Clarice lurched as she grabbed the wall's edge; her panicked mount had taken a step away from the wall. I tried to pull her up but lacked the strength.

I sucked in a great deep breath and leaped. The driver caught me easily and set me down beside him, then called to Clarice. I could see only her fingers and the backs of her hands—the right one purpled and swollen—where the fine bones stood out like ivory cords.

"Hold on, Madonna, I'll pull you over!"

Our rescuer walked to the far edge of the driver's box until his chest was pressed against the wall. He strained but could only brush Clarice's fingertips.

"God *help* me," Clarice screamed, at the same time that her horse shrieked. Men shouted on the other side of the wall.

"Get her! Hold her horse!"

"Don't let her escape!"

In desperation, the driver climbed onto the roof of the carriage and, flexing his knees, bent from his waist to reach over the ledge and catch her arms. Clarice's good hand caught hold of him; when he straightened, her face appeared over the top of the wall.

She screamed again, in fury rather than fright; her shoulders dipped beneath the wall as the men on the other side pulled at her. "Bastards! Bastards! Let me go!"

The driver staggered and almost fell, but pulled on her with such brute force that he fell back onto the carriage roof. Aunt Clarice came tumbling with him. The driver leaned down to examine her, but she sat up and struck him with her left hand.

"Go!" she snarled. She clambered down the side of the carriage and pulled me inside to sit beside her. She was gasping and trembling with exhaustion; her hair was wild on her shoulders, and the back of her gown had been torn off, exposing her petticoat.

She leaned out the door and shouted, "Out of the city, quickly! I'll tell you then where we're going!"

She fell back against the seat and stared down at her injured wrist as if astonished that it had not betrayed her. Then she stared up at the dirty wooden interior; unlike me, she made no attempt to look back at the home she was leaving.

"We'll go to Naples," she said, "to my mother's family. But not today. They'll expect us to go there." Shivering but unshaken, defeated but indomitable, she turned her fierce gaze on me. "The Orsini will help us. This is not the end, you know. The Medici will retake Florence. We always do."

I looked away. In the beginning, I had not wanted to take the knife, but it had drawn me like the darkness in Cosimo Ruggieri's eyes. Now I stared down at the palm that had wielded the blade and saw that same darkness in me. I had told myself that I did it for the House of Medici; in truth, I had done it because I was curious, because I had wanted to see what it was like to kill a man.

Like Lorenzo, I learned early that I was capable of murder. And I was terrified to think where that capability might lead.

Five

Poggio means hill, and the villa my great-grandfather built at Poggio a Caiano rests atop a sprawling grassy prominence in the Tuscan countryside, three hours from the city. The home Lorenzo obtained in 1479 had been a plain, three-storied square with a red tile roof, but in *il Magnifico*'s hands, it became much more. He encased the ground floor by a portico with several graceful arches that opened onto the front courtyard. A staircase originated on either side of the central arch and the two curved upward to meet at the grand middle-floor entrance, where a triangular pediment rested atop six great columns in the style of a Greek temple. The structure stood majestic and alone, surrounded by gentle hills and streams and the nearby Albano mountains.

No one would think to look for us there, Aunt Clarice explained, as it lay northwest of the city, and the rebels would be searching all the roads leading south. We would spend the night there, during which she would formulate a plan that would eventually take us safely to Naples.

We rolled through the open gates, coughing from the dust, and tumbled barefoot and disheveled from the carriage to be met by a dumbstruck gardener. Exhausted though we were, our nerves would not let us rest or eat. Her gaze distant, her mind working, my aunt paced through the formal, painstakingly groomed gardens while I dashed ahead of her in an effort to tire myself. Dove-colored clouds gathered overhead; the breeze grew cool and smelled of rain. I thought of the astonishment and reproach in the stableboy's eyes. I had learned a fundamental truth about killing: The victim's anguish is brief and fleeting, but the murderer's endures forever.

I ran and ran that afternoon, but never succeeded in leaving the stableboy behind. Clarice never spoke to me of him; I honestly believe that she, lost in her efforts to transform a bleak future, had already forgotten him.

When evening came, my aunt and I shared a supper of greasy soup, then went upstairs. Clarice undressed me herself. When she undid the laces on my bodice, the smooth black stone hidden there dropped to the marble floor with a click, and the battered bit of herb followed mutely. I bent to pick them up, bracing for angry words.

"Did Ser Cosimo give you those?" my aunt asked softly.

I nodded, flushing.

Clarice nodded, too, slowly. "Keep them safe, then," she said.

She sent me to bed while she sat just outside, in the antechamber, and laboriously penned letters by lamplight. I put the herb and gem beneath my pillow and fell asleep to the halting scratch of her quill against the paper.

Some time later, I was awakened by a wooden bang; an early summer storm had ridden in on a cold wind. A servant girl hurried into the room and closed the offending shutters to keep out the rain. I stared at the antechamber wall, where Aunt Clarice's shadow loomed and receded as the flame danced, and listened to the shutters' muted complaint.

My sleep, when it finally came, was troubled by dreams—not of images but of sounds: of Clarice screaming for men to let go of her skirts, of horses neighing, of rebels chanting for our downfall. I dreamt of hoofbeats and the pounding of rain, of men's voices and the faraway roll of thunder.

Consciousness returned like a lightning strike; with a start, I realized that the drum of hoofbeats, the strident cadence of Clarice's voice, and the lower one of men's were not part of any dream.

I pushed myself from bed and hurried to the shuttered window. It was low enough that I could look out easily—but the shutters were latched, and I too short to reach them. I looked about for a chair, and in that instant the door opened and a servant entered. She was not much older than I, but she was tall enough to unfasten the shutters at my impatient command and open them, then step back, her eyes enormous with fright.

I stared out. On the vast, downward-sloping lawn, two dozen men sat on horseback in four militarily precise rows, sheathed swords at their hips.

In that instant, my faith in Ruggieri's magic crumbled. The Wing of Corvus was at best a harmless piece of jet. I would never grow up to rule; I would never grow up at all. I backed away from the window.

"Where is she?" I whispered to the girl.

"Madonna Clarice? At the front door, talking to two men. They told me to fetch you.

"She is so angry with them," the girl continued. "She did not want them to wake you. She is swearing at them so, she will surely provoke them—" She pressed her hand to her mouth as if she was going to be sick, then forced herself to calm. "Last night, she summoned me and said that, if anything happened to her, I was to see you safely to her mother's people." She glanced nervously at the door. "They will come looking for you, if we don't appear soon. But . . ."

I lifted my brows questioningly.

"But we could leave by the servants' stairs," she continued. "They wouldn't see us. There are places to hide here. I think Madonna Clarice would want that."

I expected Clarice *did* want that, and that she knew if I did not appear, the rebels would torture her in the hope of learning my whereabouts; they might well kill her. Escape seemed possible but unlikely—but my disappearance would undeniably put Clarice in terrible danger. Weighing this, I moved slowly to the bed, reached beneath the pillow, and found the hidden stone. I stared at its glassy surface, a black mirror in my palm, and saw my aunt reflected there:

Aunt Clarice, lifting me up to touch Lorenzo's childish face. Clarice, lifting me out of the rebels' reach, even as they tried to tear her apart. Clarice, who could well have departed with her husband and children, leaving us heirs in rebel hands. But like her grandfather, she did not abandon those of her blood, no matter how fatally afflicted.

I placed the worthless gem upon the pillow, then pulled off the silver talisman, on its leather cord, and coiled it beside the stone. Then I looked up at the servant.

"Get my gown, please," I said. "I will be going down to meet them."

PART III

Imprisonment

May 1527–August 1530

Six

Images from that day are etched clearly in my memory: the long walk down the stairs, the sight of Clarice in the vestibule, a shawl tossed over her shoulders to hide the fact that a swath had been torn from the back of her gold gown. Her wrist—resting now in a sling—had left her pale with agony. Although the man she spoke to was more than a head taller and flanked by two aides of similar height, she seemed larger than them all. Gesturing sharply with her free hand, she railed as fearlessly at him as she had at Passerini the morning he came to tell her Pope Clement had been routed.

As I moved down the stairs, the man listening to her glanced up. He was intense and very quiet, and made me remember something Piero had once said, that a dog who did not bark was far more likely to bite. His hair and beard and eyes matched his new brown cloak. He was Bernardo Rinuccini, head of the rebel militia.

I remember how his eyes grew rounded at the sight of me, how Aunt Clarice's mouth fell open as she glanced over her shoulder, stricken and profoundly speechless.

"Promise me you won't hurt her," I told the general, "and I will go with you."

Rinuccini stared down at me. "I have no reason to hurt her."

"Promise me," I repeated, gazing steadily at him.

"I promise," he said.

I walked past Clarice to Rinuccini's side; there was horror in her eyes as she watched me slip irrevocably from her care. But the greater horror was mine, to glimpse the proud spirit behind those eyes and to mark the instant it broke.

They led me away. When I appeared in the doorway, the troops waiting on the lawn cheered. I moved quickly so that they had no cause to touch me, not until I was lifted up onto a horse and into the lap of a well-born soldier. He wore not a sword but a weapon I had never seen before: an arquebus, a contraption of wood and metal designed to blast balls of lead into distant victims, like a miniature cannon one might hold in one's hand. He regarded me with victory and loathing; never was a trophy more scorned or prized.

The ascending sun coaxed the previous night's rain from the earth; the horses moved through low swirls of mist as we rode across the quiet countryside. Numbed by the enormity of my decision, I rode in mindless dread, my back pressed to my guardian's chest.

By midmorning we had returned to the city. We headed not south to the great Piazza della Signoria and the gallows but north. As the streets were busy, we attracted much attention, but most failed to notice a little girl huddled against one of the soldiers; by the time a few had, we had already passed, and their faint curses, like stones hurled from too great a distance, did not frighten me.

Our procession turned onto an unfamiliar street lined with stone walls. They were thick and high, unbroken save for three narrow doors at long intervals.

We stopped at one of the doors. Set into it were two iron grates, one at eye level, behind which a black cloth had been hung, and an uncovered one at foot level.

An aide dismounted and called at the covered grate, while another soldier swung me down from the horse. The door opened inward, an aide pushed me inside, and someone quickly shut the door behind me.

I stumbled forward onto a stone patio that lay in the shadow of a large building and glanced up at the woman who faced me. She was worn and colorless and dressed in black but for the white wimple beneath her long veil.

She put her finger to her lips for silence, so emphatically that I followed her without a word into the building, which was as plain and aged and soundless as she. She led me up two flights of narrow stairs, then past a long row of cells, before depositing me in a tiny room, with a bed pushed against the wall opposite the window and two chairs.

The latter were occupied by two young women clad in shabby brown dresses. They dropped their mending after making the same gesture, finger to lips, before they hurried to me.

Clumsily, they began to remove my gown. I doubt they had ever seen anything as fine, for they didn't understand how to unlace the sleeves, but at last my gown slipped free and I stepped out of it into an uncertain future.

Seven

On one of Florence's most oppressively narrow streets lies the Dominican convent known as Santa-Caterina da Siena. The convent's denizens fiercely opposed the Medici and supported the rebels, no doubt because it catered to the poor. Its six boarders—girls of marriageable age or younger, from families who had discovered that it was cheaper to keep them at the convent—were born of the lowest class of workers: the dyers, weavers, and carders of wool and silk, men whose occupations stained their hands, twisted their bodies, scarred their lungs. These were men who fell sick and died young, leaving behind daughters who could not be fed. These were men who had torn down our Medici banners and ignited them out of hatred for the rich and well-fed.

Santa-Caterina stank because its ancient plumbing and sewers were in disrepair. Nuns were always on their knees scrubbing floors and walls, but no amount of cleaning overcame the smell. The inhabitants were all thin and hungry. There were no Latin lessons here, no efforts made to teach the girls letters or numbers, only work to be done. The abbess, Sister Violetta, had no energy to like or dislike me; she was too busy trying to keep her charges alive to worry about politics. She knew only that the rebels paid for my care on time.

I shared a cell—and a dirty straw mattress alive with fleas and a family of mice—with four other boarders, all of them older than I. One of them hated me bitterly, as her brother had been killed in a clash with Medici supporters. Two of them did not much care. And then there was twelve-year-old Tommasa.

Tommasa's father was a silk merchant whose mounting debts had prompted him to flee the city, leaving his wife and children to deal with his creditors. Tommasa's mother was sickly; Tommasa, too, was frail and suffered from frightening bouts of wheezing and breathlessness, especially when she overexerted herself. She had the long, thin bones and delicate coloring of a Northerner: pale hair, white skin, eyes blue as sky. Yet she worked as hard as the others without complaint, and her lips were always curved in the gentlest of smiles.

She treated me as a friend, even though her brothers were passionate advocates of the rebel cause, so much so that Tommasa never mentioned me to them.

Tommasa was my sole link to the world beyond Santa-Caterina's walls. Her mother visited weekly and always brought news. I learned how the Medici palazzo had been pillaged, how its remaining treasures had been seized by the new government. All the banners bearing the Medici crest had been torn down, and all sculptures and buildings bearing the same had been crudely edited with chisels.

I asked about Aunt Clarice, of course, and tried not to cry when Tommasa told me she was still alive, though no one knew where she had gone. Ippolito's and Alessandro's whereabouts were also a mystery.

When I commented on Tommasa's kindness to me, she was taken aback.

"Why should I treat you otherwise?" she asked. "They say your family has oppressed the people, but you are kind to me and the others. I can't punish you for something others have done."

I loved her for the same reason I had loved Piero, because she was too good to glimpse the blackness hidden in my heart.

I spent a dismal summer fearing execution and hoping for news. Neither came, and by the time autumn arrived, I dwelled in a haze of hunger and grief. I lost will and weight and stopped asking questions of Tommasa as she relayed the latest gossip.

Winter came and brought an icy chill. Our room had no hearth and was freezing; I never stopped shivering. The water froze in the tiny basin we five shared, but we were too cold to bathe anyway. The fleas guaranteed that, if I slept at all, it was poorly. The cold never eased but grew more bitter.

One morning in late December, I headed with the other girls to the refectory. As we passed by a cell, a pair of nuns were carrying out a third. The last was completely rigid, and her sisters had lifted only her head and feet, as if she were a plank of wood. The two nuns glanced up at us, their forbidding gazes intended to silence all questions.

As they passed, Tommasa quickly crossed herself, and rest of us followed suit. We held our tongues and our places until they had disappeared down the corridor.

"Did you see that?" Lionarda, the oldest girl, hissed.

"Dead," one of the others said.

"Frozen," I said. But at the refectory, as we were waiting to have our bowls filled, one of the novices in front of us fainted and was taken away. I thought little of it: I swept floors and patched worn habits, unflinching when I pricked my chill-numbed fingers with the needle. I didn't worry until that evening at vespers, when I noticed that the chapel was only half full.

I whispered to Tommasa, "Where are the other sisters?"

"Taken sick," she answered. "Some sort of fever."

That night, I counted five separate times that the nuns hurried up and down the corridor. In the morning, four of us rose from the mattress. Lionarda did not.

Her breath hung as white vapor in the frigid air above her face; despite the cold, her forehead shone with sweat. One of the other girls tried to wake her, but neither shouting nor shaking could make her open her eyes. We called for the nuns, but no one came; the cells near ours were empty.

Tommasa and I stayed with Lionarda and sent the other two girls to get help. Half an hour later, a novice came in her white veil and black apron. Silently—for it was during an hour the nuns did not speak—she slipped her hands beneath Lionarda's nightgown and ran them swiftly over her neck, collarbone, armpits. She then reached under the gown to feel the area around Lionarda's groin and drew back with a spasm of fear.

She lifted up a corner of the nightgown to reveal a lump the size of a goose egg at the top of the girl's thigh, encircled by a dark purple ring, like a perfectly concentric bruise.

"What is it?" Tommasa breathed.

The novice mouthed an answer. I looked up too late to see it, but Tommasa gasped and lifted her hand to her throat.

"What is it?" I echoed, directing the question at Tommasa.

She turned toward me, her eyes and nose streaming from the cold, and whispered:

"Plague."

After they carried Lionarda away, Tommasa and I went to the refectory for the morning meal, then headed to the common room. Sister Violetta normally assigned us our chores there at that time. But the room had become a hospital, with a score of women lying on the floor—some groaning, some ominously quiet. An elderly sister intercepted us at the doorway and gestured for us to return to our cell. There we found the other two boarders, Serena and Constantina, sewing shrouds.

"What happened to Lionarda?" Serena demanded, and when I explained, she said, "Half the sisters were missing from the refectory this morning. It's plague, all right."

We huddled on the bed, our conversation anxious. I thought of Aunt Clarice, of how devastated she would be to learn that I had died in a squalid hovel, of how Piero would cry when he learned that I was gone.

After two hours, the elderly sister appeared in the doorway to tell Tommasa her brothers were at the grate—and to warn her that she was not to speak of the sickness at the convent. Tommasa left, and within the hour returned, her eyes bright with a secret. She said nothing until midday, when she rose to go to the water closet and gestured surreptitiously for me to join her.

After we entered the foul-smelling little room, she drew her fist from her pocket, then slowly uncurled it.

A small black stone, polished to a sheen, rested in her palm. I snatched it from her and thought of how Aunt Clarice had looked at me when the Wing of Corvus and the herb had dropped from my gown, how she had gazed thoughtfully at me as I bent to pick them up.

Did Ser Cosimo give you those? Keep them safe, then.

Only Clarice could have known that I had left the stone at Poggio a Caiano. Only Clarice could have found it and returned it to me to let me know I was not forgotten. My heart welled.

"Who gave this to you?" I demanded of Tommasa.

"A man," she said. "My brothers were leaving and I had just lowered the veil over the grate. The man must have looked through the bottom grate and seen the hem of my skirt."

"What did he say?" I asked.

"He asked me whether I was friend or foe of the Medici," Tommasa replied. "And when I said neither, he asked me if I knew a girl named Caterina. I told him yes, you were my friend.

"He offered me money if I would bring you that"—Tommasa nodded at the stone in my hand—"but speak of it to no one. Is it a family keepsake?"

"It was my mother's," I lied. Tommasa could clearly be trusted, but I needed no accusations of witchcraft to add to my troubles. "Did he say anything else?"

"I told him to throw the money through the lower grate into the alms box, as an offering to the convent. And I asked him whether he had any message for you, and he said, 'Tell her to be strong a little longer. Tell her I will return.' "

A little longer . . . I will return. The words made me giddy. I tucked the stone between my apron and dress, nestling it near the fabric sash that served as my belt.

I looked up at Tommasa. "We must never speak of this, not even to each other. The rebels would kill me or take me away."

She nodded solemnly.

Despite the presence of plague and the relentless winter, I walked Santa-Caterina's halls with growing joy. Each time I slipped my hand beneath my apron, I fingered the stone, and its cold, smooth surface became Clarice's embrace.

The next morning, we four remaining boarders rose to discover that the refectory had been closed. The cooks had fallen ill, and the remaining healthy sisters were overwhelmed by the added work of caring for the sick. No doubt there were more shrouds to be sewn, but the convent's routine had been broken, so we were forgotten. We returned to our cell and sat on the lumpy straw mattress, hungry and frightened and cold, and tried to divert one another with gossip.

After a few hours, sounds echoed in the corridor: a nun's sharp voice, feet scurrying against stone floors, doors being opened and closed. I peeked down the hallway and saw a sister madly kicking up dust with a broom.

"What are they doing?" Serena called. She sat cross-legged on the bed next to Tommasa.

"Cleaning," I replied in wonderment.

More doors were closed; the frenzied sweeping stopped. I could hear Sister Violetta issuing orders in the distance but could see no one. After a time, we girls went back to our stories.

Sister Violetta suddenly appeared in the open doorway.

"Girls," she said crisply and beckoned at them with her finger, even though this hour was one of silence for the sisters. "Not you, Caterina. You stay here. The rest of you, come with me."

She led the other girls away. I waited in agony. Perhaps another sister had seen the the stranger who had looked for me; perhaps Tommasa had revealed the secret. Now the rebels would kill me, or take me to a prison even worse than Santa-Caterina.

Moments passed, until footsteps sounded in the corridor—ringing ones, the unfamiliar sound of leather bootheels against stone. A rebel, I thought with despair. They had come for me.

But the man who appeared in my doorway looked nothing like Rinuccini and his soldiers. He wore a heavy cape of pink velvet lined with ermine, and a brown velvet cap with a small white plume; his goatee was fastidiously trimmed, and carefully crafted long black ringlets spilled onto his shoulders. He pressed a lace handkerchief to his nose; even at a distance, he exuded the fragrance of roses.

Beside him, Sister Violetta said softly, "This is the girl," then disappeared.

"Ugh!" the stranger said, his words muffled by lace. "Forgive me, but the stink! How do you bear it?" He lowered the kerchief to doff his cap and bowed.

"Do I have the pleasure of addressing Catherine de' Medici, *Duchessa* of Urbino, daughter of Lorenzo de' Medici and Madeleine de La Tour d'Auvergne?"

Catherine, he said, like the man in my bloodstained dream.

"I am," I replied.

"I am—ugh!—I am Robert Saint-Denis de la Roche, ambassador to the Republic of Florence at the will of His Majesty King François the First. Your late mother was a cousin of His Majesty, and it came to our attention yesterday that you, *Duchessa*—a kinswoman—were being held in the most egregious of circumstances. Is it true that those are the clothes you are forced to wear, and this is the bed upon which you are forced to sleep?"

My fist, hidden beneath my scapular and clutching the Raven's Wing, began slowly to uncurl.

"Yes," I said.

I wanted to run my fingers over the folds of his velvet cloak, to step out of my itchy wool dress into a fine gown, to have Ginevra lace up my bodice and bring me my pick of sleeves. I wanted to see Piero again. Most of all, I wanted to thank Aunt Clarice for finding me, and that last thought brought me very close to tears.

The ambassador's expression softened. "How terrible for you, a child. It is freezing here. It is a wonder you are not sick."

"There is plague here," I said. "Most of the sisters have it."

He swore in his foreign tongue; the square of lace fluttered to the ground. "The abbess said nothing to me of this!" He took almost immediate control of his temper and fright. "Then it is done," he said. "I'll arrange to have you moved from this flea-ridden cesspool today. This is no place for a cousin of the King!"

"The rebels won't let me go," I said. "They want me dead."

One of his black brows lifted slyly. "The rebels want a secure republic, which they do not have. They need the goodwill of King François, and they will not have it until they show proper respect to his kinswoman." He bowed again, suddenly. "I shall not linger, *Duchessa*—if there is plague in this building, I must move all the more swiftly. Give me a few hours, and we will take you to a home that is more suitable."

He began to move away; I called out, "Please tell my aunt Clarice how grateful I am that you have come!"

He stopped and faced me, his expression quizzical. "I have not been in contact with her, though I will certainly try to send her your message."

"But who sent you?"

"An old friend of your family alerted me," he said. "He said that you would know it was he. Ruggieri, I believe his name was." He paused. "Let me go now, *Duchessa,* for the plague moves swiftly. I swear before God, you will not spend another night here. So be of good cheer and brave heart."

"I will," I said, but the instant he disappeared down the corridor, I burst into tears. I cried because Ser Cosimo, a near stranger, had found me and taken pity; I cried because Aunt Clarice had not. I picked up the abandoned square of spiderweb-fine lace to wipe my eyes, and inhaled the scent of flowers.

I told myself that the Raven's Wing would protect me from plague and see me freed from Santa-Caterina; I vowed never to let it go again.

But the French ambassador did not come for me that morning, nor did anyone come for me that afternoon. I sat with the other girls sewing shrouds, so exhilarated and distracted that I pricked myself a dozen times. By dusk my good spirits had faded. What if the rebels were not as desperate to please King François as Monsieur la Roche had thought?

Night fell. I refused to undress, but lay in the bed beside Tommasa and scanned the darkness for signs of movement. Hours passed, until I saw the glow of a lamp outside. I hurried into the corridor to find Sister Violetta, who smiled fleetingly at my enthusiasm and gestured for me to follow.

She led me to her cell and dressed me in a regular nun's habit and winter cloak.

"Where am I going?" I asked.

"Child, I don't know."

She guided me outside, to the door leading to the street.

A male voice on the other side heard our footsteps and asked, "Do you have her?"

"I do," Sister Violetta said and opened the door.

The man on the other side wore a heavy cloak, and the long sword of a fighting man on his belt. Behind him, four mounted men waited.

"Here now," the man said. He held out his gloved hand to me. "Keep your face covered and come quickly, and without a peep. More's the danger if you cause a stir."

I balked. "Where are you taking me?"

A corner of his mustache quirked upward. "You'll learn soon enough. Give me your hand. I won't ask nicely again."

Reluctantly, I took it. He swung me up onto his horse, then took his place behind me on the saddle, and off we rode in the company of his men.

The night was moonless and cold. We made our way through empty streets that echoed with the clatter of our horses' hooves. I tried to figure out where we were going, but the gauzy wool limited my vision.

The journey lasted only a quarter hour. We stopped in front of a wooden door set in an expanse of stone wall; I was to be confined to yet another nunnery. I panicked, and dug beneath my cloak and habit for the black stone talisman.

My host dismounted and lifted me down while one of his soldiers banged on the heavy wood. In a moment, the door swung open silently. One of the men shoved me inside and shut the door firmly behind me.

The smell of vinegar was so sharp, I lifted a hand to my nose; the fabric wound around my head and face slipped, obscuring my vision. A cool hand caught my own and drew me several halting steps forward, away from the smell. When it let go, I pulled the veil down.

In a half circle before me stood twelve nuns—tall, graceful, veiled, and cloaked in black so that their forms disappeared into the darkness. I saw only their faces, lit by the lamps three of them bore—a dozen different gentle smiles, a dozen different pairs of kindly eyes.

The tallest of them stepped toward me. She was robust, broad-faced, middle-aged.

"Darling Caterina," she said. "I am the abbess, Mother Giustina—like you a Medici. When you were born, I stood as your godmother. Welcome."

Fearless of plague, she opened her arms to me, and I ran to them.

Eight

The Wing of Corvus had not failed. I found myself in Heaven, surrounded by angels: the Benedictine convent of Santissima Annunziata delle Murate, the Most Holy Annunciation of the Walled-In Ones, and the noblewomen who had taken vows there. Most were relatives of the Medici; only a few supported the new Republic.

The convent itself had been built and supported by Medici money; the fact showed in its broad corridors and elegant appointments. That night, Mother Giustina led me to my new quarters. Fear had left me exhausted, and I noticed no details except a large bed with heavy blankets and a plump pillow. I stood obediently as a servant stripped me; I palmed the stone and peered at the quiet, solemn woman. She had not noticed, being more concerned with filling a basin with heated water. She bathed me with a cloth, then pulled a clean nightgown of fine, soft wool over my head. I tucked the black stone into a pocket as she indicated the tray of cheese and bread on the bedside table. I devoured the food, then fell into bed. The servant laid a warmed brick at my feet and tucked the thick blankets around me tightly. For the first time that winter, I stopped shivering.

I slept for hours, the Wing of Corvus clutched in my fist. When I woke the next morning, I found myself in a vast chamber, with carved wainscoting on the walls and a marble fireplace. Honeyed light filtered through the large, arched window and revealed a large table and well-padded chairs, whose dark green velvet matched the drapes and bed coverings. On the wall in front of me was a large gold cross of filigree, beneath which sat a cushioned kneeling bench.

On the wall opposite the hearth were several shelves containing books. One of them, on the lowest shelf, caught my eye: it was bound in dark brown leather, with the title stamped in gold, of a familiar heft. I flew from the bed and dragged the heavy volume from the shelf.

Ficino. *De Vita Coelitus Comparanda, Gaining Life from the Heavens,* the very copy that had sat on Piero's knees; I recognized the nicks on the leather and laughed aloud. Inspired, I scanned the shelves, hoping to find gems rescued from the Palazzo Medici. I found no more, although I discovered two other volumes with titles written in Ficino's hand.

I was still poring over the titles when a knock came on the door, and two women and a nun appeared. The women carried a tub, and the bespectacled, elderly nun smiled brightly at me. Her body was plump and rounded, and her bearing and speech marked her as highborn. In her hand was a little tray bearing a glass and a dish of sweetmeats.

"Duchessina!" she said cheerfully. "So you have discovered your library. There is a larger one in the other wing, of course, but we put a few titles here we thought you might enjoy. I am Sister Niccoletta; if you have need of anything, ask me. I brought you some small treats and sweet wine to tide you over until breakfast arrives—you must still be so terribly hungry. Afterward, we'll properly rid you of those fleas."

Little duchess. The affectionately respectful term of address made me smile. I put my hand on Ficino's work and, forgetting my manners altogether, said, "This book. How did it come to be here, in this room?"

She peered through her thick spectacles, which magnified her dark eyes. "Ambassador de la Roche brought some things for you yesterday. This must be one of them."

"This was rescued from our palazzo," I said.

"God be thanked," she replied dismissively and turned as last night's solemn-faced servant entered with a large kettle in each hand. "Dear *Duchessina,* our servant Barbara is here. You can call on her as well for whatever you need." She set the tray on my night table, then from a pocket at her waist produced a letter sealed with wax. "Your breakfast will come shortly; in the meantime, you might enjoy reading this."

Her knowing smile made me reach eagerly for it and break the seal. The handwriting was Clarice's.

I pressed the letter to my heart. "Sister Niccoletta, please, forgive my rudeness. It's just that I have not been shown kindness in such a long time that I have forgotten my manners. Thank you for everything."

She beamed. "Why, your manners are lovely! You need not apologize to me, my dear, given all you have been through." She made a small curtsy. "Enjoy your letter, *Duchessina.* I will return in an hour."

Breathless, I unfolded the letter.

My dearest Caterina,

We are horrified at the news of your incarceration, and the cruel conditions you have been forced to endure. I hope you find your new surroundings more congenial. I shall remain in constant communication with the French ambassador from this time forward to ensure that you never again endure such privation. The rebels are desperate to keep the support of King François I of France, and His Majesty wishes his distant cousin to be well cared for.

Discretion precludes any discussion of my current whereabouts; it also precludes my visiting you in the flesh. Please know that I am working without rest to obtain your release. Pope Clement has escaped the ravaged landscape of Rome. He and Emperor Charles will soon be reconciled; I shall do whatever is in my power to nurture this newfound goodwill so that it leads to the restoration of the Medici to Florence.

I have not forgotten your bravery. Hold fast and never forget the destiny to which you are born.

With sincerest affection,
Your aunt,
Clarice de' Medici Strozzi

P.S. Your uncle and cousins send their regards. Piero insists I write that he misses you dreadfully.

Reading Clarice's elegant script made me ache to see her, but I was soon distracted by a plate of sausages and apples. After I ate, I submitted to the steaming tub. Barbara washed my hair, drowning the last of Santa-Caterina's fleas, and dressed me in a tailored gown, then swathed me in fine wool shawls to protect me from the chill.

Life at Le Murate was pleasantly distracting. Every morning and evening I sat with the nuns in the refectory and drank good wine and ate good meals, often with meat and cake. Sister Niccoletta treated me like a favored granddaughter, always bringing me little gifts of candied fruits and nuts, or a bright ribbon for my hair. She and the other nuns allowed me free run of the convent.

I did not abuse their trust. I attended Mass each morning and afterward accompanied Niccoletta to the sewing room. Many of the nuns did fine embroidery, one of the skills by which they supported themselves. Without a single guiding mark upon the fabric, Sister Niccoletta could stitch a perfect lamb holding the banner of the cross, or the Holy Spirit descending as a dove from Heaven.

On that first morning I was introduced to the other seamstresses: Sister Antonia, the abbess's second, tall, poised, and elderly; Sister Maria Elena, a Spanish woman with an angelic voice who led the choir; and a boarder, Maddalena, five years older than I, with chestnut hair that fell well past her shoulders. Maddalena was a Tornabuoni—the family that had produced the mother of Lorenzo *il Magnifico.* There was Sister Rafaela, an artist whose talent with brush and paint allowed her to decorate the finished manuscripts in the scriptorum with dazzling images. And there was Sister Pippa, a handsome young woman with red-gold eyebrows and light green eyes, colorful surprises against the frame of her white wimple and black veil. A blush bloomed upon her cheeks and neck when we were introduced; shyness, I thought, until I caught the look on the face of her constant shadow, the dark-skinned Sister Lisabetta, whose gaze revealed frank hatred.

That first morning, I sat on a cushion and stared out the large windows at the withered gardens, listening to the cheering crackle of the fire while Niccoletta brought me silk floss, a needle, and scissors. She gave me a handkerchief to practice on and directions on threading the needle and taking the first few stitches. Afterward, the sisters began to whisper to each other from time to time. The sounds comforted me, until I heard Sister Pippa's pointed question:

"Ought she to be moving about freely? She is, after all, a prisoner."

Lisabetta immediately chimed in. "No one stood guard over her chamber last night. She could easily have slipped away."

Sister Niccoletta let the swath of brocade she was embroidering drop to her lap and said, in a hard tone, "She's a child, one who has been through a horrible time. She certainly doesn't need you to remind her of it."

Pippa's neck and cheeks went scarlet, and nothing more was said on the matter. I soon learned that her and Lisabetta's families belonged to the People's Party, the most radical faction within the new government.

In the meantime, twice a week, Mother Giustina had me brought to her comfortable cell, where she privately instructed me in matters of noble protocol. She had not forgotten my rank as duchess, nor the fact that I had been destined to rule Florence, and her lessons reminded me that many in the city had not given up hope that the Medici would return to power. She taught me manners at table and the art of conversation, as well as how to address kings and queens and my uncle Pope Clement.

I attended other classes with Maddalena. Sister Rosalina taught me French, given that the French ambassador paid me regular visits in order to keep King François apprised of my well-being. I was uneasy during my first lesson and did not understand why until Sister Rosalina addressed me as Catherine—Catherine, the name Ruggieri had once unthinkingly called me, the name the bloodied man had called me in my nightmare.

It was at Le Murate that I began to suffer again from evil dreams. I was perplexed until I remembered that Ser Cosimo had said the talisman would make me recall them.

Mars dwells in your Twelfth House—the House of Hidden Enemies and Dreams.

I vowed never to be separated from the talisman again; I credited it, and Ser Cosimo, with the turn in my fortunes.

Your horoscope holds many terrible challenges, and now is the first. I intend to see you survive it.

Fate had returned Ficino and the talisman to me. I could not overlook such gifts; I spent my evenings studying *De Vita Coelitus Comparanda* by lamplight. Further exploration of the bookshelf in my room revealed another present: right next to the aforementioned tone sat an ancient-looking volume titled *The Book of Instruction in the Elements of the Art of Astrology,* by an Arab named al-Biruni.

The reading was dry and daunting for one so young, but I felt my survival depended on it. At the age of eight, I memorized the twelve signs of the Zodiac, and the twelve houses, and the seven planets.

In my nightmares, a man stood calling out my name, then later lay at my feet, his face a bubbling crimson spring.

Catherine . . .

More blood was coming: The Frenchman was calling out to me for aid to stop the approaching slaughter. It was up to me to decipher the danger, and to prevent it. Fate was offering me a chance to redeem myself.

I passed a content winter. Spring brought more bulletins from Clarice about Pope Clement: he was safely in Viterbo now, and Emperor Charles was apologetic about the horrors his mutinous troops had committed on Rome. Spring also brought newsy letters from Piero: *I am so tall now, you would not know me!* The air was heavy with fragrance; I, light with optimism. I felt safe, soon to be in control of my world thanks to my astrological studies.

Then came the eleventh of May, 1528, a year to the day I first heard that Pope Clement had been routed from the Vatican. When Sister Niccoletta came to fetch me for Mass that morning, her smile was forced and tremulous. I smelled an unhappy secret; and when Mother Giustina announced that the French ambassador would meet me in the reception chamber, my foreboding increased.

I sat in the sunlit room. Ambassador de la Roche was not long in coming. He had shaved his goatee, leaving a clean chin and a razor-thin mustache beneath his formidable nose. He was dressed for spring in a farsetto of pale green brocade and yellow leggings, and when he entered, he bowed low, with a great sweep of an arm.

"Duchessa," he said, rising. He did not smile; his tone was somber. "I hope you are well."

"Very well, Ambassador," I said. "And you?"

"Quite so, quite so, thank you." He dabbed his nose with the kerchief. "Your health has been good, then? And how go your studies?"

"My health has been fine. And I very much enjoy my studies. I have excellent teachers."

"Ah," he said, nodding. "All good then." He paused.

"Please," I said, suddenly hoarse with fear. "You have come to tell me something. Just say it."

"Ah, dear *Duchessa.* I am so sorry." His tone held pity as he produced a letter from the pocket at his belt. "Dreadful news has come. Clarice de' Medici Strozzi has died."

The words were too absurd to make sense of at first; I could not speak or cry. I could only stare at the Frenchman in his ridiculously cheerful colors.

"*Duchessa,* I am sorry. You are too young to have endured so many blows. Here." He thrust the letter at me.

May 4, 1528

Dear Caterina,

I am sorry to inform you that my wife, Clarice Strozzi, died yesterday. She suffered the last week with fever, but insisted on leaving her bed to entertain a visitor from Rome.

The night before she died, she sat at her desk writing letters to those persons most able to help her cause; morning found her still at her desk, so ill that she could not rise. We helped her to her bed and summoned the physician, but by then she realized she was dying.

Even in her suffering she did not forget you. She instructed me to write this letter, and tell you that your fortunes shall soon improve.

Look to Ambassador de la Roche from this time forth. He shall see that you are cared for and protected, as King François remains your faithful ally.

I am bereft.

Your uncle,
Filippo Strozzi

Like Uncle Filippo, I was disconsolate. I buried my face in Sister Niccoletta's lap while she wrapped her arms about me. I felt abandoned: Uncle Filippo was not bound by blood to me; my welfare now depended on the vague, distant interest of the King of France.

For two days I sat in my bed and refused to eat. Surrounded by my books, I read obsessively about Saturn, harbinger of death, and of his heavy, cold attributes, and wondered how he had been placed in Clarice's chart in the hour of her demise. I read all through the night; morning found me still reading, my eyes burning from strain, when Sister Niccoletta burst in abruptly, with her reticent servant Barbara in tow.

"Duchessina," she said, "a man has come to see you to pay his condolences."

I scowled. "Who is it?"

"I don't recall," Niccoletta replied, "but Mother Giustina knows him, and says it's all right for you to speak to him at the grate. I must hurry back to the sewing room, but Barbara will attend you." She turned to the servant. "Make sure that his behavior is appropriate and that no one overhears."

Uncle Filippo? I wondered. Perhaps he had risked coming to Florence. Or perhaps—this thought brought a small thrill—Piero had managed to come see me. Quickly I asked, "Was he young or old, this man?"

Niccoletta looked blankly at me before turning to leave. "Mother Giustina did not say."

Barbara led me outside to the convent wall. The door's upper grate was curtained, but near the basket of alms—reeking of the vinegar used to prevent the spread of plague—the lower grate was uncovered. I saw a man's boots.

Barbara knocked on the door and loudly announced, "The girl is here, sir. Mind your conversation remains discreet." In a weak gesture of privacy, she took two steps back from me.

"Donna Caterina," the man said, in a voice so resonant and deep I longed to hear it sing the words, "I come to bring heartfelt condolences on the death of your aunt. These have been cruel times for you."

Had I been tall enough, I would have thrown back the veil and looked on his ugly visage—on the pitted, sickly looking skin, the crooked nose and overlarge ears—to see whether he had changed over the chaotic months that had separated us. I rose onto my toes, wanting to be closer.

"Ser Cosimo." My tone held wonder. "How did you find me?"

"Did you think I had ever abandoned you? At Santa-Caterina, I brought you the stone. I thought surely you would know who sent it. You have it in your possession, do you not?"

"I do. I'm never without it."

"Good." He paused. "And the books rescued from the palazzo . . . ?"

"That was you . . ." It had been not Clarice but Cosimo Ruggieri all along. "But how did you save the books from the rebels? And I left the stone at Poggio a Caiano. How could you possibly have known . . . ?"

"You need not worry about the *how*, Madonna. You only need know that you have never been alone, and never will be."

Tears threatened, but I censored them. "I thank you. But how can I contact you if I need you?"

"Through the French ambassador."

"Why are you so kind to me?"

"I told you before, Caterina. You and I are bound by the stars. I am simply protecting my own interests."

"The stars," I said. "I want to learn everything I can about them."

"You are only a girl of nine," he countered quickly, then added, "but a most precocious one." He sighed. "Read Ficino, then. And al-Biruni is a helpful guide."

"I have to learn," I said. "I need to know what will happen to me, whether the Pope and Emperor Charles will come to an agreement, whether I will ever be rescued."

"The Pope and Emperor will come to an agreement," Ser Cosimo said easily. "Even so, there is no point in worrying about the future now. Just know that I am at your disposal whenever you have need of me." He took a step away; his voice grew distant. "I must leave now; for your sake, I cannot risk being seen. God be with you, Caterina."

I listened to his footsteps as they slowly faded away.

"Ser Cosimo," I said and pressed my palm to the door. I did not move until Barbara caught my elbow and pulled me away.

The summer passed without further incident, as did the next fall and winter. I grew and became more proficient in French. In my dreams at night, I told the bloody man, *Je ne veux pas ces reves, I do not want these dreams.*

When summer came again, I and most of the sisters at Le Murate rejoiced to learn that the Pope would soon return to Rome; Clement had agreed to crown Charles in return for Charles's support of the Medici cause. Having lost too many battles to the Imperial forces, the French King, François, had likewise made peace with Charles and was withdrawing all support from Florence's rebel Republic.

One warm, sticky morning in June, surrounded by the sisters, I stared beyond the open windows of the sewing room to find charcoal-colored clouds billowing on the horizon: Outside the city, crops and barns were burning, set ablaze by soldiers of the rebel government. Emperor Charles was coming—or at least his troops were, led by the Prince of Orange—and the rebels did not intend for them to find succor beyond the walls of Florence.

Outside the confines of Le Murate, a militia ten thousand men strong was forming. Walking outside in the garden or on the patio, I heard the terse shouts of commanders trying to organize untrained troops. Fearful of the coming battle, hundreds fled Florence. With Maddalena standing watch, I climbed the alder in the garden and tried to look beyond the city walls but saw only rooftops and the grey haze hanging over the city. Florence stank of smoke; it clung to our clothes and hair, and permeated every corner of the convent.

September brought happy news: King François had signed a treaty with Emperor Charles. No French troops would aid the rebel Republic. I celebrated silently when I heard these things yet at the same time was afraid. I remembered the horrific Sack of Rome, when the Emperor's men ignored orders and laid siege to the Holy City, breaking down the doors of convents and raping nuns.

On the twenty-fourth of October, I sat sewing in my usual spot between Maddalena and Sister Niccoletta, both of them as anxious as Pippa and Lisabetta, who huddled over their work in silence. Sister Antonia's normally serene visage was troubled.

Beyond the window, the day was gloomy with smoke and the threat of an autumn storm; the alder had lost most of its leaves and stood bleak and jagged.

I was working on a white linen altar cloth; that morning, I fumbled. The floss seemed too thick, the hole in the needle too narrow. My first few stitches were errant and had to be snipped out.

My thimble had worn thin at the spot I exerted the most pressure. Distracted, I gathered too much fabric at once, requiring me to push hard against the thimble. As a result, the threaded eye of the needle pierced the leather thimble and sank deep into my thumb.

I let go a startled cry and jumped to my feet; the altar cloth dropped to the floor. All the nuns stopped their work to look at me. I gritted my teeth and, with a sensation of nausea, grabbed the needle and pulled hard. It came free, and I stared at the swelling pearl of blood on my thumb.

"Here," Niccoletta said. She snatched a bit of fluff from a ball of uncombed wool in the sewing basket and pressed it to my thumb.

As she did, a distant boom caused the open windowpanes to shudder. Maddalena and Sister Pippa ran to the window and peered out at the distant plume of smoke rising into the air.

"Back to your work, all of you." Sister Antonia's voice was calm. "Take care of it, and God will take care of you."

The instant she finished speaking, a second boom sounded.

"Cannon," Niccoletta whispered.

Sister Pippa remained at the window, staring as if she could somehow look beyond the convent walls. "The Emperor's army," she said, her voice rising. "Seven thousand men, but we have ten." She looked at me, her eyes bright with hate. "You'll never win."

"Pippa," Antonia chided harshly. "Sit and be silent."

The cannon sounded a third time; simultaneously a fourth rumble came from the opposite direction: Florence was surrounded. Lisabetta jumped to her feet and hurried to Pippa's side.

Pippa's cheeks were scarlet with fury. "They won't let you go free."

"Pippa!" Antonia snapped.

Pippa ignored her. "Do you know what the Republic plans for you?" She sneered at me. "To lower you in a basket over the city walls and let the Emperor's men blast you to pieces."

Sister Niccoletta rose urgently. "Pippa, stop it! Stop it!"

"Or to put you in a brothel so you can play whore to our soldiers. Then Clement won't be so quick to marry you off to his advantage!"

Niccoletta lunged and slapped Pippa full in the face.

"Enough!" Sister Antonia cried. She moved between the two women; she was taller than either, and more formidable. Niccoletta sat back down beside me and put an arm about my shoulder.

Pippa stared defiantly at Sister Antonia. "You'll regret coddling her. She's an enemy of the people and will come to a bad end."

Sister Antonia's face and eyes and voice were stone. "Go to your cell. Go to your cell and pray for forgiveness for your anger until I send for you."

In the hostile silence that followed, cannon thundered.

At last Sister Pippa turned away and left. After a dark glance at Antonia, Lisabetta went back to her chair.

"And you," Sister Antonia said, more gently, to Niccoletta, "will need to make your own prayers when you are in chapel."

We all sat then, and took up our work again. I had forgotten about my thumb, and in the excitement, the bit of wool had fallen off. When I gathered the altar cloth in my hands, I stained the linen with blood.

The cannonfire continued until dusk. That afternoon, Maddalena's panicked mother came to the grate and confirmed what we suspected: The Imperial army had arrived and had surrounded the city.

That night I penned a letter to Cosimo Ruggieri. My correspondence with him had been limited to the subject of astrology, but desperation caused me to open my heart.

I am terrified and alone. I was foolish enough to think that the arrival of the Imperial troops would make me safer. But war has rekindled the people's hatred toward me. I fear the Raven's Wing alone is not enough to shield me from this fresh danger. Please come, and set my mind at rest.

My esteemed Madonna Caterina,

War brings dangerous times, but I assure you that the Wing of Corvus has guarded you well, and will continue to do so. Trust the talisman; more important, trust your own wits. You possess an intelligence uncommon in a man, unheard of in a woman.

Only wait, and let events play themselves out.

Your servant,

Cosimo Ruggieri

I felt abandoned, betrayed. I gave up my books, made no effort at my studies. In the refectory I sat beside Niccoletta and stared down at my porridge; food had become nauseating, unthinkable. I did not eat for three days. On the fourth day, I took to my bed and listened to the shouts of soldiers, the song of artillery.

On the fifth day the abbess came to visit. She smelled faintly of the smoke that permeated Florence.

"Dear child," she said, "you must eat. What do you fancy? I will see it brought to you."

"Thank you," I said. "But I don't want anything to eat. I'm going to die anyway."

"Not until you are an old woman," Giustina said sharply. "Don't ever say such a thing again. Sister Niccoletta told me what Sister Pippa said to you. Horrible words, inexcusable. She has been reprimanded."

"She was telling the truth."

"She was repeating silly rumors, nothing more."

Exhausted, I turned my face away.

"Ah, Caterina . . ." The bed shuddered gently as she sat beside me. She caught my hand and took it between her own cool ones. "You have been through too much, and these are terrible times. How can I comfort you?"

I want Aunt Clarice, I began to say, but such words were vain and heart-wrenching.

I looked back at her. "I want Ser Cosimo," I said. "Cosimo Ruggieri."

It was enough, Mother Giustina said, that she had tolerated the astrologer's one visit and, indeed, that she had permitted me to study astrology although it was an inappropriate subject for a woman, much less a young girl. She had conveyed Ser Cosimo's letters to me only because he had been a friend of the family. But there were rumors of his alliance with unsavory individuals, and of certain acts. . . .

I faced the wall again.

Giustina let go a troubled sigh. "Perhaps earlier, before your aunt died, we should have tried harder. . . . But even then, the rebels watched our every move, read every letter sent you. We could never have gotten you past the city gates. And now . . ."

I would not look at her. In the end, she agreed to allow further communication.

Within three days—during which I remained abed but allowed myself a few hopeful sips of broth—Sister Niccoletta arrived at my bedside, fresh from outdoors. A bitter storm had brought freezing rain; tiny beads of ice melted upon her caped shoulders. In her hand was a folded piece of ivory paper, and even before she proffered it to me, I knew its author.

My esteemed Madonna Caterina,

The good abbess Mother Giustina has informed me of your malaise. I pray God you will soon find health and cheer again.

There is no cure for these uneasy times save caution and wit, but I would be happy to provide another talisman should it give you comfort. One under the augury of Jupiter would encourage, in some small way, good fortune, but

I crumpled the letter into a ball and, while Sister Niccoletta watched wide-eyed, cast it into the fire.

Afterward, I shunned even broth and water. Within a day, the fever came. Outside my window the wind howled, swallowing the boom of the cannon. The thrill of the sheets against my skin set my teeth chattering; my body ached from the cold, but the blankets gave no warmth. Firelight stung my eyes and made them stream.

I began to lose myself—lose the walls and the bed and the baying wind. I traveled to the stone wall enclosing the rear of the Medici estate, where the stableboy appeared, miraculously alive, the dagger's hilt still protruding from his neck; we argued a time over the necessity of his death. The scene shifted: I stood on the battlefield where my bloodied Frenchman lay. During my long and vague conversations with him, murmuring crows huddled before the hearth, casting long shadows over the crimson landscape, speaking senselessly. Perhaps I cried out Clarice's name; perhaps I cried out Ruggieri's.

When, tearful, aching, and uncertain, I discovered I was still in my bed at Le Murate, it was still dusk. The light was still too bright, the fire too cold, the sheets too painful against my skin.

Barbara looked down at me, one of my better gowns in her arms.

"You're better," she announced. "You should sit up awhile, and be properly dressed."

The suggestion was so absurd that I, in my weakness, could not reply. I tried to stand but could not, and sat trembling in the chair while Barbara coaxed my body into the gown and laced it up.

My bed was too distant, my legs unreliable. I sank back in the chair, unable to fight off the cup lifted to my lips. Cup and chair and Barbara: These things seemed solid at first glance, yet if I stared too long they began to shimmer.

"Stay there," Barbara ordered. "I'll return soon." She stepped outside and closed the door.

I clutched the arms of the chair to keep from sliding off, and let myself be dazzled by the fire's sparks of violet and green and vivid blue.

The door opened and closed again. A raven stood in front of the hearth—one tall and caped with a hood pulled forward, obscuring its face. Slowly it lowered the cowl.

I was alone with Cosimo Ruggieri.

Nine

I blinked; Ruggieri's apparition did not fade. He looked older, having grown a thick black beard that hid his pockmarked cheeks. In the hearth's orange glow, his skin took on a devilish hue.

Delirious, I trembled in my chair. He could not be standing there, of course. The nuns would never permit him behind the cloister walls.

"Forgive me if I have startled you, Caterina," he said. "The sisters told me you were very ill. I see that they were telling the truth."

My head lolled against the chair. Speechless, I stared at him.

"Stay just as you are," he said. "Don't move. Don't speak." He let the cloak slip from his shoulders and drop to the floor. All black, his clothes, his hair, his eyes—there was no color to him at all. On his heart rested a coin-sized copper talisman, unapologetic magic. He moved to the room's center, just in front of my chair. Facing the fire, he drew a dagger from his belt and pressed the flat of the blade to his lips, then lifted it high above his head with both hands, the tip pointing at the invisible sky.

He began to chant. The sound was melodious, but the words were harsh and utterly incomprehensible. As he sang, he lowered the blade, gently touching the flat to his forehead, then to the talisman over his heart, then to each shoulder, right and left. Again he kissed the dagger.

He then took a step forward to stand an arm's length from the hearth. He sliced the air boldly, then jabbed the knife in its center and called out a command. Four times he did the same: carving great stars and joining them with a circle. I huddled in the chair, entranced. In my feverishness, I imagined I could see the faint hot-white outline of the stars and circle.

Ser Cosimo returned to the room's center and flung out his arms, a living crucifix. He called out names: Michael, Gabriel, Raphael.

He turned and knelt beside the arm of my chair, his tone gentle. "Now we are safe," he said.

"I'm not a stupid child," I told him. "I won't be soothed by lies."

"You're frightened of the future," he countered. "Afraid you don't possess the strength to survive it. Let us learn something of it together." He tilted his head and looked into me. "A question. Formulate your fears into a question."

Uneasy, I asked, "A question for whom?"

"A spirit," he answered. "One of my choosing, for I know those whom I can trust."

The skin on my arms prickled. "You mean a demon."

He did not deny it but gazed steadily at me.

"No," I said. "No demons. Ask God."

"God does not reveal the future. An angel might—but angels are too slow for our purposes tonight." He looked away at the shadows veiling the western wall. "But there are others who might . . ."

"Who?"

He stared at me again. "The dead."

Aunt Clarice, I meant to say. But something raw welled up from my core, a hurt so deeply buried that, until that instant, I had never known it was in me.

"My mother," I said. "I want to speak to her."

The emotion of the moment gave me strength. I got to my feet beside Ser Cosimo and turned toward the western wall, opposite the hearth. Ser Cosimo produced a stoppered vial, opened it, and dipped the tip of his index finger in it, then traced upon my forehead a star.

I smelled blood and closed my eyes, dizzied. I had gone too far, let myself slip again into the grasp of evil. "There is blood in this," I whispered and opened my eyes to see his response.

Ruggieri's eyes were wide and strange, as if his spirit had suddenly expanded and become a force greater than himself.

"Nothing comes without cost," he said and traced a star upon his own forehead, leaving a dark brown smear. Then he sat down at my writing desk.

"Paper," he demanded.

I took a clean sheet from the drawer and placed it in front of him. Before I could move my hand away, he caught it and pricked my middle finger with the tip of the dagger.

I cried out.

"Hush," he warned. I tried to pull away, but he held my hand fast and milked my finger until a fat drop of blood dripped onto the page. "My apologies," he murmured as he let go and I put the offended digit to my lips. "Fresh blood is necessary."

"Why?"

"She will smell it," he answered. "It will draw her."

He set the dagger down, then closed his eyes and breathed deeply. His head began to sway.

"Madeleine," he whispered. My mother's name. "Madeleine . . ." His eyelids trembled. "Madeleine," he said, then groaned loudly.

His torso and arms stiffened and twitched; this continued a moment, until he slumped in the chair and released a harsh, involuntary sigh.

Of apparent separate volition, his right hand groped for the quill and dipped the nib in the ink. For moment, the pen hovered over the page as the hand that held it jerked spasmodically. Suddenly his hand relaxed and began to write with impossible speed.

I gaped as the letters poured onto the page. The script was distinctly feminine, the language French—my mother's native tongue.

Ma fille, m'amie, ma chère, je t'adore
My daughter, my beloved, my darling, I adore you

My eyes filled with silent tears; they sprang pure and hot from a wound I had never known existed.

A woman, yet greatest of all your House
You will meet your benefactor
A question

The pen hovered over the paper; Ruggieri's hand trembled. A pause, and then another spasm of writing:

A question

"Will the rebels kill me?" I asked. "Will I ever be freed?"

The hand hesitated, then jerked and began to write.

Do not fear, m'amie, *Silvestro will see you safely returned*

The quill fell and left a dark blot upon the paper. Ser Cosimo's hand went fully limp, then curled into a fist.

"What more?" I cried, desperate. "There must be more . . ."

Ser Cosimo's head lolled upon his shoulders, then steadied. His eyes opened—blank and clouded—then slowly cleared until he saw me again.

"She has gone," he said.

"Call her back!"

He shook his head. "No."

I stared down at the impossible writing. "But what does it mean?"

"Time will make it clear," he said. "The dead see all: Yesterday, today, tomorrow are all the same for them."

I lifted the paper from the desk and held it to my heart; Ruggieri, the desk, the floor, suddenly began to whirl. I staggered; the room tilted sideways, and I fell into darkness.

I woke in my bed. Sister Niccoletta sat beside me, reading the small psalter in her hands; light streamed through the window and glinted dazzlingly off one lens of her spectacles. She glanced up and smiled warmly.

"Sweet girl, you're awake." She set aside her book and laid a cool palm upon my forehead. "The fever's broken, praise be to God! How do you feel?"

"Thirsty," I said.

She turned her back to me to fuss over a pitcher and cup on the nearby table. I sat up and quickly patted my chest, the last place I remembered putting my mother's letter, but felt only the silk amulet that held the raven's wing. I panicked. Had Ruggieri's visit been the product of a fevered dream?

I propped myself up with my palms behind me. They slid against the sheets and beneath my pillow, where my fingertips grazed the sharp edge of paper.

I pulled it out quickly. It was folded in half, with the writing on the inside so that I could not make it out, but I recognized the large blot of dark ink.

Ma fille, m'amie, ma chère, je t'adore

As Sister Niccoletta turned with the cup in her hand, I slipped the letter beneath the blankets.

"I'm hungry, too," I told her. "Would it be possible to get something to eat?"

I kept my mother's letter beneath my pillow and every night tucked my hand there, palm resting upon the only memento I had of her; the rebels had taken all else. It brought warmth and sadness and a wistful welling of affection; it brought comfort the way no talisman could.

Christmas came and Christmas passed, and the new year of our Lord 1530 arrived. In February, Pope Clement crowned Charles of Spain Emperor of the Holy Roman Empire. Clement had fulfilled his end of the bargain; now it was time for Charles to deliver Florence into Medici hands.

In those early months, the cannon were silent. The Imperial commander realized that his advantage lay in striking not at Florence herself but at those towns that supplied her with arms and food. The summer before the siege all crops grown outside Florence's walls had been torched months before the harvest, all livestock slaughtered. To eat, Florence relied upon supplies smuggled from Volterra. For goods, for news, for troops, she relied upon Volterra.

As the weather warmed, the Imperial forces attacked our lifeline. We sent a garrison to defend our sister; Volterra survived the first battle. Deciding that the Emperor's army had been decisively defeated, our garrison commander—against orders—left for the comforts of home. Hearing this, the Prince of Orange laid siege to the town a second time.

I was at my embroidery when Mother Giustina appeared in the sewing room doorway. Her expression was troubled but furtively hopeful.

"Volterra has fallen," she said.

Without help from the French and now without sustenance or arms, the rebel leaders faced certain defeat.

I sat listening to the sisters' unhappy murmurs and thought very hard.

My hair fell past my hips, fine and thin, the color of olive bark. That day it was gathered up into a large net that rested heavily on the nape of my neck. I unfastened the net and shook my hair free, then took up the scissors and began to snip. It took a long time; the scissors were made for embroidery and could take only small bites. After each cut, I carefully placed the ribbon of hair neatly at my feet.

The thunderstruck sisters watched silently; only Mother Giustina understood. She waited in the doorway, and when I was fully shorn, she said tersely, "I'll find you a habit."

I took the veil but not the vows. I was an impostor, but not even Sister Pippa complained.

Meanwhile, citizens grew desperate. Without Volterra's grain stores, there was no wheat; without the hunters' catch from the forest beyond the city walls, there was no meat. The poor were hit first and hardest, and began starving in the streets. Plague flourished, prompting Mother Giustina to remove the alms box and board up the lower grate.

In the first days of July, I received my last letter from Ser Cosimo:

> *I will not be corresponding for a while. This morning I saw my neighbor sitting propped against his front door, eyes closed as though he were sleeping. I thought hunger had made him faint. Fortunately, I had not advanced too far before I saw the buboes upon his neck. I called out to those inside but heard no reply.*

I went home immediately and bathed with lemon juice and rose water, a remedy I highly recommend. As a precaution, burn this letter and wash your hands.

I have confidence we will meet again in the flesh.

At dusk on the twentieth of July, I sat in the refectory flanked by Maddalena and Sister Niccoletta at the supper all sisters shared. Per custom, we observed silence as we dined on our *minestra,* whose broth now lacked meat or pasta.

The eastern wall of the refectory bore a fresco of the Last Supper; the adjacent wall was broken by a large window overlooking the patio and the convent door, its grates now boarded shut.

Atop my scapular, the work apron worn over the habit, I wore a golden crucifix, but beneath the habit I wore Ruggieri's black amulet. I had assiduously studied my nativity until the greater details were committed to memory, and had followed the position of the planets and stars over the days and nights. Mars, hot red warrior, was conjunct Saturn, harbinger of death and destruction, and passing through my ascendant—Leo, the marker of royalty. Such a transit warrants danger and ofttimes violent ends. And Saturn, silent and dark, had sailed into my Eighth House, the House of Death. Like Florence's, my stars boded catastrophic change.

When I heard the pounding at the convent gate, I felt little surprise. For a moment, we women sat very still and listened to it echo off the worn cobblestone.

Sister Antonia directed a pointed look at Mother Giustina; the abbess nodded, and Antonia rose and walked out of the refectory, her gaze guarded and avoiding mine. As she did, masculine voices at the door began to shout.

I set down my spoon. The walls that for two and a half years had afforded protection were now a trap. I jumped up, thinking to run, knowing I could go nowhere.

"Caterina," Mother Giustina warned. When I gaped at her, she ordered sternly, "Go to the chapel."

Outside at the gate, Sister Antonia cried out, "You cannot come inside. This is a nunnery!"

Something slammed against the door, something heavier and thicker than a human fist. Giustina was on her feet.

"Go to the chapel," she repeated and then ran, veil and full sleeves fluttering, to join Antonia. Halfway across the cobblestone patio, she called out to the men behind the wall, but the battering was so loud her words were lost.

Sister Niccoletta rose and seized my arm. "Come." She pulled me with her toward the refectory door, and suddenly we were encircled by others—Maddalena and Sister Rafaela, Barbara and Sister Antonia and Sister Lucinda—all of us moving together.

Lisabetta and Pippa remained at the table. "They've come for you," Pippa gloated. "They've come and God will see justice done."

The others engulfed me. We swept out into the corridor, past the archway that opened onto the patio, past the nuns' cells.

Behind us, the hammering abruptly stopped, giving way to voices calling back and forth over the wall: Mother Giustina's, a man's. The sounds faded as we moved deeper inside the convent, passing the scriptorum and emerging from the other end of the building. Outside, the dying light colored the clouds in sunset shades of rose and coral against a greying lilac sky.

We crossed the walkway and entered the chapel, the candles already lit for vespers, the air hazy with frankincense. The sisters brought me to the altar railing and formed a half-moon barrier around me. I knelt trembling at the railing; Saturn weighed so heavily on me I could not breathe. I reached for the rosary on my belt and began to recite from memory but stumbled over the words. My mind was not on the beads in my hand but on the black stone over my heart; my prayers were not truly to the Virgin but to Venus, not to Jesus but to Jove.

Giustina's shouts filtered in through the open doors. "You commit sacrilege! She is a child, she has done no one harm . . . !"

Bootheels hammered against stone. I turned and saw them enter: men with heads unbowed, hearts uncrossed, as though these walls were not hallowed.

"Where is she?" one demanded. "Where is she, Caterina of the Medici?"

I crossed myself. I rose. I turned and looked beyond the shoulders of my sisters at four soldiers armed with long swords—as if we were a danger, as if we might give fight.

The youngest of them, all gangling limbs and nerves, had eyes as bright and wide as mine. His chin was up, his hand on his hilt. "Back away," he told my sisters. "Back away. We must take her, by order of the Republic."

Niccoletta and the others stood fast and silent. The soldiers drew their swords and advanced a step. A collective sigh, and the women scattered.

All of them, except Niccoletta. She stepped in front of me, her arms spread, her voice hard. "Do not lay a hand on this child."

"Move away," the young soldier warned.

I caught hold of Niccoletta's arm. "Do as he says."

Niccoletta was stone, and the soldier so nervous, he swung his sword. The flat hit Niccoletta's shoulder and dropped her to her knees.

The sisters and I cried out at the same instant Niccoletta did. I knelt beside her. She was speechless, gasping in pain, but there was no blood; her spectacles were still in place.

The other more seasoned soldiers elbowed the younger man back before he could do further harm.

"Here now," one said. "Don't press us to violence in God's house."

As he spoke, two more soldiers entered, followed by a dark-haired man with silver in his trimmed beard and an air of authority. He had come to take me to die.

Mother Giustina, red-eyed and resigned, walked beside him.

With one hand, I gestured at my white veil and raised my voice; it echoed, clear and ringing, throughout the chapel. "What sort of excommunicated fiend would enter a sanctuary to drag a bride of Christ from her convent? Would dare to drag her to her doom?"

The commander's eyes crinkled in amusement.

"I dare do neither," he said, in a tone so good-natured that it broke the spell of fear. The women, arms raised in protest, slowly lowered them; the soldiers sheathed their weapons. "I have simply come to transport you, Donna Caterina, to a safer place."

"This place is safe!" Mother Giustina countered.

The commander turned to her and politely said, "Safe for her purposes, Abbess, but not the Republic's. This is a den of Medici sympathizers." He settled his gaze again on me. "You see that we have sufficient force to take you, *Duchessa.* I would sincerely prefer to use none."

I studied him a long moment, then lifted my fingers to Sister Niccoletta's face and stroked it; she touched her forehead to mine and began to cry.

"Stop," I said softly and kissed her cheek. Her skin was powder-soft and weathered, and tasted of bitter brine.

Ten

The commander asked me to dispense with the habit and change into a regular gown, but I refused. He did not ask a second time. Haste was critical, and when, for the first time in two and a half years, I stepped outside Le Murate's walls into the street, I understood why.

Eight soldiers on horseback had fanned out in a half circle around the cloister gate. Four of them held torches; four of them brandished swords against a crowd thrice their number but steadily growing.

As the soldiers and I passed through the gate, a man in the crowd shouted, "There she is!"

I could not see much of the crowd beyond the men on horseback, only a leg here, an arm there, a glimpse of a face. Color fled in the wake of twilight, leaving behind black and grey.

In the center of the group of soldiers, two men held the reins of unmounted horses and a donkey. One of them handed off his reins to the other as he caught sight of us and hurried over.

"Commander," he said apologetically. "I don't know how word got out . . ."

No, it's her, it is! The little nun—

The Pope's niece—

Pampered in a rich nunnery all this time while we starve!

The commander's face grew still, save for a muscle that spasmed in his cheek. He looked out at his men and said softly, "I chose you because I thought you could hold your tongues. When I learn who has done this—I care not why, I care not how—I will see him swing."

Death to the Medici! a woman cried.

A hurled stone struck just inside the ring of soldiers; it skipped and clattered to a stop near my feet.

Bastards! Traitors!

Give her to us!

The commander looked down at it, then back at his second. "Get her mounted," he said. "Let's move on before it gets worse."

The troops ran to their horses. The second, a large, sullen-faced man, took my elbow as if I were an unruly commoner and swung me up onto the donkey. The animal looked reproachfully back at me, showing large yellow teeth that worried the bit.

The commander, now astride a pale grey stallion, rode up alongside me and called to his men. We began to move: the commander and I side by side, each flanked by a mounted soldier. In front of us, behind us, men rode three abreast.

Before all the men were in formation, three street thugs dashed between the horses' bodies; one reached for me, the tips of his fingers grazing my leg. I cried out. The commander bellowed and leaned toward him with such urgent ferocity that the filthy youth shrank back, and was trampled by a horse.

Abaso le palle! someone shouted. *Death to the Medici!*

The soldiers closed ranks around us, and we made our way down the broad Via Ghibellina at an earnest trot. The crowd followed us for a while, hurling curses and the occasional missile. We soon outpaced them and made our way onto a quieter thoroughfare. We passed monastery walls, cathedrals, and rich men's houses, the windows dark because the owners had fled in the face of the siege.

I clutched the saddle horn and slapped, stiff with dread, against the donkey's saddle. Too late today for a public execution; it would have to wait until morning—unless a quick and private death awaited.

The streets grew narrower. The grand estates gave way to shops and tradesmen's houses.

As we turned onto a broader avenue, our caravan slowed. In the near distance, black forms blocked the street. They had been waiting silently in the dark.

"*Damn* you," the commander cursed his men. "Before God, if one of you is the traitor, I'll send you to Hell myself . . ."

Death to the Medici, someone in the darkness said uncertainly.

The cry erupted with fervor: *Abaso le palle! Down with the balls!*

A hail of stones followed.

Beside me, the commander reined in his stamping horse and bellowed, "This prisoner is being transported at the command of the Republic! Anyone who interferes is a traitor!"

"*You* are the traitors," a woman's voice cried.

She stepped forward into the torchlight, a starving wraith wrapped in filthy rags. Beneath her jutting collarbones, her torn bodice had been rolled down to expose one breast, where a weakly wailing infant refused to suckle. She glared at me, her eyes two wild black holes.

"Medici bitch!" she roared. "You kill me, you kill my child! Your soldiers starve us, while you grow fat! *You* should die! *You!*"

You, the crowd echoed. *Death to the Medici!*

Two youths ran out of the dark to accost the soldier on my left. One grabbed his heel in the stirrup and pulled him down; the other struck him with a club. He fell sideways in the saddle, grappling with the first youth.

"Get his sword!" someone shouted, and the crowd rushed forward.

The commander barked orders and reined his horse in until his leg pressed against mine. The fallen soldier had managed to unsheathe his sword and held the youths at bay.

A grizzled beggar dashed into the light, gripped the skirt of my habit, and tugged mightily; the donkey brayed and I screamed. My saddle slipped, and the world canted sideways in a frightening whirl of animal hide and swords and filthy limbs.

My legs became tangled in the stirrups; my shoulder struck bone and flesh. I looked up in midfall and saw the beggar's yawning grin, studded with cracked and rotting teeth, maggots in a putrid hole. I felt his hands on me and screamed again.

Suddenly he disappeared; I kicked free from the stirrups and was guided up by strong hands onto my feet. The commander's right arm pressed me close; his left hand brandished his sword. On the stones before us, the beggar lay bleeding. The soldiers encircled us, holding back the now-quiet crowd.

The commander pointed the tip of his sword at the beggar's head and thundered, "The next one who touches her, I'll kill." He lowered his voice. "She's just a girl. A girl at the mercy of the same politics you poor bastards are."

He mounted his stallion, then gestured at his second in command, who lifted me so that the commander could pull me up into his saddle. We began to move again. The commander's arms were on either side of me as he held the reins, and momentum pushed me back against his chest, warm and hard.

Now and then, I caught a whiff of raw meat left too long in the sun. The commander pulled out a square of linen and handed it to me.

"Put it over your nose and mouth," he said. "There's plague in this neighborhood."

I put it over my nose and breathed in the antiseptic fragrance of rosemary.

"You're still trembling," he said. "It's all right now. The street rabble, I won't let them harm you."

I lowered the kerchief. "That's not what I fear."

He grew quiet, then said softly, "We don't know what to do with you. Were it my choice, I'd free you now. It's only a matter of time."

Eager, wistful, I half turned in the saddle. "You really think I'll be freed?"

The same muscle in his cheek twitched. "A cruel thing for a child," he said. "You've been our prisoner—how long now? Three years? With luck, you'll outlive me, *Duchessa.* Me and every one of these poor bastards here." He indicated his troops with a jerk of his chin. "Your friends outnumber ours now."

Hope tugged at me. "Don't lie," I said.

His mouth stretched in a cynical grin. "I'll lay you a wager that, within two months' time, you and I will see our fortunes reversed."

"And what are the stakes?" I asked.

"My life."

I didn't properly understand his reply then, but I said, "Done."

"Done it is," he said.

I settled against him. Whether he had lied or not, he had put my mind at ease.

"For our wager," I said lightly, looking out at the shopfronts and walls as the torches' yellow glow swept over them, "if you lose, whose head shall I ask for?"

The instant he opened his mouth, I knew what he would say.

"Silvestro," he said. "Silvestro Aldobrandini, a humble soldier of the Republic."

I thought of my mother's letter, lying beneath my pillow at Le Murate, forever lost.

Our party encountered no more challenges, and we made our way quickly to the northern quarter of San Giovanni. Once there, we turned onto the narrow Via San Gallo and came to a cloister wall, behind which Sister Violetta was waiting to receive me.

It was the convent of Santa-Caterina, where I had spent the first months of my captivity. Ser Silvestro had seen me safely returned.

Eleven

As she closed the wooden gate on Ser Silvestro, Sister Violetta received me as she had before, finger to lips. Her lantern revealed the toll the past three years had taken; she was even gaunter now. She turned and led me upstairs to my old cell. A young woman with pale golden hair sat on the straw mattress; when the glow of the lantern found her, she lifted a thin arm and squinted at the light. Like Violetta's, her face bore the pinched look of the hungry, but hers was growing into womanly beauty.

"Tommasa?" I asked.

She let go a gasp of recognition and embraced me as Sister Violetta again signaled for silence, then turned and disappeared down the corridor.

Tommasa broke the silence as soon as Violetta's footsteps faded. "Caterina!" she hissed. "Why did they bring you back? Where have you been?"

I took in the filthy straw mattress, the stink of the sewer, and slowly sat down on the edge of the bed. Back at Le Murate, Sister Niccoletta was surely weeping, and I wanted to weep, too. I shook my head, too heavyhearted to speak.

Tommasa was too lonely to be silent. Most of the sisters and all of the boarders had succumbed to plague, she told me, and because of the siege, the convent's larders were almost bare.

I lay awake all that night on the hard, lumpy straw, listening to Tommasa's soft snores. All the while, I thought of Sister Niccoletta and Mother Giustina, and the life I had lost at Le Murate.

When morning came, I learned the new terms of my imprisonment: I was not to do chores, nor eat in the refectory, nor attend chapel. I was to remain day and night in my cell.

A miserable fortnight passed. There were no books at Santa-Caterina, and my requests for mending to pass the time were ignored. I lost weight on watery gruel. My only distraction was Tommasa, who returned in the evenings.

One hot August morning, the cannon started booming again, so loudly the floor vibrated beneath my feet. Sister Violetta, hollow-eyed with fear, appeared in the corridor outside to confer with my guardian nun. After several concerned glances in my direction, Violetta stepped forward and shut the door to my cell. Had there been a bolt or lock, she would have used it. From that point on, the door remained closed. Tommasa did not return, and I spent the night alone on scratchy, sour-smelling straw, vacillating between hope and terror.

The next morning, I woke again to the thunder of cannon; the merciless assault against Florence's walls had begun. My guardian sister failed to bring food. When night fell, the fighting and the cannon ceased.

On the second day, there were only the cannon, closer than ever; on third morning, I woke to silence. I got out of bed and knocked on the door. No one responded; as I caught the handle of the door, a bell began to toll.

It was not a church bell marking the hour or summoning the faithful to prayer. It was the low, sad chime of the Cow—the bell in the tower of the Palazzo della Signoria, the Palace of Lords, the bell that called all citizens to the town's central square.

Overwhelmed by joy, I threw open the door to glimpse my captor disappearing swiftly down the hallway. I followed. We came upon other sisters, all rushing to the patio beside the convent wall. From there they ascended a steep staircase built into the side of the convent. I elbowed my way up the stairs to the slanting roof, dizzyingly free and open to the sky and the city; I spread my bare arms to the breeze. Florence sprawled out around me, her walls surrounded by rolling hills, once green but now dark earth, raw from the tread of enemy boots and the wheels of artillery.

On roofs throughout the city, people were gathering. Some were pointing to the south, beyond the river, at Florence's walls and their most ancient gate, the Porta Romana. There, just inside the city walls, huge white flags billowed as they slowly neared the gate. Soon they would pass outside, to the waiting enemy.

Down below, people swarmed into the streets; beside me, the nuns sobbed openly. Their hearts were broken, but mine was sailing on the wind with the flags.

Overcome, Sister Violetta sank onto her knees and stared out at the swelling white harbingers of defeat.

"Sister Violetta," I said.

She stared at me, her gaze blank. Her mouth worked for an instant before she was able to say, "Remember us kindly, Caterina."

"I will," I answered, "provided you tell me how to get to Santissima Annunziata delle Murate."

She frowned and finally saw my tousled braid and dingy, sleeveless nightgown, its hem lifted by the wind, the outlines of the black silk pouch visible beneath the fraying linen at my breasts.

"You can't go out onto the streets," she said. "You're not even dressed. There will be soldiers. It isn't safe."

I laughed, an unfamiliar sound. I was bold, unstoppable. Mars had just surrendered its hold on me, and now lucky Jupiter was ascendant. "I'm going, with or without your help."

She told me. South and east, down the Via Guelfa, past the Duomo, to the Via Ghibellina.

I hurried down the stairs, ran across the patio, slid the bolt on the thick convent door, and stepped out into the Via San Gallo.

It was early but hot, the cobblestones beneath my bare feet already warm. The street was alive with noise: the low-pitched toll of the Cow, the clatter of hooves, the rumble of excited voices. I had expected to find a populace shuttered indoors, hiding in fear from the same army that had savaged Rome; instead, people streamed out of their houses. Their poverty caused my giddy fearlessness to waver. I rubbed elbows with the well-dressed merchants and the starving poor, their children's bellies bloated from hunger. Some headed with me, toward the tolling Cow in the Piazza della Signoria, but most headed due south on the Via Larga, toward the southern gate and the Imperial army. Toward food.

Republican soldiers moved against the crowd—some on foot, some mounted. None looked up at me. Their heads were bowed, their gazes downcast as they headed wearily home to await their conquerors and certain death.

I ran unnoticed, sweat streaming from my temples, the tender soles of my feet bruised and cut. The throng swept along faster and faster, as a cry went up.

The gates are open! They're coming in!

I turned to see Ser Silvestro headed in the direction opposite mine, slouching astride his stallion, riding very slowly. His bare head was bowed; at the crowd's shout, he lifted his chin, acknowledging the inevitable, then dropped it again.

Chance, some might call it, or luck. But it was Jupiter, touching us both with its beneficence, bestowing us upon each other.

I hurried to him; his weary horse paid me no mind.

"Ser Silvestro!" I shouted giddily. "Ser Silvestro!"

He did not hear; I reached out and touched his boot in the stirrup. He started and scowled down at me, ready to shout at the urchin who disturbed him—then recoiled and looked more closely at me.

"Duchessina!" he exclaimed in amazement. "How can it be . . . !"

Without ado, he reached for my hands and I grasped his, and he lifted me up onto his saddle.

I turned round to look at him. "Do you remember our wager?"

He shook his head gently.

"You should," I admonished. "The stakes were your life." And when he looked blankly at me, I added, "You said that, in two months' time, our fortunes would be reversed. Two months, but only three weeks have passed since we met."

His features relaxed into a pale, unhappy smile. "I remember now," he said heavily. "I suppose, since it has been three weeks and not eight, I have lost."

"To the contrary, you have won," I said. "You need only take me to the convent of Le Murate to collect."

PART IV

Rome

September 1530–October 1533

Twelve

I made good on my bargain with Ser Silvestro. His comrades met their deaths at chopping blocks and gallows; he was fated to join them until I dispatched a letter to the Pope. His sentence was commuted to exile.

When Le Murate's door opened to me, I ran into Sister Niccoletta's waiting arms; we held each other fast and I laughed at the pools of tears collected on her spectacles. Within two days, Roman legates arrived with gifts of cheese, cakes, lambs, pigs, pigeons, and the finest wine I have ever tasted. While the rest of the city mourned defeat, those at Le Murate celebrated my return with a feast.

Fortunately, our invaders were not the wild, angry troops that had decimated Rome. The occupation of Florence was orderly. The Imperial commander who brought greetings from the Pope and Emperor Charles kissed my hand and addressed me as *Duchessa.*

On the fourth morning after the Republican surrender, a carriage took me to the Strozzi family villa. There, two men waited in the reception hall, one of them the gray-haired, sunken-cheeked Filippo Strozzi. As I entered the room, he embraced me more enthusiastically than he ever had before. He had reason to be glad: Florence and Rome were in the throes of rebuilding, and Filippo, kinsman by marriage to the Pope and a banker with money to lend, was positioned to become dazzlingly rich.

The other man was young, short, barrel-chested, and wearing a blinding grin. I failed to recognize him until he cried, his voice breaking with emotion, "Cat! Cat, I thought never to see you again!"

I had no words. I hugged Piero tightly, reluctant to let go of him. When we sat, he pulled his chair next to mine and held my hand.

My joy at the Imperial victory was tinged with sorrow at the realization that I would have to leave Le Murate, but I comforted myself with the thought that I would soon return home to the Palazzo Medici with Uncle Filippo and Piero.

"Duchessina," Filippo said, "His Holiness has sent you gifts."

He fetched presents: a silk damask gown of vivid blue and a choker of pearls from which hung a pea-size diamond.

"I shall wear these," I said, delighted, "when we dine together again at the Palazzo Medici."

"Pope Clement bids you wear these when you go to meet him in Rome." Filippo cleared his throat. "His Holiness wishes the heirs to remain in Rome until such time as they are ready to rule."

I cried, of course. I had to be pried away from Piero after we said good-bye.

Back at Le Murate, I mourned bitterly. I wrote impassioned letters to Clement, begging to stay in Florence. It didn't matter. By the end of the month, I was forced to say farewell to Sister Niccoletta and Mother Giustina and my beloved Piero.

I was orphaned again.

Rome sits upon seven hills. After hours of rolling green countryside, I glimpsed the first of them, the Qirinal, from the window of the carriage that carried Uncle Filippo, Ginevra, and me. Filippo pointed at an approaching expanse of worn, unremarkable brick, sections of which had dissolved with age and sprouted greenery.

"The Aurelian Wall," he said reverently. "Nearly thirteen hundred years old."

Moments after, we reached the wall and passed beneath a modern archway: the Porta del Popolo, the Gate of the People. Beyond, a sprawling city stretched to the horizon, dotted with campaniles and cathedral domes rising above the flat roofs of villas; white marble glittered beneath a hot September sun. Rome was far larger than Florence, far larger than I could have imagined. We rolled through common neighborhoods, past shops, humble homes, and open markets. The poor traveled on foot, the merchants on horses, the rich in carriages, a preponderance of which belonged to cardinals. Yet the streets, though busy, were uncrowded; a third of the buildings were still empty three years after the devastation wrought by the Emperor's troops. Rome was still licking her wounds.

As the districts grew wealthier, I saw more evidence of the Sack. The gaudy villas of cardinals and of Rome's most influential families exhibited damage: Stone finials and cornices had been smashed, wooden doorways scarred. Statues of gods were missing limbs, noses, breasts. Over the entrance to one cathedral, a headless Virgin held the Christ child in her arms.

Hammers rang on every street; wooden scaffolding embraced the façade of every other building. Artists' shops were crowded with clients arguing over commissions, apprentices grinding gems, sculptors chiseling huge chunks of marble.

At last the carriage slowed, and Uncle Filippo said, "The Piazza Navona, built on the ruins of Emperor Domitian's circus."

It was the largest square I had ever seen, wide enough for a dozen carriages to travel side by side. Ostentatious villas, newly built, lined its perimeter.

Filippo pointed to a building at the far side of the square and proudly announced, "The Medici Palace of Rome, which rests upon Nero's baths."

The new palace, of pale stucco edged with marble, had been built in the popular classical style—square and flat-roofed, three stories high. The carriage rolled into the long, curving driveway, then stopped, and the driver jumped down to call at the front door. Instead of the expected servant, a noblewoman appeared.

She was my great-aunt Lucrezia de' Medici, daughter of Lorenzo *il Magnifico* and sister of the late Pope Leo X. Her husband, Iacopo Salviati, had recently been appointed Florence's ambassador to Rome. Elegant, thin, and slightly stooped, she wore a gown of black and silver striped silk that precisely matched her velvet headdress and hair.

At the sight of Uncle Filippo helping me from the carriage, she called out, smiling, "I have been waiting all morning! How wonderful to finally set eyes upon you, *Duchessa!*"

Aunt Lucrezia led Ginevra and me to my new apartments. I had come to think of my room at Le Murate as lavish; now, I entered a sunny antechamber with six padded velvet chairs, a Persian rug, a dining table, and a large cherry desk. Paintings covered the marble walls: an annunciation scene, a portrait of Lorenzo as a young man, and one of my mother, an arresting young woman with dark eyes and hair. Lucrezia had brought the painting out of storage for me.

She explained that my great-uncle Iacopo was meeting with His Holiness that very hour, arranging a time for my audience. She left me in the company of a seamstress, who fitted me for several fine gowns.

Before supper, Lucrezia's own lady-in-waiting arrived. With Ginevra's help, she laced me into a woman's gown of daffodil yellow brocade. An inset of sheer silk, fine as a spider's web, stretched from the low bodice to my neck. My hair was smoothed back at the crown with a band of brown velvet edged with seed pearls.

Sheepish in my grand costume, I followed her down to the family's private dining chamber. At its entrance, Aunt Lucrezia and Uncle Iacopo, an authoritative, balding old man, greeted me. They led me inside, to my place at the long, gleaming table, and I found myself staring across it at Ippolito and Sandro.

I had known they would be there, of course, but had not allowed myself to think about it because facing them was simply too awful: I could never forgive them—but they were now the only family I had.

Now nineteen, Sandro looked more than ever like his African mother, his clean-shaven face dominated by heavy black brows and great dark eyes ringed by shadows; he wore a drab, old-fashioned *lucco,* the loose tunic of a city elder.

"Cousin," he said formally and bowed on the other side of the table, keeping his distance, at the same time that Ippolito came grinning round the table.

Beneath an attractively hawkish nose, Ippolito's mustache and beard were blue-black and full, his large eyes brown and rimmed by thick lashes. Dressed in a tight-fitting green farsetto to show off the broadness of his shoulders and narrowness of his waist, he was, simply, beautiful.

"Caterina, sweet cousin!" he exclaimed. The diamond on his left ear flashed. "How I have missed you!"

He reached for me. In my mind's eye, I saw Aunt Clarice staring down in horror at a tangle of hastily discarded leggings and tunics; I put my hand up to keep him from touching me, but he bent down and kissed it.

"The *Duchessina* is tired," Aunt Lucrezia pronounced loudly. "She is glad to see you both, but she has been through too much; let us not tax her. Take your chair, Ser Ippolito."

We sat down. The food was exquisite, but the sight of it nauseated me. I went through the motions of putting a small bite into my mouth and chewing it, but swallowing it made me want to cry.

Conversation was polite, dominated by Donna Lucrezia and Ser Iacopo. The latter asked what I thought of Rome; I stammered replies. Donna Lucrezia inquired politely about the cousins' studies; Ippolito was the quicker to answer. A lull followed, during which I felt Ippolito's steady gaze on me.

Softly, he said, "We were all horrified, of course, when we heard that the rebels had taken you prisoner."

I pushed back my chair and ran from the table, out the French doors that opened onto a balcony overlooking the city; thousands of windows flickered yellow in the darkness. I crouched in the farthest corner and closed my eyes. I wanted to vomit up the food I had just eaten; I wanted to vomit up the last three years.

I heard footsteps and looked up at Ippolito's silhouette, backlit by the glow from the dining room.

"Caterina . . ." He knelt beside me. "You hate me, don't you?"

"Go away." My tone was ugly, raw. "Go away and don't ever speak to me again."

He let go the saddest of sighs. "Poor cousin. It must have been dreadful for you."

"They might have killed us," I said bitterly.

"Do you think I feel no guilt?" he countered, with a trace of vehemence. "Consider my point of view: I was about to make a very dangerous escape, one I might well not have survived. I didn't tell you for fear you would be endangered. We dressed like common thugs; our accomplices were thieves and murderers. We didn't feel safe with them ourselves. What would they have done to a young girl?"

"They tore her gown when we were climbing the wall to escape," I hissed. "It broke her heart to lose Florence. It broke her heart, and she died."

His features, faded by darkness, twisted with anguish. "It broke *my* heart to leave you both. I thought the rebels would rightfully blame us, pursue us, and let the both of you go free. I thought that, by confiding nothing, I had protected you. Then I heard you were imprisoned. And when Clarice died, I . . ." He turned his face away, overcome.

I startled myself by reaching toward him—but when he faced me again, I withdrew my hand, uncertainly.

"Sweet little cousin," he said. "Perhaps in time you will be able to forgive me."

In the end, Ippolito led me back into the dining room. Supper continued in subdued fashion. Afterward, I went up to my room, unnerved yet relieved by the ease with which Ippolito had coaxed me back. That night, as I struggled to fall asleep in my fine new bed, with Ginevra snoring enthusiastically out in the antechamber, I recalled the regret and sorrow in Ippolito's voice when he spoke of Clarice and wondered what might have happened had I not drawn my hand away.

The next morning, wearing Clement's gifts—the blue gown and diamond pendant—I climbed into a gilded carriage with Filippo, Lucrezia, and Iacopo. We rolled over the Ponte Sant'Angelo, the bridge named for the giant statue of the Archangel Michael atop the nearby fortress of the Castel Sant'Angelo, his huge wings sheltering the wounded city.

The bridge spanned the river Tiber, which separated the Holy See from the rest of the city. The Tiber was so crowded with merchant ships—a thousand sails, so close together they might have all been one monstrous vessel—I could scarcely see the muddy water, which stank of garbage.

The Ponte Sant'Angelo took us into Saint Peter's Square—in fact a circle, its circumference ringed by massive stone colonnades; at the far end stood the new Basilica of Saint Peter. Built in the shape of a Roman cross, it rose above the colonnades embracing it. The beggars and pilgrims, monks and cardinals upon its sprawling marble steps were gnats in comparison. Like the rest of Rome, Saint Peter's was undergoing repairs—it had served as the stables for Lutheran invaders during the Sack—and its flanks were covered with the ubiquitous wooden scaffolding.

Our carriage stopped on the Basilica's northern side. Ser Iacopo led the way as Filippo, Lucrezia, and I passed porticoes, courtyards, and fountains *en route* to the Papal Palace, surrounded by the famed Swiss Guard, clad in broad stripes of yellow and blue, with plumes of Medici red on their helmets. When the Emperor's troops swarmed Saint Peter's Square, forcing Clement to run for his life, the Swiss soldiers had died almost to a man defending him.

The guards knew Ser Iacopo well and parted smartly to permit us entry. We ascended a great marble staircase, Donna Lucrezia whispering in my ear, pointing out landmarks as we made our way past priests, bishops, and red-robed cardinals. On the second landing, a pair of closed doors were bound with a chain: the infamous Borgia Apartments, sealed off entirely since the death of the criminally inclined patriarch Rodrigo, better known to the world as Pope Alexander VI.

Soon we arrived at the suite directly above the Borgia Apartments: the Raphael Rooms, named for the artist who had adorned their walls. In the alcove just inside, a frail, white-haired cardinal frowned as he listened intently to an urgently whispering widow. Ser Iacopo gently cleared his throat; the ancient cardinal smiled up at Ser Iacopo and asked eagerly, "Ah, Cousin . . . Is this she?"

"It is," Ser Iacopo replied.

"Duchessina." The old man bowed stiffly. "I am Giovanni Rodolfo Salviati, at your service. Welcome to our city."

I thanked him, and he staggered away bearing news of our arrival. A moment later, Cardinal Salviati returned and beckoned to us with a gnarled finger. We passed through an outer chamber so thoroughly covered with murals I could not absorb them all.

The door to the adjacent chamber lay ajar; the Cardinal paused on the threshold. "Your Holiness? The Duchess of Urbino, Caterina de' Medici."

I walked into a work of art. The floor was shining inlaid marble arranged in varying geometric designs, and the walls . . .

The walls. Three were covered in painted masterpieces limned by gilt and encased in marble lunettes; the fourth was lined from floor to ceiling with ornately carved shelves that held hundreds of books and countless stacks of scrolls yellowed by the centuries. The ceiling was a riot of marble molding and painted allegorical figures, gods, and haloed saints; in its center was a small cupola, where four plump cherubs supported the gold and crimson shield bearing the papal tiara and keys.

I had grown up in the Palazzo Medici, surrounded by the art of the masters—Masaccio, Gozzoli, Botticelli—but the mural on the chapel walls in Florence had been its one real glory, set above wainscoting of dark wood, the better to show it off. In Rome, there was no wainscoting, no thumbnail of space that was not astoundingly glorious. Over every door, every window, in every corner was a glorious masterwork.

I leaned my head back, giddy, until Lucrezia plucked my sleeve. At a magnificent mahogany desk sat my kinsman Pope Clement, the erstwhile Giulio de' Medici, whose family name had purchased him a cardinalship and then the papacy, even though he had never been ordained a priest. A quill was in his right hand, and in his left a document, which he held at arm's length, squinting with the effort to read it.

Since the Sack of Rome, Clement had, like mourning prophets of old, refused to cut his beard or hair. His wiry beard now touched his heart, and his wavy, silvering hair fell past his shoulders. His red silk robe was no finer than those worn by the cardinals; only his white satin skullcap hinted at his status. His eyes held an unspeakable weariness, the exhaustion caused by much grief.

Uncle Filippo cleared his throat, and Clement glanced up and caught my gaze; the mournful eyes brightened at once.

"My little *Duchessina,* is it you at last?" He dropped the quill and paper, and spread his arms. "Come kiss your old uncle! We have waited years for this moment!"

Having been carefully coached by Donna Lucrezia, I stepped forward and fumbled for his hand; when he realized my intent, he held it still so I might kiss the ruby ring of Peter. But when I knelt to kiss his feet, he reached down and pulled me firmly to mine.

"We chose to see you here rather than in public audience so that we could dispense with such formalities," he said. "We have been through too many horrors, you and I. For now, I am not Pope, and you are not a duchess; I am your uncle and you my niece, reunited after a long sorrow. Kiss me on the cheek, dear girl."

I kissed him and he took my hand. When I drew away, tears filmed his eyes.

"God has taken pity on us at last," he sighed. "I cannot tell you how many nights' sleep was stolen from us by the knowledge you were in rebel hands. We never forgot you, not for even one day, nor ever ceased praying on your behalf. Now you must call us Uncle, and always think of us as such. We will see you rule in Florence."

He looked to me, expectant, and I, overwhelmed, could say only "Thank you, Uncle."

He smiled and gave my hand a squeeze before letting it go. "Look at you," he said. "You are wearing our gifts. The color suits you, and the jewels." He did not tell me I was beautiful; that would have been a lie. I was old enough to look into a mirror and see that I was plain.

"Donna Lucrezia," he asked, "have you arranged for her tutors, as I requested?"

"We have, Your Holiness."

"Good." He winked at me. "My niece must become proficient in Latin and Greek, so as not to scandalize the cardinals."

"I know Latin very well, Your Holiness," I said, "having studied it for many years. And I have a smattering of Greek."

"Indeed?" He lifted a skeptical brow. "Then translate this: *Assiduus usus uni rei deditus et—*"

I finished for him. "*Et ingenium et artem saepe vincit.* It is Cicero." *Patient study of a single subject trumps brains and talent.*

He let go a short laugh. "Well done!"

"If it please Your Holiness," I began timidly. "I should like to continue my studies of Greek. And of mathematics."

"Mathematics?" He lifted his brows in surprise. "Do you not yet know your numbers, girl?"

"I do," I answered. "And geometry, and trigonometry, and algebra. It would please me to study under a tutor with advanced knowledge of these subjects."

"On her account, I ask forgiveness," Donna Lucrezia interjected swiftly. "The nuns said she liked to do calculations to plot the courses of the planets. But it is not a fit preoccupation for a young lady."

Clement did not glance in her direction; he was too busy appraising me with faintly narrowed eyes. "So," he said finally. "You have the Medici head for numbers. What a fine banker you would make."

My great-aunt and great-uncle laughed politely; Clement kept his gaze fixed on me.

"Donna Lucrezia," he said, "give her whatever she asks in terms of her studies. She is very bright, but malleable enough, I think. And Ser Iacopo, do not limit your conversation with her. There is much she could learn from you about the art of diplomacy. She will need such skills to rule."

He rose and, against the protests of his aides about the pressing nature of business, took my hand and led me through the Raphael Rooms. He paused to explain each work of art that provoked my curiosity, and in the Room of the Fire in the Borgo, pointed out the many images of my great-uncle Leo X on the walls there.

Clement spoke wistfully of the loneliness of his position, of his yearning for a wife and family. He would never bestow upon the world a child, he confided sadly, and wished that I might be as a daughter to him, and that he might be to me the father I had never known. His voice caught as he said our time together would be short. Too soon, my native city would be ready to receive my husband and me as its rightful rulers. He, Clement, could only hope that I would remember him fondly, and permit him to gaze on my children one day with grandfatherly pride.

His speech was so eloquent, so poignant, that I was moved and stood on tiptoe to kiss his bearded cheek. I, malleable girl, believed it all.

Thirteen

A small crowd had been invited to the palazzo that evening to more properly celebrate my arrival. Donna Lucrezia had taken care to ensure that at least one representative was present from each of the city's most influential families—the Orsini, Farnese, delle Rovere, and Riario.

I smiled a great deal that night as I was introduced to dozens of Rome's luminaries. Uncle Filippo, bound to leave the following morning, knew everyone well and was clearly at ease in Roman society. Sandro's manner with the guests was far less stuffy than it had been the previous evening; he actually grinned and displayed some wit.

As we were seated at the table and wine was poured, Ippolito remained noticeably absent. I was disappointed; I wanted to tell him that I had decided to forgive him. And I suspected my blue dress was quite fetching.

Supper was served. His Holiness had sent over a dozen suckling pigs and a barrel of his best wine. I was rather nervous at first but soon became lost in conversation with the French ambassador, who complimented my feeble efforts at his native tongue, and with Lucrezia's grown daughter Maria, a gracious woman. I was enjoying the people, the food, and the wine, and had forgotten about Ippolito until I caught sight of him in the doorway.

His doublet was bright blue velvet, the same shade as my gown, with the pearl button at the neck undone; his short black hair was tousled. The conversation ebbed as others noticed him.

"My apologies to the assembled company," he said, with a sweeping bow. "And to our dear hostess, Donna Lucrezia. I was forgetful of the hour."

He quickly took his place at table, directly across from Sandro and at some remove from me. Chatter resumed, and I returned my attention to my plate and the French ambassador.

Five minutes later, I heard a shout. Ippolito had jumped to his feet so quickly that he had knocked over his goblet; a garnet stain was spreading across the table, but he cared not at all.

"Son of a whore," he said loudly, his wild-eyed gaze fastened on Sandro. "You know very well what I am speaking about. Why don't you tell *them*?"

Across from him, his cousin sat deadly still. "Sit down, Lito."

Ippolito gestured sweepingly at the other diners. "Tell them all, Sandro. Tell them how you are ambitious—so very, very ambitious—but too craven to be so openly."

Ser Iacopo rose from his chair and, in a voice of well-honed authority, said, "Ser Ippolito, sit *down*."

Ippolito's body was taut with the effort to contain a torrent of hatred. "I will sit down when Sandro speaks the truth publicly," he announced. "Tell us, dear cousin. Tell us all what you are willing to do to see me brought down."

He lunged across the table, rattling plates and cutlery and nearly overturning a flaming candelabrum, and caught the neck of Sandro's tunic.

Uncle Filippo was instantly at his side. "Come away," he commanded.

He seized Ippolito's elbow and pulled him upright. Ippolito jerked free; his mouth curled in a snarl. I thought he would strike Filippo, but his anger turned abruptly sullen and he strode from the room.

Still seated, Sandro watched him go with a guarded expression. Dinner continued, the conversation at first subdued but soon regaining its earlier liveliness.

After the meal and hours of small talk, I made my way back up the stairs to my chambers. Ginevra had forgotten to pack some items for Uncle Filippo, who was leaving early, but she had promised to come undress me within the hour. A hallway sconce had been lit in consideration of my unfamiliarity with the terrain, and it cast a sharp shadow in the alcove near my door; a figure stepped from it into the light.

I recognized Ippolito at once. Had I not drunk a good deal of wine myself, I might have noticed that his eyes were red, his words slurred, his balance precarious. His hands were steepled contritely at his heart.

"Caterina," he said. "I came to apologize for my behavior at supper."

"You need not apologize to me," I responded lightly, "but Donna Lucrezia is another matter."

He smiled ruefully. "She will be satisfied only if I spend the rest of my life trying to make amends."

"Why were you so angry at Sandro?"

He pulled me toward the door with the intent of leading me into the antechamber. I balked; Ginevra might be back at any time, and if she saw me alone with a man in my room, cousin or no, she would think it improper.

"Not in there," I hissed, but he laid a finger to his lips and drew me just inside the door.

The bedroom beyond was dark, but the lamp on the antechamber desk had been lit. Ippolito stepped conspiratorially close and took my hands. I did not pull away, as propriety demanded; I was giddy from the wine and his presence.

"You were so angry," I whispered. "Why?"

He tensed. "Sandro, the bastard, tells terrible lies about me to His Holiness. And His Holiness, who is partial to Sandro, believes them."

"What lies?"

His lip tugged downward. "Sandro wants His Holiness to believe that I am nothing but a drunk, a womanizer, that I am failing at my studies . . ." He let go a low, bitter laugh. "And here am I, stupid enough to drink too much wine, because I am so angry!"

"Why would Sandro say such things?"

"Because he is jealous," Ippolito said. "Because he wants to poison Clement against me. He wants to rule alone." His expression grew even darker. "If he dares speak ill of *you* to Clement, I . . ." He tightened his grip on my hands. "Your years of imprisonment haven't hardened you, Caterina; you have the same kind heart."

He fell silent and stared intently into my eyes. In his, I saw the same light I had seen in Aunt Clarice's, when she had kissed Leda for the last time.

"That is why I love you," Ippolito said. "Because you are nothing like him. Because you are utterly brilliant yet completely guileless." He lowered his face to mine. "Can you be loyal, Caterina? Can you love me?"

"Of course." I didn't know what else to say.

He leaned into me, his hips pressed to mine. He was tall, and the top of my head barely reached his collar. He put one hand on my shoulder, and let it slide down inside my bodice; the other cradled the nape of my neck.

It occurred to me that I ought to run away, but the feel of his hand on my bare flesh was intoxicating. I leaned back against his hand and let him kiss me. The act involved a good deal of heat; I instinctively wrapped my arms around him.

He kissed my ears and closed eyelids, then parted my lips with his tongue. He tasted of the Pope's wine.

"Caterina," he sighed.

I heard Ginevra's step on the distant landing and pulled away from him; he slipped out of my antechamber just in time to escape her detection.

A heady year passed, one of banquets and balls. I was convinced that I would marry Ippolito and return to Florence. Each day, I grew more to look like a woman; each day, Ippolito won me by increasing degrees, with compliments and tender glances. On my birthday, he presented me with a pair of earrings, diamonds cut in the shape of tears. "To better show off your lovely neck," he said. My face was not pretty, but he had found other features to honestly compliment: my long neck, my small feet and elegant hands.

Donna Lucrezia frowned; the gift was one a lover might give his paramour, or a man his betrothed, but our engagement was not yet official. She had reason to be concerned. The week before, upon dismounting after a vigorous ride, I realized my petticoats were wet. I went to my bedchamber and discovered, to my astonishment, that they were soaked with blood. Alerted by the chambermaid, Donna Lucrezia came to explain the distasteful facts of monthly bleeding. Afterward, she lectured me at length on the need for virtue—for political purposes as much as religious ones.

I scarcely listened. Whenever we found ourselves alone, Ippolito fell on me with kisses and I heatedly returned them. With each encounter, I permitted another liberty. At supper, the memory of such ardent moments left us grinning across the table at each other. Increasingly, I sent my lady-in-waiting, Donna Marcella, off on meaningless errands while I stole away to those areas of the villa frequented by Ippolito.

On one such occasion, I found him in a corridor near his private chambers. We went straightaway into each other's arms. When his hand burrowed beneath my skirts and petticoats, I did not stop him; when his fingers reached between my legs and stroked the mound of flesh there, I moaned. Suddenly, he slipped one finger inside me, and I was lost. I bore down with my full weight as it moved, slow and probing at first, then faster.

We were too far gone to hear footsteps until it was too late. There we were, Ippolito pressed hard against me, his hand beneath my skirts; and there was Sandro, close-mouthed and wide-eyed. Sandro stared at us and we stared at him, then Sandro turned and walked away.

I pushed free from Ippolito, my desire transformed into something sickening and ugly.

"Damn him," Ippolito breathed, still trembling. "He will use this against me, I know it. But if he dares use it against you, there will be hell to pay."

Hell was a long time coming. In the interim, I continued my occasional brief encounters with Ippolito, though I remained alert to avoid detection. Ippolito grew more passionate, more intense in his declarations of love, and I, certain we would be married within a year, allowed his fingers and lips full access to my person.

Ippolito, however, desired more—but Donna Lucrezia had impressed upon me the fact that I could now become pregnant. I kept my ardent cousin at bay, though I grew increasingly tempted to give him what he most wanted.

Winter came—mild and sunny, a cheerful contrast to cold, gloomy Florence. At Christmas we attended a large banquet at the Papal Palace, held in Raphael's glorious Room of the Fire in the Borgo. Afterward, as the guests mingled in the magnificent surroundings, Clement took me aside. The roar of convivial conversation around us guaranteed that his words would be heard by us alone.

"I hear you are much taken with our Ippolito," he said.

Sandro, I realized, had revealed everything. Mortified, furious, I glanced down at the marble floor, unable to formulate a coherent reply.

"You are too young to be mooning over a rake like him," Clement admonished. "Besides, you have inherited the brains and tenacity for which the Medici are famed. Ippolito did not, and so it falls to you, as young as you are, to be the wiser one. He pursues you not for love but because youth makes his blood run hot. Shun him now so that, when his ardor cools, you will still have his respect. Otherwise—I tell you as a man who understands these things—you will find yourself badly used. Do you understand me, Caterina?"

I mumbled, "I do, Your Holiness."

"Then promise me. Promise me that you will keep your virtue and spurn his embrace."

"I promise, Holiness," I said.

I was at the age of foolishness, when I believed my elders incapable of understanding the exceptional nature of the love Ippolito and I shared. And so I lied, bald-faced, to the Pope.

Late that evening, accompanied by my lady, Donna Marcella, I was ascending the stairs to my chambers when Sandro came up behind us.

"Good evening, Caterina," he said, with unsmiling reserve.

I gave him a withering stare before turning my back to him.

"Donna Marcella," Sandro said softly, "I should like to speak privately with my sister."

Marcella—a cautious woman twenty years my senior—hesitated as she studied Sandro. He was slight, less solidly built than his cousin, with light umber skin and tight black curls, and the broad nose and full lips of his Moorish mother. The authority in his huge dark eyes made her yield. She had pledged to serve as my constant chaperone; however, from Sandro's manner, and from my own, it was clear nothing impetuous could ever happen between us.

She turned to me. "I will wait for you in your chambers, *Duchessina.*"

When she had left, Sandro said, "I know that you hate me, but in the end, you'll see that I acted in your best interests. Ippolito is using you without any thought for your feelings."

"I won't listen to your lies," I said. "You hate Ippolito because you are jealous."

He sighed. "I don't hate him," he said patiently. "Lito hates *me.* Any jealousy in the equation is his, not mine." He hesitated again. "I am by nature cool. I look different from you both, and I have never forgotten it. But you and I are more alike. You're lovesick now—but you have the intelligence and detachment needed to rule."

My voice was ugly. "Then why did you carry tales about us to the Pope?"

"Because regardless of what you think and what Ippolito might say, I care about you. And if I read the signs aright, you're allowing yourself to be put in a dangerous situation. Don't let yourself be hurt."

"How *dare* you."

I turned and began again to climb the stairs. He advanced a step or two behind me.

"He loves wine and women too well," Sandro said. "Or are you so smitten—like the rest of them—that you haven't noticed?"

When I hurried my pace, he made a last, desperate effort to shock me. "When he comes to you again, ask him about Lucia da Pistoia. Ask him about Carmella Strozzi, and Charlotte Montblanc."

"You lie!" I would not turn around.

"You're being played, Caterina."

I spoke over my shoulder, harshly, venomously, wanting to wound him as badly as he had me. "You are no brother of mine."

"You're right, of course," he said softly. "I suppose everyone knows it by now."

I did not understand at all but was too upset to pursue an explanation. I lifted my skirts and ran up to my room. Alessandro did not follow, but I felt his presence, lonely and disapproving, behind me on the stairs.

The new year of 1532 came, followed by an early spring. Donna Marcella rarely left my side; Ippolito and I were reduced to stealing glances over supper. Eventually, he recruited one of the chambermaids to deliver his impassioned letters to me, and return my lovesick responses to him.

Finally he wrote that he had petitioned Clement to allow us to become betrothed and said His Holiness had indicated an affirmative reply was forthcoming. A betrothal was as binding as a marriage: Once it was accomplished, no one, not even Clement, would keep us from each other. I quickly penned a reply expressing my eagerness. Within a day, I received another missive:

> *Why must we wait for Clement, or any ceremony? I will find a way so that we can be alone and undisturbed in each other's arms until dawn. I am only awaiting the right opportunity.*

I stared down at the paper in my hands with queasy excitement. If we were discovered, Donna Lucrezia would be scandalized, and Pope Clement furious.

I had done my best to dismiss Sandro's words, but now they echoed dismally in my memory.

Ask him about Lucia. And Carmella. And Charlotte . . .

Several weeks of fervid correspondence ensued. In early April, Donna Marcella took ill and went to the countryside, leaving me in the care of one of the chambermaids, Selena. That afternoon, Selena combed lemon juice through my hair. I settled into an inconspicuous corner of the courtyard on a coverlet spread on the grass and absorbed sunlight in the hope of coaxing some gold from my drab locks. I sat for an hour and was getting up to leave when the sound of Ippolito's voice made me pause.

He and Sandro passed by, sweating and disheveled from the hunt, and so absorbed in lighthearted conversation that neither saw me.

Happily, Ippolito was the closer to me, his body blocking me from Sandro's view. I ventured a small, timid wave; Ippolito paused at the entrance to the palazzo and made an excuse to Sandro, who continued on.

Before I could get to my feet, Ippolito was beside me on the coverlet, his face incandescent with hope.

"Tonight, Caterina. I will come to your bedchamber tonight. You don't know how hard it's been all day—knowing this and trying to hide my excitement from Sandro, from everyone."

I pressed a palm to my sun-warmed cheek. "It's too dangerous," I said. "They'll discover us." My protest sounded distant and small.

"They won't."

"And if I become with child?"

He brightened. "Clement will see us wed all the sooner. Only grant me this one night, and when we are married, I'll reward your generosity a thousandfold." He pressed his lips to the insides of my wrists, one by one. "Say you'll wait for me tonight."

"I'll wait," I answered, with a thrill of longing and guilt.

Fourteen

That night, I lay in my bed with agonizing expectancy. What if we were discovered? Might Clement's anger be so great he would deny us our right to Florence? My fear paled beside the memory of Ippolito's deft tongue and fingers. When the soft knock came on my antechamber door, I sat up listening to the whisper of Selena's sheets as she rose, to the tread of her bare feet on the marble floor, to the creak of the door.

Ippolito's silhouette appeared in my bedchamber doorway. "Caterina," he whispered. "At last."

He strode to the bed, pulled back the covers, and slid next to me to lie on his side, propped upon one elbow.

Ippolito, I tried to say, but he hushed me and ran the flat of his palm from my neck to my thigh, up and down, languidly, only the thin lawn of my nightgown separating us. His mouth was open, his breath quick and reeking of wine. I was entranced, but the spell was broken when he said, brusquely, "Sit up."

I did. With surprising skill, he pulled my nightgown over my head and upraised arms; I was suddenly naked, sheepish. He, however, was inflamed, and while I sat, he pressed his face against my small breasts and began to suckle them.

I seized his head and buried my spread fingers in his hair, thinking to pull him away out of embarrassment. But as his tongue and teeth worked my nipple, I felt as though an invisible cord ran from that tender spot directly to my womb and tugged at the muscles below, causing them to twitch deliciously. When he was satisfied, he ordered, "Lie back."

I complied. He rose to his feet and pulled his loose shirt over his head; balancing on one foot at a time, he pulled off his leggings. He was very unsteady and fell twice against the mattress, but at last he was free.

Male genitalia are, at first glance, odd-looking. Beneath a thick spray of black hair at Ippolito's groin, a shaft of flesh emerged, tilted upward at an angle I estimated to be thirty degrees. It unnerved and fascinated me. As I lay back, Ippolito stepped up to the edge of the mattress; I reached out and squeezed it hard. It was firm as brick, yet velvety to the touch. He flexed it so that it pulsed once, twice in my hand, and we both giggled softly.

"Kiss it," he said. The idea was unappealing, if not appalling, and I balked. He caught the braided hair at the base of my neck and pulled my head toward it. "Kiss it," he repeated. His words were slurred, his eyes half-closed; for the first time, I saw how very drunk he was.

He pulled my hair again, hard enough to cause pain, and I indulged him. I kissed it, briefly, softly, wrinkling my nose at the tickle of wiry hair, careful not to turn away too quickly from the smell of musk. It was not all that he wanted, but he chose to let it pass and pressed my shoulders against the mattress.

Then he spat into his palm and slicked the shaft. I stared at that strange, seductive, glistening bit of flesh and—quite insanely—wished to feel it inside me. He wedged both hands between my thighs so that they were obliged to part until I lay with my legs spread wide, forbidden fruit ready to tumble from the tree.

He slipped his middle finger deep inside me, plumbed a bit, then plunged a second finger in with it, causing me to draw in my breath sharply. A third finger soon followed. Despite my excitement, I groaned at the discomfort, but he pumped his hand steadily until I relaxed and grew still.

As he drew his fingers out, with a moist, sucking sound, he smiled evilly and said, in full voice, "The goose is not too young. She is fully cooked and succulent, and waiting to be pierced."

He eased himself down on me and pushed his legs between mine; propping himself up on one hand, he spat again into the other and applied it as before.

"I will visit tomorrow, and the night after," he said, stumbling over the words. "Again and again, so long as Donna Marcella is ill. Let me lie with you tonight many times, and take care, once I release my seed, to remain flat and still. The sooner you conceive, the sooner Clement will marry us."

He put his free hand around the rod, which probed hard and smooth against my thigh, between my legs, searching.

It was Lorenzo's blood, I think, that pulled me up short—his talent for political manipulation and for recognizing the same when he witnessed it. Perhaps too, Ser Iacopo's careful tutelage in diplomacy had paid off, in teaching me that social niceties often masked the basest of political goals.

Clement's warning, and Sandro's, and Ippolito's sudden urge to impregnate me all converged with the Medici nose for deception.

I tried to clamp my legs shut, but Ippolito's bulk intervened. I slipped my hand between my womb and his turgid flesh.

"What of Lucia?" I asked.

He let go a gasp that was also a nervous laugh and rested on both hands again. "She's a liar; the child isn't mine."

All at once the lovesick veil lifted, and I saw things as they were: Ippolito had felt the need for a great deal of wine before coming to me. Indeed, our most lascivious encounters had occurred when he was drunk. His own answer apparently startled him; he grinned stupidly at it, then at me.

"And who is Carmella?" I demanded. "And Charlotte?"

"Caterina," he cajoled, smiling. Then, realizing that I was furious at his inadvertent admission, and that he would lose me, he feigned anger. "Who told you such lies? It was Sandro, wasn't it, trying to ruin things for us both!"

"Get out," I said. "You are drunk and despicable. Get out now."

"You can't deny me this," he hissed threateningly. "You can't. You are my birthright."

"I am not," I countered with equal ferocity.

He seized my wrist with such force that I yelped. With one hand, he pinioned both of mine above my head; with the other, he grasped the shaft of flesh with the clear aim of pushing it inside me.

Many thoughts are born in the time it takes to draw a breath, and during that time, I weighed my options. I could submit and pray I would not be impregnated and, in the morning, seek Donna Lucrezia's protection; I could continue struggling, which would obviously fail; or I could scream in earnest, which would bring Selena running in from the antechamber. None of these appealed, as they all gave Ippolito enough time to deflower me. Given my earlier flirtatious behavior, no one would believe me innocent. That left only negotiation—but Ippolito was too frenzied for discussion.

I spat as much saliva as I could muster into his eyes. He obeyed the natural reflex to wipe them, which left him off balance, allowing me to drag my prized virginity up toward the pillows.

Before he could gather himself, I said, "I will struggle. And scream. And tell the truth, that I was raped. You are drunk, after all."

"You little bitch." His tone was soft and filled with wonder.

"Sandro will support me," I said. "He will say that you are worried, with good reason, that your drunkenness and womanizing have sullied your reputation and given Clement pause."

I didn't want to be right; I wanted very much for Ippolito to laugh gently and explain my reasoning away with better logic of his own. But his long and guilty silence shattered the fantasy that I was brilliantly loved, that I would soon have a home and family of my own. I was, after all, a homely girl, and he the most handsome man in all the world.

I crawled as far away as I could, sat up, pressed my back against the headboard, curled my arms about my legs, and wished to die. But like Sandro, I was cool and hid my hurt.

"Shall I continue?" I asked him. "Shall I take this to its natural conclusion, that whoever marries me will be seen as the more legitimate ruler of Florence?"

He sat up and stared at me. He was drunk, impetuous, and cruel, but he was not a monster. The flesh between his legs had shrunk into a sad, dangling thing. At my question, he shook his head.

It was a gesture of defeat, but I misread it and countered hotly, "Alessandro is my brother, true, but only my half brother. An exception from Clement and we could be wed."

Without smiling, he let go a soft, bitter laugh. "You're wrong," he said.

"I am *not.*"

"You are wrong," he repeated. "Sandro is not your brother. He's Clement's bastard, born while His Holiness was still a cardinal and foisted off on us. Perhaps now you better understand my concern."

For a long time we sat breathing hard as we stared at each other. I think he considered forcing himself upon me again, but had lost the taste for it.

"I don't mean to hurt you," he said finally. "I *do* care for you, and there is real heat between us. Can't I be with you tonight? Clement will come to his senses and wed us, install us in Florence, all the more so if you are pregnant . . ."

"No," I said.

He hesitated, then made as if to reach for me.

"No," I repeated. "I'll scream for Selena."

He rose and dressed without another word. I waited until he was out the door and well down the corridor before I began to cry.

Sandro had done me a kindness. Three months after my nocturnal encounter with my cousin, Pope Clement announced that Ippolito was to become a cardinal and would serve as Papal legate to Hungary. He was to be properly schooled, then sent off within a year.

Alessandro left for Florence soon after the announcement to acquaint himself with the politics of the city he would soon govern.

I did my best to lose myself in my studies. The sordid unraveling of my first love affair had wounded me, but I found comfort in the fact that I still had Florence. I aspired to become worthy of ruling a city, of being a fitting partner to Alessandro, who had shown himself to be wise and decent.

Clement sent me home to Florence that April to attend Alessandro as he was installed as the first Duke of Florence, a title bestowed on him by Emperor Charles as part of the treaty with Clement after the Sack of Rome. Bedecked in ermine and rubies, I stood proudly beside my cousin during his installation; in that moment, Ippolito faded into a youthful indiscretion.

An obscenely magnificent banquet followed the ceremony. Late that evening, I stood in my bechamber as Donna Marcella unlaced me from my complicated finery. I was still exhilarated, reluctant to retire, and chatted with Maria about the day's events.

"When do you think His Holiness will announce our engagement?" I asked her.

"Engagement?" She seemed honestly puzzled by my question.

"Mine to Sandro, of course."

Maria glanced away quickly as she sought the proper words. "His Holiness is considering several possible suitors for you."

I had to repeat the words silently to myself three times before I fully understood them.

"I'm so sorry," Maria said. "They said nothing to you, then?"

"No," I answered slowly. "No, they did not."

Pity sullied her features. "Alessandro has been secretly betrothed since last year to Margaret of Austria, the Emperor's daughter. His Holiness will make the official announcement soon."

I was humiliated, privately seething, but I continued to attend public functions at Sandro's side, aware that I was there not as a partner but as a symbol. I was the ghost of my father—my father, whose birthright was Florence. As his sole legitimate heir, I alone should have ruled—but I was female, a politically unpardonable sin.

With each day, my concern over the future grew. At thirteen, I was of marriageable age, but if Sandro was not to be my groom, then who was? Maria confessed that Clement was entertaining a proposal from the Duke of Milan, an ailing, elderly man with fewer wits than the coins in his empty coffers. Although Clement was not infatuated with the idea, he had been forced to consider it because Emperor Charles wanted the match, as the Duke had always been a staunch Imperial supporter. The thought so disgusted me that Maria spent a fruitless hour trying to soothe me.

"God willing, he will not be the final choice," she said. "Let us just say that he is the least of the options. There are other suitors—one so marvelous I have been sworn to secrecy. His Holiness is working hard to negotiate to your very best advantage."

"Are any of the men from Florence?" I had lost everyone; my home was all I had.

She did not understand the significance of the question; she shook her head and smiled mischievously. "We mustn't speak of it any more, my dear. No point in raising your hopes only to have them dashed."

Too late, I wanted to tell her. I thought of the day I first met His Holiness: how he had asked that I look upon him as a father and confessed his sorrow that he would never have a child of his own. Even then, he had been negotiating with Emperor Charles to find his son Alessandro a proper bride, one who brought the greatest possible prestige to the new young Duke. I was simply another gem in Clement's crown, one with which to bargain—just as I had been for the rebels. The circumstances of my captivity were much improved, but I was a prisoner of politics no less.

I survived an uneasy fall and Christmas. An outward observer might have envied me; dressed in ermine and thread of gold, I danced and dined with dukes, princes, and ambassadors. The new year brought a fresh spasm of celebration. Late in January 1533, Iacopo and Lucrezia arrived from Rome in their gilded carriage.

They brought news from His Holiness: I saw it in Lucrezia's smug, secretive smile. The morning after their arrival, they summoned us to a reception chamber; only Iacopo, Lucrezia, Maria, and I were allowed entry—and Alessandro, of course, who had set aside his obligations to come.

I sat between Maria and Lucrezia while Ser Iacopo stood in front of the snapping hearth. A shaft of winter sunlight caught his hair, white as cotton. He cleared his throat, and I died, thinking of the Duke of Milan.

"I have an announcement," he said, "a very happy one, but my words must be kept scrupulously secret. No one else must learn it, or it will all be in sore jeopardy."

"We can trust everyone here, Uncle," Alessandro prompted impatiently. "Please continue."

"A betrothal has been arranged," Ser Iacopo said and broke into a maniacal grin. "My dear *Duchessina,* you are to wed Henri, Duke of Orléans!"

The Duke of Orléans: The title sounded familiar, but I could not place the man.

Donna Lucrezia, who could bear the excitement no longer, looked at my blank expression and exclaimed, "The son of the French King, Caterina! The son of King François!"

I sat, silent and dazed, unable to grasp the implications of this news. Maria was clapping her hands for joy; even Sandro was smiling.

"When is this to happen?" I asked.

"This summer."

Ser Iacopo retrieved two boxes from a nearby table—both inlaid with mother-of-pearl in the shape of a fleur-de-lis—and presented them to me. "Your prospective father-in-law, His Majesty King François, offers you these gifts on his son's behalf."

I took them. One box held a necklace of gold with three round sapphire pendants, each big as a cat's eye; the other framed a miniature portrait of a somber, hollow-cheeked youth.

"He is young," I said.

Donna Lucrezia squeezed my forearm enthusiastically. "Henri de Valois was born the same year as you."

"He was to have married Mary Tudor of England," Maria added. "Until King Henry put aside her mother, Catherine of Aragon. That ended *those* negotiations." She reached out and grasped my hand, and clicked her tongue at finding it limp. "Caterina, aren't you excited?"

I didn't answer. I looked levelly at Ser Iacopo and asked, "What are the terms of the arrangement?"

The question took him aback. "Your dowry, of course. It is a sizable sum."

"It's not enough," I said, even though I knew that France's wealth had been greatly reduced by years of war; King François could certainly use the gold. "I'm only a commoner—not much of a match for a prince. There are other girls with larger dowries. What else do I bring?"

Ser Iacopo looked at me, amazed—though he should not have been, as I was his earnest pupil in the art of political negotiation. "Property, Duchess. King François has always yearned for holdings in Italy. Pope Clement has promised to deliver Reggio, Modena, Parma, and Pisa; he will also provide military support to France in order to take Milan, Genoa, and Urbino. These terms are confidential; even the news of the betrothal itself cannot be revealed for some time. Emperor Charles will not relish hearing that the Duke of Milan's offer has been spurned."

"I understand," I said. I smoothed my palm over the surface of the box, pausing at the raised mother-of-pearl and tilting it gently so that it flashed, muted velvet shades of icy blue and rose.

"But are you not happy, Caterina?" Donna Lucrezia prompted loudly. "Are you not pleased?"

I opened the box again to stare at the young man inside. His features—even and unremarkable enough to be termed good-looking, if not handsome—were compressed into a stiff expression intended to convey stern regality.

"I am pleased," I announced, though I still did not smile. "King François was my mother's kinsman; I should be happy to call him father-in-law. He saw me removed from cruel conditions to the kind haven of Le Murate, for which I am forever grateful."

I set down the box, which prompted Maria and Donna Lucrezia to descend on me with tears and kisses. Lucrezia told me, quite ecstatically, that Pope Clement had recruited the most fashionable noblewoman in all Italy, Isabella d'Este, to choose the fabrics and designs for my wedding attire and trousseau. I was to have a new tutor, fresh from the French Court, who would accelerate my instruction in the language and customs of my new country.

Ser Iacopo had pressing matters to discuss with Alessandro on behalf of His Holiness; we women were dismissed as the men prepared to leave for Sandro's offices. At the doorway I lingered, gesturing to Lucrezia and Maria to go ahead of me, and waited until Sandro neared. Iacopo lowered his gaze and said, "I shall wait for you, Ser Alessandro," then continued down the corridor.

When all were out of earshot, I said to Sandro, "You *knew*. Even a year ago, as you warned me to stay away from Ippolito. You and Clement knew even then."

"I was not certain," Sandro answered. "François's offer had just been made, but we had no way of knowing whether it would be successfully negotiated. I wanted to tell you, but I was sworn to secrecy. The agreement was finalized less than a week ago."

"You always planned I should never have Florence," I charged. "You and your father."

He drew back slightly at the venom in my tone but answered calmly, "It was decided the instant Clement set eyes on you. I am shrewd enough to govern a city. But you . . . You're brilliant; God help the world once you learn the art of cunning! I have no need of a wife with more brains than I. I can secure my father Florence. But *you* . . ."

"I can bring him a nation," I finished, bitter.

"I'm sorry, Caterina," Alessandro said, and for an instant, his cool reserve slipped, and I saw that he truly was.

It was a long day with Donna Lucrezia and Maria, and I went to bed after an early supper. Alone, I tried to take stock of my new fate, though it seemed hazy and unreal. How could I leave everything and everyone I had known and loved to go live among foreigners? The picture of the aloof, uneasy boy in the wooden box gave me no comfort at all. Eventually, exhaustion trumped anxiety and I dozed.

I dreamt that I stood in an open field, staring into the coral rays of the failing sun. In front of its great, sinking disk stood the black silhouette of a man broad-shouldered and strong. He faced me, his arms stretched out, imploring.

Catherine, ma Catherine . . .

The utterance of my name in that foreign tongue no longer seemed barbarous. I called a reply.

Je suis ici, je suis Catherine . . . Mais qui etes-vous?

Catherine! he cried, as though he had not heard my question.

My ears roared. The landscape altered magically until he lay writhing at my feet, his face still in shadow. As I tried vainly to make out his features, blood welled up from his face like water from a burbling spring.

I knelt beside the fallen man. *Ah, monsieur! Comment est-ce que je peux aider? How can I help?*

His face lolled out of the shadows. His beard was caked with thickening blood, his head limned by a dark red halo. His eyes, wild with agony, finally beheld mine.

Catherine, he whispered. *Venez a moi. Aidez-moi.*

Come to me, help me.

A great convulsion seized him; he arched like a bow. When it released him, the air in his lungs rushed out with an enormous hiss and he fell limp, mouth gaping, eyes wide and unseeing.

I glimpsed something troublingly familiar in his lifeless features—something I did not recognize, something I recognized all too well—and cried out.

I woke to find my lady-in-waiting, Donna Marcella, standing over me.

"Who?" she demanded. "Who do you mean?"

Disoriented, speechless, I stared at her.

"The man," she persisted. "You were calling out, 'Bring him here at once!' But whom should I bring, *Duchessina*? Are you ill? Do you require a doctor?"

I sat up and put my hand to my heart, where the Wing of Corvus lay.

"Cosimo Ruggieri, the astrologer's son," I said. "Come morning, have him found and brought to me."

Fifteen

Ruggieri could not be found. An old woman came to his door and said that the day after the siege, Ser Cosimo had disappeared. Two and a half years had passed without word from him.

"Good riddance," she said. "He went altogether mad—raving about wicked, horrid things, refusing to eat or sleep. I'd be surprised if he were still alive."

The news devastated me, but I had no time to indulge in disappointment. I had ceased being Caterina, a thirteen-year-old girl, to become an entity: The Duchess of Urbino, future wife of the Duke of Orléans and daughter-in-law of a king. Like any precious object, I was on constant display.

For my fourteenth birthday in April, a reception was held at the Palazzo Medici and attended by His Holiness, who had made the long trip from Rome. Weighed down by jewels, I held Pope Clement's hand as he presented me to each distinguished guest as "my darling Caterina, my greatest treasure."

Surely there was no greater treasure than that which was heaped on me now; I suspected His Holiness had leveraged half of Rome and his papal tiara to cover the expense. Later I learned that Sandro—that is, Duke Alessandro—had forwarded the taxes paid by the citizens of Florence to help with the costs.

Swaths of brocade, damask, lace, and silk arrived, hand-picked by the stylish Isabella d'Este. Heaps of jewels—rubies, diamonds, emeralds, necklaces and belts of gem-studded gold, and a pair of earrings made from pear-shaped pearls so huge I wondered how I should wear them and still hold my head up—were spread out for my inspection. When I was not sorting through precious stones or metals or fine cloth, I met with a tutor to sharpen my proficiency in French and the protocol of the French Court. I learned French dances and practiced them until my legs ached. I learned King François was overly fond of the hunt, and so I mounted a stallion and practiced jumping—and, as a necessary corollary, falling. The tutor remonstrated when I used my sidesaddle; it was indecent, he charged, as it permitted glimpses of my calves. He recommended a ridiculous contraption—a little chair, so unsteady that the rider would be thrown if she urged her mount to more than a slow walk. I would have none of it.

There were countless public appearances. If my presence had lent legitimacy to Alessandro's rule before, it lent the aura of royalty to it now. I hung on his arm, a shiny political bauble, and stood by his side to welcome his betrothed, Margaret of Austria, to Florence; I sweetly kissed her cheek.

Those frantic days left me too exhausted to think. Summer came all too quickly, though I earned a respite when the wedding location was changed from Nice to Marseille, and the date from June to October.

Inevitably, however, the first of September arrived, and I departed Florence in a sumptuous coach, accompanied by a gay caravan of nobles, servants, and grooms, and a dozen wagons loaded down with my belongings and gifts for my new family. In my excitement, I had never considered that I might not return to the land of my birth; it was not until we reached the city's eastern gate that my throat constricted and I turned, panicked, to stare behind me at the slowly retreating orange dome of the great cathedral and the winding, grey-green Arno.

Aunt Clarice was gone, Ippolito fickle, and Sandro cunning; I would miss none of them. But as Florence shrank from view, I wept as I thought of Piero—and of the wise-eyed boy Lorenzo, high upon the chapel wall of the Palazzo Medici.

I traveled by land to the coast, and from there, by sea to Villefranche to await His Holiness, who intended to perform the religious ceremony himself.

Clement had decided that my marriage to Henri, Duke of Orléans, would be a gilded spectacle such as had never been seen. When the papal flotilla arrived, I boarded His Holiness's ship to find it entirely upholstered in gold brocade. We sailed for two days to Marseille, and when we dropped anchor, three hundred cannon boomed over the joyous clamor of cathedral bells and blaring trumpets.

Marseille was sunny and scented with brine, with clear blue seas and sky. We made our way through streets lined with cheering Frenchmen, to the plaza known as the Place-Neuve. On one side of the avenue stood the King's magnificent Palace of the Comtes de Provence, on the other, a temporary papal mansion of timber. The two were united by a vast wooden chamber that spanned the entire square. It was here that the banquets and receptions would take place.

I made my entrance into Marseille on a roan charger caparisoned in gold brocade. The awkward throne the Frenchwomen used was proffered me, but I refused it in favor of my own sidesaddle; if the cheering crowds were scandalized to see a woman riding a horse in that fashion, they hid it well.

My destination was the papal palace of wood on the Place-Neuve. When I dismounted, I was led quickly to the reception hall. Three hundred souls, the eminent men and glittering women of the French Court, had gathered there. They had come to weigh me as though I, too, were a gem to be set within His Majesty's crown.

I swept past six hundred eyes, past the cat-eyed, haughty women with their insolent smiles. Their tight-fitting bodices ended in widows' peaks at their breathlessly cinched waists; they were all thin, and strangely proud of it. Their tight sleeves were not separate from the gown but sewn onto it, with small puffs at the upper arm. Their collars were high, ruffed at the neck like the men's, but open at the throat and plunging in narrow vees to the décolleté. Stiff, curving bands of fabric smoothed back their hair to midcrown and covered the remainder in velvet or gossamer veils. They were beautiful, sleek, and blatantly confident, and I a clumsy, unfashionable foreigner in my large sleeves and loose-waisted gown.

I shook off their stares and fixed my gaze on His Holiness, who sat in a golden throne upon a high dais. Beside him, at a respectful remove, stood King François I and his three sons: Henri; eleven-year-old Charles; and the fifteen-year-old Dauphin, heir to the throne, named François after his father.

Clement's face was luminous. In six years' time he had gone from prisoner in a ravaged city to puppetmaster of a king.

As my name—*Caterina Maria Romula de' Medici, Duchessina of Urbino*—was announced, I kept my face downcast, my gaze demure.

"Caterina!" Clement exclaimed, drunk with achievement and joy. "My darling niece, how beautiful you are!"

I ascended three of the five steps leading up to the dais, then knelt. Prostrating my upper torso upon the stairs, I took Clement's slippered foot into my hands and pressed the velvet-clad toe to my lips.

"Rise, *Duchessina*," Clement said, "and greet your new family."

A great hand upon my shoulder guided me to my feet. Before me stood a very tall man with a short dark beard along his jawline, so wiry it puffed out like uncombed cotton. His thick neck made his head seem small by comparison; his nose was very long, his eyes and lips small. The grandeur of his costume—a tunic of bronze satin with insets of black velvet embroidered with scrolling leaves—made me draw in a breath of admiration. His posture and movements reflected self-aware dignity and supreme confidence as he smiled at me.

"Daughter," King François said, his voice welling with affection, "how sweet your demeanor, how humble! Surely I could have found no better bride for my son in all of Christendom!"

He embraced me impetuously, then kissed my mouth and cheeks with wet lips.

"Your Majesty." I executed a low curtsy. "How grateful I am to you for rescuing me from my dire prison; I am happy to be able to thank you in the flesh."

The King turned to his son, his tone critical. "Here, Henri, is true humility; you could learn much from your bride. Embrace her gently, with affection."

Henri lifted his miserable gaze from the floor. He wore his fourteen years awkwardly—his nose and ears were too large for his eyes and chin, though time would likely see them better matched. He was bony, gangly, with a boy's narrow chest and back, a fact that the full sleeves and padded shoulders of his satin doublet sought to disguise. His brown hair was clipped short in the Roman style.

He was a poor substitute for my charming, handsome Ippolito, but I smiled at him. He tried to do the same, but his lips trembled. He hesitated for so long that a murmur passed through the crowd; I lowered my gaze, embarrassed.

The King's eldest son, the Dauphin François, stepped between us.

"*I* must kiss her first," François announced loudly, in a voice as polished as any courtier's, yet good-natured. He had full cheeks, ruddied by fresh air and good health, and flax-colored hair.

"We want her to feel welcome," François added, winking at me, "but I fear the bridegroom's nerves are so unsteady, he shall put a fright into her instead."

The King looked annoyed at this breach of propriety, but François kissed me quickly, then handed me to his youngest brother, Charles, an imp with pale ringlets.

Grinning wickedly, Charles kissed me on both cheeks with such an exaggerated smacking sound that some in the crowd tittered.

"Don't worry," he whispered. "I'll soon prove that he can laugh."

He drew back and presented my hands to Henri. The King beamed; apparently, he approved of Charles's every action.

Panicked, Henri looked to his older brother; the Dauphin gave him a nod of gentle encouragement. Henri's expression hardened with determination as he turned back to me, but terror flickered in his eyes as he leaned down to kiss me; his breath smelled agreeably of fennel seed.

"Duchess," he began, reciting a speech from memory. "With all my heart, and with the good wishes of all my people, I welcome you to my father's kingdom, and to . . ." He faltered.

"To our family, the Valois!" the King snapped. "Have you no brains? You've only practiced it a hundred times!"

Henri glared up at his father with sullen hatred. The unpleasant moment was broken suddenly by a loud, stuttering fart. I thought that someone in the royal party had just embarrassed themselves until I saw young Charles's smug grin. His tactic worked: Henri broke into a charming smile and giggled; King François relaxed and gave Charles a reproving but affectionate nudge. The Dauphin smiled, relieved for his father and brother.

Henri gathered himself and, in better humor, said, "Catherine, welcome to our family, the Valois."

Catherine, he said, and like that, Caterina was no more.

His voice was too deep to be a boy's, too wavering in pitch to be a man's. Though I had never heard it before, I knew it. His voice and face were young now, but given time and maturity, they would change. Somewhere, between my bridegroom's voice and his father's, somewhere between his features and the King's, were those of the man who had cried out to me in my dreams.

Catherine

Venez a moi

Aidez-moi

That evening, in my gilded, timber-scented chamber on the Place-Neuve, I wrote another letter to the magician Ruggieri. There was little point to the exercise, save to vent my desperate foreboding: Ruggieri was at worst dead, at best mad and missing. He could not help me, trapped in a foreign land and a blood-soaked dream that threatened to become waking.

I paused in midstroke of the quill, set it down, and crumpled the page before feeding it to the hearth. I took a fresh sheet and addressed it to my cousin Maria. I asked that she send me *De Vita Coelitus Comparanda,* by Marsilio Ficino, and the letters from Ser Cosimo Ruggieri on the art of astrology.

When the time came to sign the letter, I paused, then scrawled in bold letters:

Catherine
Duchesse d'Orléans

PART V

Princess

October 1533–March 1547

Sixteen

Three days of celebration followed—banquets, jousts, and balls. My betrothed participated reluctantly in them all. I, too, participated with only half a heart. The thought that Henri was the man in my nightmare had terrified me, and I had no one to confide in, no one who might say, with a laugh, that I was tired and anxious and so had let my imagination run unfettered.

Queen Eléonore, my soon to be mother-in-law, served as my chaperone. Three years earlier, she had married François, as reluctant a bridegroom then as his son was now. Ravenous to plant the French flag in Italian soil, François had unwisely taken on the Emperor's forces and suffered a catastrophic defeat at Pavia, where he was captured. He had purchased his freedom with hundreds of thousands of gold ecus and a promise to marry Emperor Charles's widowed sister, Eléonore.

Like her brother, Eléonore was Flemish, fluent in French, and well-versed in Parisian culture and customs but altogether unlike the sparkling, sly-eyed women of her husband's court. Her chestnut hair was worn in an unforgivably old-fashioned Spanish style: parted down the middle, plaited, and wound in two thick coils covering her ears. She was solid, thick-limbed, and graceless, her movements lumbering, her eyes bovine.

I liked her. Her silence, patience, and virtue were genuine. She had waited a short distance from her husband and his sons, and when King François brought me to her, she had gazed up at him adoringly. He did not so much as glance at her to acknowledge her presence and uttered with bored carelessness, "My wife, Queen Eléonore." She had embraced me with unsullied sincerity and introduced me to King François's daughter, ten-year-old Marguerite; another girl, thirteen-year-old Madeleine, was sick with consumption and home abed.

Early in the morning on the day of the secular ceremony—the third day of my stay in the palace on the Place-Neuve—Queen Eléonore came to my chambers as I was being dressed.

Her smile was kind and simple, her gaze steady. "You have no mother, Catherine. Did anyone speak frankly to you of the wedding night?"

"No," I said, and at the instant I uttered it, realized I should have lied; I had no desire to listen to a lecture on the rudiments of sexual congress. I felt I had learned all I needed to know from my encounters with Ippolito.

"Ah." She looked on me with gentle pity. "It is not such an unpleasant thing; some women, I hear, enjoy it. Certainly the men love it so." She proceeded to tell me that I should insist that my husband not waste his seed but put all of it in the proper receptacle, and that I must lie flat afterward for a good quarter hour.

"It is important that you give birth as soon as possible," she said, "for I think they do not love you until you give them a son." I heard the wistfulness behind her words. François had adored his first wife, Queen Claude, the mother of his children, dead for almost a decade.

Eléonore placed her hand upon mine. "It will all go well. Before it happens, I will make sure that you take a little wine so that you are comfortable." She patted my hand and rose. "You will have many sons, I know it."

I smiled at the notion. My husband to be was not fond of me now, but I would have his children—a family truly my own, from which I would never be separated. And I would never, like poor Queen Eléonore, have to compete with a ghost.

The betrothal ceremony was a simple matter of signing the weighty marriage contract and standing silently beside Henri while the Cardinal de Bourbon intoned a blessing over us. We were taken then to the great hall where I had first been introduced to the King and his family. Henri and I were prompted to kiss, the signal for the trumpets; the noise made us both start.

A ball commenced. I danced with Henri, and the King, and then Henri's brother, François.

It was clear that Henri and his older brother were close. The Dauphin's presence usually provoked an honest smile from my bridegroom; from time to time they shared a secret joke told by a single glance. The golden-haired François—the Dauphin, I prefer to call him, to spare confusing him with his father—was more talkative than Henri and passionately loved books and learning. He also enjoyed history and explained to me the evolution of his title. Five centuries earlier, the first count to rule the region Vienne, in western France, bore the symbol of a dolphin upon his shield, hence becoming the Dauphin de Viennois. The name stuck, even two hundred years later, when the position fell to the eldest son of the French king.

As the Dauphin spoke engagingly to me, I sensed a faint discomfort that never left him except when he and his brother Henri were alone. His discomfort was greatest in the presence of his father, who never missed an opportunity to criticize his two older sons, or to praise his youngest—nor did Henri ever miss a chance to direct spiteful glances at his father. I wondered, as I glided beside the Dauphin in a sedate Spanish pavane, whether he was the king that the astrologer Ruggieri had seen in my moles. Perhaps I was marrying the wrong son.

That night, I returned to my temporary suite and Henri to his father's palace. I was awakened three hours before dawn, when the women came to dress me. Seven long, tedious hours passed before I was ready and word was sent to the King.

On that day I suffered more glory than anyone ought. My poor skull was already laden with gemstones when one of the women set the golden ducal crown upon it, weighing so heavily I could scarcely hold my head up. Gold brocade robes, trimmed in purple velvet and white ermine and studded with rubies, hung from my shoulders. I dreaded the prospect of standing upright in them for hours.

At last King François arrived. His Majesty wore white satin embroidered with tiny gold fleurs-de-lis, and a cloak of gold. He was jubilant but, to my surprise, a bit nervous; when he saw my trembling, he kissed me and lied, saying that I was the most beautiful creature he'd ever seen.

Joking and laughing in an effort to jolly me, he led me down the stairs to the chapel erected near the Pope's chambers, where the bulk of the nation's wealth was displayed on the persons of three hundred guests. The sun's rays streamed in through the great arched windows; at the altar, ten tall candelabra bloomed flame. Dazzled, I clung to the King's thick forearm, matching my steps to his sedate pace.

Henri waited at the altar. At the sight of us, resentment rippled across his features. Whether it was directed at his father or at me, it didn't matter: Henri hated the very idea of marrying me.

Before the King handed me off to his son, he kissed my cheek and whispered, "Remember, you are my daughter now, and I shall love you as such until the day I die."

I stood on tiptoe to return his kiss and then went to stand beside my husband.

Henri was less grandly appointed than the King, but grand enough in a white satin doublet with black velvet leggings and black sleeves, slashed so that his white undershirt showed through. He, too, wore a ducal crown and cloak of gold.

At my approach, he hid his hostility. His carriage was graceful and proud, though he clasped his hands so tightly that the whites of his knuckles showed. When I came alongside him, he turned and knelt on the purple velvet cushion at the altar.

I did the same and stared up at Pope Clement. Captured in a pane of light, his face looked unhealthy and waxen, his lips grey; the white in his beard had overtaken the black. Yet his eyes were radiant. My match with Henri was his crowning achievement. I hated him for condemning me to live the rest of my life in a foreign land with a stranger who resented me for the very reason I resented him: We were pawns forced upon each other.

The ceremony was interminable, with much standing and kneeling and far too many prayers. My betrothed and I recited our vows in turn, and exchanged rings; Henri's touch was cold. Pope Clement recited much Latin, scribed many signs of the cross over our heads, and then it was done. At his urging we turned, bright with relief, to face the crowd.

Henri scanned the first row of observers, anxious to catch someone's gaze. Between Queen Eléonore and her stepdaughters stood a pale-haired noblewoman. She was not natively beautiful; it was her serene, elegant bearing and delicate bones that made her seem so. I had seen her before, mostly at my husband's side, explaining the finer points of protocol to him. She was well past the age to be Henri's mother, and I thought little of the eager look he gave her as we moved toward the aisle, little of the approving glance she offered in return.

But as we passed by, her expression seemed to shift, perhaps only a trick of the sun and candlelight reflected in hueless eyes. For an instant they seemed gloating, calculating, but as I looked sharply at her, her eyes softened and she glanced away, humble, servile.

Only then did I take note of her gown. She wore a widow's colors, white and black: white satin for the bodice and undergown, black for the overskirt and the sleeves—slashed so that the white of her chemise showed through. White satin and black velvet, the very fabrics Henri had chosen for his wedding day.

A banquet followed the ceremony. The King's family and I dined on a platform, the better to be seen by the hundreds of souls crammed into the great hall. Relieved of my heavy crown and cloak, I sat between Henri and the Dauphin. My new husband had few words for me but many for his brother; in François's presence, Henri transformed into a laughing, affectionate youth.

The feasting began at midday and ended at dusk. I changed into a gown of green, my official color. Corsages of red velvet roses were fastened in my hair and on the black brocade mask that hid the upper half of my face. Weakly disguised, I returned to the banquet chamber, where a masquerade ball had already begun. I danced with the King and Dauphin—parrying verbally as if we did not easily recognize each other—and with my taciturn husband, who came alive only in the presence of his brothers or the blond widow.

I drank little wine that night. I was tempted, knowing what was to come, but reasoned that I would be better off if I were in full control of my emotions. I was apparently one of the few to come to that decision; by the time Queen Eléonore came to fetch me, the din in the great hall was so loud we did not speak, as our voices would have been lost in the roar. She led me out into the corridor, where an entourage of ladies waited. Some had accompanied me from Florence; others, including the elegant, fair-haired woman dressed in white and black mourning, belonged to Eléonore's retinue. Her perfume, the essence of lily of the valley, preceded her person and lingered in the air behind her.

The ladies escorted me to Prince Henri's chambers, which were chilly despite the snapping fire in the hearth. His great bed, supported by four posters of carved mahogany, had been covered with Isabelle d'Este's fashionable ebony sheets. A thick fur coverlet was neatly folded at the foot. Rose petals, the last of the season, had been strewn by a careful hand upon the black silk.

The bed hangings—all venerable tapestries in shades of forest and scarlet, aglint here and there with thread of gold—displayed pastoral scenes in which women strummed lutes and danced and picked fruit from trees while wearing great tall caps pointed like narwhal tusks, reminders of the previous century's fashion.

I stood next to the fire as the women coaxed me from my sleeves and bodice and skirts. Clad in my chemise, I remained still as the ladies picked gems, one by one, from my hair and brushed it out until it cascaded down my back. I was obliged to remain motionless a bit longer, as the black-and-white widow pulled my chemise up over my head.

I was naked as Eve in the sight of a half dozen strangers—I, to whom my own body was an unfamiliar sight, untouched since Ippolito's embraces. I was still thin then, ivory kneecaps and hip bones straining against pale olive flesh. I pressed my right palm to my left breast, concealing my right breast beneath my forearm; with my left hand, I cupped the delta of thin golden brown hair at the juncture between my legs, and so I staggered awkwardly to the bed as the elegant widow pulled back the top sheet.

The black silk was so cold I shivered while the women arranged my hair upon the pillow and drew the sheet up so that it just covered my breasts.

The widow retreated. Queen Eléonore leaned down and pressed her lips tenderly to my forehead.

"It will all go quickly," she whispered. "Don't be afraid."

She pulled the bed hangings together, leaving me in solitary darkness. The women retired to the antechamber; I heard their soft laughter as they scattered nuts onto the floor to mask the sounds soon to be made by the newlyweds.

All of Pope Clement's yearnings for power, all of King François's hopes for glory, all the glittering pomp of the past several months had been nothing but fantasy, a bright, hectic dream. Now stripped bare of my gems and silks, I woke to reality, wherein a homely, frightened girl waited in darkness for a sad, reluctant boy. I thought of Clement and François, full of wine and self-congratulation, and felt gnawing bitterness.

Footsteps came, followed by the creak of the antechamber door. His Majesty's booming voice was so cheerful that it dispelled the solemnity the Queen had left behind.

"Greetings, ladies! We have come in search of my son's wife!" His words were slurred.

Feminine voices replied, followed by a ripple of restrained laughter at the crackle of nuts beneath royal boots.

The bedchamber door opened as someone entered. On the other side of the bed hangings, fabric rustled, then sighed as it fell. The tapestries snapped open so suddenly I clutched the sheet at my bosom.

Henri stood nude at the bedside. Swift as a shot, he stretched out beside me and pulled up the covers, but not before the firelight revealed a long, slender torso punctuated at the groin by a thin tuft of ash brown hair. He did not look at me but stared straight up at the green velvet canopy above our heads.

Seconds later, King François entered. His head was uncovered, his hair tousled as he leaned heavily on the arm of the wizened, white-haired Cardinal de Bourbon. Both men were breathless from coarse laughter; the King paused at the sight of us naked children. Perhaps he also saw our mortification; his gaze softened as he withdrew his grip from the older man's forearm. "Bless them, Eminence," he urged the Cardinal softly. "Bless them, then begone. My word will be sufficient."

The Cardinal took his leave. When he had gone, the King turned to his son.

"I remember too well my wedding night with your mother, how young and frightened we both were," François said. "The law requires me to witness the coupling, but the instant it's done, I'll leave you in peace. In the meantime . . ." His voice dropped. "Kiss her, boy, and forget I am here."

Henri and I rolled onto our sides to face each other; he set his trembling hands upon the rounds of my shoulders and pressed his lips against mine—a perfunctory, passionless kiss. He was as trapped within his resentment as I was within mine, yet one of us was obliged to break free.

I closed my eyes and thought of Clarice's mouth blooming upon Leda's, of Ippolito's skillful tongue and fingers. I cupped Henri's face in my hands as Clarice had Leda's and pushed my lips against his, then delicately parted them with my tongue. He tensed and would have recoiled had my touch faltered, but I persevered until he responded with kisses of his own. As his confidence and mine increased, I rolled him onto me, slipped a hand between his legs, and felt the flesh there stir.

I sensed nearby movement and opened my eyes to see King François looming; he drew the bedsheet down until his son's buttocks were exposed.

When Henri and I both looked up at this intrusion, the King dropped the sheet and stepped back, mildly chagrined.

"Don't stop! I'm only making sure it's properly accomplished. I will disturb you no more." He moved away toward the hearth.

Henri's cheeks went mottled scarlet. Because I was obliged, I reached between his thighs and stroked him until he grew again; and he was obliged, when he was ready, to part my legs and settle himself between them, as Ippolito had done so long ago, but there was no sweetness, no heat, no yearning.

At the moment of penetration, my resolve wavered and my body tightened; I cried out at the pain. Henri must have feared losing his confidence, for he began to pump wildly. I held on, gritting my teeth. Within a minute, his passion crested and he reared his torso backward, his eyes rolling up against his fluttering lids. Simultaneously, something warm trickled between my legs.

Henri pulled away and lay on his back, gasping.

"Well done!" King François clapped his hands. "Both riders have shown valor in the joust!"

I pulled the sheets up and turned my face toward the distant wall. After an all-too-audible whisper to his son that virgins were prone to weep after such events, the King left.

In the silence that followed, I knew that I should falsely compliment Henri on his lovemaking, yet exhaustion so overwhelmed me I felt I could not move; it was accompanied by a painful constriction of the muscles in my throat, the certain precursor of the tears the King had mentioned.

I lay silent, hoping that Henri would leave me to my self-pity, but he said, very softly, his gaze directed at the ceiling, "I'm sorry."

"You didn't hurt me, Your Highness," I lied, without turning to look at him. "I cried out only because I was startled."

"I wasn't speaking of that," he said, "although I'm sorry for that, too." He paused. "I'm sorry that I haven't been more pleasant. You've been so kind. My brothers and sisters like you very much, and so does my father."

I stared at the tapestry bed hanging in front of me, at the play of the firelight on the threads of shining gold woven in among those of burgundy and forest green. "And you?" I asked.

"You're charming," he answered shyly. "Dignified, yet cordial. Everyone at Court is very impressed. But . . . I know I'm not as cheerful as my brothers, a fact that annoys my father. I'll try to do better."

"You need not apologize," I said. "I know you didn't want this match. I'm a foreigner, a commoner, and ugly . . ."

"Don't speak of yourself in such a manner!" he exclaimed indignantly. "I forbid it. Your looks are pleasing enough; one doesn't need to be pretty to be handsome." His words were so honest and guileless that I was moved to roll over and face him.

"Oh, Henri," I said, reaching for him, but I had moved too quickly. He flinched and recoiled in such involuntary disgust that I withdrew at once. His gaze met mine, but he didn't see me: instead, he stared at something beyond me, something hideous. I saw the poorly veiled loathing in his eye and shrank from it.

How, I thought, *shall I ever be able to tell you of my bloody dream, if you will not love me?*

He dropped his gaze. "Please, I . . . I'm sorry, Catherine, truly I am. I'm just so very tired."

"I'm tired, too," I said tightly. "I think I would like to sleep." I turned my back to him.

He hesitated—trying, perhaps, to think of the words to ease my hurt—then finally turned away. He lay awake for some time, but in the end, sleep took him.

Had there been a place within my new home to find solitude, I would have gone there; but the room where I had spent my last virginal days in the temporary palace was full of servants, the corridors full of revelers. Women stood watch in our antechamber; if I had risen, or stirred, they would have known. I remained all night where I least wanted to be—in Henri's bed.

It was there, in the hours before dawn, that an ominous thought jerked me from a light doze.

Perhaps what Henri had seen, when he recoiled from me in disgust, was not his hated father or an unwanted marriage. Perhaps, with his innocence and sensitivity, he had looked beyond those things at the dark blot on my soul.

Seventeen

In the weeks that followed, Henri never came to my quarters or summoned me to his. He spent his time hunting, jousting, or playing tennis with his older brother. Many times I sat with the gentlemen of the chamber in the great indoor gallery and watched Henri and François. One brother would lift the ball high in his left hand and bellow: "*Tenez!* I have it!"—a warning to his opponent that he was about to smash the ball against the high stone walls. That either ever managed to avoid being struck by the madly ricocheting projectile—or braining one of the spectators—was a testament to his skill.

Young François, pale and golden in contrast to his dark brother, won the crowd's affection and sympathies, grinning at his errors and bowing to the audience immediately after their commission. In his presence, Henri came alive. He was athletically gifted, while François was shorter, heavier, and not as lithe. Henri could easily have taken every game but often made intentional errors so that his brother could win.

When Henri was not engaged in sport, he spent a great deal of time with the blond widow from Queen Eléonore's entourage. Young François, by contrast, liked to dine with his sisters and many days shared lunch with us.

On one such occasion, I asked him about the widow. She was Diane de

Poitiers, wife of the late Louis de Brézé, a very powerful old man who had been the Grand Seneschal of Normandy. Her grandmother had been a de La Tour d'Auvergne, which made us second cousins. At the age of fourteen, Madame de Poitiers had come to Court to attend the King's first wife, Claude. In the twenty years since, she had earned a reputation for dignity and temperance, dressing modestly and eschewing the white face paint and rouge used by the other women. A pious Catholic, she was scandalized by the infiltration of Protestants into Court.

"In which subject does she instruct my husband?" I asked François.

I speared a piece of venison—I had brought my own fork from Italy and still suffered the bemused glances of the French for using such an exotic implement—and paused before taking a bite.

Young François held his meat in his fingers and bit off a large chunk before answering. "In protocol, comport, and politics," he said, chewing, his words muffled. "She's quite good at all three." He swallowed and shot me a curious glance. "You needn't be jealous. The lady is famous for her virtue. And she's a good twenty years older than Henri."

"Of course I'm not jealous," I said, with a little laugh.

François dismissed the thought with an easy smile. "You must understand, Henri was only five when our mother died. He had always been very attached to her, so the loss was particularly hard on him. Madame de Poitiers looked after Henri and tried to be like a mother to him. That's why he looks to her for approval now."

François was not the only dear friend I discovered in my new family. The King's sister Marguerite, Queen of Navarre—that tiny country south of France and north of Spain, bordering the Pyrenees—lived at Court with her five-year-old daughter, Jeanne. Marguerite and I adored each other at first glance; our affection was strengthened when we discovered our shared passion for books. Marguerite was tall, warm, and sparkling, with such prominent cheeks that, when she smiled, they partially eclipsed her eyes.

Like her brother, she had been born in Cognac, not far from the central eastern coast, where Italian art and letters were properly appreciated, and she had insisted that King François bring the aging Florentine master Leonardo da Vinci to France and pay him handsomely—"even though," she said, with gentle, rueful humor, "he was too old and blind to do much painting." He had brought with him some of his best works—including a small, lovely portrait of a smiling, dark-haired woman, one of my favorites, which still hangs at the Château of Amboise.

"However," Marguerite warned, "don't believe the King when he tells you that Leonardo died in his arms. My brother likes to forget that he was not in Amboise at the master's final hour."

She also spoke with pride of her brother's work to create the grandest, most complete library in Europe—housed at the country Château at Blois. I promised that at my first opportunity I would visit it.

Meanwhile, I settled into an ostensibly magnificent life. We quit Marseille's sunny coastline for the country's wintry interior as King François grew restless after a month or two in any one location.

Before I arrived in France, I had thought I lived in luxury, with my needs attended to by many servants, but my error was one of scope. In Italy, power was scattered and a ruler's subjects few. The Sforzas ruled Milan; the Medici, Florence; the d'Estes, Ferrara; a hundred different barons ruled a hundred different towns. Rome lay under the authority of the Pope; Venice, under that of a Republic. But France was a nation with a single monarch, and the greatness of that fact struck me when I first traveled with François I's Court—not so much a court as a city of thousands.

Most of the royal employees served in one of three domains: the chamber, the chapel, or the hostel. Under the first, the Grand Chamberlain supervised the provision and maintenance of clothing, the ritual of dressing the King, and all activities related to the King's personal toilette. Its staff included valets, gentlemen of the chamber, cupbearers and bread carriers, barbers, tailors, seamstresses, laundresses, chambermaids, and fools.

The domain of the chapel, managed by the Grand Almoner, included the King's confessor, dozens of chaplains, almoners, choirs, and the King's reader.

The domain of the hostel, run by the Grand Master, fed the King and his enormous entourage. There were other lesser domains, including those of the stables, which encompassed the royal messengers; the hunt, which cared for the dogs and birds; and the fourriers, who faced the harrowing task of moving the Court and its belongings from location to location. In addition, there were councillors, secretaries, notaries, bookkeepers, pages, apothecaries, doctors, surgeons, musicians, poets, artists, jewelers, architects, bodyguards, archers, quartermasters, sumpters, and squires.

And these were only those who were in the King's employ. There were also those who attended his family—his sister, children, and cousins—as well as the foreign dignitaries and ambassadors, and all of the King's friends whose boon companionship pleased him.

I left Marseille in a sumptuously appointed carriage and turned to look at the winding caravan of wagons, horses, and heavy-laden mules behind me. Twenty thousand mounts, five hundred dogs, and as many hawks and falcons, as well as a lynx and a lion, traveled with our circus. We stayed at various lodgings—mostly the châteaux of nobles happy to entertain the Crown—until we made our way into the Loire Valley.

The royal Château at Blois was magnificent and contradictory. To one side stood a red-brick castle built by François I's predecessor, Louis XII, and inherited by his daughter, Claude. It was here that Jeanne d'Arc received a blessing from the Archbishop of Reims before leading her troops into battle. Claude had been fond of the property, and when she married François—thus securing his claim to the French throne—he added a modern four-story palace.

The palace was unlike Italian palazzi. The interior apartments were connected to all other areas not by corridors but by spiraling staircases. My first few days at Blois, I was constantly short of breath, but within a week, I was running up and down the steps without a thought. The King was so fond of spiral staircases that he had a massive, dramatic one—adorned with statues, in Gothic fashion—placed outside at the building's center.

The King's and Queen's apartments were on the second floor—as was, in flagrant violation of tradition, that of François's mistress, Madame d'Etampes. The children's apartments were all on the third floor. Persons of lesser importance lived on the ground floor, where the refectories, kitchen, and guardroom were also located. Numerous outbuildings housed cardinals, clerks, courtiers, bookkeepers, doctors, tutors, and a host of others.

Night had fallen by the time I ate and saw my trunks unpacked. I was shown my spacious apartment, next to that of Henri's sisters, by lamplight;

the King was expected on the morrow and would take up residence in his. I was used to a bedchamber and antechamber, but now I had a bedchamber, an antechamber, a garderobe large enough to hold all my clothes as well as a sleeping servant, and a cabinet, a small, private office. On the brick over my bedroom fireplace was the golden image of a salamander—King François's personal symbol—and beneath it, the motto *Notrisco al buono, stingo el reo,* "I feed off the good fire and extinguish the bad."

I dismissed all the French attendants and called for one of my own ladies-in-waiting, Madame Gondi, to undress me.

Marie-Catherine de Gondi was an astonishingly beautiful woman of thirty with prematurely silver hair and delicate black eyebrows. Her skin was flawless, save for a tiny dark mole on one cheek, near the corner of her lips. She was well-educated, intelligent, and possessed of a natural daintiness that held no whiff of affectation.

She was French but with a comforting difference: She had lived in Florence for many years before joining my entourage, with the result that she spoke fluent Tuscan. I was not of a mind to speak French that night, and her conversation was a comfort to me. After she undressed me, I asked her to read to me and gave her a copy of one of Aunt Marguerite's poems, "*Miroir de l'Ame Pecheresse,* Mirror of a Lost Soul."

She read for some time, and I sent her to bed as the poor woman was exhausted after a long day of travel. I was still restless and recalled what Aunt Marguerite had told me about the royal library. I wrapped myself modestly in a cloak and, lamp in hand, made my way onto the spiraling staircase that exited my apartment.

The layout of the château was confusing, but after several false starts, I found the staircase that led me to the library. The room was vast and as dark, on that moonless night, as a high-ceilinged cave. I held my brave little lamp close, my hand in front of me to prevent any immediate encounters with walls or furniture.

As I sensed a looming presence in the darkness, I reached out and felt the smooth edge of molded wood and silk-covered spines—a shelf of books. Eagerly, I moved closer and lifted the lamp, whose glow revealed a wooden case stretching from floor to ceiling; in the shadows, even more cases stretched back into infinity. The books were all of a uniform size, bound in different colors of watered silk. There were the obligatory editions of Dante's *Commedia,* Petrarch's *Trionfi* and *Canzoniere,* and of course Boccaccio's *Decameron.*

There were also titles I had never seen before: a newly bound volume of *Pantagruel,* by Rabelais; *Utopia,* by Sir Thomas More, and an astonishing collection by Boccaccio, *De claris mulieribus, On Famous Women.*

I soon stumbled onto greater riches: a copy of *Theologica Platonica de Immortalitate Animae, Platonic Theology of the Immortal Soul,* by Marsilio Ficino. I pulled it down at once, of course, and might have stopped my searching right there, but my appetite was whetted. A chill coursed through me at the sight of *De Occulta Philosophia Libri Tres* by Cornelius Agrippa. I had just stumbled onto the King's occult collection, and a lifting of my lamp revealed volume after volume on the subjects of astrology, alchemy, qabala, and talismans.

In my mind, I heard the magician's voice: *The Wing of Corvus Rising, from Agrippa, created under the aegis of Mars and Saturn.* Instinctively, I lifted a hand to my breasts, between which the talisman hung.

It seemed to me that the sudden appearance of these works by Ficino and Agrippa was a providential indication: If Henri was the bloodied man in my dream, I needed all the secret wisdom I could find.

This notion filled me with an eerie excitement; I opened Agrippa's book and began to read. I was so utterly carried away by the words that I did not hear the creak of the door, with the result that when the King himself appeared in the darkness—hair uncombed, nightshirt hid beneath a gold brocade dressing gown—I gasped as if I had seen a specter.

King François laughed; the yellow glow from the lamp in his hand had a ghoulish effect on his long face.

"Don't be frightened, Catherine. My supper awakens me far too often now that I am grown old."

"Your Majesty." I shut the book and curtsied awkwardly. "I must compliment you on your library. I'm enormously impressed by your selection of titles. And I've barely begun to explore it."

He lowered his lamp and grinned, pleased, then glanced at the books in my hand.

"Agrippa, eh? That manuscript is rare—it has yet to be formally published—but I was lucky enough to obtain one of the few copies in circulation. Quite esoteric choices, Neoplatonism and astrological magic, for a young lady. How do you find Agrippa?"

I paused. Many priests disapproved of such subjects; indeed, many argued that these topics were blasphemous. It occurred to me that, although the King might see fit to include such titles in the royal library, he might not necessarily approve of them—or of my taking them to read.

"I find it fascinating," I said stoutly. "I am a student of astrology and related subjects, and fond of Ficino. In fact, I brought one of his works from Florence, *De Vita Coelitus Comparanda.*"

His eyes widened and lit up. "That would be the third volume—"

"Of *De Vita Libri Tres,* yes. I'll write my family in Florence and ask for the first two volumes. And I shall make all three of them a present for your library."

He lunged at me and kissed each of my cheeks in rapid turn. "My darling! I could ask for no better gift! But I cannot ask you to give away one of your own country's national treasures."

"I'm French now," I said. To my mind, the House of Medici and the royal House of Valois were one and the same.

He embraced me with real warmth. "I will accept your generous gift, my daughter. But I would not see the books sent here, where we will be spending only a month or two. Have them sent to Fontainebleau, near Paris. You and I will be there by the time the books arrive, and thus will be able to enjoy them immediately." He paused. "You needn't read the books here, child; take them to your room and keep them as long as you'd like." He moved back toward the shelves. "And now, some reading for me."

Lifting the lamp, he squinted at the titles.

"Ah," he said at last. "Here." He drew a book from the shelf. The title was in French, the subject Italian architecture. "I'm of a mind to do more building at Fontainebleau."

I moved to stand beside him and spied a treatise about Brunelleschi, who had designed the great dome for Florence's cathedral. I retrieved the book from the shelf and opened it.

He turned his head sharply as he registered my interest. "So," he asked, "you enjoy philosophy *and* architecture? Not generally subjects of interest for a woman."

I must have blushed, given the sudden rush of warmth to my neck and cheeks. "It is Brunelleschi, Sire, and I am from Florence. But I should think anyone would be curious to learn how such a huge cupola stands without any visible support."

He gave a toothy grin of approval. "Tomorrow, the third hour after noon, go to the royal stables and join me for a ride in the countryside."

"Your invitation honors me, Your Majesty," I said and curtsied again. "I won't be late."

By the time I finally drifted off to sleep in my bed, Agrippa's book open on my lap, I had made a decision: If I could not win Henri, then I would win his father, in the hope of reconciling them—and, of course, reconciling Henri to me.

As Madame Gondi directed my ladies in dressing me the next morning, I asked her to find a French hood for me. I had been wearing my hair in the fashion of an Italian married woman, up with brooches, but all the French women had shoulder-length hoods—veils actually, affixed to stiff, curved bands of velvet or brocade, worn at midcrown over smoothed-back hair. I had told King François that I was now French, and the hood was a physical reminder of my first loyalty.

In a matter of minutes, Madame Gondi appeared with a white veil attached to a dove grey band. I felt odd wearing it, as if I were wearing a disguise at a masque.

The days at Court fell into a predictable pattern based upon the King's movements. After rising, the King met with his secretaries and councillors. At ten o'clock, he went to Mass, and at eleven, he ate lunch in his reception hall. He was the sole diner, with nobles, petitioners, and servants standing in solemn attendance. Often, a bishop would read aloud to him from a text of His Majesty's choosing. Afterward, the King held audiences or heard complaints. In the afternoons, he would emerge for exercise—a ride, a hunt, a walk, a game of tennis.

I shadowed the King that day in the hope of encountering Henri, but he and his older brother were off elsewhere.

By afternoon, the November sky held grey clouds that promised drizzle.

Even so, my mood had brightened. My favorite mount, Zeus, a black-maned chestnut gelding, had traveled with me to France. I missed him, and the exercise, terribly. I also hoped that my husband might be among the riders.

But when I arrived at the stables at the appointed hour, Henri was not there. Nor was the Dauphin, nor young Charles, nor any of the gentlemen of the court. With the exception of the grooms—one of whom stood holding the reins of the King's restless, large black charger—His Majesty was the only man present.

He was quite distracted by the five lovely women who accompanied him, all laughing and chattering like bright, beautiful parrots—save one, who had just stepped onto a small stool set before her waiting mare with the intent of ascending the padded, thronelike perch that was a French ladies' saddle. Her back was to the others—a fact that tempted the King. He wound his arm around the waist of a different woman standing beside him and pulled her body against his in lascivious fashion, then, with incriminating deftness, slipped his hand inside her bodice and squeezed her breast. She displayed no embarrassment, even when she lifted her gaze and saw me.

"Sire!" she exclaimed, with mock reproval, and coyly slapped his hand. She was dark-haired and stout, with prim lips braced by dimples. "Your Majesty, you are a wicked man!"

"I am," the King admitted cheerfully, "and only the kiss of a good Christian woman can save me. Marie, my darling, rescue me!"

Eager not to be seen by the woman settling on the saddle, Marie gave him a swift kiss on the lips and glanced pointedly at me.

I curtsied. "Your Majesty," I said loudly.

Instantly, five pairs of feminine eyes marked my French hood.

"Daughter!" the King exclaimed, smiling, and took my hand. "How fashionable you look, and how French! Welcome to our little band! Ladies, this is my darling daughter Catherine. And these, Catherine, are Madame de Massy, the Duchess de Montpensier, Madame Chabot, and Madame de Canaples."

I nodded at each of them in turn. Madame de Massy, perhaps eighteen and the most hesitant of the group, had milky blond hair and eyebrows so fine and colorless as to be invisible. Beside her, already mounted, Madame de Montpensier—a handsome woman with a square, masculine jaw—bowed politely in the saddle but could not entirely repress her smirk at my discomfort over finding the King with his hand in a woman's bodice. Madame Chabot, wife of an admiral, smiled faintly as though bored and beyond it all. Madame de Canaples—Marie, as the King had called her—looked on me with smug, heavy-lidded eyes.

The King gestured at the woman who had been mounting the grey mare when I arrived. "And this is my beloved Anne, also known as the Duchess d'Etampes." He glanced at her with a foolish, lovesick grin.

All of the women's glances followed his, looking to Anne for a cue. The Duchess sat upon her little riding throne, her feet on the high footrest, which forced her knees to bend so that her skirts spilled down to cover her legs. Thus situated, she could not reach the reins but folded her gloved hands while a mounted groom came alongside and took the reins for her.

She was a fragile creature, tiny, with large golden brown eyes and rouged lips that were full and astonishingly mobile, curving easily in sly amusement, or twisting in contempt, or pursing in disdain. Her copper hair was crimped into soft, frizzy clouds at her temples and parted severely down the middle; the band of her French hood was of gold filigree fashioned to resemble a tiara. From her chin to the tip of her riding boots, she was swallowed by a high-collared coat of the same cut and fur as the King's. She accepted his adoration as her due, with no more acknowledgment than a pleased sidewise glance.

When I neared, she turned her head deliberately to take me in, as a cat would prey, then swept her gaze over me: me, in my plain, shapeless cloak and my foolish French hood covering my very Italian hair; me, with my unforgivably olive complexion and bulging eyes.

"Madame de Massy," I said politely, with a nod. "Madame Chabot. Madame de Montpensier. Madame de Canaples." I turned to the Duchess and said, simply, "Your Grace."

The Duchess's lips tightened into a rosebud of a smile, as though she was struggling to repress a laugh at my thick accent.

"Your Highness," she said, in a voice deeper than expected from so small a throat. "We are honored to have you ride with us this day."

It was at that instant that my own horse, Zeus, was led out, snorting an eager greeting. I ran to him and stroked his dark muzzle, whispering of how I had missed him.

"Whatever is *that*?" the Duchess asked, with a nod at my sidesaddle.

The King more courteously echoed the question.

"My own design, Your Majesty," I answered, "so that I might mount and ride in modesty and without assistance." I demonstrated. "I put my left foot in a stirrup, here, and grasp the pommel . . ." With a small bound, I swung myself up onto Zeus and settled into place. The act permitted only the most fleeting glimpse of my calves, which were covered in white stockings. "I put my right leg around the horn, at the pommel. It holds my right knee fast, you see, so that I don't fall." I gathered up the reins and waved off the groom who wanted to take them.

"Brilliant!" said the King. "But surely you cannot ride as swift as a man."

"Sire, I can."

"Certainly when you ride at such speed, your legs will show," said Marie de Canaples.

"A pity," the Duchess said slyly, "to distract the King from such a fair face."

Marie grinned; her eyeteeth were sharp, like a fox's.

I flushed at the insult and looked to the King, but he offered no protection. Like the others, he was watching to see how I handled myself.

"Your Majesty," I said pleasantly. "Shall we ride?"

The King led us south, away from the château and steep hills, toward the broad river.

Our pace was unbearably sedate. The women's mares were content to be led by the grooms, but the King's stallion and my gelding were straining at the bit. To ease the tedium, Marie told a story of how one devious young woman, new at Court, had invited her paramour to a great banquet. As her husband dined nearby, her lover crawled beneath the table and, hidden by her voluminous skirts, pleasured her while she ate.

We made our way onto the long wooden bridge across the river, which took several minutes to cross. I looked back over the river, its blue broken here and there by golden sandbanks, to see the houses and church spires and hills behind us, and the great white rectangle of the royal château dominating the city.

The King grew bored; his gaze was on the dense woods waiting on the other side. The instant we made it to the other shore, he broke into a trot. The grooms quickened their pace a bit, which caused the women to bounce in their saddles.

"Your Majesty!" the Duchess called after him, with overt irritation. "The doctor didn't want you to ride at all today—you mustn't overtax yourself!"

In reply, His Majesty gave a laugh that terminated in a small cough and grinned over his shoulder at me. "Catherine! Let's see if you can truly keep up with a man!"

I grinned back at him and signaled Zeus with my heel.

I expected the King to lead me on a chase through the open meadow along the riverbanks; instead, he rode at a gallop straight into the thick woods. I drew in a breath and followed—ignoring, as he did, the women's warnings. I rode headlong into the forest of bare-limbed beech, oak, and fragrant pine. Luckily, the trees were all a century or more old, with branches high enough that I was not immediately knocked from my mount. Even so, I had to lean low to avoid some of them—not an easy feat when one is astride a horse at full gallop.

King François whooped at the realization that I had given chase and urged his stallion to go faster. Reveling in the sting of cold air on my cheeks, I followed him through the thick of the woods—hares and birds scattering before us—until he swerved and broke clear to ride alongside a neatly tilled vineyard. I followed in close pursuit but, in the end, couldn't catch him; Zeus's stride was shorter than that of François's huge charger. Even so, I refused to yield him more distance.

When he circled to retrace his path through the woods, I followed, encouraging Zeus to go as fast as he dared. I ducked at a low-hanging limb of a pine, then looked up to see the King veering sharply: The Duchess and the others had entered the forest and were heading directly toward us.

Immediately after his change in course, the King crouched low as the black charger surged upward over an obstacle.

The trunk of an ancient oak had split and fallen, blocking our way; the bare fingers of its upper limbs had caught on those of a neighboring tree, so that it hung high above the ground.

I saw the obstacle the second after it would have been possible to steer my horse away from the fallen limb and the nearby band of riders. I knew Zeus's limits, and this pressed them sorely, but the time for decision was past: I had no choice.

The horse's muscles strained beneath me; the spectators gasped. The fall happened, as falls do, so quickly that I had no time to be frightened. The world whirled as my body collided with Zeus's lathered flank, the jagged edges of wood, the cold, damp earth.

For an instant I couldn't breathe, then just as suddenly I was gulping in air.

King François stood over me, his long face made even longer by his gaping mouth. "Good God! Catherine, are you all right?"

The Duchess stood beside him, her mouth open in a tiny circle. The other ladies were still mounted.

My skirts were bunched up about my hips, exposing my petticoat, my stockinged calves, and my knee-length pantaloons of fine Italian lace, part of the exquisite trousseau chosen by Isabella d'Este. I made a sound of disgust as I pushed myself up and quickly rearranged my skirts.

The instant she realized I was unharmed, the Duchess said, in a low voice, "So. You did indeed distract the King from your pretty face. Such comely legs." A ripple of repressed laughter made its way through the women on horseback behind her; humor glinted in the King's eye, but he dutifully extinguished it.

I pushed the grooms' proffered hands away as I got to my feet. Zeus stood nearby, breathing heavily but exhilarated after the fine run, his reins held by the youngest groom.

"I'm fine, Your Majesty," I said.

I brushed dead leaves and splinters off my cape. The jagged limb, broader than my thigh, had caught my right shoulder, gouging the wool; had I been unprotected by the thick fabric, the branch would have torn open my gown to leave a serious wound. As it was, my shoulder ached from a bad bruise. My French hood had been pulled off completely; the punctured veil fluttered from the offending branch like a flag of surrender. One of the grooms fetched it like a trophy. It was torn, so I told him to hold it.

The King took my hand. "I can't believe you tried to take that tree. You must be more careful."

"My horse is a good jumper, Your Majesty," I said. "Under better circumstances, he could have cleared it."

A curious look came over him; he cocked his head, and the beginnings of a faint grin showed at one corner of his mouth. "You jump?"

"I do. Or at least I did, before coming here. Have you never seen a woman on horseback take a hedge?"

He gave a small laugh. "I didn't know it was possible. Of course, my sister has always said that, given the opportunity, women would be better at the hunt than men." He paused. "Perhaps I will have you accompany me on a hunt sometime."

"Nothing would please me better, Sire."

As we left, he rode next to me, and we made our way out of the woods at our original slow amble. The Duchess brooded silently, ignoring Marie's attempts at conversation. We cleared the forest and made our way onto the open, grassy riverbank. The King led us back toward the bridge, but the Duchess resisted.

"Canter along the shore, Your Majesty," she said, with feigned cheer, "and let us have a contest to see who can best keep up with you."

The King turned back in his saddle to look at her. "Anne, don't be foolish."

The Duchess turned to the groom holding her mount's reins and pointed. "Ride faster. There, along the banks."

The groom looked uncertainly to the King, who gave no signal, then again at the Duchess before leading her horse away from the group at a steady trot.

"Come, Your Majesty!" she called. "Give us chase!"

"Anne," the King said again, though she was already out of earshot. His expression was slightly pained as he spurred his charger and rode after her.

I would not compete directly with Anne; I followed slowly as the King broke into a canter and easily outpaced her mare. Once he had committed himself, he did so with boyish abandon.

"Faster!" she urged her groom. "Faster!"

The other women took up the cry. The most ridiculous of races commenced, with the Duchess well behind the King and the other women following, bobbing madly on their little thrones. The Duchess was not content with a brisk trot and insisted on more speed until the nervous groom finally broke into a canter. As he did so, she leaned forward to grasp her mare's white mane.

The result was utterly predictable. I spurred Zeus into a gallop, arriving just as the groom noticed he was leading a riderless mount; the King, caught up in the moment, was still happily cantering away.

I let go a shout, dismounted, and hurried over to the Duchess. She lay on her side, her crimson skirts and petticoat hiked up to reveal thin white legs—and much more. When Madame Gondi had first come to serve as one of my ladies of the chamber, she had remarked on my pantaloons, not just their fine lace and embroidery but the fact that French women did not wear them at all. Now I saw the proof, as the Duchess d'Etampes pushed herself up and, finding that she was entirely exposed, pulled down her skirts. I repressed a smile; her hair was not naturally copper but dull brown like mine.

She was undamaged, with her hood still in place, but would not rise until she was sure that the King had marked her fall. As the others rode up, I offered her my hand.

"So," I said loudly, "I see that you, too, have decided to distract the King from your pretty face."

François and his ladies giggled. As Anne rose, her hand in mine, fury sparked in her eye, tempered by approval that my barb had cleanly hit its mark. To ease its sting, I murmured of her bravery and took care, as we rode back over the bridge toward home, to remain well behind the King so that the Duchess could take her place beside him.

For I suspected, even then, that if I fell out of Anne's favor, I would fall out of the King's, and lose everything.

Eighteen

That evening the King hosted an intimate family supper, which included his children; his sister Marguerite and her daughter, Jeanne; and the Grand Master—the stodgy, grey-haired Anné Montmorency, who was included in almost everything because he was trusted with the keys to the King's residence. Queen Eléonore came with her most trusted lady-in-waiting—Henri's tutor, Madame de Poitiers. My husband arrived late and shared a hostile glance with his father before taking his seat between his aunt Marguerite and me. I greeted Henri eagerly; in response, he averted his gaze.

The King began to speak: He had been quite impressed by my courage in attempting a difficult jump, and the grace with which I took my fall. He related the incident with some embellishment and a good deal of humor, describing in comic detail the Duchess's desperate bouncing upon her saddle and subsequent fall—referring to her simply as "one of the ladies" so as not to embarrass the Queen.

Henri clearly understood which lady had been indicated, however, and while the others laughed at his father's amusing tale, he frowned.

The King went on to describe my saddle and said that, with the urging of "one of the ladies," he had ordered the Master of Horses to have several copies of it made "so that the women of the realm might keep pace with their king."

Queen Eléonore, Madame de Poitiers, and Grand Master Montmorency all smiled with brittle disapproval but dared not appear unenthusiastic. But Henri scowled at the story; something deeply vexed him. I tried to divert him with talk of amusing things, but the more I spoke, the darker his mood grew.

After supper, I found him in the outdoor courtyard, lingering at the foot of the steps leading to our separate apartments, I hoped with the aim of speaking privately to me. After Queen Eléonore and the royal children had made their way past us up different staircases, I confronted him.

"Your Highness," I said softly, "you seem displeased with me. Have I offended you?"

He was growing so quickly that each day brought fresh changes. He was already taller than the day we had met, and his jaw had grown longer and squarer, making his nose less prominent and his face almost handsome. His hair had been cut quite short, but he had let it grow since our wedding so that it now fell against the neck of his collar. Though his beard was still patchy, he had managed to grow a respectable mustache.

I expected him to flush and stammer and quickly take his leave. Instead, he turned on me with heat. "That harlot, that whore—how could you befriend her? She's a viper, a vicious creature!"

Dumbstruck, I blinked at him. I had never before heard him speak in anger, or use harsh language.

"Madame d'Etampes?" I asked. "You think I am her friend now?"

"You rode with her." His tone was cold, accusatory.

"The King invited me to ride. I didn't seek her company."

"You helped her up when she fell."

"What was I to do, Your Highness?" I countered. "Spit on her as she lay?"

"My father is a fool," he said, trembling. "He permits her to use him. You can't imagine . . . At Queen Eléonore's coronation, my father viewed her procession through the city streets from a great window, in full public view. And *she*"—he could not bring himself to say the Duchess's name—"*she* convinced him to let her sit in the window with him and seduced him, made him do horrid, lewd things, while everyone—while the Queen, who passed by—watched." He fell silent and glared at me.

"Are you telling me not to ride with His Majesty when he invites me? Are you giving me an order?"

He turned swiftly, with a jerk, and began moving toward the staircase.

"No, of course not," I called out after him. "An order would require you to be a husband. It would require you to care."

I pressed my fist to my mouth to stifle the next angry word and ran up a different set of stairs to my apartments. Without a word to my ladies, I swept into my bedchamber, slammed the door, and fell onto the bed.

Only a few moments had passed when a knock sounded at my door. Thinking that it was Madame Gondi, I called sharply that I did not want to be disturbed.

But the voice at my door belonged to the King's sister. "Catherine, it's Marguerite. May I come in?" When I didn't answer, she added softly, "I saw you with Henri just now. I might be able to help."

I cracked open the door to avoid raising my voice. "There's nothing you can do," I said. "He hates me, and that's the end of it."

"Oh, Catherine, it isn't that at all." Her voice held such knowing compassion that I let her in. She led me over to the bed to sit on its edge beside her.

"I had no more say in this marriage than Henri did," I said hotly. "But I don't hate anyone for it. Of course, he's handsome and I'm homely. I can't remedy that."

"Never let me hear you say such a dreadful thing again," she said sternly. "You make a fine appearance. It has nothing to do with you—not in the personal sense."

"Then why does he run from me?"

Marguerite drew in a deep breath, the better to tell a long tale. "You know that the Duchess of Milan was our great-grandmother. That's why King Charles invaded Italy, and King Louis after him, to claim hereditary properties that rightfully belonged to France."

I nodded. Like most Italians, I had been raised to hate the French kings for their incursions; now I was obliged to retrain my sympathies.

"It's also the reason my brother invaded Italy nine years ago. It was a matter of honor." She paused. "François is very brave, but sometimes foolhardy. When he was fighting Emperor Charles's army at Pavia, he led a charge into the open. He thought the enemy was retreating, but he was badly mistaken. His men were all killed, and he was taken prisoner. He languished in Spain for a year, until an agreement was reached for his release.

"My brother had to agree to give up many things in order to win his freedom. One was the whole of Burgundy. Another was his sons—the Dauphin François and Henri."

My eyes widened. "They were held prisoner?"

Marguerite's expression grew distant and sad. "France languished badly in the King's absence. And so he made many unpleasant concessions: to marry Charles's widowed sister, Eléonore, to hand over Burgundy . . . and to hand over his sons."

She fell silent. I recalled the morning I had awakened at Poggio a Caiano to see rebel troops on horseback lined up on the sprawling lawn. I thought about the night I had ridden with Ser Silvestro through the streets of Florence, jeered at by a hate-filled crowd.

Marguerite continued. "Henri was barely seven years old when he and the Dauphin took their father's place as the Emperor's prisoners. They were held in Spain for four and a half years. When he left France, Henri was a cheerful boy—a bit shy, and sometimes melancholy over his mother's death, but generally happy. The imprisonment changed that. The King has often said that the Spanish must have sent back a different boy."

"So his father's desire for lands in Italy," I said slowly, "led to the imprisonment of Henri and his brother. And our marriage took place because the Pope guaranteed the King those lands."

Marguerite nodded sadly. "Perhaps now you understand why the King favors his youngest son, Charles. The Dauphin has forgiven his father, though he has not forgotten, but Henri has done neither. His hatred toward the King hasn't eased with the passage of time; if anything, it's grown worse, especially now that you two have married." She sighed. "I know that this doesn't make your situation any better, but perhaps understanding Henri will make it more bearable."

I brought Marguerite's large, smooth hand to my lips. "Thank you," I said. "It's already more bearable. And perhaps you've helped me to make it better."

The next day, I put aside my wounded dignity. Early in the morning I asked Madame Gondi to locate a French ephemeris. I knew Henri's birth date—the thirteenth of March, 1519, the same year I was born—and decided to chart his nativity myself so that I might better understand his character.

Afterward, I shadowed the King, following him to Mass at ten o'clock, standing in attendance at his lunch at eleven while listening to the bishop read from Thomas Aquinas. I didn't do so merely out of the desire to grow close to the father in the hope of reconciling him to his son, though that was still part of my aim. I wanted to better understand the workings of government, to fathom the forces that shaped nations and separated children from their fathers.

During his lunch, the King spotted me and invited me to ride with him that afternoon. By three o'clock, I was at the stables and highly amused to see the Duchess sitting upon her mare, outfitted with a hastily constructed sidesaddle. The other ladies were forced to ride slowly, led by their grooms, but Anne and I trotted alongside the King, making plans for a future hunt. Though I cannot say she exuded warmth, she accepted me well enough to engage in lighthearted verbal parries. I was now a member of the King's inner circle.

That evening, the family met again for dinner. Aunt Marguerite cast a knowing glance at me as she took her place. I sat beside her.

Henri was, again, a few minutes late. This time, his manner was subdued as he apologized to his father and quickly took his chair. I was greatly relieved when my greeting was kindly returned.

After supper, we made our way into the courtyard, lit by blazing torches upon the winding staircases that led up to our separate apartments. It was a cold night, very clear and quiet save for the murmurs of the other diners saying their good nights. Henri said my name, softly, and I turned to see him summoning his courage by averting his gaze toward the star-littered sky.

"I'm sorry, Your Highness, for my ill-considered retort last evening," I said.

"You mustn't apologize for anything, Catherine," he said. His eyes were very, very black; I had thought, until that moment, that they were dark brown. "It's I who am sorry, for all my selfish, unkind behavior since you have come."

His sincerity unnerved me; I cast about for an appropriate reply. Madeleine's sudden laughter floated down from the staircase above us as she and her sister made their way up to their apartment, accompanied by their little cousin, Jeanne. Behind us, Montmorency called to the King as they left the dining room.

Henri glanced quickly in both directions, then back at me. "May I accompany you to your chambers? I should like to speak to you alone."

"Yes," I said quickly. "Yes, of course, Your Highness."

We climbed the stairs in awkward silence. Henri went only as far as my antechamber and seated himself near the fire. I gestured for all of my ladies to leave.

When we were alone, Henri cleared his throat and stared into the hearth. "I'm sorry for losing my temper. Madame d'Etampes manipulates my father shamelessly and has hurt many of her fellow courtiers. Last night, I was thinking only of my own feelings and did not take yours into consideration."

"I am Catherine," I said. "I am not Italy."

He drew back, startled; his cheeks bloomed red. "I see that now. I have also seen how my father mistreats Queen Eléonore, how he ignores her, even though she greatly desires his attentions. When she enters a room, he acts as though she's not even there." He shook his head. "I don't want to be cruel like him."

"She is a foreigner, and unlovely," I said, "and your father a victim of political circumstance. He didn't want to marry her."

"His own greed obliged him," Henri countered with sudden heat. "His craving for Italian property—it's an insanity with him. He bankrupted the royal treasury in pursuit of it; he almost died for it, at Pavia. Like a fool, he rode ahead of his men into the thick of battle."

He turned his head away in an effort to hide his bitterness.

"Henri," I said, "this anger will destroy you if you let it." I paused. "I learned only yesterday of your imprisonment in Spain."

He jerked his head back to face me. "And were you told, too, how my father betrayed us once he gave us to the Emperor? How he left his own sons to rot, to die, to be—" He broke off, bitter.

"No," I murmured. "No. I was not told."

Henri looked down at his hands and squeezed them into fists, then stared into the fire; a distant look came over him.

"They made the exchange at a river," he said. "My mother was dead by then; only Madame de Poitiers came to say good-bye. She kissed the top of my head and told me that I would return soon, that she would count the days. My brother and I were put in a small boat. The Spanish were waiting on the other shore, but we couldn't see them. It was early morning and the fog was thick, but I could hear the lapping of the water. Just as we pushed off, I glimpsed my father like a ghost in the mists, waving to us from the bow of a nearby ship. He was crossing at the same time."

He let go a long, wavering sigh. "The Spanish treated us kindly at first. We stayed in the palace with the Emperor's sister, Queen Eléonore. Then, suddenly, we were sent to live at a fortress, in a filthy little room with a dirt floor and no windows. If we uttered a single word in French, we were beaten; we were allowed to speak only in Spanish. When I had finally learned enough to ask the guard why we were being mistreated, he told me that my father had violated the conditions of his release. He had promised that, once he was freed, he would go to Burgundy to prepare it for a peaceful takeover by the Emperor's forces.

"Instead, my father went to Burgundy and fortified it for war. He never intended to let the Emperor have it. Knowing this, he had surrendered me and my brother to the Spanish."

I drew in a sharp breath. I saw clearly the political expediency of the act: how King François had gambled that the Emperor would not kill his sons, and how he saw that a vast Imperial stronghold in Burgundy—the very heart of the nation—would threaten all of France. Yet that made it no less horrifying, no less cruel. I rose from my chair and slipped to my knees beside Henri; I reached up for his clenched fist. He flinched, so absorbed in the memory that my touch startled him, but he let me take his hand and gently uncurl it, and kiss the palm.

"Henri," I said softly. "We have much in common, you and I." And when curiosity flickered in his gaze, I explained, "I spent three years a captive of the Florentine rebels."

His lips parted as he blinked in surprise. "No one told me," he said. "No one dares speak of my imprisonment to me, so perhaps they were afraid to tell me of yours."

He seized my hand and squeezed it hard. He looked at me and for the first time saw me, Catherine, and not the Pope's niece, the foreigner, the hateful obligation.

"Catherine, I am so sorry. I would not wish for anyone . . ." He trailed off. "Was it terrible?"

"At times. I was always afraid for my life. I was betrayed, too—by my own cousins, who escaped and left me behind, knowing I would be taken prisoner. One of them now rules Florence. But I can't waste my time hating them."

"I've tried not to hate my father," he said, "but the sight of him fills me with such anger . . ."

"You need him," I said gently. "He's your father, and the King."

"I know." He dropped his gaze. "I hate him only because I love my brother so much. For the Spanish, tormenting the Dauphin was the same as tormenting the King, because they knew he would rule France someday. So they singled him out. They defiled him." His voice broke on the last two words. "Sometimes there would be as many as five men—always at night, when they were full of wine. We were isolated, in the mountains, with no one to hear him scream but me." He looked up at me, his face contorted, his black eyes liquid. "I tried to stop them. I tried to fight. But I was too small. They laughed and shoved me out of the way."

He let go a hoarse sob. I rose, wound my arms about his shoulders, and kissed the top of his head as he pressed his face to my bosom.

His words were muffled. "How can people be so evil? How can they want to hurt others so badly? My gentle, good-hearted brother, he can forgive them all. But I can't . . . And our father hates us, because each time he looks at us, he's forced to remember what he's done."

"Hush," I said. "Your brother François wakes each morning happy. He let go of his suffering long ago. For his sake, you must stop clinging to yours."

He pulled back to look at me as I held his hot, damp face in my hands. "You're like him, kindhearted and wise," he said. He reached up and brushed my cheek with his fingertips. "So beautiful of spirit that all the other women at Court are hideous by comparison."

I drew in a breath, voluntarily captive. I know not who moved first, but we kissed each other with sudden heat and fell by the fire. I lifted my skirts and petticoat; when I pulled off my pantaloons and flung them so carelessly that they landed on his head, he giggled.

This time when he took me, I was ready. I rode him with wild desperation, abandoning myself with spectacular result. No one had told me that women could gain as much pleasure as men from the sexual deed, but I discovered the fact that day, to my astonished delight. I suppose I cried out rather loudly, for I remember Henri laughing wickedly while I was in the grip of unbearable pleasure.

When we were spent, I rang for my ladies to undress me while Madame Gondi fetched one of Henri's valets to do the same for him. After the servants departed, we lay together naked in my bed. I permitted myself to do what I had longed to do since coming to France: I ran my palms over the contours of my husband's body. He was so very tall, like his father, with long, sculpted legs and arms. And he touched me—my breasts, and my legs, muscular and shapely—and pronounced them to be perfect.

"You are so brave and good," he said. "You endured prison, and coming to France, a strange land, and have been patient with me . . ." He rolled on his side to face me. "I want to be like you. But there are times I think I'm going mad."

"You're unhappy," I countered. "It's not the same thing."

"But I remember all the terrible things my brother went through—and I grow frightened that they'll happen again. So frightened that I can't trust anyone, that I can't even speak kindly to you when I want to . . ." He looked away, haunted.

"It won't happen again," I said. "It's past."

"How do you know?" he demanded. "If Father was captured again—if something happened to François . . . It might not be the same thing, but it could be even worse."

He fell back against the pillow, his eyes wide at the thought. I wrapped my arms around him.

"Nothing bad will happen to you," I whispered, "because I won't let it." I kissed his cheek. "Let me give you children, Henri. Let me make you happy."

The tension in his face dissolved, giving way to trust, and I dissolved with it. I laid my head upon his shoulder as he whispered, "Oh, Catherine . . . I could love you. I could so easily love you . . ."

He fell asleep in that fashion. And I, swooning with infatuation, reveled in the feel of his warm flesh against mine. Filled with blissful thoughts, I dozed.

In the middle of the night, I woke in a mindless panic and lifted my head from Henri's shoulder to stare down at him. In the dimness, blood bubbled up from his face—the stranger's face, the one from my dream.

Catherine. Venez a moi. Aidez-moi.

I understood my life's purpose in that crystalline instant.

"I heard you far away in Italy, my love," I whispered fiercely. "You called to me, and I have come."

At the sound of my voice, Henri stirred and stared up at me with eyes that were black and haunting as the Raven's Wing.

He slept the rest of the night beside me, but when I woke to the first light of morning, he was gone.

Nineteen

When I saw Henri had gone, I rose quietly, so as not to wake Madame Gondi, sleeping in the adjacent garderobe.

I had discovered three volumes on astrological magic by Cornelius Agrippa in the King's library and brought them all to my cabinet. I went into the tiny office, lifted the first volume from the shelf, and began to thumb through it. I no longer believed in coincidence. Chance hadn't presented me with the magician any more than it had brought me Henri—or Agrippa's masterwork there upon His Majesty's library shelf.

Until that morning I had been reluctant to try to create a talisman myself. I doubted the books contained all the information necessary for dealing with the intangible world. But the convergence of Henri's need and the appearance of Agrippa's tomes convinced me that I was destined to do this.

I found what I wanted in volume two: Corvus the Raven is a constellation near Cygnus the Swan. The Raven's stars are ruled by morbid Saturn and bloodthirsty Mars; yet combined as they are in a star named Gienah, said Agrippa, they "confer the ability to repel evil spirits" and protect against "the malice of men, devils, and winds." When the figure of a raven is drawn over the constellation, Gienah glitters in its wing.

The image required was that of the raven. The stone required was black onyx; the herb daffodil, burdock, or comfrey; the animal a frog—specifically, its tongue. On a night when Gienah was rising and favorably aspected to the Moon, the stone should be inscribed with a sigil, fumigated, and consecrated.

This was my task, then—to obtain a ring fitted to Henri's finger, construct a raven's image, collect the stone and herb and frog, and perform the ceremony. First, however, I needed to locate Gienah, track its movements, and determine when, over the next months, it rose conjunct the Moon.

I felt purposeful that day, believing that the bloody burden I had carried for so long would soon be lifted. I never dreamt that I was instead taking another step toward the heart of the magician's sinister and ever-widening circle.

In the meantime, my fortunes bloomed while Florence's withered. I received a letter from my dear cousin Piero. He lived in Rome now with his father, Filippo, and his brothers. They had been forced to flee Florence. Sandro, it seemed, had become a murderous tyrant and profoundly suspicious of his relatives—to the point of accusing Piero of plotting to seize control of the city. Others who had provoked Alessandro's distrust had been executed or poisoned, or had simply disappeared.

It is a good thing you and Ippolito live some distance from him, Piero wrote, *or you would not both still be alive.* So many disaffected had left Florence out of fear or protest that there was talk of raising an army to retake the city.

I wrote Piero at once, inviting him to come with his family to France, as I longed to see them; in truth, I also wanted them to see me happy.

In King François, I had found the father I had always longed for. To my delight, he invited me to his morning meetings with his councillors, so that I might see how the business of the nation was transacted. I learned how the King worked with Parlement, the Treasury, and his Grand Council.

Every day at his lunch, the King bade me sit nearby, a special honor. When the King's reader was silent, we conversed about His Majesty's building plans for Fontainebleau, or about which Italian artisan he should hire for a particular project, or about a work of literature we both had read.

He was as affectionate to me as he was to his own daughters, whom he visited regularly. He would gather them both upon his lap, although they had grown too large to fit. When he sat smiling at us, I glimpsed the same bright, loving boy I had seen in my Henri. At the same time, he was ruthless in the council chamber; the well-being of the nation took precedence over any individual claim of the heart.

And though I heard often about his insatiable lust, he guarded his family from it, though there were times when I came up unawares to find him with his hand in a courtier's bodice or up her skirts. Madame Gondi told me that when she had first come to Court, His Majesty had cornered her and caressed her, saying that he could not live without her love.

"Did you submit?" I asked, shocked.

"No," she said. "His Majesty's weakness is women, and when a woman weeps, he becomes utterly helpless. It's how the Duchess d'Etampes controls him. And so I wept as I told him that I loved my husband and could not betray him. His Majesty accepted my explanation and retreated with an apology."

Such stories troubled me, but I found myself making allowances for him despite myself, for I loved him dearly.

Best of all, I felt my love for Henri was requited. He now smiled shyly and met my gaze, albeit with endearing timidity. And he came often—though not often enough to suit me—to my bedchamber.

I was thoroughly enamored. I understood his pain now: His anger was born of protectiveness and love. If mention of an Italian campaign brought a flash of heat into his eyes, it was only because he worried about a coming war's effect upon his brother.

The King finally publicly announced the full details of our wedding arrangement: Pope Clement had already paid half of the exorbitant sum agreed upon as my dowry; in addition, Clement and King François both proclaimed Henri to be Duke of Urbino by virtue of his marriage to me. Milan was to be ours, too, and Piacenza and Parma; His Holiness the Pope asserted our right to the territories and would supply additional troops to aid in the conquest.

In preparation, King François began to build an army.

Meanwhile, the Court followed the King northward from the Loire countryside to Paris. The city was not as sprawling as Rome, but it was ten times more crowded; the narrow streets were always congested, the half-timber houses crammed side by side. But spring brought enchanting, sweet-smelling blossoms and temperate weather, even though the sky, placid one moment, could release a sudden shower the next. The Seine, grey-green in gloom, quicksilver in sun, was too shallow to permit nautical traffic; some days revealed so many golden sandbanks I felt I could simply walk to the opposite shore. The river cut the city in half; in between nestled the island of Ile-de-la-Cité, home to the massive, magnificent cathedral of Notre-Dame and the ethereal, dainty Sainte-Chapelle, with its fiery circular windows of stained glass.

I could see their spires from the high, narrow windows of the Louvre. It was my least favorite royal residence—old and cramped, with tiny apartments. Over the centuries, the size of the Court had greatly increased, though the Louvre, on the Seine's bank, had no room to expand. The only way to increase the number of chambers had been to decrease the size of each. It had only a token cobblestone courtyard instead of the vast green expanses found at the countryside châteaus.

The city itself I adored. Paris was not as sophisticated as Florence, nor as jaded. It emanated an excitement that attracted the best artists from all over Europe. There were many Italians, thanks to King François's determination to bring the best artists, architects, and goldsmiths to France. Everywhere I went, I found scaffolding and at least two Italians arguing over the best way to decorate or rebuild a particular section of the old palace.

In my cramped cabinet at the Louvre, I drew the likeness of a raven in black ink upon white parchment. A Parisian jeweler had supplied a polished, faceted onyx; an apothecary furnished ground cypress wood, of the nature of Saturn, and the poisonous root of hellebore, ruled by Mars. I found an errand boy willing to kill a frog and cut out its tongue without impertinent questions. I placed it alongside the stone and incense in one of the compartments hidden in the wooden wainscoting near my desk, where it browned and withered.

I charted Gienah's movements through the night sky and calculated when it would rise conjunct the moon. The most propitious time would not arrive for months.

Cosimo Ruggieri, then, had prepared my stone for me well in advance—weeks, or even longer. He had known all along that I would need it, and had merely been waiting for the opportunity to deliver it into my hands.

We did not remain long in Paris that spring of 1534. Like me, the King disliked the lodgings and soon forsook them for the Château at Fontainebleau, south of the city.

If the Louvre was the smallest royal residence, then Fontainebleau was certainly the largest. The massive four-story stone structure took the shape of an oval ring, with an interior courtyard. It was large enough to house a village and too small to accommodate King François's Court; a west wing and connecting structure had to be built. François hired the famous Fiorentino to paint frescoes, framed by gilded molding, on the walls. Under the King's direction, the château began to glitter, thanks to the famous goldsmith Cellini.

I summoned Cellini to my cabinet and presented him with a sketch of the golden ring, its heart empty to receive a stone. When it was done, I paid him handsomely and put the ring in the hidden compartment with the rest of my secrets.

As spring turned to summer and summer turned to fall, the King went hunting at every opportunity—accompanied by *La Petite Bande,* as he called us ladies. All of us now rode sidesaddle, and each woman showed her determination to keep pace with the King.

One afternoon in late September, we were in pursuit of a stag. I was happy that day, comfortable in my new life. The weather was exquisite with a comfortable breeze and sun, and I was laughing with Anne as we galloped together after the King.

Suddenly, a bell began to toll; someone of import had died. We called off the hunt and rode in, subdued and curious. The stable master had no idea what had happened.

I dismounted and walked back to my chambers, where Madame Gondi waited in the doorway. Her recent tears had washed away some of her face paint, leaving rivulets of pink beside the chalky white. The other ladies and the servants were all crying.

"What is it?" I demanded.

She crossed herself. "Your Highness, I am so sad to be the one to tell you. It is your uncle, the Pope."

I was shocked and sorry, but I didn't cry. It is a devastating thing for the faithful when a Pope dies, and he was also my relative. But I still resented his choice of his own illegitimate son, Alessandro, to rule Florence.

Once the shock had worn off, I grew uneasy. Clement had died with only half my dowry paid and none of his promises of military support to King François fulfilled. In the chapel, I prayed that his successor would be a friend to France and to me—but God, I knew, never heard me.

Seven nights after the Pope's death, the moon rose with the star Gienah her close companion. At forty-three minutes past midnight, I went into my windowless cabinet and opened the hidden compartment with a key.

I had turned my desk into a makeshift altar, with a censer from the chapel in its center, in front of my drawing of the raven. After lighting the coal in the censer, I sprinkled the cypress wood shavings and the dried leaves of hellebore over it. Acrid smoke billowed out immediately. As my eyes streamed, I took up a jeweler's awl and the polished onyx. On the stone's backside I etched the sigil for Gienah, then held the stone up to the smoke and repeated the name of the star. Using one of Cellini's fine pliers, I set the stone into the ring and applied pressure to the golden prongs until the gem was held fast.

It was done unremarkably, without any whiff of the unworldly. I repeated the ritual of lighting the incense and invoking Gienah for seven nights, at forty-three minutes past midnight. I had worried that I might not remember to rise at the appointed time, but in fact, I could not forget.

Within two weeks, Alessandro Farnese was elected Pope and took the name Paul III. If his election caused King François a moment's unease, His Majesty never showed it but treated me as warmly as ever. On the last day of October, the Eve of All Saints, we shared lunch and a spirited conversation about the works of Rabelais, and whether they were heretical. My heart was light that afternoon when I went to the stables, ready to ride with the King and his band.

As I neared, the ladies—except for Anne—were hurrying back to the château, their faces drawn with fear. Marie de Canaples gestured frantically; I didn't understand until later that she had been trying to warn me.

At the stables, grooms were leading agitated horses back to their stalls. A trio stood near the entry: Grand Master Montmorency, the Duchess d'Etampes, and the King. The Duchess was silent and distraught, Montmorency dignified and immovable, his gaze downcast.

The King was roaring and slashing the air with his riding crop. As I approached, he turned it on one of the grooms, who was not moving fast enough to suit him; the lad let go a cry and picked up his pace.

I stopped a short distance away. The Duchess's eyes widened as she, too, made a surreptitious attempt to wave me off.

"Nothing!" the King screamed, spraying spittle. He slashed the air again, then turned his whip on the ground, sending tufts of grass flying. "She brings me nothing! Nothing! She has come to me naked, that girl!"

I recoiled; the movement caught François's eye. He whirled on me, his stance challenging.

"Stark naked, do you understand?" His voice broke with ugly emotion. "Stark naked."

I understood completely. I curtsied low and full, then turned and walked back toward the château with as much dignity as I could feign.

Mésalliance: the French use the word to describe an ill-conceived royal marriage. It was on every courtier's lips, every servant's, though no one dared utter it aloud to me.

The French people had tolerated me but never loved me. I had been for them a necessary evil—a commoner who had promised, but failed, to bring gold to fund a bankrupt nation, and the troops to fulfill François's dreams of Italian conquest. It would be so easy to put me aside; after all, I had yet to bear children.

Madame Gondi, my able and eager spy, now confessed the truth: The French loved the Florentines for their art, their fine cloth, their literature—but they hated us as well. Backstabbers, they called us, poisoners whose inherited penchant for murder made us dangerous even to our families and friends.

Many at Court were eager to see me gone; before my arrival, many had vowed that they would rather have their knees broken than bow them to the child of foreign merchants.

But I loved Henri desperately; I had found a life in France and couldn't imagine another, especially now that Florence was no longer mine.

The next morning, I went to Mass with the King and followed him to his lunch. In the afternoon, I went, head up, chin lifted, to the royal stables.

King François was there, and the thin, elegant Duchess and plump Marie de Canaples. They all smiled at me, but their warmth had cooled to a distant politeness. Once again, I had become inconvenient.

Soon Henri's ring with the talisman of Corvus was ready. I decided to present it to him one evening after we had lain together. Henri rose from the bed and pulled on his leggings. I sat upon the bed watching, still naked, with my hair falling free to my waist.

Before he could reach for the bell to summon his valet, I said, "I have a gift for you."

He stopped and gave me a curious little half smile. I moved quickly to my cupboard, produced a little velvet box, and handed it to him.

His smile widened and grew pleased. "How very thoughtful of you." He opened the box to find the gift, wrapped in a swatch of purple velvet.

"A ring," he murmured. His expression remained carefully pleased, but a slight line appeared between his eyebrows. It was a very plain gold ring with a small onyx—an unremarkable piece of jewelry, more fit for merchant than for a prince. "It is handsome. Thank you, Catherine."

"You must wear it always," I said. "Even when you sleep. Promise me."

"To remind me of your devotion?" he asked lightly.

Foolish girl, I did not respond smiling and teasing, as I should have to convince him, but hesitated.

A shadow fell over his face. "Is this some sort of magic?"

"There's nothing evil in it," I countered quickly. "It will bring only good."

He held it to the lamplight, his expression suspicious. "What is it for?"

"Protection," I said.

"And how was it made?"

"I did it myself, so I can swear that it isn't evil. I used the power of a star; you know how I like to follow the heavens."

A corner of his mouth quirked in a skeptic's smile. "Catherine, don't you think this is superstitious?"

"Indulge me. Please, I only want to keep you safe."

"I'm young and healthy. I don't want to hurt your feelings, but this is nonsense." He put the Raven's Wing back into the box and set it on the table.

"I've dreams about you," I said, with unhappy urgency. "Many dreams, worrisome ones. Perhaps God sent them. Perhaps God sent me here, to see you safe. Take the ring, Henri, I beg you. I went to great trouble to make it."

He let go a sigh. "All right. I'll wear it, if it gives you that much comfort." He retrieved the ring, slipped it onto his finger, and held his hand to the lamp. "I suppose it can do no harm."

"Thank you," I said and kissed him, deeply relieved. My job was done; whatever happened to me from that moment on no longer mattered. Henri was now safe.

One year bled into the next. The King grew increasingly distant, and the Duchess and her ladies began whispering into each other's ears in my presence. The simple act of my walking into a room abruptly sealed speakers' lips.

In October of 1535, the Duke of Milan died without an heir, leaving his city ripe for the plucking. Even without papal assistance, King François could not resist so succulent a plum. He sent his new army toward Milan.

In retaliation, Emperor Charles invaded Provence, in France's south.

The King was desperate to fight against the Imperial invaders himself, but Grand Master Montmorency convinced him otherwise while delicately avoiding mention of the fact that the last time the King had led his troops into battle, he had been captured. To everyone's relief, the King appointed the experienced, cautious Montmorency as Lieutenant General, to take charge of the armed forces.

But François wished to be near the fighting, the better to advise. In the summer of 1536, his elder sons went with him, and so did I, followed by a skeleton Court. We stayed first in Lyon, then went to Tournon, then down to Valence, in the Midi, as the French call the Mediterranean-like south, moving at a safe parallel with the fighting.

The Dauphin remained in Tournon to nurse a slight case of catarrh—an excessive precaution, but the King was adamant. Young François made a joke of it, of course, and left me laughing as our carriages rolled away.

At Valence, I rode alongside Madame Gondi through forests of pine and eucalyptus and inhaled the scent of wild lavender crushed beneath the horses' hooves. I never rode long or ventured too close to the banks of the Rhone, where the mosquitoes were thickest. The sun and river conspired to leave the air ruthlessly sultry. We stayed at an estate set atop a promontory, with sweeping views of the valley and river. In the late afternoons, as the heat was breaking, I sat with my embroidery in the vast reception chamber adjacent to the King's quarters, perched upon a window seat overlooking the river.

The King spent long hours in his cabinet conferring with his councillors and, surprisingly, Henri. He and his father remained recluses, eating in private, forgoing audiences, even missing Mass; the Cardinal of Lorraine, one of his councillors, would interrupt the long sessions to grant the King absolution and administer the Sacrament.

This manner of life continued for a week, until the morning I woke in my bed to hear heart-wrenching keening. I threw on my dressing gown and ran downstairs toward the source.

At the reception chamber near the King's apartment, I paused on the threshold to see the Cardinal of Lorraine. Though it was barely dawn, he was already dressed in his scarlet robe and skullcap, but he had not shaved; the first rays of the sun glinted off the grey stubble on his cheeks. At my approach, he turned, his gaze dulled by horror.

Beside him, the King was on his knees near the edge of the little window seat where I liked to embroider, dressed in only his nightshirt and dressing gown, his hair uncombed. He reached up suddenly to clutch his skull, as if to crush the misery there, then just as quickly let it go and pulled himself up onto the velvet cushion. There he knelt, his arms spread to the river and the sky.

"My God," he cried. "My God, why could you have not taken me? Why not me?"

He collapsed in a storm of tears.

I began to weep myself. This was not a commander's regret but a father's sorrow. Poor sweet Madeleine, I thought; she had always been so sickly. I began to move toward His Majesty, but the Cardinal sharply waved me off.

Still bowed, the King lifted his head just enough for his words to be understood. "Henri," he groaned. "Bring me Henri."

The Cardinal disappeared, but his mission was unnecessary. Within seconds, Henri appeared of his own accord, fully dressed and ready for a dire emergency; he, too, had heard the King's cries. He walked over the threshold, our shoulders brushing, and shot me a questioning gaze for which I had no answer.

At the sight of the King doubled over in misery, Henri rushed to his side.

"What is it?" he demanded. "Father, what has happened? Is it Montmorency?"

He put his hand upon the King's shoulder, and the old man reared up onto his knees.

"Henri . . ." The King's ravaged voice was quaking. "My son, my son. Your older brother is dead."

François, my smiling, golden-haired friend. The room whirled; I caught the edge of the doorway and let go a torrent of involuntary tears.

"No," Henri snarled and lifted an arm to strike his father. Before the blow could land, the King seized his son's forearm and held it fast. Henri strained against his father's strength until both were trembling. Abruptly, Henri dropped his arm and began to shriek. "No! No! You can't say such things! It's not true, it's not true!"

He reached for a nearby chair and overturned it with such force that it skittered across the stone. He reached, too, for a large, heavy table, and when he could not upend it, he fell to the floor.

"You can't take him," he sobbed. "I won't let you take him . . ."

I ran to him and gathered him into my arms.

He was limp. In his eyes was a shattered vacancy, a fathomless despair—a look I had seen only once before. His spirit had broken, and I did not have the means to mend it.

I guided him to his father and retreated to the threshold to give them their privacy. I was a latecomer, an interloper in terms of their grief.

Once the King had calmed enough to speak, he said, "My son. You are the Dauphin now. You must become as good as your brother François was, and as kind, so that you are loved as much as he was. You must never give anyone cause to regret that you are now the first heir to the throne."

At the instant I heard it, I thought only that His Majesty was cruel and unthinking to say such things to Henri at this time of terrible sorrow. How could one speak of political matters when one's own son was dead? Indeed, I thought so for some days, until after we had laid poor François to rest in a temporary tomb.

Until one afternoon shortly thereafter, when Madame Gondi was speaking of some trivial matter and addressed me as *Madame la Dauphine.*

The sound of it stole my breath—not because I craved the power that would come when I was Queen, nor because I feared it, but rather because I realized that the astrologer and magician Cosimo Ruggieri had, from the very beginning, been right about everything.

Twenty

I penned another letter to Cosimo Ruggieri, explaining my new circumstances and asking him to join me at Court to serve as my chief astrologer, though I had little hope. Ruggieri was dead or mad, but I had nowhere else to turn. With increased power came increased vulnerability. Like Henri, I felt there were few I could trust. One was Ruggieri, who had long ago proven his loyalty to me.

I was uneasy, and rightly so.

I saw the details of young François's death as straightforward, but the King and many of his advisers and courtiers thought otherwise.

Left behind at Tournon, François had appeared to recover quickly from the catarrh. He'd felt so well, in fact, that on one of the hottest afternoons of that miserable August, he had challenged one of his gentlemen of the chamber to a strenuous game of tennis. The Dauphin had won handily.

Afterward, however, he felt strangely winded. Thinking it was the heat, he ordered his Page of the Sewer, Sebastiano Montecuculli, to bring him a glass of cold water. Soon after drinking it, the Dauphin collapsed and fell ill with a high fever. Fluid filled his lungs. Pleurisy, one doctor said; the other had doubts. Neither could save him.

Perhaps it was because Montecuculli was Florentine, and had come to France as one of my entourage, but Henri could hardly bear to look at me and stopped visiting my chamber.

The King was desperate to blame someone for his suffering. Montecuculli was the convenient choice, poison the convenient charge—the man was, after all, Italian. When he was arrested and his belongings examined, a book on the properties of chemical agents—some nefarious—was discovered, along with a paper granting him safe conduct through Imperial strongholds. His death was inevitable.

Montecuculli was anxious for a swift execution instead of the torments reserved for those guilty of regicide, so he confessed his guilt immediately, claiming to be a spy acting on Emperor Charles's orders, with his next target the King.

The seventh of October brought cloudless blue skies. I mounted the pine-scented steps of the hastily constructed dais behind Queen Eléonore and Diane de Poitiers; Marguerite—not quite thirteen then—followed me, plucking anxiously at my skirts. We had come to Lyon—close enough to Valence for the King to receive any important news of the war but far enough from the fighting to ensure everyone's safety.

More than two hundred courtiers awaited us on the dais. All wore black—like the four coal-colored stallions, caparisoned in the same color, who paced anxiously in the empty plaza in front of us. Only Madame de Poitiers had diluted her black with an underskirt of white, and a grey band on her hood. To me it seemed that Madame was admitting to no fresh sorrow; the scent of her lily of the valley perfume, especially strong that morning, seemed an affront to the somber proceedings.

We royals—as well as Madame de Poitiers—had been provided with padded chairs at the very front of the crowd. We found our places but remained on our feet as we awaited the King and his two surviving sons.

Charles climbed the stairs to the dais first. He was fourteen; over the past year, he had sprouted in height until he stood only half a head shorter than the King. Like his late brother, he was golden-haired and blue-eyed, with a round, handsome face, a gift from his mother.

Behind him came his father. In the past two months, large shocks of white had appeared at the King's temples; the hollows beneath his eyes had deepened. Rumor said that his insides were rotting, that he had developed an abcess in his privates. I prayed this was untrue, for I loved him so. Once he had mounted the steps and taken his chair, the King stared straight ahead but, blinded by grief, saw nothing.

In one sense I was relieved to be spared his gaze, for I feared it might have held recrimination. A fortnight earlier, an outraged Emperor Charles had responded to the charge that he had ordered the Dauphin's assassination: "Had I wished to," he declared, "I could easily have murdered father and son years ago, when both were in my possession." His agents at the French Court spread the rumor that I, a power-hungry Medici, had persuaded Montecuculli to poison the Dauphin, with the full support of my husband.

King François loved me and did not believe this accusation, yet it pained him all the same. The day the rumor surfaced, he withdrew even further from me, avoiding my gaze and my questions, until I became for him the same mute, invisible creature I was now for my husband.

Henri, now the Dauphin, mounted the stairs last. His grief was so black, so pervasive, that he had refused visitors since his brother's death. There was no cold light of vengeance in his eyes that morning, or even grim satisfaction, only uncertainty tinged with fresh grief. The thought of more suffering, more death, brought him no joy.

I did not smile as he stepped onto the platform but directed my most loving gaze at him. He saw it, and at once averted his eyes, as if he could not bear to look on me. The ring with the black stone, the Wing of Corvus, which he had faithfully worn every day since receiving it, was gone. His finger was bare.

Such tiny gestures—a shift of the eyes, the missing ring—left me crushed. I hung my head and did not lift it when little Marguerite, thinking I mourned her lost brother, squeezed my hand and told me not to be sad.

Once the King and the Dauphin were seated, the rest of us followed suit. A shout came from a guard in the plaza, one of the King's kilted Scotsmen, who stood beside the four grooms with their restless black stallions.

In response to the summons, a solemn group walked into the center of the open. First came the scarlet-clad Cardinal of Lorraine and the Captain of the Scottish guards, consummately masculine despite his kilt and flowing auburn hair. Behind them followed two guards, who flanked a prisoner.

This was Sebastiano Montecuculli, the unfortunate soul who had set a glass of cold water into the Dauphin's sweating hands. Montecuculli was a count, of considerable grooming, education, and intelligence. He had so charmed the Dauphin that the latter immediately offered him the only available position in his household, Page of the Sewer, which consisted of bearing the prince's cup. I knew that if young François had been alive to see the cruelty visited upon his unfortunate page, he would have been horrified.

Montecuculli had been a handsome, lively man of some thirty years. Now he was stooped, his legs crooked, his gait stiff and halting from the iron shackles at his ankles and wrists. I would never have recognized him: His face had become puffed and purple; the bridge of his nose had been smashed flat. Whole handfuls of his long hair had been pulled out, leaving large patches of bare scalp encrusted with dried blood. His captors had left him only a nightshirt, stained with blood and excrement, to cover himself. It fell just to his knees; the slightest breeze lifted the hem to expose his genitals.

The Cardinal of Lorraine and the captain approached the dais as the guards dragged Montecuculli toward the King. The Page of the Sewer fell to his knees, partly in supplication, partly from weakness. In a loud voice, the Cardinal implored him to confess his sin.

Montecuculli had already retracted his earlier confession to the crime. When torture was applied, he confessed readily, but when it was removed, he disavowed all guilt. He looked to the King and tried to reach out with his trembling, shackled arms, but could not raise them.

"Your Majesty, have mercy!" His words were slurred and barely comprehensible, the result of the recent loss of many teeth. "I loved your son and never wished him harm! Before God and the Virgin, I am innocent and I loved him!" Sobbing violently, he fell forward onto the cobblestone.

Every face turned to the King. For a long moment, François sat motionless save for a muscle spasming in his cheek, then made a sharp downward motion with his hand.

The captain nodded to his men. The guards tried to pull Montecuculli to his feet, but the poor man's legs had given way; he was dragged back to where the horses waited. As the guards pushed him down against the cobblestones, he began to shout:

Ave Maria, gratia plena, Dominus tecum . . .

His captors unfastened his shackles and stripped away his filthy nightshirt, revealing skin that was completely mottled in shades of red, purple, green, and yellow. Montecuculli continued to pray so wildly, so swiftly that the words ran together.

Mater Dei, ora pro nobis peccatoribus, nunc et in hora mortis nostrae . . .

Mother of God, pray for us sinners, now and at the hour of our death.

At the captain's bidding, the grooms led the four stallions into position around the naked, supine man: north at Montecuculli's right hand, south at his left, northwest at his right foot, southwest at his left. A leather strap—thick as my arm, corded and reinforced—was fastened to each horse's harness by a series of heavy buckles. At the end of each strap was a collar of leather and iron.

When one guard first tried to set Montecuculli's wrist into a collar, the unfortunate prisoner howled and bucked and flailed, requiring an additional two men to hold him down while four worked quickly to slip on the collars, tighten and buckle them securely: one at each wrist and one at each thigh, just above the knee. The Scotsmen finished their work and quickly receded to a place of safety with their captain.

One man—the executioner, with a long whip in his hand—stayed behind. Though he addressed the prisoner in a low voice, no doubt making the traditional request for forgiveness, Montecuculli was too tightly in terror's clutches to stop screaming. The executioner lifted his head and called a command to the grooms, who mounted their horses. Each horse took a single step forward in one of the four directions, and Montecuculli, spread like a starfish, lifted slightly off the ground.

Beside me, little Marguerite began to weep softly.

The executioner—a handsome young Scot with a close-trimmed golden beard and emotionless expression—looked to the King. François let go a long breath and gave a slow, single nod.

The executioner moved out of the horses' paths and as far away from the prisoner as he could, then struck the animals' rumps with the whip. Urged by the lash and their riders, the horses took off at full gallop.

Marguerite buried her face in my lap and clutched my skirts, but I was compelled by position and by horror to watch.

Blood sprayed, crimson fireworks. In one second, two, Montecuculli's arms had been torn off at the shoulders, his legs torn away at the groin, the large thigh bones yanked clear of the hip sockets. Momentum caused the abandoned torso to roll once, twice, before finally coming to rest faceup. What was left was a frightful, inhuman thing, spurting blood from each of four gaping holes edged by raw, jagged flesh. A strand of glistening intestine slid out from the largest of them as the torso convulsed against the cobblestones like a fish plucked from the sea.

He was alive. Montecuculli was still alive.

Not far off, the stallions had been reined in, and the riders and horses slowly returned, each dragging a limb behind them so the prisoner might see. One trotted up and positioned the bloodied stump of a still-twitching leg, with the ivory ball of the thighbone protruding from the top, next to the dying man's face.

In the crowd of courtiers behind me, a man retched.

I sat still and composed, my hand upon little Marguerite's shoulder as she sobbed into my lap. I watched every hellish, interminable second until Montecuculli stopped screaming, until his mutilated body stopped spasming, until his corpse stopped spewing blood.

When His Majesty, apparently satisfied, rose, I stood with the others. I looked at my husband and read in his features no less grief; if anything, this day had added to it. I stared hard, too, at King François's expression. His was no longer the face of the loving father; it was that of a relentless ruler with a thirst for revenge that had yet to be quenched.

After the execution, the King went to Mass and took the Sacrament without hesitation. If he felt any compunction over the page's death, it was not great enough for him to confess it.

After Mass, we all retired to our chambers. I went to my cabinet and continued my calculations for Henri's nativity.

Saturn is a cold, brooding, dismal planet. It augurs burdens and loss, and fosters melancholy. A birth chart heavily marked by Saturn indicates an unhappy life and the early deaths of loved ones. Any planet that appears in the house or sign it rules will have its attributes greatly magnified. And my poor Henri's Saturn appeared in the sign it ruled, Capricorn.

Seeing this, and meditating on all the wounds this day had pricked, I decided to commit a forward and impetuous act. I left my chambers and went to my husband's. I did not plan what I wanted to say; I only wanted to offer comfort, perhaps distract him with pleasant talk. In truth, I hoped that such comfort might bring him again to my arms.

By then it was late afternoon, but Henri was not in his chambers; his valet claimed to have no knowledge of his whereabouts. After charging the man to send word when his master returned, I returned to my cabinet.

I dined alone and afterward, told Madame Gondi that I wished to be notified when Henri had retired. Hours passed, but I refused to be undressed; by then, I began to worry.

It was very late when I got word that he had gone to his apartment. Concerned, I went and knocked upon his door.

A different valet answered and was astonished to find me standing there; Henri was inside, his collar undone and leggings removed. He was exhausted, though his mood was more pleasant than it had been earlier. When he saw me in the doorway, fully dressed, his eyebrows lifted with alarm.

"Catherine! Is everything all right?"

At least now he was willing to look at me.

"All is quite well." I turned to the valet. "Monsieur, please wait outside until I call for you."

After a nervous glance at Henri, who nodded, the valet stepped into the corridor.

My husband gestured for me to sit beside him. I did, and could not help noticing how strong the lines of his face had become, beautifully framed by his dark beard, and how perfectly his black eyes reflected firelight. Simply being alone with him, and so close, disarmed me, made me remember the day he had taken me on the floor in front of the fireplace. I looked down at my hands and felt a rush of warmth rising from the base of my spine.

"I didn't mean to disturb you at such a late hour. Forgive me," I said. "I only wanted to say that I know how very difficult today must have been for you."

"Thank you," he said, with a very faint note of impatience. He was tired and eager for me to leave; he held a kerchief, which he kept squeezing.

I realized it might end right there, and so I said boldly, "I've missed you, Henri. I've been so worried; I can see you haven't eaten and fear you might make yourself ill." I did not ask after the ring, for I did not want to put him on the defensive too soon. "I am . . . I wanted . . . Might I embrace you? Simply as a member of the family, to show my affection and concern?"

He rose, too quickly. "Of course, Catherine," he said and began to avert his eyes out of nerves.

He was very tall. I wrapped my arms about him and pressed my cheek against his chest. I kept the embrace gentle and closed my eyes, hoping my own ease would relax him—but I soon snapped them open again.

He stank of lily of the valley.

Aghast, I pulled away. He was dressed in the same clothes he had worn to the execution: a black doublet with black velvet sleeves—slashed, so that the white satin of his undershirt could be pulled through. White, like Madame de Poitiers's underskirt. On the table beside him sat his black velvet cap, with a single grey feather—to match the grey band on Madame's hood.

"Her," I whispered. "You have been with *her.* Is that why you took off my ring?"

His face colored crimson. He stared at the floor, too ashamed to look up at me; he opened his palm to reveal a wadded kerchief, white silk edged in black, embroidered with a large *D,* and threw it, in admission, at the table.

"You," I said, "you who hated your father because he was unkind to the Queen. Now you are obliged to hate yourself."

"I didn't want it to happen, Catherine," he said softly; his voice trembled. "I didn't ever want to hurt you."

"She means to use you," I said savagely. "Now that you are Dauphin, she surrenders her virtue to you. She lures you."

"No." He shook his head. "She loved me when no one else did. Loved me, and François, as if she were our mother, even after Father gave us over to the Spaniards. When she heard that François had died, it nearly killed her. She loved him as I did. She understands what it was for me to lose him, more than anyone else."

My voice grew ugly. "A mother does not comfort her son by spreading her legs."

His head jerked as if I had struck him.

"Out of kindness to you," he said hoarsely, "I resisted temptation as long as I could. We both fought it . . . until grief finally broke us. Today was the first time we sinned, and God has already punished me by sending you here, so that I might see how I have hurt you." For the first time, he looked hard into my eyes. "I tried so very hard to love you, Catherine, but she had my heart long before you arrived. I know it's sinful—and if I am damned for it, then I am damned. But I cannot live without her anymore."

As I stood speechless, he fetched an item from his dressing table and pressed it into my palm: the talisman ring.

"Take it," he said. "It is a foul superstition and ungodly. I should never have agreed to wear it."

I curled my fingers over the unwanted gift. A blade would have caused less pain; I bled tears and could not stanch their flow. Unwanted, unlovely, I had only ever had my dignity, and now that was lost, too.

I whirled about and ran sobbing back to my apartment, and did not stop crying even when Madame Gondi sent the ladies of the chamber away, even when she kissed the backs of my hands, even when she put her arms around me and wept, too.

From that day forward, Henri wore only Diane's colors, white and black. Perhaps envious of his son, His Majesty, bored and lustful, summoned his mistress to be near him—against his doctors' advice.

The morning after her arrival, I rode with the Duchess d'Etampes and her inseparable companion, the dimpled Marie de Canaples. The latter had grown plumper, while the Duchess, in her lover's long absence, had grown thinner and sharper. As I approached the stables, the two ladies were murmuring furtively, heads together; at the sight of me, they broke apart quickly. The Duchess smiled at me with lips pressed tightly together, as if she had swallowed a dove; Madame de Canaples grinned at me with her sharp little fox teeth. Our conversation during that ride was strained, with both women coy and distant. When the ride was over, I walked away while the two of them whispered and laughed behind me before I was even out of their sight. I knew I would not go with them again.

I was fool enough to think that they shunned me because they had heard of my tearful encounter with Henri—no doubt the news was all over Court about my husband's affair with Madame de Poitiers, and I last to discover it.

But there was more behind the Duchess's sly smirk. I should have listened more carefully to Madame Gondi's cryptic statements, as she dressed me for supper, that there were those in Court who whispered against me. I see now that she was trying to warn me, but I waved away her words.

That evening, the King hosted a small banquet at the château, attended by many members of the Guise family. The Guises were descended from the royal House of Anjou, with a distant claim to the throne. It behooved the King to maintain good relations with them; that night, he entertained the Duke, his wife, and their daughters, Renée and Louise. Renée was still young, but Louise was a dark-eyed beauty of marriageable age. Young Charles, who had begun the previous year to notice women, was clearly smitten by her.

As soon as was courteously feasible, I retreated to my chambers, too disheartened to indulge in after-dinner chatter. To distract myself, I continued the work I had begun on Henri's natal chart. In time, my anguish eased and I grew lost in concentration. I remained at the task late into the night, stopping only long enough to let Madame Gondi and a lady of the chamber undress me and brush out my hair.

I sat at the little desk in my cramped cabinet and studied Henri's nativity. He was an Aries—a headstrong sign ruled by Mars—and his ascendant was, like mine, Leo, a clear marker of royalty.

My focus that night was the Fifth House of our nativities, the House of Children. I hoped to find happy news there, the promise of heirs. But in Henri's case—and eerily, in mine as well—the house was barren of planets and fell under the zodiacal sign of Scorpio, ruler of secrets and lies, of things buried, of the darkest magic.

This crushed the fragile hope I had been nursing for the past several hours. Not only were there no signs of children but that area of our lives was ruled by deceit and dark forces. I grew frightened and tried to convince myself that I had misinterpreted the ominous nature of Scorpio in relation to the Fifth House. I had brought Agrippa's writings to Lyon and decided to consult one of his books in the hope that I could ferret out something to indicate a brighter future. There was a small library where we were staying, and my large trunk of books had been stored there. I slipped on my dressing gown and stole outside.

My apartment was on the third floor. A spiraling outdoor staircase connected it to a courtyard on the second floor, which housed the King's and Queen's apartments as well as the library. I hurried silently down the staircase, lamp in one hand. It was a still, clear, star-littered night in late November, with a huge waxing moon that cast shadows in my path. My dressing gown provided little warmth, and the stone banister was freezing beneath my bare hand; my teeth were chattering by the time I reached the second-floor courtyard.

I scurried through the large entryway, flanked by two tall junipers, and nodded to the guards, accustomed now to my nocturnal excursions. After several moments of digging through the library stacks, I was able to find the second volume of Agrippa. I tucked it beneath one arm and, with the lamp in my other hand, went back out into the night.

I did not get far. Before I moved past the junipers flanking the recessed entryway, I heard laughter floating through the still air. It came from the loggia that opened onto a terrace behind the King's apartment; the terrace looked out onto the very stretch of courtyard I needed to cross.

Instinct prompted me to lower the lamp and wait in the junipers' shadow. The laughter grew louder as a woman's form, backlit by the moon, ran out onto the terrace.

A man's voice called to her from the loggia. "Anne! Anne, what are you doing?" The King's indignance was tempered by slightly drunken good humor. "It's freezing cold!"

She spread her arms and whirled, a dark silhouette dressed in nothing but a chemise that ended above her hips; she was bare from the waist down. Her loose hair fanned out about her shoulders. "It's wonderful! I feel revived! You had me sweating so."

"Anne . . ." His Majesty's voice turned petulant.

"François," she mimicked, then laughed. "Come take me here, beneath the moon."

He came to her—his black form tall and thick, hers small and spritelike—and lunged suddenly for her with a roar. She ran from him at first but let him catch her easily at the terrace's edge. She put her palms upon the waist-high stone railing, facing it, with her back to the King.

"Your Majesty, claim your prize."

He went to stand behind her, his hands on her hips, ready to enter her, but she pulled away, suddenly coy. "Only if you promise to heed my advice."

He groaned. "Woman, don't torment me . . ."

"Louise is a lovely girl, don't you think?"

"You're lovelier." He put his hands around her waist and lifted her to her tiptoes in the hope of piercing her, but she wriggled around to face him.

"He's been through so much sadness," she said, suddenly serious. "He deserves a beautiful woman with royal blood."

"Don't vex me, Anne. I want nothing to do with the Guises. Henri's cousin Jeanne—she's almost of marriageable age, and brings with her the crown of Navarre. She'd be a much better match for him. But Catherine is a sweet girl. Give her time, and let's not speak of this now . . ."

"It must be Louise," she countered firmly. "She would give you grandchildren who would unite the Houses of Guise and Valois. No more struggles between them for the Crown . . ."

François sighed, a bit annoyed; his dark silhouette stilled. "This is very premature. I haven't even made up my mind yet."

"But you *must* repudiate her," Anne said swiftly. "The people don't like her, Henri can't abide her . . . What does she bring you? Only disappointment."

"Enough!" François commanded.

Their forms merged in a kiss, then the King abruptly turned her so that her back faced him and bent her at the waist. She clutched the stone railing as he pushed his way inside her and began to thrust.

She let go a little gasp, then a laugh; her breath rose and hung above her head, mist in the cold night air. "François! You're like a bull!"

I blew out my lamp and averted my eyes. For agonizing moments I listened to their passion. Soon I began to shiver uncontrollably, not entirely from the cold.

Twenty-one

I didn't read Agrippa's book on astrology that night; my mind and heart were racing far too swiftly to concentrate on anything but what I had overheard. Instead, I lay awake, staring up at the tapestry canopy over my head.

Without children, without Henri's heart, I had no defense and no supporters. King François would petition the Pope and have the marriage annulled on the grounds that I was barren. Mine would not be the first royal union to end in such a manner. I would be banished—to Italy, I supposed, though I could never return to Florence so long as Alessandro ruled.

And Henri—my beloved, faithless Henri—would no longer have me by his side to protect him, as I was meant to do. Without me, he would die just as he had in my dream, bloodied and helpless.

I was not on particularly close terms with God, given my hard early lessons that the universe is neither safe nor just. But I prayed to Him who ruled the stars and planets. I promised that if I could remain near my darling Henri, I would be willing to surrender anything, including every last scrap of my pride.

In the morning I rose exhausted but resolute and penned a short letter to His Majesty requesting a private audience. I would not, like my enemies, resort to a whispering campaign, going about to the King's favorites begging for their support. François had called me his daughter; he had claimed to be my father and my friend. I would speak directly to him, or to no one at all.

The reply came quickly. The King agreed to see me directly after the morning ritual of his dressing.

I wore no jewels that morning, only black mourning for the Dauphin. His Majesty received me alone in his private cabinet, accessible only by royal invitation. It was cramped but handsome, the walls covered in carved panels of glowing cherrywood, some of which hid compartments for the storage of secret documents. A large mahogany desk dominated the room; on its polished surface rested a map—of Provence, where the fighting was, I supposed—but it had been scrolled so that I could not see what was marked there. Apparently I could not be trusted with state secrets.

François sat behind the desk. His long face was marked by excess, the cheeks heavy and ponderous, the eyes puffy. The white that had appeared in his temples upon the Dauphin's death now glistened in his dark beard as well. He was dressed simply, for work and not pleasure, in a plain doublet of black.

"Catherine. Please, sit." His mouth smiled, but his eyes were guarded.

"If it please Your Majesty, I will stand," I said. I hoped my suffering would be over quickly.

"As you wish," he said. Knowing what I had come to discuss—and thinking his position contrary to mine—he was consummately regal. He was prepared to behave as a king, to do what was best for France; to achieve that aim, he had abandoned even those of his blood to his enemies. I, a newcomer and foreigner, had no hope.

I abandoned all pretense. I said, "Your Majesty, I love you. And I love your son. I know I am a liability to you both now. And so . . ." My voice broke; I silently cursed myself for my weakness. When I had gathered myself, I looked up at François again. His expression was hard, cautious.

"And so I will not object to the repudiation. I accept that you must do what is politically expedient, and I harbor no resentment."

His jaw went slack. My unexpected words disarmed him.

"I only ask . . ." The words caught in my throat, which tightened. I repeated the words, and when the barrage of tears came with them, I lowered my face to hide them and forced myself to continue. "I only ask that I be allowed to serve in whatever lowly capacity pleases you and your son. That I not be sent away. I would happily serve the woman who becomes Henri's wife. If only I could stay . . ."

I sank to my knees; I covered my face and sobbed. I was humiliating myself, yet I did not care. I thought of Henri bleeding, dying because I had been sent away and had failed to save him.

When at last I looked up, sodden and gasping, François was standing rod-straight behind his desk. An intense emotion was filling him, slowly widening his deep-set eyes and quickening his breath—yet whether it was fury or fear or revulsion, I could not have said. I could only kneel, dabbing at my eyes and waiting for the storm to erupt. I huddled in self-hatred and burning resentment, that my fate was not my own, nor even God's, but held in the hands of men: the rebels, the Pope, the King.

A muscle in François's jaw twitched, as it had that bright October day when he had seen Montecuculli ripped apart.

"Catherine," he whispered, and emotion—doubt and sadness, then resolution—played upon his features. He came around the desk and gently lifted me up by the shoulders.

"No saint was ever more humble," he said. "May we all learn from you. It is God's will that you be my son's wife and my daughter. I tell you now that there shall be no more talk of repudiation in my Court."

He kissed my cheek and took me in his arms.

Had I tried to manipulate him—had I gone to him and wept for pure show, and not meant my words with my whole heart—he surely would have sent me away, just as he would have if I had begged to remain Henri's wife. But on the day we first met, His Majesty had loved me for my humility; he had only to be reminded of it.

I was safe—but only for a time. Until I bore Henri's child, I was vulnerable. The Duchess would not easily surrender her campaign against me, and Louise of Guise was still so very young.

I was deeply relieved when King François chose to marry Jeanne to a German duke willing to pay an outrageous dowry; war was a costly business, and at that moment, François needed money more desperately than heirs. As a young woman, Jeanne was not pretty: Her nose was long and bulbous, her lips and chin too small. But her intellect was keen, like her mother's, and her green eyes, slanting and thick-lashed, were strikingly beautiful. I bade farewell to her as she boarded the coach to Düsseldorf; I thought we would never meet again.

Perhaps uncomfortable that I would not soon be repudiated, Henri asked to join the fighting in Provence. The King refused him at first, saying he had just lost one son and would not risk another. But Henri was so determined that he prevailed and joined Lieutenant General Montmorency in the south.

While Henri was away, I had time to think clearly about my predicament. My husband was loyal by nature; now that he had given his heart and body to Diane de Poitiers, he would no doubt be repelled by the thought of sharing either with another woman. Yet if I were to conceive an heir, Henri would need to come to my bed frequently once he returned from the war.

Not long after my encounter with the King, I went to Queen Eléonore and asked if I might enjoy the company of her lady-in-waiting Diane de Poitiers for an hour.

The Queen consented graciously, though she and her entourage understood how very strange my request was. Madame de Poitiers and I were perfectly cordial to each other when our paths were forced to cross, but in all other instances we avoided each other, and everyone knew why.

Madame de Poitiers rode full astride, like a man, unashamed of her calves and ankles. Like me, she would not be led, and she held her reins with no uncertain grip. Her horse was white, perhaps chosen carefully to match her widow's trousseau. It was a colorless sight on a day uncommonly cold for the Midi: Diane in her black and white, the grass frosted, the sky a burdensome grey. Despite the intemperate weather, I had asked her to ride. I led her away from the palace grounds and human ears. A groom followed at a distant pace, given the possibility of encountering a wild boar. When the time came for earnest conversation, I lifted my gloved hand so that he remained behind, and we women trotted off until he appeared no larger than a pea. I wanted no one to be able to read our faces.

Diane de Poitiers was not quite forty, and the gold in her hair was tempered by silver. But her skin was still firm—except around the eyes, where the troubled light revealed fine creases. Her complexion was even, without the broken veins or blotchiness that reveal a fondness for wine.

As I stared at her, struggling to perceive what qualities my husband so loved, her answering gaze was steady and calm. She was unafraid—balm, surely, for Henri's fearful, uncertain soul. I despised her at that moment, almost as greatly as I despised myself.

I smiled at her and said easily, "Shall we speak?"

The degree of her smile matched mine. "Of course, *Madame la Dauphine,*" she replied. "Let me first thank you for the opportunity to ride. I have been eager for the exercise, but none of the other ladies will accompany me because of their belief that the cold is unhealthful."

"The pleasure is mine." My little smile faded. "We have much in common, Madame. A grandmother, and a love for riding. A love, even, for the same man."

Her expression remained unflinching and serene as she faced me, waiting.

"Louise of Guise is a beautiful girl, isn't she?" I continued. "So fresh and young. Any man would deem himself lucky to have such a stunning bride."

"Yes, *Madame la Dauphine,*" she dutifully replied.

My black steed paced, impatient; I reined him in.

"But I've heard she is quick-tempered and somewhat demanding," I remarked. "She would make a difficult wife, perhaps, for a husband to manage."

"Yes, Madame. I've heard the same." Her eyes were mirrors, reflecting me back to myself, revealing nothing of what lay beneath their polished surface.

"I have been told," I said, "that I am patient. I have never enjoyed causing trouble for others. I only hope that my children are as agreeable."

"I pray they are, *Madame la Dauphine.* And I pray that they are many."

Her face, her eyes, her soft and gracious tone were unchanged, as if she had just remarked on the weather. She might have been utterly sincere or utterly false. I tried to imagine how someone who showed so little feeling could inspire such passion in my husband.

"I will have no children at all," I said, "if my husband will not come to my bed." I felt an exquisite tightening of my throat and waited until my composure was sure.

Perhaps she sensed my anguish; for the first time, her gaze wavered, and she looked beyond me at a copse of bare-limbed trees.

"If he will not come to me," I said, "we both know that I shall have to leave." My tone became candid. "I do love him. For that reason alone, I will never make things unpleasant for him or for those fortunate enough to share his affections—even if it breaks my heart. The Dauphin's will must be respected."

She eyed me, faintly frowning, a hint of cautious wonder in her gaze.

"A laudable attitude," she said.

"Louise of Guise's would not be so gracious."

Nearby, the underbrush crackled, and a bevy of quail took flight. Crows settled on the silver branches and scolded the invisible culprit below. Our distant chaperone craned his neck, on the alert, but the disturbance was not repeated and the crows grew silent. Diane and I watched them for a moment before turning back to each other.

The faint lines that had appeared on her brow smoothed as she made her decision. "The House of Valois must have heirs," she said, and for an unsettling instant I thought she referred to my inability to provide them and agreed with those who would repudiate me. But then she added softly, "He will come to your bed, Madame."

"I have never taken my agreements with others lightly," I said. "And I have heard that you are a woman of honor."

"You have my word, Madame."

We rode back to the palace without speaking. I was in no mood for idle conversation now that my humiliation was complete.

On the way, something feather-light and cold stung my cheek. I looked up at the threatening sky and saw what was, for the Midi, impossible: snowflakes sailing down, white and soft and soundless.

In time, Henri returned from the war. As Dauphin, he was supreme military commander of the French forces in Provence, but aware of his inexperience, he consulted his lieutenant general, Grand Master Montmorency, on every maneuver. His deference paid off: Our army decisively defeated the Imperial invaders. As a result, Henri and Montmorency became close friends and were welcomed home as heroes. The King had nothing but praise for both of them.

The crucible of war had transformed Henri into a man and brought him confidence. It also left him determined to hide his affair with Madame de Poitiers no longer. He proudly wore her colors, white and black, and adopted as his emblem the crescent moon—symbol of Diana, goddess of the hunt.

But within days of his return, Henri appeared at my bedchamber door. He brought with him resignation, not joy, but neither did he bring resentment. Diane had surely told him everything; I think he was relieved that I would cause them no trouble.

His manner was removed but kindly. The sight of his body—utterly a man's now, with a full, muscular back and chest—made me ache with longing. Each time I lay with him, I convinced myself that surely this time I would say or do the very thing that would win his heart; and each time he rose from my bed too quickly, I lay watching him, replete yet shattered. Never did pleasure bring so much pain.

A year passed, then two, three, four, and I did not conceive. I consulted the King's astrologers and had dutiful intercourse with Henri at the recommended times. I uttered pagan chants and spells; Madame Gondi put a mandrake root beneath my mattress; I followed Aristotle's advice and ate quail eggs, endive, and violets to nauseating excess. Following Agrippa, I made a talisman of Venus for fertility and put it beside the mandrake. All of it availed nothing.

Anne, the Duchess d'Etampes, began to whisper again into the ear of her lover and anyone else who would listen. The Court parted into two camps: those who supported the aging King and his devious paramour, and those who looked to the future and supported Henri and Diane de Poitiers. The Duchess was extraordinarily jealous; she perceived Diane as her rival and wanted to see her cast down. The best way to do so, she had decided, was to bring Henri a new wife—one headstrong and willful, who would not accept Henri's mistress as graciously as I had. And if this caused harm to me, favored too well by the King, so much the better.

So I watched over the barren days and months and years as the smile His Majesty directed at me grew fainter, as the warmth in his eyes and embrace slowly cooled. The talismans, the physicians, the astrologers . . . all had failed. Yet in my mind I kept returning to the memory of the night my late mother had spoken to me. Her words had been uncannily accurate; as I could not trust the living, I decided to trust the dead.

I had been very ill the night that the magician had summoned her, so I could not remember the proper chants or gesticulations. I recalled only that Ruggieri had anointed us with what seemed to be old blood.

I saved some purplish black menstrual blood and, on a chilly day in March, 1543, in the privacy of my cabinet, I anointed my forehead with it, then pricked my finger with an embroidery needle.

Fresh blood was required, Ruggieri had said. The dead would smell it.

At my desk, I squeezed my finger, milking several fat red drops onto a small piece of paper. I dipped my quill into it and scratched out a message:

Send me a child.

I cast the paper into the hearth. The fire jumped as it caught and blackened at the outer edges, curling inward as the flame raced toward the center.

"Ma mere," I whispered. *"M'amie, je t'adore. . . .* Mother, hear my prayer and send me a child. Tell me what I must do."

The ash fell onto the glowing logs; pieces of it broke off and whirled about before sailing up the flue.

I repeated my plea, staring into the writhing flames. I did not address myself only to my mother, to the dead, to God or the Devil. I spoke to whoever might answer. My heart opened until there was no separation between it and the power that fueled the universe. With my will, my desire, I clutched that power and would not let go.

Heaven—or Hell—opened in that instant. I knew not which. I knew only that I touched *something*; I knew only that my plea had been heard.

The next day, I followed the King's movements until the afternoon, when I was required to hold audiences. As Dauphine, I had many petitioners, mostly Florentines asking for assistance. Enthroned, I listened to each sad tale.

The first was that of an elderly Tornabuoni widow, related to the Medici by marriage. She had lived in her deceased husband's villa until Alessandro's henchmen seized the property after illegally taxing her into bankruptcy; she had left the city with nothing. I granted her sufficient funds so that she could live comfortably in one of the better convents outside Paris.

There was also a banker with a wife and six children who had long ago worked as an apprentice to Uncle Filippo Strozzi, which had been enough to endanger his life. He had fled Florence with his family, leaving behind all his assets. I promised to find him work in the Treasury.

There were several others, and after a few hours, I grew tired.

Madame Gondi said, "I will tell the others to return tomorrow. But there is one, Madame—a rather strange-looking gentleman—who insists that he be seen today. He says that you know him and will be glad to see him."

I had opened my mouth to ask the name of the impertinent beggar when revelation suddenly stole my voice. When it returned, I told Madame Gondi to bring him to me.

He entered wearing red and black, the colors of Mars and Saturn; he was fully a man now, but there was no meat on him, and his striped doublet hung upon his bony frame. His face was gaunt and sickly pale against his blue-black brows and hair. At the sight of me, he doffed his cap and bowed very low.

"Madame la Dauphine," he said. I had forgotten how very beautiful his voice was, how very deep. "We meet again at last."

I stepped down from my throne. When he rose, I took his cold hands in my own.

"Monsieur Ruggieri," I said. "How I have prayed that you would come."

Twenty-two

I immediately appointed Cosimo Ruggieri my court astrologer. He brought with him no belongings, as though he had materialized from the ether with no purse, no trunk, no wife, no family.

I led him at once to my cabinet. I asked after his past: He had left Florence for Venice and, on the day of his arrival there, had fallen ill with plague. From Venice he had gone to Constantinople and Araby, though he would not explain why or what had happened there. I told him of my joy at receiving, during my imprisonment, the volume of Ficino and the Wing of Corvus. I told him how my mother's words had proven true, how a man named Silvestro had saved me from a hostile crowd. I shared with him the details of my self-education in astrology, and my efforts to cast nativities.

If anything in my long tale surprised him, he did not show it. Never once did he remind me of his prediction that I would become a queen.

At last I said, "I have had a recurring dream ever since you gave me the Raven's Wing. I dream of a man with his face drenched in blood. He calls out to me in French. He is dying, and it is my duty to help him—but I don't know how." I lowered my gaze, troubled. "It's Henri. I knew the instant I met him. I feel bound to protect him from a gruesome fate."

He listened dispassionately. "Is that all? Only Henri, in your dream?"

"No," I said. "There are others in the field—hundreds, thousands, perhaps, but I cannot see them. The blood . . . it swells like the ocean." I lifted my fingers to my temple and massaged it, as if to work the memory loose and make it fall away.

"This is your destiny," he said. "Yours is the power, Madame, to spill that ocean . . . or to stanch its flow."

I wanted suddenly to weep. "But Henri . . . Some ill will soon befall him. If I can stop it, then perhaps the others won't die. Tell me what will happen to him, and how I can stop it. You're the magician—there must be spells to protect him. I tried; I made a talisman myself, another Wing of Corvus, but he wouldn't wear it."

"A simple talisman, a simple spell, could never be enough," he said.

I flared. "It was enough for me, when I was in the hands of the rebels."

"You faced danger of the sort that could be overcome, with the potential for a long life. But Prince Henri . . ." Regret flickered in his gaze. "His life will end too soon, in calamity. Surely you have read his stars."

His words stole my breath. I had read the sinister signs, but I had never permitted myself to believe them.

"If simple magic will not do," I persisted, "then what will? Exchange my life for his. You have the knowledge, surely."

He recoiled from the suggestion. "I have the knowledge. But there are others in your dream, yes? What of them?"

"I don't care," I said, miserable.

"Then France will be torn apart," he replied. "For they are as much your responsibility, as much a part of your fate, as Prince Henri is."

"They are another reason, then, why I must stay," I said. "But there are those at Court who intend to see me cast aside and Henri wed to another. He'll be left unprotected without me. I must have his child. I *must*." The muscles of my face hardened. "Only tell me what I must do to keep Henri alive, and to have his child."

He considered this a long time before replying. "We cannot outwit fate forever. But we can bring Henri more years than he might otherwise have had." He paused. "Is that truly your will? To bear the Dauphin's child?"

It seemed a ridiculous question. "Of course. I would do anything. I already *have* done everything: I've made talismans, cast spells, worn disgusting poultices, and drunk mule's urine. I know of nothing else to do."

He considered this, then said slowly, "And the child must be the Dauphin's."

It was a statement, yet I heard the question buried in it, and my face grew hot. *How dare you,* I wanted to say—but this was Ruggieri, and propriety was immaterial. No secret was hidden from him, no topic too wicked to be broached.

I blushed and said, "Yes, it must be. He is my husband. And . . . I love him."

He cocked his head at the desperation in those last three words. "I am sorry to hear this," he said softly. "It complicates matters."

"How so?"

"Surely you have studied your own nativity in regard to children," he said. "Surely you have studied Prince Henri's. Scorpio rules your Fifth House," he continued, "and that of your husband. You are far too intelligent to miss the implications: barrenness—or, if you wish, lies and deceit. The choice is yours."

"I won't accept either," I countered. "There has to be a third way."

"There always is." He leaned forward, his skin sickly pale against his blue-black hair. "But it depends entirely on what you are willing to do."

Despite the crookedness of his nose and the pitting in his cheeks, his voice and manner were magnetic, intoxicating. Beneath an icy surface ran a hot current, one that would pull me under if I dared test it.

"Anything," I said, "except to lie with another man."

He nodded slowly. "Then I warn you, *Madame la Dauphine,* that to get blood, you must give blood."

An unpleasant thrill coursed through me at his words: He spoke of the very darkest sort of magic. But I had always felt that my soul was already lost.

"I will give every last drop," I said, "to save Henri."

His gaze revealed nothing. "Ah, Madame. Here is where a strong will and a strong stomach are needed, for it is not your blood of which we speak."

I resisted for weeks. I met with Ruggieri daily, consulting him on trivial matters and begging for instruction in the magical arts. As to the latter, he refused:

I knew too little, and he too much; it was far safer for him to cast spells at my request.

"It is enough," he said, "that one of our souls is imperiled."

During those weeks, I lived in uneasy dread. Madame Gondi reported to me that the Guises—family of the nubile Louise—had met secretly with the King to discuss, again, the possibility of a marriage contract with Henri. It was almost enough to make me consider Ruggieri's suggestion that I be impregnated by another man.

But even though Henri had betrayed me, I could not do the same to him. The House of Valois was mine now; and I longed for a son with Valois blood who would inherit the throne. I had found my home, and would not be taken from it.

In the end, I yielded to the unthinkable. In the middle of the night, I took up my quill and listened to the scratch of the nib as my hand wrote impossible, barbarous things.

I sent for Ruggieri early the next morning and met him in my cabinet. Behind the locked door, I handed him the paper, folded into eighths, as if that somehow decreased the enormity of the crime.

"I've thought it through carefully," I said, "and these are my restrictions."

The paper whispered in his fingers. He frowned at the message, then lifted his dark gaze from the page.

"If I follow them," he said, "I cannot say what effect they might have upon the outcome."

"So long as we meet with success," I said.

He refolded the paper and slipped it inside his breast pocket, his gaze never straying from mine; his eyes were black, like my Henri's, though they lacked any light. His lips moved faintly toward a smile.

"Oh, we shall meet with success, Catherine."

I did not see his use of my given name as impertinence. We were equals now, after the grisliest of fashions. I had given Henri my heart, but only Ruggieri knew the evil it contained.

I trusted only Madame Gondi to make the arrangement directly with the Master of Horses. She ordered her own mount saddled and brought to the far side of the stables, where it could not been seen from the palace windows. A scandalous thing for a woman to be riding near dusk, alone; the Master no doubt assumed an illicit rendezvous was in the offing. He was not wrong.

Madame Gondi rode out of sight of the stables and past the gardens to the nearest copse of trees; beneath their shelter, she and I made the exchange. We both wore black; someone watching from a distance would think that the woman who rode into the woods was the same woman who rode out.

Hours earlier, morning had revealed the strangest of spring skies, troubled and overcast, with a diffuse coral glow where the sun should have hung; now, at dusk, that glow had slipped to the horizon. The air was cool and redolent of rain. I rode well beyond the woods; several times I reined my borrowed horse to a stop, thinking to turn around, but the thought of Henri spurred me on.

Eventually I came upon an unkempt vineyard flanked by an orchard of dying pear trees, their gnarled limbs speckled with feeble, struggling blossoms. On the outskirts of the orchard, a black figure held up a lantern. As I neared, I discerned Ruggieri's face, phosphorescent in the yellow glow. He turned and walked slowly past the trees to a thatch-roofed cottage of crumbling brick. Candlelight shone dimly through cracks in the drawn shutters.

I dismounted; Ruggieri set the lantern on the ground and helped me down, catching both my hands in his. For an instant he stared at me, his complicitous gaze intent, searching for something he did not find.

He had not wanted me to come. I wasn't needed, he said, and there was always the chance of danger, both magical and practical. I felt that his real reason was to spare me upset, and the revulsion of seeing firsthand what he was capable of, yet I had insisted. I did not want the crime I was about to commit to be distant, a mere tale without the attending visceral reality.

I did not want to be able to do such a thing again.

The sudden coldness in his gaze stole my breath; the talon touch of his fingers, separated though they were from mine by two layers of gloves, chilled me to the core. He was capable of acts worse than murder, and I was alone with him, where no one could hear my screams.

I thought to pull away, to jump onto Madame Gondi's horse and ride off. But the magician's eyes were powerful, compelling. With a dreamer's languid helplessness, I followed him to the entrance of the cottage.

Ruggieri flung open the rotting portal to reveal a single room with a dirt floor half covered by a large piece of slate. The pale walls were covered in pigeon droppings, the hearth so long unused that greenish mold had sprouted from the bricks. Someone had painted a perfect black circle on the slate, one large enough to comfortably contain two men lying end to end. Unlit candles, each on a brass holder tall as a man, rested at four equidistant points on the circle's circumference.

On a small table pushed against the wall beneath the shuttered window, a lamp revealed the room's other contents: two stools, a shelf holding half a dozen books and several instruments, including a double-bladed dagger, a censer, a goblet, a quill, inkwell, parchment, and several small stoppered vials. A large pearl on a silver chain and a polished onyx lay beside the censer. The table and stools rested on the dirt floor, the shelf upon the slate, just inside the circle in front of one of the large candles.

A young woman with her back to us sat at the table. Her thick, waving hair—a gold so pale it was almost silver—fell heavily to her waist. She paid us no notice but continued to address herself to a roasted duck. Our shadows fell upon the wall near the table; the girl saw them, set down the half-eaten drumstick in her hand, and turned.

She was only twelve or thirteen years old. Her face was abnormally broad, and her blue eyes wide-set, tiny slanting almonds in a pale expanse. The bridge of her nose was flattened; the tip of her tongue protruded between her lips. At the sight of me she let go an agitated grunt and gesticulated at Ruggieri.

He shook his head and swept his arm in a downward, dismissive manner, but she continued to stare at me with a dull, clouded gaze. I had seen such children before, usually in the arms of older mothers.

"She is a deaf-mute," Ruggieri said, "born an imbecile."

He smiled sweetly at her and gestured for her to come to him. She rose and turned toward us, revealing breasts too ripe for one her age, pushed high above her tightly laced bodice to create the illusion of greater volume. These were set over a swollen belly, which strained so hard against the waistline of her gown that the seam had torn. She looked to be more than halfway through her confinement.

Sickened, panicked, I turned to Ruggieri. "She is too young!"

"How many years would you buy?" he challenged coolly. "She is a trained prostitute; her guardian used her for income until her pregnancy became obvious. Now she is outcast and wandering, and will certainly starve or be raped and murdered. Even if the child is born . . ." He let go a small sound of disgust. "What sorts of lives will they have if I put her back on the village streets? You told me that our use of her must come as a kindness. In her case, it will."

I took a step away from him and thought of the girl's slack face and vacant eyes. "I can't do this," I whispered.

Ruggieri's black eyes flared; beneath his calm tone lay an undercurrent of coiled violence. "Leave if you must," he said, "and your Henri will die before you can give him sons."

I stood frozen, unable to answer.

By then, the girl had eaten most of the duck and turned her attentions on Ruggieri. Without preamble or finesse, she pulled up his doublet and wormed a hand down his leggings. He pulled away and caught her wrist.

"She is quite insatiable," he said, studying her with perfect detachment. "She had just finished servicing one gentleman when I discovered her, and it has taken me a great deal of effort to avoid her advances." He held the girl's wrist tightly until she began to struggle, at which point he glanced over his shoulder at me. "Go stand inside the circle."

I went to stand in the circle's heart. A breeze had stirred, sending cold drafts through holes in the thatched roof and rattling shutters, yet I felt the sudden nauseating weight of suffocation.

Ruggieri let go of the girl's wrist and smiled as he pinched her cheeks playfully. This relaxed her, though when he moved the plate of duck beyond her reach, she grew anxious. He sat down beside her, his arm about her shoulders, and lifted a cup of wine to her lips. Again and again he urged her to drink, which she did without hesitation.

Abruptly, the girl swayed upon the stool and would have fallen had Ruggieri not caught her. He gathered her up and carried her into the circle, where he laid her, limp as a corpse, onto the slate. Her eyes were open and glittering, her breath shallow and slow.

"Don't move," Ruggieri whispered hoarsely at me. "Don't speak or in any way interfere. Above all else, do not step outside the circle."

He pulled a metal basin and a folded sheet of yellowed linen from the shelf, then unfurled the cloth and dragged the girl onto it.

As he had on the night he had summoned my mother's ghost, he unstoppered a vial and anointed his forehead and mine, then lit the censer on the bookshelf. Smoke streamed languidly up from the coals, carrying the resinous smell of myrrh and something earthier, deeper, faintly putrid. He lit the candles with the lamp, starting with the one behind the makeshift altar and proceeding clockwise until each bore a flame. Then he blew out the lamp.

By then the sky outside was dark; despite the draft, the filmy air blurred the edges of all objects, rendering the scene indistinct. Ruggieri's cape and doublet merged into the blackness so that his face, alabaster against his beard and eyes, appeared to float.

It seemed unreal—the girl's flaccid body at my feet, the curling smoke that veiled the candles' glow, the magician's tools upon the shelf—and the vastness of our crime a distant thing. Ruggieri took up a dagger—double-edged, black-hilted, wickedly sharp. Holding it in both hands, he plunged it above his head as if to pierce the sky and chanted loudly as he lowered it to touch the flat to heart and shoulders. He seemed to grow physically larger, all-powerful, more than human. When his eyes snapped open, fierce and focused and impersonal, I thought I looked upon a god.

Abruptly, he began to retrace the circle, above and parallel to the black line on the slate, pausing at each of the candles to slash a symbol with the dagger. At each candle, he thrust the dagger forward and boldly intoned a name, until he again stood in front of the altar.

He dropped to one knee beside the girl and slid his arm beneath her shoulders to prop her torso against his chest. When her head lolled forward, he wound her thick golden hair around his left hand and pulled her head back to expose her white throat.

The girl was still awake, wide-eyed at the sight of the knife. She whimpered; a shudder passed through her as she tried vainly to move her limbs.

Supremely commanding, infinitely assured, Ruggieri called out a foreign word, harsh and sibilant, then made a nick with the dagger beneath the girl's ear. She moaned ferally as darkness streamed down her neck onto her collarbone and between her high, full breasts.

The magician thundered the word again.

The candles dimmed, then brightened; the smoke thickened and began to swirl. I fancied that a shape was forming within it, that something unspeakably cold and heavy and cruel had just entered the room, raising the hairs on my arms.

Ruggieri called out the term of the agreement: this woman's life for Henri's; her child for an heir.

Clutching the girl's hair, Ruggieri maneuvered her throat over the basin and plunged the dagger's tip into her throat, then made a swift, certain slash beneath her jaw to the opposite ear. The blood spilled out in a sheet, striking the basin with a tinkling sound. Ruggieri's eyes narrowed at the spray, but his face was immobile, the corners of his lips pulled down by infinite determination.

It was how I should have killed the stableboy. I stared down at the blood. It did not frighten me as much as the knowledge that I could so casually command it, that I could look upon it and not be dismayed. The anticipation had been hard, but at the actual moment of the killing, I remembered how very easy it was. A flash of Ruggieri's knife, and she was gone.

When the spilling stopped, he pulled the girl's head up; it dropped back against him to expose the raw, gaping grin beneath the jaw. He let go of her hair and torso and let her drop lifeless to the floor. Her face was white as bone, her neck black with blood; her gaze was fixed on some far distant sight.

Ruggieri went down on both knees over her as if he meant to pray, but instead he slid the dagger beneath her tight bodice and pulled; the thin fabric ripped easily. She wore no chemise; her breasts were round and very firm, the skin a lovely lunar white, so translucent that one could glimpse a vein here and there leading to the large pink nipples. Her body, though unwashed, was young and perfect and plump.

Ruggieri smoothed a hand over her belly as if reading a map with his fingers. With the finesse of an experienced surgeon, he inserted the tip of the dagger beneath her breastbone and drew it neatly down over the mound of the unborn child to her pubis. The knife left a red stripe in its wake, which blurred as her gown absorbed the blood; there was less of it than I expected. He set the knife aside and tried to part the flesh with his fingers, but it did not yield easily because she wore a good deal of fat. He took up the knife again and cut more carefully. I covered my nose at the smell.

Amid a stew of quivering fat, raw muscle, and glistening entrails, something lay exposed: the curve of a tiny red skull, the corner of a purple shoulder smeared with birth cheese. Ruggieri worried his fingers deeper into the woman's womb and pulled. The silent child emerged with a sucking sound, its bloodied cord intact. I could not see its face, and the magician did not clean it but set it aside on the sheet, a sad little unborn corpse with a great head and frail limbs, still connected to its mother.

At Ruggieri's soft gasp I looked up. His hands disappeared again inside the dead girl, and when he lifted them up they bore a second red tangle of flesh and bone, this one smaller than the first. Again his hands disappeared, and again brought forth a child.

"Triplets," he said, amazed. "Chance smiles on you, Catherine."

Four lives to buy Henri's, and three sons.

"Never again," I whispered. "Never."

The magician knew well what I meant; my words replaced his sudden lightness with something very dark.

"How often," he said, "I have uttered those words myself."

I remember little of the ritual afterward. Ruggieri applied a drop of the girl's blood to the onyx, then a bit of blood from each child to the pearl. When the circle was broken, we left the bodies on the slate and Ruggieri lit the lamp. We sat on the stools while he explained that I must lie with my husband as soon as possible, then handed me the two tainted stones: The pearl was mine, the onyx Henri's. I was instructed to hide the latter where my husband spent most of his time. I was to wear the pearl always, and never let it from my sight.

As the magician spoke, rain drummed on the roof and crashed against the stones outside. He opened the shutters just enough to admit the sound of a downpour and distant thunder.

"Madame Gondi's horse," I said, absurdly worried that it might get wet when my bloodied victims lay nearby.

"Stay," Ruggieri ordered. "I'll lead it beneath the eaves for shelter. You'll need to remain here until the storm passes."

He pushed open the door and disappeared into the darkness.

I stood at the window, though the night and rain blotted out sight and sound. He was gone for so long that a sudden paralyzing fear stole my breath: Something old and shrewd and evil waited outside in the darkness for me.

Cosimo Ruggieri was an inhuman fiend: I had just witnessed the proof. He had once said that he had protected me because it served his best interests; what might serve them now?

The rain crashed down harder. Childishly, knowing I could not be heard, I cried out to him. Ruggieri appeared upon the threshold abruptly, as though the utterance of his name had forced him to materialize.

Water pooled upon his shoulders; beads of rain coursed down his cheeks. I was still trembling and tried to cover my fear of him by sneering, "Poor man. Do you cry now, for her and her children?"

He stepped inside the door. The edges of his eyelids and nostrils were red; he was indeed weeping.

"Don't tell me you feel remorse," I said.

He looked up at me with a face I had never seen, one wearing Ruggieri's features, but younger and haunted by many ghosts; in its eyes was self-loathing that verged on insanity.

"For no one else, Catherine," he said hoarsely. "For no one else." Words welled up and caught in his throat, bitter things he could not bring himself to expel.

I heard but refused to understand. I shook my head and backed away from him. "No. No, that isn't true. This isn't the first time you've done something so horrible. I heard of your crimes when I was only a girl."

"When you were in the hands of the rebels," he hissed, "how do you think I protected you? How do you think I knew of the danger that was coming?"

The talisman, I wanted to say. *It was the talisman that kept me safe.* I closed my eyes and felt it hard against my heart, hiding the wickedness that lurked beneath. I did not want to know what he had done to charge it.

He bowed his head; the words he had fought so hard to contain finally tore free. "Only ever out of love, Catherine."

The girl's mutilated body and those of her unborn children lay inside the circle, the candles extinguished. The lamplight chased away all sense of unreality, leaving behind a stark heaviness. Pierced to my bones, I sank onto the stool, the one on which the girl had sat as Ruggieri plied her with tainted wine.

Love.

Do not tell me that you did this for me. I understood suddenly how my husband would feel were I to confess my crime. The magician's words, uttered more than a decade earlier, returned to me:

We are tied, Caterina Maria Romula de' Medici.

Aghast, I said, "I love only Henri. I will forever love only Henri."

His face was taut with grief, his voice shatteringly mournful.

"I know, *Madame la Dauphine.* I have read your stars."

Twenty-three

The rain did not last long. Numbed, I rode back to the palace, stopping a short distance away to hand over the horse's reins to Madame Gondi, who returned it to the stables. I said nothing to her, but even in the darkness, she must have read the horror in my bearing.

I went directly to my chamber, and did not go down for supper; I was still too shocked to be charming and talkative. I fastened the pearl pendant around my neck with trembling fingers.

Despite my disquiet, I needed to lie with Henri that night. I made a chambermaid wait while I penned a note urging my husband to come to my chambers immediately after supper, implying that some emergency had occurred.

One of the ladies undressed me to my chemise, then left while Madame Gondi brushed out my hair, still damp from the drizzle on my ride home. Her eyes held many questions, but she came and went in silence.

After a time, Henri knocked on my bedchamber door; I opened it myself. He hesitated on the threshold, his face sun-browned from the hunt, a slash of concern separating his brows. His eyes were easily read: He had not wanted to come, but Diane had sent him.

"Are you unwell, *Madame la Dauphine?*" he asked formally. He held his brown velvet cap a bit nervously in both hands.

Before his arrival, I had thought that my nerves would fail, that I would be unable lure him into a liaison. But at the sight of him, a surge of feral heat swept over me—wild and foreign, from someplace far outside me—carrying away with it all my notions of propriety and dignity. I wanted to devour him alive.

I put a finger to my lips and reached past him to close the chamber door.

He was embarrassed by my forwardness and eager to leave; I would not let him. Like the imbecile prostitute, I snaked my hand beneath the waistband of his leggings, found the flesh between his legs, and closed my fingers around it; with my other hand, I pulled his leggings down to the middle of his thighs.

I knelt before him and did something I had never done: I lowered my head and took his swelling flesh into my mouth, at the same time glimpsing a veil of waving golden hair where my own mousy brown should have been.

My actions caught him off guard. At first he tried to push me away, then held very still, and finally seized my skull and groaned as his cap fell to the floor, forgotten. His shaft was veined and purple and more swollen than I had ever seen it—like me, hardened by blood and ready to burst. I moved my mouth up and down, so fast that I cut my upper lip and tasted blood. I rose quickly on my toes, seizing Henri's shoulders and pulling him down to kiss his mouth and tongue, to make him taste blood, too.

This time, he did not pull away. My madness infected him, and he lifted me off my feet into his arms, our tongues entwined, our bodies pressed so fast together that the effort made us tremble; so tightly, Ruggieri's pearl burrowed painfully between my breasts.

I pulled back with a mighty sigh, then caught Henri's hands and led him shuffling to the bed, his erect shaft an arrow pointing upward to lift the hem of his doublet. He waited for me to lie down as I always had; instead, I pushed him onto the bed and stripped away his leggings, then pulled off my chemise. I spread him like Montecuculli waiting for the final crack of the whip, then straddled him. I was wet and he slipped in easily; the emphatic pleasure of it made us both gasp.

The power that seized me was white-hot and inhuman; its sway allowed no resistance, no thought, no emotion save desire. It was coarse and ugly and beautiful; it bloomed with life and stunk of death. I was no longer Catherine, no longer in my chamber. The breath of a hundred men warmed my face, the touch of a hundred hands groped my breasts, my vulva; I was ablaze, unashamed. I wanted them all to pierce me. I desired the entire world.

I pinned Henri's legs and pressed my mouth hard against his to taste death and iron. I ground my body against his; I sank my teeth into his shoulder and laughed when he cried out. I laughed, too, when he pulled me from the bed and pressed my face and breasts against the cherry paneling on the wall to impale me from behind.

It was tainted and impure and intoxicating. I reared against him, groaning, reaching behind me to dig my nails into his hips, to bring him deeper inside me. And when I could take no more—when desire had reached its loveliest, ugliest peak, he convulsed, crushing me against the wall, and roared in my ear. I screamed, high and shrill with unbearable pleasure, unbearable horror. For buried within this surfeit of mindless, pulsating heat was a tiny cold black center, one that contained the glistening purple skull of an unborn child.

Thought returned, in the guise of Ruggieri's silent whisper:

Only ever out of love.

Henri pulled out his shriveling flesh. I felt the weight of liquid dropping inside me and realized it was his seed. For a moment, I considered letting it flow out and away, but its loss would have healed nothing. I staggered to the bed and lay down, protective of the fluid within my womb and repulsed by it.

Henri fell beside me on his stomach, his expression one of wonder and disbelief.

"Catherine," he whispered. "My shy, innocent wife, what has taken hold of you?"

"The Devil," I said flatly and did not smile.

He recoiled faintly at the darkness in my tone. He was unsettled, rightly so, but also entranced, and the next evening found him again in my arms. By then, I had given the charged onyx to Madame Gondi and instructed her to hide it beneath Diane's mattress.

Three weeks passed, during which my husband visited my bedchamber nightly. Voracious, I flung myself at Henri every time he passed over my threshold. My appetite knew no bounds; I demanded that he penetrate every orifice, examine with his fingers and tongue every inch of my flesh, and I did the same to him. Alone with any man—Ruggieri, or a groom or page or diplomat—I would find myself suddenly overcome by blazing desire.

One morning, Madame Gondi was reading aloud my list of appointments for the day while Annette, one of the ladies of the chamber, was lacing my bodice. I was exhausted from my antics with Henri the night before. He had paid a great deal of attention to my breasts, and they ached so much that I scolded Annette to be gentler. The words had scarcely left my lips when I felt a surge of heat, followed by a chill and urgent nausea. I pressed my hand to my mouth and lurched toward my basin, but in midstep I stopped and retched violently. Just when I thought I was recovered, a fresh wave seized me and brought me to my knees.

A basin appeared near me, and I maneuvered myself over it to vomit repeatedly. Eyes and nose streaming, I looked up to see Madame Gondi crouching beside me. Her expression held no concern; to the contrary, she was grinning broadly, and it took me, stupid girl, long seconds to understand and smile back at her.

Our first son was born at Fontainebleau on the nineteenth of January 1544. It was late afternoon when he appeared; the winter sun had already set, and the lamps were lit, casting long shadows. His first wail was high and weak. I was not comforted until he was placed in my arms and I saw for myself that he was a normal infant, if frail. We named him after the late Dauphin and the King, who was pleased beyond description.

Such a strange and wondrous thing, to be a mother! With Clarice, Ippolito, King François, and Henri, I had never received constant affection. But nestling my tiny son against my bosom, I was filled with urgent tenderness, a love that defied all restraint, and knew that it was requited.

"Ma fils," I whispered into the translucent little shell of his ear. *"M'ami, je t'adore . . ."* The words of endearment in a foreign tongue came easily to my lips, though I had never heard them uttered—only seen them written on parchment, in Cosimo Ruggieri's hand.

Little François was beset by fevers and colic, though the French astrologers claimed that he would be a long-lived monarch, greatly loved by his subjects, and would have many siblings. I did not ask Ruggieri to cast his nativity; I knew he wouldn't lie to please me.

I was deeply relieved. With my son's birth, I had purchased the King's loyalty and Henri's gratitude; I had also hoped this would win his love, but he turned increasingly to Diane.

I swallowed my pride and took pleasure in my infant son and in the company of the King, who now lavished gifts on me as if I were his paramour. I spent most of my hours with His Majesty, learning all that I could of government.

I also met daily with Ruggieri, who presented me with a tiny silver talisman of Jupiter to put beneath the baby's crib to bring good health. We never mentioned the murders or his earlier confession of love. At times I would laugh at his dry wit or smile, and the veil of his composure would lift fleetingly to reveal tenderness, but I always pretended not to see it.

Diane continued to make good on her promise to me: Henri visited my bedchamber faithfully. By then my wild ardor had cooled, but that did not stop me from conceiving again.

I was heavily pregnant when my dear friend, Jeanne, returned to Court. Her marriage to the German Duke had been annulled, in part because Jeanne had failed to conceive, but mostly because King François had failed to deliver on promises of military support. I was glad to see Jeanne again; she remained my constant companion and was at my side when I gave birth the following year to my daughter Elisabeth.

Elisabeth was sickly, like little François, and it was some time before we were certain of her survival. She was a docile, content infant who rarely cried; I held her in my arms as she slept and looked down on her sweet, placid face, finally able to believe that my crime was justified.

But the joy brought by Elisabeth's arrival was dimmed by tragedy. The English had invaded the French region of Boulogne, and in the autumn of 1545, Henri's younger brother had joined the battle. During a respite in the fighting, Charles and his companions had come upon a dwelling whose inhabitants had died of plague. Believing himself to be immortal, like so many youths, Charles entered the house fearlessly, mocked the piteous corpses, and used their pillows to playfully beat his men. Within three days he was dead.

His death stole the last of the King's physical reserves. For many years,

François had suffered from an abscess in his privates and infections of the kidneys and lungs; now he worsened dramatically, though grief did not permit him rest. For two years, he traveled compulsively through the countryside, hunting despite his illness; I rode with him. Near the end, he could no longer bear the pain of sitting in the saddle but followed the hunt in a litter. I ignored the chase and trotted slowly alongside, chatting with him while Anne and his band of fair ladies galloped ahead after the prey. Henri had gone to visit Diane in her château at Anet, leaving me to look after his ailing father, but there was nothing I would rather have done.

We moved from lodge to lodge. At Rambouillet, I was riding alongside François when he fainted in his litter. I instructed the pages to take him to his chamber and summon the physician. I expected him to rally; he had fallen desperately sick several times over the past year but had always recovered.

While the doctor was examining His Majesty, the Duchess d'Etampes stormed into the antechamber where I waited.

"What has happened?" she demanded. "Let me go to him!"

Anne was quivering, imperious, still enviably beautiful, but her indignance was born not of honest concern for François but of a selfish desire to ensure her protector still lived. Over the past several months, she and Diane had begun to exchange public insults while secretly lobbying against each other. The courtiers' loyalties were shifting from the ailing King to the Dauphin, with the result that Anne's influence had lessened. Rather than accept the inevitable change, she had grown frantically demanding.

The physician emerged from the King's bedroom. The hair beneath his black velvet skullcap was white; bags of shadowed flesh hung under his eyes. I rose to my feet when he entered, but at the sight of his grief-dulled gaze, I sank back into my chair.

His voice broke as he relayed to me the results of his examination: François's body could bear no more. Although the King was only fifty-two, infections had overwhelmed him. He was rotting from the inside out.

"You lie!" Anne hissed. "He has always recovered. You underestimate his strength!"

I turned to her. "Get out," I said softly. "Get out, Your Grace, and do not set foot into this room until you are called for, else I will summon the guards."

She gasped as though I had struck her. "How dare you," she said, her jaw slack with outrage, but I heard uncertainty in her tone. "How *dare* you . . ."

"Get out," I repeated.

She retreated as far as the corridor, muttering curses beneath her breath.

I ignored her and turned back to the sorrowful, rheumy-eyed doctor. "Are you certain?"

He nodded gravely. "I do not expect him to survive more than a few days."

I steepled my hands, pressed them to my lips, and closed my eyes. "My husband must be sent for at once. He is at Madame de Poitiers's château at Anet . . ."

"I will see that the Dauphin is notified, Madame," the doctor responded kindly. "In the meantime, His Majesty has asked for you."

I banished imminent tears and eased my taut, vacant expression into one more pleasant, then rose and went into the bedchamber.

François was propped up on the pillows, his face grey against the white linens. It was the end of a cold, damp March, and a fire roared in the hearth, leaving the room oppressively warm, yet the King shivered beneath many blankets. The curtains had been drawn and the lamps left unlit, to avoid paining his eyes, which cast the room in twilight. The lines in his brow conveyed misery, but he was altogether lucid, and when he saw me, he managed a wan smile.

I did my best to smile back, but he was not fooled.

"Ah, Catherine," he said, his voice wavering and reedy. "Always so brave. There's no need to dissemble; I know I'm dying. Cry if you wish, my darling. I won't be frightened by your tears."

"Oh, Your Majesty . . ." I clasped his hand. "I've sent for Henri."

"Do not tell Eléonore." He sighed. "I regret that I've treated her badly, especially when I see what you've endured."

I averted my eyes. "It's nothing."

"Oh, but it is. Perhaps . . ." His face crumpled—in physical pain, I thought, until he opened eyes gleaming with tears. "Had I not sent him away to be the Emperor's hostage, perhaps he would have grown to be a different man. But he is weak . . ."

His teeth began to chatter. I tucked the blankets tightly about him, then wrung out a towel from a basin of water and set the damp cloth upon his forehead. He sighed with relief.

"That woman . . ." His lip curled. "She rules him, and so will rule France. Henri has made the same mistake I did. Mark my words: She'll seize all the power she can; she's ruthless, and Henri too much a fool to see it."

The speech exhausted him; he broke off, panting, until he could catch his breath.

"Don't let Anne in here," he said finally. "I have been such a fool." He squeezed my hand. "You and I are alike. I see it in you. You're strong enough to do what is best for the nation, even if it breaks your heart."

"Yes," I said, very softly.

He looked at me with wan affection. "Promise me, then. Promise me that you'll do what is best for France. Promise me that you'll keep the throne safe for my son."

"I promise," I whispered.

"I love you more than my own child," he said.

At that, my composure broke and I sobbed openly.

The physicians bled the King with leeches and dosed him with quicksilver, but he worsened markedly. By morning, he did not know me. Toward the afternoon he grew lucid again and asked for a priest.

Henri arrived late that night. He and his father wished to be alone, without witness to their grief or final words to each other. The Duchess d'Etampes hovered silently in the corridor, her eyes wide with shock.

I sat on the floor in the King's antechamber, my back pressed to the wall, and wept into my hands. François had been my protector and dearest friend. I remained huddled on the floor throughout the long night, listening to the rise and fall of Henri's voice on the other side of the closed door. In the morning, the King's confessor, the Bishop of Mâcon, arrived. I tried to see past the door as it opened, and glimpsed Henri's haggard face, his black eyes raw with grief.

The King never called for me again.

When Madame Gondi came for me at noon, I was too weak to resist but let myself be guided to my room and washed and dressed in clean clothes. I could not rest, but returned to the King's apartments and settled again on the floor near the entrance to his bedchamber. The Duchess d'Etampes again appeared, dazed and carelessly dressed and minus her white face paint and rouge. She did not dare speak to me, but held vigil in the corridor.

In the next room, Henri let go a heartbroken wail; I lowered my face into my hands and wept. The Duchess seemed strangely unmoved until the door to the King's bedchamber opened and the red-eyed Bishop of Mâcon emerged. He turned to me, his head bowed.

"His Majesty the Most Christian King François is dead."

I could not speak, but in the hallway, the Duchess d'Etampes let go a scream.

"May the earth swallow me up!" she wailed—not in grief but in terror. She had abused her power as the King's mistress to harm many and insult all. Apparently she had thought that François would never die, that retribution from her enemies would never come—and now she was unprepared. I remember her dry-eyed panic well—how she clutched first her cheeks, then her head, as if to keep it from suddenly flying off, how she seized her skirts and ran away, her progress hobbled by her fine high-heeled slippers. It was the last time I ever saw her.

I sat down upon the cold floor a princess and rose from it a queen, but took no joy in the fact. As it would the Duchess, change would bring me catastrophe.

PART VI

Queen

March 1547–July 1559

Twenty-four

My husband was transformed by the King's death. Henri wept for his father, but along with his grief came a curious lightness, as if all his anger and pain had died with the old man.

His first official act was to dismiss his father's ministers and summon the former Grand Master, Anne Montmorency, to the palace. Montmorency had fallen out of favor with the King, though his friendship with my husband had remained steadfast.

Montmorency was like Henri and Diane in many ways: conservative, dogmatic, resistant to change. His very being reflected those traits: He was solid and square of build and pompous of bearing, with a long, old-fashioned grey beard and outdated clothes. Henri named him President of the King's Privy Council, a position second only to the King. Montmorency at once moved into the apartment adjacent to the King's—the one hastily vacated by the Duchess d'Etampes, who had fled to the countryside.

I did not like Montmorency, though I respected him. I saw arrogance in his narrowed, deep-set eyes, in his bearing and speech. He was quick to dismiss the opinions of others but was loyal and did not, like so many others, see Henri's accession as an opportunity to increase his own wealth.

The same could not be said of Diane de Poitiers. Not only did she convince Henri to give her all of the Duchess d'Etampe's assets but Diane asked for and received the breathtaking palace at Chenonceaux—royal property that was not Henri's to give. In addition, Henri gave her the taxes collected upon his accession, a veritable fortune. He even gave her the Crown Jewels, an insult I did my best to bear gracefully while my friends howled at the injustice.

To me, Henri gave an annual allowance of two hundred thousand livres.

He also indulged in political matchmaking: He married his cousin Jeanne of Navarre to Antoine de Bourbon, First Prince of the Blood, who would inherit the throne upon the death of Henri and all of his sons. Bourbon was a handsome man, though very vain; he wore a fluffy hairpiece to hide his balding crown and a gold hoop in his ear. By then he had converted to Protestantism, then recanted, then called himself a Huguenot again, as it suited his political aims. I despised his inconstancy but was glad that the marriage brought Jeanne to live at Court again.

Henri also increased the status of the Guise family, a branch of the royal House of Lorraine. His closest friend was François of Guise, a handsome, bearded man with golden hair and magnetic grey-green eyes, who laughed easily. He was warm, charming, and sharp-witted, the sort of man who exuded importance and commanded attention; he could silence a crowd by the mere act of entering the room. Henri elevated him from Count to Duke, and appointed him to the Privy Council.

Henri likewise appointed Guise's brother Charles to the Council. Charles, the Cardinal of Lorraine, was a dark-haired, dark-eyed, brooding political genius known for his duplicity. Their sister, Marie of Guise, was the widow of King James of Scotland and served as regent for her five-year-old daughter, Mary, Queen of Scots.

At the time, Scotland was in turmoil, and the girl Mary was in great danger in her own country.

"Let her come to live with us in the French Court," my Henri said, "where she may grow to her majority in safety. When she is old enough, she will marry my son, François."

Some considered that to be a wise strategy: As a Catholic, Mary was the only monarch of England recognized by the Pope; if she married our son, he would have a claim to the English throne as well as to that of Scotland.

Mary arrived at Blois swathed in tartan, a dark-haired porcelain doll with wide, fear-filled eyes. She knew very little French; she would loose a tumble of harsh, guttural sounds, too coarse to be words, yet those in her entourage understood them. She brought with her bodyguards, brawny, kilted giants with greasy auburn hair and narrowed, suspicious eyes, who frankly stank. The Scots scorned bathing and manners—all except for Mary and her governess, Janet Fleming, a white-skinned beauty with green eyes and hair like sunlight. Madame Fleming was a young widow who quickly absorbed much of French culture and relayed it to her charge.

I was predisposed to like Mary, even to love her: I felt a kinship with this child whose own countrymen had threatened her with death and forced her to flee her home. I understood what it was to be hated and frightened and alone in a foreign land. When I learned of her arrival, I hurried to welcome her.

I entered the nursery without fanfare to see Mary standing beside François, eyeing him critically. She was slight and imperious, with a haughty lift to her sharp chin.

At the sound of my step, she turned and, in thickly accented French, demanded: "Why do you not curtsy? Do you not know that you are in the presence of the Queen of Scotland?"

"Yes," I said easily, with a smile. "Do you not know that you are in the presence of the Queen of France?"

She was thoroughly taken aback; I laughed and kissed her. She returned the kiss, guarded little creature, with lips that smelled of fish and ale; her stiff posture conveyed an intense dislike. She was two years older than my François but already thrice as tall. At three years of age, my son looked barely two, and his intellect was even younger. At times I looked into his dull, unfocused eyes and saw the ghost of the murdered imbecile.

Henri doted on Mary, saying that he loved her more than his own issue because she was already a queen. I bit my tongue at the insult to my children. François and Charles of Guise were delirious at their niece's good fortune: When Henri died, our son would be King and his bride, Mary, would become Queen of France as well as of Scotland.

My husband's accession brought other changes as well. The old King's little band of women was scattered, with the Duchess d'Etampes disgraced and living in anonymity; her closest friend, the dimpled, coquettish Marie de

Canaples, had been denounced as an adultress by her husband and banned from Court. Two of the women had left for Portugal with Queen Eléonore, who had had enough of France and wished to live out her days far removed from intrigue.

On the day my husband was crowned, I sat in a tribune in the cathedral at Reims and fought not to weep as Henri marched to the altar. It was not only pride that triggered my unshed tears but also the gold embroidery upon my husband's white satin tunic, directly over his heart: two large *D*'s back to back, intertwined, over which was superimposed the letter *H*. This was to become his symbol, as the salamander had been his father's, and for the rest of my life I found myself surrounded by Diane and Henri's monogram in tapestry and stone and paint adorning every château. I told myself that I did not care, that I had what I wanted most: Henri's life, and the chance to give him children. Even so, it stung no less.

My own coronation took place two years later, at the cathedral of Saint-Denis, just outside of Paris.

I entered heralded by trumpets, my bodice glittering with diamonds, emeralds, and rubies; my deep blue velvet cloak glinted green with the play of the light. Escorted by Grand Master Montmorency and flanked by Antoine de Bourbon, the most senior Prince of the Blood, I glided to the altar. Beneath my gleaming bodice, the magician's pearl—which had brought me thus far—hung between my breasts.

I genuflected and proceeded to my throne, mounted on a platform draped in gold cloth; the steps leading up to it were covered in the same blue velvet as my cloak. The Cardinal de Bourbon—Antoine's brother—presided over the ceremony. I knelt and prayed on cue, my voice strong as I answered the Cardinal's questions in the affirmative. I had wedded Henri fifteen years ago, and now I was marrying France.

The ancient crown Antoine de Bourbon set upon my head was so heavy that I could not bear it. A second lighter crown was produced, which I wore for the rest of the ceremony.

After Mass was said, I and three other noblewomen were given precious items to place upon the altar in offering before the Holy Sacrament was administered. Diane was chosen to follow directly behind me because my husband had given her the duchy of Valentinois, which elevated her rank and fortune substantially. Before the ceremony, he had also announced that she was now one of my ladies-in-waiting—a fact that offended me no small amount, as it would greatly increase the amount of time Diane would spend in my presence.

I processed down the long aisle with a golden orb in my hands; when I arrived at the altar, I deposited it with the Cardinal de Bourbon, then turned and waited for the other women.

They were long in coming. Diane was to have followed closely but instead moved at a ridiculously languid pace, her gaze directed heavenward, her face aglow with feigned beatific rapture. As she passed beneath the loge where my husband sat, she stood completely still for a long moment—drawing the attention of the entire assembly—then slowly paraded past him.

I watched with rage, though my expression remained consummately dignified. I had thought that Diane would be satisfied with obscene riches and Henri's love—but these were not enough. She wished to steal what little attention I received, even on this day; she wished to make it clear who truly ruled the King.

I reflected, at that instant, on how very easy it would be to kill her—to ask Ruggieri for a potion, or a poisoned glove, or a spell—especially since I had broken through that seductive barrier twice before. But I would never kill to exact personal revenge, only to save those I loved, the same as Cosimo Ruggieri.

Perhaps there is a kinder place in Hell for us.

Twenty-five

The years that followed were difficult. Jeanne's mother, the warmhearted, brilliant Queen Marguerite of Navarre, died shortly before Christmas 1549, leaving her daughter and all those who knew her bereft. Henri spent his days and most of his nights in the company of Diane, while I found joy only when I retreated into the simple pleasures of motherhood.

Henri was frugal and did not waste his days pursuing every pretty woman who caught his eye. Yet unlike his father, he possessed a zeal for persecuting Protestants—a zeal created and nurtured by Diane. Perhaps she thought that burning heretics would make God forget that she was a whore. She shrouded herself in a cloak of piety and virtue, and delighted in drawing a sharp contrast between Henri's "morality" and his father's debauchery. But like his father, Henri was ruled by his mistress: Diane wanted lands seized from Protestants and placed in the hands of Catholics, and Henri accomplished it. She desired to see Protestants imprisoned and executed, and so it was done—although there were many Protestant sympathizers at Court, including Montmorency's young nephew Gaspard de Coligny, Antoine de Bourbon, and the King's own cousin Jeanne of Navarre, who had embraced Martin Luther's teachings during her stay in Germany. Nobility conferred protection; only commoners risked persecution.

Every morning after meeting with his advisers, Henri went to Diane's chambers to discuss government business; he took no action without her approval and delegated so much power to her that she signed royal documents in the King's stead.

Like his father, Henri failed to see the jealousy his mistress's power generated among his courtiers. Nor did he see the dissatisfaction brewing in the countryside, where Protestant villagers were outraged by the new laws forbidding their form of worship. Paris was almost entirely Catholic, so Henri did not listen to the advisers who warned him that his harsh intolerance of the new religion was fostering rebellion. He listened only to Diane, who in turn listened to the Guise brothers. Like Diane, they despised Protestantism and were eager to influence the Crown.

The people's hearts began to turn from Henri, and the Protestants grew to hate him. I spoke privately with him on the matter several times; King François had taught me the importance of earning the people's love. Perhaps I was too direct, for Henri dismissed me abruptly, accusing me of overestimating my own intelligence and underestimating Diane's.

I spent years eclipsed by Diane, years during which my intellect and capabilities were ignored, years when I saw the country harmed and greedy, calculating nobles rewarded by my ingenuous husband. I yearned to speak out but complained to no one, for I had purchased with the prostitute's life exactly what I had requested: I was Henri's wife and mother to his children—and not a whit more.

Diane continued to keep her promise and sent Henri to my bed. I did not realize then that she was so confident in her position that she had begun to shun my husband's physical attentions, and that Henri had begun to look in other arms for solace.

Our son Charles-Maximilien—as sickly as his predecessors, with a red-violet, walnut-sized birthmark just beneath his nose—was born in 1550, three years after Henri assumed the throne. We built a large nursery in the palace King François I had renovated at Saint-Germain-en-Laye, just west of Paris, where Henri had grown up. The chateau was built around a central courtyard, with sweeping lawns that spurred Mary to chase François, but running made my elder son gasp so horribly that he fainted. In the days just after Charles's birth, I watched from my window as Mary ran alone, a swift, solitary little figure on the grassy expanse.

My husband became a solicitous father during Charles's early months, visiting the nursery almost daily. He abandoned the old King's itinerant habit, keeping the Court at Saint-Germain for the children's sake. After Diane broke her leg in a fall from the saddle and went to her château at Anet to recuperate, Henri remained with me at Saint-Germain. I admit, his choice pleased me—until I learned its true cause.

On the first cold night of autumn, I sat in my chamber in front of the mirror while Madame Gondi brushed out my hair. It was late, but I was enjoying our conversation about how little François had been allowed to hold his infant brother, Charles, for the very first time, and how he—after being convinced that the baby's red birthmark was not catching—had kissed Charles and solemnly pronounced him acceptable.

As Madame Gondi and I were speaking, I heard a woman's heartbroken wail coming from the nursery above us. I ran out of my chambers and up the stairs, propelled by maternal urgency.

On the landing, one of Mary's Scottish bodyguards stood beneath the lighted wall lamp. He had heard the cry but had not reacted to it; in fact, he was restraining a knowing smirk.

I ran past him toward the double doors of the now quiet nursery. Just beyond, two figures stood in the wavering light cast by a sconce in front of the closed door of the chamber inhabited by Mary's governess. They were arguing—and at the realization, I stopped half a corridor away in the shadows.

It was Montmorency, broad-shouldered and gray-bearded, his back pressed against the door, his hand upon the latch, and Diane, who leaned heavily upon a crutch tucked under one arm. Apparently she had just traveled all the way from Anet and had rushed into the château without pausing to remove her cloak. The lamplight revealed shadowed hollows beneath her eyes and the slackness of age along her jaw. The hair at her temples was more silver now than gold. She was dressed elegantly in a high ruffed collar of exquisite black lace, accentuated by a large diamond brooch at her throat, and ivory satin skirts embroidered with gold scrollwork. But even such sartorial glory could not hide the fact that she was worn and frazzled, her dignity replaced by shrewishness as she tucked into Montmorency.

"You insult me, Monsieur, with your lies!" she hissed, shaking her forefinger at the Grand Master. "He is in there—I know it! Open the door—or move aside, and I will do it myself."

Montmorency's voice was soothing. "Madame, you are beside yourself. Please lower your voice, lest you wake the children."

"The children!" She released an exasperated gasp. "I am the only one here thinking of the children!" She lurched forward, balancing on the crutch, and reached beyond the solid Grand Master for the door. "Open it now or I will go in myself! I demand to speak to Madame Fleming!"

The door behind Montmorency swung inward, causing him to take a staggering step backward, almost colliding with the man emerging from the governess's room: my husband. Unlike Diane, Henri was in his prime, with his father's long, handsome face and full, dark beard, his attractiveness enhanced by the sort of deep relaxation he showed on returning from a particularly vigorous hunt. His head was bare, his hair tousled; his doublet rode up a bit at the hips. At the sight of Diane, he smoothed down the hem. The room behind him was dark as he shut the door, and Montmorency moved to block it.

At the sight of the evidence that her suspicions were true, Diane averted her face in pain. The three players stood stunned and silent in the face of disclosure until she lifted her wounded countenance again.

"Your Majesty!" she exclaimed, anguished. "Whence do you come?"

At the sight of his livid paramour, Henri directed his attention to the carpet beneath his feet.

"I've done nothing wrong," he murmured, so softly that I strained to hear. "I was only speaking with the lady." Poor guileless Henri, too slow to concoct a feasible lie.

"Speaking!" Diane hissed. "Let me go ask Madame Fleming the subject of your conversation!"

She started again for the door, but Montmorency's bulk stymied her.

"This is unseemly," he scolded her. "You have no right to speak so to the King!"

Henri turned on him with a dangerous look, and Montmorency fell silent at once.

"Your Majesty," Diane said, more quietly yet no less indignantly, "you have betrayed your dear friends the Guises and their niece Queen Mary with such behavior. You have betrayed your son the Dauphin as well, for he is to marry the child who has that—that *woman* for a governess. As for myself—I will not even speak of the hurt."

I marked that she had not thought to mention the betrayal of the King's wife.

"I mean to hurt no one," Henri said, but he could not look at her. "Please, can we discuss this tomorrow? And not here, in the hall, lest we wake the children . . ."

"But it is on their account I must raise the alarm." In the most politic of strokes, Diane loosed her wrath on the Grand Master. "I was told of this. Told that *you,* Monsieur Montmorency, have encouraged this affair. *You* have betrayed the Guises, and thus His Majesty, more than anyone by facilitating an infidelity that has dishonored everyone." She pivoted on her crutch toward Henri. "Do you not see, Sire, that their niece, innocent little Mary, is being raised by a whore? How shall they feel when they learn the truth? If the Grand Master had your interests at heart, he would advise you to avoid that woman."

"It's not his fault," Henri said softly. "It's all mine. Forgive me, Madame, and do not be angry; I can bear anything but your displeasure."

She lifted her chin, composed and regal once more, and told Montmorency, "You have served the King badly and disgraced his friends. Do not cross my path again, Monsieur, or speak another word to me, for I will not hear it."

Montmorency—outraged, yet biting his tongue—looked to the King for support. Henri averted his eyes and gave the Grand Master a short, dismissive nod.

A muscle deep in Montmorency's great square jaw twitched, just above the line of his beard, but he was a man of grace and self-control. He left quickly, his gaze downcast so that he would not have to see Diane gloat.

I remained motionless in the corridor; when Montmorency passed me, he started, but I put a finger to my lips. He could well have alerted Henri to my presence, but he was still angry at Diane and perhaps hoped she might say something to further provoke my hatred. He continued on, leaving me to listen alone.

After Montmorency's departure, Diane spoke first, raw and uncertain.

"Do you love her?"

Henri's countenance displayed the same contrition I had seen when he had first confessed his love for Diane.

"No," he whispered. "No, of course not." His voice rose to a murmur. "It was purely . . . purely the flesh, nothing more. And I *am* ashamed. I had hoped to be able to end it before I hurt anyone. Before I hurt you. But now I can only beg for your forgiveness."

Diane cooled in the face of the King's groveling. "Do not ask my forgiveness, Sire. Ask the forgiveness of your dear friends the Guises, and of little Mary."

He hesitated. "Promise you won't say anything to the Guises."

She studied him a long moment, then answered slowly, "I will say nothing to anyone if you promise that this crime will never be repeated."

He let go a long sigh at the thought of abandoning such pleasure, then squared himself and met her gaze directly. "I swear before God it will not."

Satisfied, she nodded, dismissing him as if she were the monarch and not he, and began to move away haltingly on her crutch.

Henri called softly to her, "Will you be . . . ?" Awkward, he let the question trail.

Diane did not turn back to look at him. "I will be recuperating in my quarters adjacent to the Queen's." The words were frosted, a rebuke.

Henri heard the rejection in them; his shoulders slumped as he turned away. Diane moved toward me and the spiraling staircase that led to my wing, while my husband went in the opposite direction and disappeared quickly. Her progress was slow and her focus on the coordination of the crutch with her step. She did not see me hidden in the shadows, waiting for her to pass. I meant to gloat, to revel in the dark joy that my rival had finally tasted a sip of the bitter draught I had swallowed for so many years. Yet when our gazes met—hers startled, mine knowing—I saw only myself, wounded and unloved.

She must have glimpsed compassion in my eyes, for her own expression softened. She bowed as best she could before continuing on at her painfully slow pace. Pinned carefully at her throat to hide the slackening skin beneath, the diamond caught the lamplight and flashed.

By late December, I knew I was pregnant again and decided to share the happy news with my husband on Christmas Day. That morning, I went to the royal nursery accompanied by Jeanne, Diane, Madame Gondi, three ladies-in-waiting, and a male attendant. This entourage was required to carry all the gifts for the children, including a large rocking horse with a horsehair mane. As always, Jeanne was eager to accompany me to the nursery, as she longed for children of her own.

The day had dawned grey and cloudy; the château's tall rectangular windows overlooked a bleak courtyard of brown grass edged by bare-limbed trees. But the nursery's reception chamber was cheery: Scores of candles burned, their flames dancing in the windowpanes and on the marble floor; a massive Yule log blazed in the hearth. A long table was heaped with glazed chestnuts, walnuts, apples and figs, and little pastries.

The children greeted us with enthusiastic cries. François was not quite seven, with a domed forehead and wide-set, dull eyes; he was smaller than his five-and-a-half-year-old sister, Elisabeth, who was a sweet, dainty child. The two rushed to me as the wetnurse went to fetch the infant Charles from his cradle.

Eight-year-old Mary, the little Scottish Queen, remained at a distance, her expression wary. She was already quite tall, and her imperious manner made her seem far older than she was; many who saw her playing with François thought they were separated by several years. On that day she wore her hair up, several times braided and coiled and wound about with dark pearls. A tartan shawl was fastened to her chest with a round silver brooch. She reminded me of myself at that age—yearning to be a careless child, free with my affections, yet knowing that my life was threatened by those who hated me.

As I bent down to embrace François and Elisabeth, Mary called out to Diane, "*Joyeux Noël*, Madame de Poitiers! What word from my dear uncles?"

"They are riding with the King, Your Majesty," Diane said, smiling. "But they will join us within the hour."

"Good." Mary sighed and presented herself to me for the unwanted kiss. *"Joyeux Noël, Madame la Reine."*

"Joyeux Noël, Mary," I replied. It troubled her, as it always did, that I did not address her by her title, but I preferred to remind her that she was a child, and not yet Queen of France.

The governor of the nursery, Monsieur d'Humières, emerged from one of the children's chambers. A small, quick man given to emphatic gestures, he hurried into the room and bowed.

"*Madame la Reine,* a thousand pardons, but I received word that His Majesty suffered a minor fall during the hunt. He wished for you to know that he and the brothers Guise will be late as he is meeting now with the physician."

Mary's face fell. Poor, infatuated François tried to comfort her, but he often stuttered and could manage only a pitiful repetition of the first sound in Mary's name: "M-m-m-m—"

She silenced him with a kiss.

I did my best to distract the children with the presents. François received his first, a wooden sword copied after his father's real one, with a painted gold hilt. I gave him stern direction as to its careful use, knowing all the while that it was only a matter of time before someone received a minor injury. Elisabeth's rocking horse was so popular that the children argued over who should ride it first.

Then came Mary's present. Jeanne held the large wooden box, with holes drilled along the sides, and had remained at a distance so that the children could not hear the scratching and thumping. But as she stepped forward, a distinct whine emanated from the box's interior, causing Mary's sallow face to light up. The girl hurried to remove the top and freed the little black-and-white spaniel pup within.

She took it into her arms and beamed at me. "Thank you, thank you! May I keep it here, in the nursery?"

I smiled back. "You may indeed."

The rocking horse and sword were abandoned in favor of the dog. François had to be shown how to pet it gently; Elisabeth was timid, so I showed her how the puppy could be coaxed to sit nicely for a bit of apple.

During this happy domestic scene, Mary's governess began conversing loudly with one of her peers in the doorway of Charles's bedroom. I paid little attention to the stream of guttural consonants and trilled *r*'s.

Monsieur d'Humières approached her and her companion and hissed, "Stop this rude behavior! Go present yourselves to the Queen!"

I ignored it all. Since their arrival, the Scots had proven loyal only to Mary and resentful of the due owed my husband and me; their behavior sometimes brought the members of our separate courts to blows.

Madame Fleming replied in tortured French: "I cannot be silent; I am proud, Sir, to announce that I have conceived a child by the King."

I had been offering a piece of apple to the puppy; at that, my arm fell to my side. I caught Diane's gaze, then Jeanne's, and saw from their sickened expressions that they, too, had heard.

Monsieur d'Humières murmured something in a low, scandalized tone.

By this time, Madame Fleming had entered the room, her faint smile one of smug defiance. Diane had once been pretty, but Fleming was a golden-haired work of art, a radiant, emerald-eyed goddess in a green satin gown, with a shawl of blue and green tartan pinned at her shoulder.

"Madame la Reine," she said sweetly and bowed very low. "I have heard a rumor that you are with child. If so, I understand your joy, for I, too, am pregnant by His Majesty."

Jeanne let go a hiss of outrage. Diane was too stunned to emit a sound. Fleming tossed her head, gloating.

Monsieur d'Humières had come into the main chamber, his wildly gesticulating hands filling the air like a scattering flock of birds. "How dare you! How dare you, Madame, insult the Queen! Apologize at once!"

I gestured for Madame Gondi to attend the children and rose. With Diane close behind me, I caught Fleming by the elbow and guided her back to the nearest bedroom.

Once inside the door, I said, my voice low and not particularly pleasant, "It shows incredibly poor taste to discuss such matters in front of the children. You are an unmarried woman, and your condition is nothing less than scandalous."

Fleming did not cower. She was tall, as were all the Scots, and she gazed down her pretty nose at me with contempt.

"You speak of scandal," she said. "Yet you visit the children with the King's former lover."

Former lover . . . Diane gaped, incensed, at the words.

"You will regret that remark," I said evenly. "And you are never to speak of your condition in front of the children again, or you will have me to deal with—and I am not so easily influenced as His Majesty."

Fleming retorted, "Mary, Queen of Scots, is my sovereign, Madame. I answer only to her."

Diane stepped forward and slapped Fleming swiftly, resoundingly. Fleming shrieked and pressed her hand to the offended cheek.

"Forgive my outburst, *Madame la Reine,*" Diane said, glowering at the startled governess, "but I will not suffer such heinous impertinence toward my queen."

"You are forgiven," I answered, my gaze fixed on the governess. "Madame Fleming, you are correct: You are Queen Mary's subject. But I am her guardian, which makes me your employer. I would counsel you to remember that."

I turned my back to her and called for Monsieur d'Humières, who appeared, groveling. Fleming, her eyes filled with tears from Diane's stinging blow, her tongue bristling with Scottish curses, hurried out of the room toward the common chamber and the children.

I said, "Monsieur, please make sure that she goes to her own room and remains there until I give orders to the contrary."

"At once, at once, Your Majesty," he said, and the three of us returned to the common nursery.

In keeping with her abysmal judgment, Fleming had gone directly to Mary, and as the puppy and the other children quailed, stormed, and wept in front of her. Mary at first stroked the puppy in her arms, but as Fleming continued her tirade, Mary grew quite still, her expression darkening.

When Diane and I approached, with Monsieur d'Humières preceding us, the governess fell silent. Mary scowled at us.

"How dare you," she said, her voice low and shaking. "Madame de Poitiers, how dare you strike Miss Fleming! Apologize at once!"

"There is no need for an apology," I countered firmly. "Your governess gave ample provocation. Madame Fleming, go to your chambers and await word from me."

Mary bristled. "She will do nothing of the kind. I want her to stay here."

I studied the tableau—the furious girl, the weeping governess, François frightened into hiccups, Elisabeth hushed—and sighed. "Mary," I said, "there can be no winner when two queens argue. But you are still a child, and I your guardian." I turned to the agitated Monsieur d'Humières. "Monsieur, please escort Madame Fleming to her room."

"No!" Mary cried. She hurled the puppy to the floor with such vehemence that the poor thing yelped.

Elisabeth picked the little dog up and saw that it was not hurt. The temperamental act—involving as it did an innocent creature—set my teeth on edge. I whirled on Mary, ready to chastise her, but she let go a torrent of words.

"She will do as *I* say! I am twice queen, and born to it—not a commoner, a merchant's daughter who made a match far beyond her station!"

Thus I learned how I was perceived—by the Scots and by the Guises, who were waiting for the moment their niece would take the throne of France. Suddenly fierce, I stepped up to Mary and, gazing deep into her hostile little eyes, said very softly, "Yes, I fought my way up from a lower station—all the more reason for you to fear me, my spoiled girl. I *will* win."

Her lips pursed at that, but she recoiled without answer. I turned to Elisabeth and said, "The dog is now yours."

In the end, I summoned one of my own guards to escort Fleming to her room and prevailed upon Monsieur d'Humières to confine Mary to her own chamber. When my husband at last arrived in the nusery with the Guises, limping on his bandaged ankle but cheerful, I allowed Mary to come out so long as she agreed to behave.

Madame Fleming's name did not surface in the conversation. But several times during that long morning, I caught Mary studying my face, her eyes narrowed by a yearning for vengeance.

Twenty-six

Given the unpleasantness in the nursery, I waited to share my news with Henri; that evening, I invited him to my chambers.

He arrived limping on a crutch, thinking that I had invited him to my bed despite his injury. Once the door was closed, I took him into my arms and returned his kiss. He smelled of wine and was flushed from having drunk more than usual, most likely to dull the pain from his ankle.

When I drew back from the embrace, I said, "Henri, before we become distracted . . . I have both happy and unhappy news to share with you."

He tensed at once. "Well, then. Let me hear the unhappy news first."

"The happy is better first this time, I think. I am pregnant again, dear husband."

As eager as I was to tell him, I was also reluctant. Each time he had learned I was carrying a child, Henri had forsaken our marriage bed, underscoring the reality that he had relations with me solely to produce heirs.

He grinned, teeth flashing against his dark beard, and wrapped his arms around me. "Once more you delight me. And what a good mother you are; I saw, in the nursery, how well the children behave."

He kissed me repeatedly—I giggled at the tickle of his wiry beard—then I pulled away and grew solemn.

"Ah," he said. "Now the unhappy news?"

"Now the unhappy," I confirmed. "Janet Fleming is pregnant as well."

His eyes widened with shock in the instant before he turned his embarrassed gaze downward. He dropped his arms and took a step back.

I gestured at a chair. "Please sit, Your Majesty. This matter bears discussion."

He sat down hard; the impact forced a breath from him. "How did you . . . How did you learn this? From Diane?"

"No. From Madame Fleming herself."

His jaw slackened. "She *said* it outright to you?"

"She is quite boastful of it."

"I had hoped you would never know," he said, flushing. "I am not proud of it. I can only beg your forgiveness, and tell you that I promised Diane a fortnight ago that I would have nothing more to do with Janet Fleming. And I have kept my promise."

My manner was infinitely calm. "I did not summon you to accuse you, although I can thoroughly understand Madame de Poitiers's heartache. I ask rather for your help."

He stared at me, astonished. "You're not angry?"

"Only hurt. But there is a matter far more important than my personal unhappiness, or even Diane's," I said. "Madame Fleming is so proud of her condition that she has told everyone. Even Mary and the children know."

"You're jesting." He shook his head in amazement. "I can't believe she would speak of it so freely. How horrible it must be for you. Yet here you are, so calm and understanding . . ." Something in his tone made me think Diane had not reacted quite as well.

"You must send her away, Henri, at least until after the baby is born. She will only cause you embarrassment—not to mention the scandal she visits on Mary and the Guises."

He stared out the window as he considered this. "Mary will not allow it," he said at last. "She loves Madame Fleming."

"Mary is a child," I countered, "and must trust you to do what is best."

He thought for a moment, then gave a slow, reluctant nod. "I will see Madame Fleming sent to the country for her confinement. Of course, I will see that her child is well cared for."

"Of course. Thank you."

"I do not deserve such a patient wife. I cannot—" He broke off, suddenly very near tears encouraged by pain and wine.

"Is all well between you and Diane?" I asked softly.

"Since I gave up Janet Fleming," he answered, "I have been faithful to you alone, Catherine."

Hope, an emotion long buried, stirred within me. "Did Diane cast you from her bed because of the affair?"

His cheeks grew scarlet, the way they had when we'd first met, when he was a shy, tongue-tied boy.

"Long before it, actually. Almost a year before. She . . ." He struggled silently as words and emotions warred. "Somehow, I lost her heart. She is so cold sometimes, so distant. I have given her property, and gold, and honors, everything she ever wanted, and more. . . . Yet she turns me away. She tells me we are no longer children, that we no longer need indulge in even the smallest gestures of affection. I find myself begging for a smile."

I understood his hurt too well. "You have been ill-used for years."

"I can't believe that," he said. "I know that she honestly cared for me. Perhaps she still does. But she is older now, and tired, and I too impatient, so I responded to Madame Fleming's advances. Like a fool, I convinced myself that this beautiful creature was attracted to me, not to the crown I wear. But she is nothing more than an agent of the Guises, determined to enslave me further to their cause."

He shook his head in self-disgust. "As much as I despised my father for his faithlessness, here I am an adulterer, played for a fool by women. I should have sought love in the one place where it has always been constant and patient. Do not think I am blind to your suffering, Catherine. Do not think I am not desperately grateful for you."

He was still seated; I put a hand upon his shoulder and kissed the top of his head. He wrapped his arms around my waist and pressed his face to my bosom. I thought that was the end of our encounter, that he would go, as he always had, and leave me to my empty bed until our child was born. Instead he rose and kissed me tenderly.

"I said once that I could easily love you, Catherine," he whispered. "And I see now that I do."

I drew him to the inner chamber, to my bed. There was a poignant sweetness to our lovemaking, that we should have faltered so many times before finding each other.

In the days that followed, I said nothing to anyone, though surely Madame Gondi suspected that things had changed between Henri and me. My pregnancy had been announced, yet my husband still came almost nightly to my room. For the first time, Henri noticed the pearl that hung above my breasts and reached for it—but I drew his hand away and distracted him with kisses.

Although Diane de Poitiers no longer possessed the King's heart, she continued to possess enormous political power, and my husband lacked the will to cast off her yoke. In public, we played out a great farce: Honors were still paid to the King's mistress, and I was treated as second to her—when, in fact, my husband and I had become lovers. In private, Henri and I discussed Diane's pervasive control of the government and how he might reclaim it, but he lacked the will and the heart to upset her. He did, however, resist giving her any more riches and honors.

Diane's response was to draw closer to the Guises. Unfortunately, during the Fleming affair, Henri had agreed to appoint the golden-haired François of Guise to be his Grand Chamberlain. The Chamberlain oversaw the running of the King's apartments and was always in possession of the keys; in addition, his signature was required on certain royal documents. It was a position more of status than of power, but if anyone could use it to seize more of the latter, it was Guise.

Henri did not tell me of the appointment until it was a fait accompli. He rightly surmised that I would object and chose to wait until we were in bed together after an evening of gentle lovemaking. He kissed my belly and spoke sweetly to the child inside me. I was thoroughly charmed and smiling—until he abruptly confessed to Guise's appointment. The news brought me out of the bed and onto my feet.

Henri waited until I had vented my displeasure, then argued that a move against Diane and François of Guise would upset the delicate balance at Court and throw the government into confusion. That was true, so I calmed and discussed with him what was best for France. Unfortunately, he did not agree that Diane's and the Guises' conservative Catholicism presented the greatest danger; he agreed with them that Protestantism should not be tolerated at all, which frightened me.

From that time on, I grew fearful of the conflict that would come if the Guises' desire to persecute the Protestants was indulged, but I let myself be mollified during my pregnancy by Henri's doting caresses and pushed away all thought of impending political catastrophe.

When our new son was born, Henri was present, laughing and squeezing my hand. Edouard-Alexandre was healthier than my other children, and Henri and I freely lavished affection upon him. Edouard was by far the most handsome, and his presence always reminded me of the loveliest days of my life. Henri and I spent much time together in the nursery, and Henri spent an hour every evening discussing affairs of state with me.

Such an idyll could not last long. When Edouard was only a few months old, my world was again shaken.

For years, my husband had exchanged insults with Emperor Charles, who had held the child Henri and his brother prisoner. A rational man, Henri resisted going to war for slight cause; however, in 1552, the year after Edouard was born, my husband yielded to pleas for help from German princes who hoped to oust the Emperor from their country. They were Lutherans, outraged by the Catholic Emperor's attempts to suppress their religion.

To my astonishment, Henri cooperated with them, agreeing to weaken the Emperor by fighting him on France's northeastern border with an eye to reclaiming the towns of Cambrai and Metz, among others. If Diane saw any irony in the King's rush to aid Protestants in order to defeat a good Catholic, she said nothing. Henri decided that French soldiers would go to war.

And he intended to join them. This terrified me, for it meant that he would leave behind the safe haven created by the onyx talisman hidden beneath Diane's bed.

My anxiety was not helped when I received a letter from the venerable Luca Guorico in Rome. Ser Luca was greatly respected for his work in judicial astrology, the branch that studied the influence of the stars on the fates of individuals. When my great-uncle Giovanni de' Medici was only fourteen years old, Luca Guorico had predicted that he would become Pope—and indeed,

Uncle Giovanni became Pope Leo X. Guorico had also predicted Alessandro Farnese's ascension to Pope, and his death, with uncanny accuracy.

When Madame Gondi placed an envelope from Rome into my hands, I broke the wax seal with trepidation. Inside was a letter to me and a second sealed letter, folded into thirds, addressed to my husband.

Your Most Esteemed Majesty, Donna Caterina,

Please forgive my boldness in writing you, and not your husband directly. I have heard that His Majesty is indisposed to heed the advice of astrologers, and so I turn to you for help, for I know that you are quite knowledgeable about astrology and sympathetic to its aims.

I have charted the progression of your husband's stars over the course of the next several years. As a result, I am convinced of the need to warn King Henri to exert extreme caution at certain times and in specific situations.

The danger to His Majesty is great. May I prevail upon you, Your Majesty Donna Caterina, to present the enclosed letter to him, and to use your influence to persuade him to heed its advice?

The temptation to break the seal on the second letter and read it was nearly overwhelming, but I set the letter aside and waited until Henri came to my chambers to discuss the affairs of the day.

When he entered my room, I handed him the sealed document in lieu of a greeting. "You have received a letter from Rome, Your Majesty. From Luca Guorico."

"Do I know him?" he asked wearily, settling into a chair as he took the letter. He had spent a long day in his cabinet discussing plans for the war, first with his loyal old friend Montmorency, then with François of Guise—the two advisers were so politically opposed that Henri did not meet with them together, as the discussion would quickly degenerate into argument.

"The famous astrologer," I prompted. "The one who said my uncle Giovanni would become Pope."

"Ah," he said dismissively and slipped the letter into his belt. "I will deal with the machinations of fate later. I am done with serious thinking for the day."

"Please!" At the unintended sharpness in my voice, he glanced at me in mild surprise. "Please," I said more gently, "will you not at least look at it?"

"Catherine, you brood too much about these things."

"Monsieur Guorico also wrote to me." I settled into the chair beside him. "He has discovered something in your stars and means to warn you."

"Warn me of what?"

I looked pointedly at the letter in his hand. "He did not tell me."

"I will read it then," he sighed. He opened the letter and scanned it. As he read, a line above the bridge of his nose gradually deepened.

"It's nothing," he said. "He warns me against single combat—against duels, not battles, so there is no danger in my going to the front. And it is nothing I need worry about for many years." He refolded the letter and stuffed it into his belt.

It was impertinent even for a queen to violate the King's privacy, yet I could not restrain myself. "Please, Henri, I must know what he has told you."

"Look at the fear in your eyes," he chided. "You have gotten yourself agitated over nothing. Why do you continue to believe in such things?"

"Because astrology is like medicine, Henri—a gift from God to aid the suffering. I have seen the proof with my own eyes."

He snorted. "It's that sickly looking magician who shadows you like a ghost. Why do you surround yourself with such people? There's nothing of God in him—he looks more like he speaks daily to the Devil."

"Monsieur Ruggieri saved my life in Florence," I countered hotly. "He gave me a talisman. I never would have survived without it."

"You would have survived just as well with nothing." Henri shook his head. "That man fills your head with strange notions. I've a mind to send him away."

The French doors leading to the balcony were shut; night had left the glass unrevealing, but I studied a point far beyond it.

"When I was a girl," I said quietly, "just before the rebels imprisoned me, Ruggieri gave me a talisman for protection." Henri began to interrupt, but I stayed him with my hand. "He also told me that I would never rule Florence. He said that I would move to a strange land and marry a king." I did not add what had finally convinced me: Ruggieri's summoning of my dead mother, and her prediction that Ser Silvestro would rescue me. Henri remained silent, but one corner of his mouth quirked with ill-concealed skepticism.

I continued. "He also spoke to me about the dreams that have tormented me since that time. I dream that you lie bleeding and I must save you, but I don't know what to do. You speak to me in French—and always did, even before I learned the language. The day we first met, I recognized you, because I had already known you for years."

"Catherine . . ." Henri's tone held both disbelief and dawning amazement.

"I have tried . . ." I faltered as a wave of emotion broke over me. "All my life, I have tried to understand what I must do to protect you. It's what God means me to do. So don't scoff, and don't push me away."

"Catherine," he said, this time gently. He could see that I was distraught and took my hand.

Tears slid down my cheeks, though my voice remained calm. "That's why I wanted Ruggieri to come to France—to save you from evil, not to bring it—and that's why I'm so curious to know what Luca Guorico told you. I would die for you, Henri."

I did not say, *I have already killed.*

We were silent a long time—I, struggling to gather myself, he, clasping my hand.

"Then we will not send Monsieur Ruggieri away, since his presence comforts you," he said at last, "though I do not believe in his methods." He took the folded letter from his belt and handed it to me. "Because you are so desperate to help, I will not hide this from you."

I unfolded it with an unpleasant thrill.

Your most greatly esteemed Majesty,

My name is Luca Guorico. Her Majesty Donna Caterina may have told you that I am a horoscopist who focuses my art on determining the fate of illustrious persons.

After studying your stars, I must warn you urgently to avoid all combat in an enclosed space. Duels and single combat present the greatest peril, and could lead to a mortal blow to the head.

This danger remains constant but will be magnified greatly a few years hence, in your fortieth year, as the result of an evil aspect made by Mercury to Mars as the latter moves through your ascendant, Leo the royal lion. I warn you in hopes that foreknowledge and caution will allow you to survive this treacherous period. This is quite possible, for my investigation has revealed that you survived an earlier period of comparable risk without incident.

May God bless and guide you and see you safely through all hazards.

For a few moments, I sat with the letter open on my lap before turning to Henri, who now sat beside me.

"Promise me that you will never go to war again," I begged.

His brows lifted. "Of course I'm going. I *must* lead the troops. Didn't you read the letter carefully? War doesn't occur in enclosed areas, and I'm not challenging anyone to a duel."

The same anguished helplessness I felt in the dream tugged at me. Henri was so close, yet there was nothing I could do to keep him there beside me; he would—like my mother, my father, Aunt Clarice, and King François—slip too easily from life into shadowy memory.

"War is unpredictable. What happens if you find yourself in a building, faced by a single assailant?" I demanded. "If I lose you . . ."

"Catherine," he soothed. "We've only just found each other, after all this time. I promise that you won't lose me. Not now."

"Then take a talisman with you."

"I need no such thing," he answered gently. "If God sent you to protect me, then He will hear you. Pray for me, and that will be enough to bring me home safely."

He would not listen when I tried to explain that God did not hear my prayers.

Twenty-seven

Before he left for the war in the northeast, Henri appointed me his regent. With the country mine to run, I discovered that I had both the taste and the aptitude for it. My memory was keen, and I enjoyed the exercise of recalling each word uttered by Henri's advisers. Coupled with my gentler, more diplomatic method of governing, this talent won me support and admiration. I pored over each letter Henri or his generals sent from the front and made sure that funds and supplies were constantly available for them; I even grew bold enough to offer military advice.

Victory came quickly; within months, the towns of Toul, Verdun, and Metz were ours. My husband distinguished himself in battle, as did François of Guise, and the campaign further solidified the friendship between them.

Henri left for war in late January and returned to my arms in late June, brimming with optimism. By August I was pregnant again. This time I did not remain sequestered in my chambers or the nursery but sat in on cabinet meetings with Henri and his ministers. Montmorency and Diane soon learned that I was no longer the silent, invisible Queen.

Henri began to spend more time with the First Prince of the Blood, Antoine de Bourbon. I approved heartily of this, for Bourbon despised the Guises. He was also a Protestant again by that time, as was his wife, Jeanne.

I hoped that Henri's relationship with the man would soften his prejudice against non-Catholics.

While Henri spent more time with Bourbon, I spent a good deal of time with Jeanne. She assisted the midwife at the birth of my daughter, whom I named Marguerite, in honor of Jeanne's mother, though we all called her Margot. In the difficult hours before Margot's birth, Jeanne confessed that she had just learned of her own pregnancy.

My dark-eyed, dark-haired Margot, as precocious and stubborn as her own mother, was born on the thirteenth of May, 1553. Jeanne's son, Henri of Navarre—named to honor both his grandfather and my husband—was born seven months later, on the thirteenth of December. I remained beside Jeanne throughout her labor, just as she had stayed with me throughout mine. And when I first held her squalling newborn son, love pierced me as keenly as if he were my own.

Even then, I believed the two children were linked by fate. When Jeanne's father died a year later, leaving her Queen of Navarre, she chose to remain in France for her son's education. Little Henri, or Navarre, as I sometimes called him, grew up at the Court and spent his days playing with my children in the royal nursery and sharing their tutors. He and Margot became especially attached to each other.

For many years, I would not understand just how intricately their fates were intertwined, or how deeply both were bound to the coming bloody tide.

This is how a dozen years of my marriage passed. As I lived them, I perceived them to be difficult and tumultuous, but perspective has revealed them to be sweet and halcyon compared with the evil that followed. I was deeply relieved that Henri did not return to war, though he and Emperor Charles remained enemies. Shortly after Margot's birth, a new queen ascended the throne of England: Mary Tudor, champion of Catholicism, determined to purge her country of the Protestant blight. Perhaps we should have been glad of the fact, but when Mary wed King Philip, uniting the thrones of England with Spain to create an invincible military giant, I grew uneasy.

Three years after Margot's birth, I became pregnant again. My stomach grew so distended that I soon realized I carried more than one child. A strange dread settled over me during my confinement. I had labored hard to forget my crimes, but the memory of them began to overwhelm me. My fear was underscored by an event in the last moments of my last pregnancy.

Henri had continued his father's tradition of collecting a copy of each book printed in France; my librarians knew to bring works of interest to my attention.

Such was the case with a volume titled *Les Prophéties,* written by Michel de Nostredame—in the Latin, Nostradamus—a physician renowned for saving victims of plague. Monsieur de Nostredame's work consisted of hundreds of verses—four-lined quatrains—each of which contained a prophecy. The references were oblique, arcane. I understood little of what I read until I reached the thirty-fifth quatrain.

On a warm night in June, I was lying propped up against the pillows in my bed, uncomfortable and sleepless because of the weight in my belly and the relentless kicking of two pairs of little legs. I had chosen to give birth at the Château at Blois, and that night, the dank air rose from the Loire River, bringing with it the stink of decay. I had trouble balancing the heavy book on my swollen stomach and was about to give up the effort when I turned the page, and my gaze fell upon these lines:

The young lion will overcome the old, in
A field of combat in a single fight. He will
Pierce his eyes in a golden cage, two
Wounds in one, he then dies a cruel death.

I sat up with a gasp, recalling the words penned by the great astrologer Luca Guorico:

I must warn you urgently to avoid all combat in an enclosed space. Duels and single combat present the greatest peril, and could lead to a mortal blow to the head.

Fear wrung my midsection like a sponge. I cried out at the sudden physical spasm and let the heavy book slide off my lap.

The labor of childbirth had always gone easily for me, but the agony that gripped me now was malicious, dire and unknown. I climbed out of the bed, but when my foot touched the floor, pain felled me.

I went down shrieking for Madame Gondi, for Jeanne, and, most of all, for Henri.

I am stout in the face of pain, but this labor was so cruel and protracted that I thought I would die before the first infant was born.

Jeanne sat beside the birthing chair, and Henri visited me at the beginning of the labor, gripping my hands when the pains worsened and encouraging me throughout the long morning and into the heat of the summer afternoon. We pretended that the added agony I experienced augured nothing ominous, that it was only because there were two children instead of one. My longest previous labor had endured ten hours—but when ten hours had passed, then twelve, without progress, our anxiety increased. When the evening lamp was lit, I was no longer able to maintain a cheerful front. Henri paced helplessly until I grew peevish and told him to leave. Once he had gone, I lost myself to the pain, barely aware of Jeanne's soft, perfumed hands bearing cool compresses, of the midwife's whispered instructions. I fainted, and woke to find that I had been spirited from the wooden chair to my own bed.

The first infant, Victoire, arrived at dawn, almost thirty-six hours after the initial excruciating spasm. She was weak and grey, with a sickly mewl, but her arrival brought joy to Jeanne and the midwife, who thought that this signaled the end of my travail. But her birth brought only a glimmer of relief before the savage pain returned.

I slid into delirium. I cried out for Aunt Clarice, for Sister Niccoletta, for my dead mother; I cried out for Ruggieri. I must have called out for Jeanne, for when I came to myself, she was clasping my sweaty palm.

The hairline part at the center of the velvet drapes glowed with dying orange light. I felt the midwife's rapid breath upon my legs, smelled a familiar perfume, heard soft weeping. I wanted to tell Jeanne that I was going to name the second girl for her but found I could not speak.

The lamplight caught the curve of Jeanne's cheek, turned the crimped curls at her temple into a glowing halo. Her voice was stern, as if she were explaining a hard fact to an unreasonable child.

"Catherine, the midwife must remove the baby now, to save your life. Squeeze my hand, and yell if you must. It will be over quickly."

I gripped Jeanne's hand. The midwife's deft hands added to my anguish; I ground my teeth when her fingers found the unborn child inside me and remained silent when I felt that child turned.

The midwife's hands came together inside me, clutching little limbs. They moved swiftly, sharply; I heard—no, *felt*—the crack of tiny bones and screamed at the realization that the little girl was still alive, and they were maiming her, killing her, in order to save me. I flailed and shrieked and thrashed against those who wept as they held me down.

I wailed at Jeanne that God was punishing me because I had purchased my children with the darkest magic. I begged her to let me die instead, to put things right; I begged her to go to Ruggieri, to have him undo the spell.

I remember nothing more.

The infant Jeanne died at birth as a result of the wounds inflicted by the midwife. I hovered in feverish limbo for two weeks, then rose from my bed to learn that Victoire, the twin who had survived, was dying.

I went to my tiny, gasping daughter. For three days I sat in the nursery, holding her in my arms, staring into her pinched yellow face, feeling as though my heart were melting and spilling out all my love onto her. I whispered apologies into her perfect little ear; I begged for forgiveness. She breathed her last with her father standing close beside us.

I sat motionless by the infant's body for hours. No one, not even the King, disturbed me.

In my sorrow, I did not see the pane of light that appeared when the nursery door was cracked open; I did not hear the feather-light tread upon the marble. But I sensed someone beside me and looked down at my elbow to see a little boy plucking my sleeve. It was Henri of Navarre, then two and a half years old, his round head covered with dark curls, his little brow furrowed with worry.

"*Tante* Catherine," he lisped. "*Chère Tante,* don't be sad."

"But I *must* be sad," I told him. "Your little cousin Victoire has died."

"Ah," he said, considering this, and fidgeted a bit before adding: "But she didn't know us, so she won't miss us in Heaven."

I could answer only with tears.

Stricken at the sight of them, he exclaimed with anguished sincerity, "Poor *Tante*! I can pretend to be one of the babies that you lost. And I promise to be very, very good."

I put my arms around him.

"My little Henri," I said. "My darling, my own."

Ruggieri and a thousand others sent condolences the following day, but I was of a mind to receive no one. Instead I summoned Madame Gondi to my cabinet and dictated a letter to Michel de Nostredame of Provence.

During the weeks I awaited a reply, I began again to dream.

Twenty-eight

I received the great prophet Nostradamus as I would a dear friend or relative: informally, in the comfort of my antechamber. As the door swung open to admit him, I sat alone beside the cold hearth—I had dismissed everyone, even Madame Gondi—and forced a wan smile.

He entered limping, leaning heavily upon a cane; evidently, God was more interested in relaying visions of an ominous future than in relieving gout. He was astonishingly unremarkable-looking: short, stout, and grey-haired, with an unfashionably long beard and drab, worn clothing rumpled by travel.

"Madame la Reine," he said, in the soft voice of a southerner; his face was round and fair, his eyes, gentle and devoid of self-importance. He had been born a Jew, but his father had converted to Christianity and adopted the most Catholic of surnames, in honor of the Virgin. He removed his cap and, balancing precariously on his cane, bowed; his thinning hair spilled forward to hide his face.

"I am honored and humbled that you would summon me," he murmured. "I pray to be of service to you and to His Majesty in whatever manner pleases you. Ask for my life, and it is yours." His voice and hands trembled. "If there is any question of heresy or devilry, I can only say this: I have endeavored all my life to serve God alone, and wrote down the visions at His express bidding."

Madame Gondi had told me that he had been obliged to move from village to village in Provence to avoid arrest; I realized, with a surge of compassion, that he was terrified. For all he knew, he was walking into an inquisitional trap.

"I do not doubt that, Monsieur de Nostredame," I said warmly, smiling, and extended my hand. "That is why I have asked for your help. Thank you for traveling such a distance, in your discomfort, to see us. We are deeply grateful."

He let go a shuddering sigh and tottered forward to kiss my extended hand; his hair brushed softly against my knuckles. As he straightened, he turned his head and caught sight of the window; he forgot his nerves entirely and grew very focused, very calm.

"Ah," he said, as if to himself. "The children."

Outside, on the sprawling grassy courtyard, Edouard and little Navarre were tearing after Margot, ignoring the warnings of the governess to slow down. It was midmorning, hot and sultry, yet strangely grey; dark clouds had gathered early over the river Loire in anticipation of a sudden August storm.

I managed a faint smile at the sight. "His Highness Prince Edouard likes to chase his little sister."

"The two younger ones—the little boy and girl—appear to be twins," the prophet said, his sloping brow furrowed.

"They are my daughter Margot and her cousin, Henri of Navarre."

"The resemblance is remarkable," he murmured.

"They are both about three years old, Monsieur; Margot was born on the thirteenth of May, Navarre on the thirteenth of December."

"Tied by fate," he said. He looked back at me with pale grey eyes that were very large and frankly piercing, like a child's. "I once had a son," he said sadly, "and a daughter."

I had heard of this: Renowned as a healer and physician, he was famed for saving many sick with plague—but when his own wife and children were stricken, he had been unable to save them.

"Forgive me for mentioning my own sorrow, *Madame la Reine,* but I learned recently that you mourn the loss of two little girls. There is no worse tragedy than the death of a child. I pray that God will ease your grief, and the King's."

"Thank you, Monsieur de Nostredame," I said, then changed the subject quickly, so that I might not cry. I gestured at the chair across from mine, with the footstool placed there expressly for him. "You have suffered enough on my behalf. Please sit down. Shall I tell you when the children were born?"

"You are too gracious, Your Majesty. Yes, that would be lovely." He settled into the chair and propped his foot up on the footstool with a little groan.

"Do you require pen and paper, Monsieur?" I asked.

He tapped his forehead. "No, I shall remember. Let us start with the eldest, then."

I told him the specifics of the boys' births. I did not give him the girls', as, under Salic law, a woman could not ascend the throne of France.

"Thank you, *Madame la Reine,*" Monsieur de Nostredame said, when we were finished. "I will give you my full report within two days. I have already done some preparations, since the dates of the boys' births are widely known."

He did not make as if to rise, as one might have expected; he gazed at me with those clear, all-seeing eyes, and in the silence that followed, I found my voice.

"I have evil dreams," I said.

He tilted his head—intrigued, but not at all surprised. "May I speak candidly, then, *Madame la Reine*? I am not the first astrologer to chart the children's nativities. You already have this information, do you not? You called me here for another reason."

I nodded. "I've read your book," I said and recited the thirty-fifth quatrain, about the lion dying in a cage of gold.

His gaze grew clouded. "I write what God bids me, Madame la Reine. I do not presume to understand its meaning."

"But I do." I leaned forward, no longer hiding my desperation. "My husband—he is the lion in the verse. I dreamt—" My voice broke.

"Madame," he said gently, "you and I understand each other well, I think—better than the rest of the world understands us. You and I see things others do not. Too much for our comfort."

I turned my face from him and stared out the window at the garden, where Edouard and Margot and little Navarre chased one another around green hedges beneath a hidden sun. I closed my eyes and saw instead a great scorched battlefield, where my husband thrashed, drowning, in a swelling tide of blood.

"I don't want to see anymore," I said.

"God does not give us that choice."

"The King will die," I said, with faint heat. "That is the meaning of the thirty-fifth quatrain, is it not? My Henri is destined to die too young, a terrible death in war, unless something is done to stop it. You know this; you have written of it, in this poem." I leveled my gaze at him. "And I have dreamt, since I was a small girl, that a man who cried out to me in French would die in a pool of blood upon a battlefield. I did not know who this man was until I met my husband."

"I am sorry, Madame," he responded sadly. "If God has sent you these visions, you must strive to discover why He has done so. You have the responsibility."

"I have a responsibility to keep the King safe," I said. "I have a responsibility to my children. And I have spent my life trying to understand, trying to learn what I am to do."

Monsieur de Nostredame lowered his gaze to the pattern on the carpet. His expression remained placid; he might have been praying.

"Perhaps," he suggested, "you are meant to do nothing. Perhaps you are meant only to write your visions down."

My tone grew brittle. "Or perhaps not all of your prophecies come true. Perhaps they are meant as warnings, just as my dreams are warnings, so that danger can be averted. Is that not possible, Monsieur?"

He did not look up. His features had grown slack, his breathing slow and deep.

"Ah!" he exclaimed, his eyelids fluttering. "How the blood wells! How it streams from his face!"

"Yes," I whispered, then more loudly: "Yes. But this danger can be avoided. The future can be changed, can it not?"

"Yesterday, today, tomorrow," he murmured, "all are the same in the Almighty's eyes. Just as one cannot change the past, so one cannot change the ordained future."

My hands tensed upon the arms of the chair. "My husband has been warned that he could sustain a mortal wound in battle. His stars are instructive: If he avoids battle and does not lead his men into war, then he will be safe. This is the very basis of astrology, Monsieur. You must tell me whether war is coming again for France. You must tell me what can be done to stop it."

"War comes," he said. "War always comes, and there is little you or I can do to stop it."

"But surely you know when," I said. "When did you first have this vision of the two lions, Monsieur? Many years ago?" I told myself that it must have come before Ruggieri had cast the spell using the prostitute's blood, before we had made Henri safe.

"Five years ago," Monsieur de Nostredame replied. "But even now, I see it with the eye of spirit. The prophecy holds."

"This cannot be true! Please, Monsieur . . . Henri is my life, my soul. If he dies, I would not want to live. You must tell me what more I can do."

His eyes snapped full open. His stare was wide and frank. "One does not thwart God, Madame."

"But God is merciful."

"God is just," the prophet answered softly.

"And He listens to prayer," I countered. "Therefore, if one beseeches Him heartily enough—"

"As Christ beseeched Him, in the Garden of Gethsemane?" His tone remained gentle. "Prayed to be spared a bitter death—knowing that crucifixion was inevitable?" He shuddered, then just as abruptly went limp in the chair. When he spoke again, it was with another's voice.

"These children," he sighed. *"Madame la Reine,* their stars are marred. These children should not be."

I put a hand to my heart, where the pearl hung, and feigned anger. "What a horrible thing to say to a mother. What a cruel thing."

He ignored the lie. "The tapestry of history is woven of many threads, Madame. Let even one be exchanged for another that is weak and flawed, and the veil will tear." His eyes, now fire-bright, focused on me. "The veil will tear, and blood be loosed, more blood than you have seen in any dream. Reparations must be made."

I stared at him, sickened. No doubt, with the eyes of spirit, he saw her just as I did: the prostitute, her dull eyes wide at the touch of Ruggieri's blade against her throat. Yet I could not bear to confess the truth aloud, even to him.

I whispered, "I do not understand..."

"You think that you are heartless, Madame," he said. "Far from it. Beware of tenderness. Beware of mercy. Do not spare those who have your heart. Even so, restitution will not come easily. More blood will be spilled."

Restitution: He spoke of Henri and the children, I knew. He wanted me to abandon my loved ones. He wanted me to undo the spell. I rose abruptly, forcing him to emerge from his reverie, to fumble for his cane, to struggle to his feet.

"Our audience is over, Monsieur," I said coldly. "You are quite right—I have many astrologers and have no need of your services at this time. Please rest tonight at Blois before continuing on your way. May your journey home be pleasant, and may God protect you."

He looked on me with empathy so deep it broke my heart.

"It was hard," he whispered. "So hard, when I lost my wife and children. But it was God's will, Madame. God's will."

It was the man who spoke, not the oracle, but I could not bring myself to reply. Seething, imperious, I rang for Madame Gondi, then watched as she led the prophet away.

I returned to my chair, lowered my face, and dug the tips of my fingers into my brow, my temples. I remained thus, my mind and emotions a swirl of confusion, until a peculiar instinct prompted me to rise.

I went to the large window overlooking the courtyard where the children were playing. There had been some emergency: Edouard and Charles were shouting and pointing at a pile of rocks while the governess comforted wailing Margot. The situation must have been serious, for Jeanne herself had appeared on the grassy lawn and was kneeling beside her son, talking to him.

Nostredame appeared, leaning hard upon his cane, and made his way laboriously across the lawn until he stood a polite distance from Jeanne. He spoke to her; whatever he said made her rise and smile, then watch curiously after him as he retreated. The sight filled me with dread: Other than Ruggieri, Jeanne was the only person who knew I had resorted to dark magic in order to conceive. How much more horrified would she have been had I confessed that I had bought my children with the blood of others?

I hurried out of my apartment and down the spiraling stone staircase to the courtyard. By the time I had crossed the grassy lawn to arrive at Jeanne's side, the seer was gone, no doubt on his way to his guest chamber.

"Maman!" six-year-old Charles bellowed rudely, so excited that he had forgotten his manners. "*Maman,* Margot was almost bitten by a snake!"

My shock was genuine. "A snake? Where is it now?"

"Gone," Edouard said, as I deflated with relief. "Margot climbed onto that pile of rocks"—he pointed—"and while she was standing there, Henri told her to get down, because the snake was near her foot, ready to bite her!"

"Henri!" I exclaimed. "How good of you to save Margot!"

Little Navarre blushed and turned back to his mother's arms. Jeanne gave him a squeeze and beamed proudly. "He's a brave, good boy," she said.

I turned to give Margot a hug and listen to her excited rendition of the story; when she was done, Edouard whispered in my ear.

"The snake was under the rocks, *Maman.* Little Henri couldn't have seen it. None of us could see it until Henri took a stick and pushed the rock away. But he knew exactly where it was. He told Margot to get away from it."

I smiled indulgently, certain that I was listening to a child's embellished tale. "How amazing."

"Henri sees things," Edouard hissed. "Things that aren't there."

"Very good," I said, my tone dismissive. I signaled for the governess to collect the children and distract them so that I might speak to Jeanne privately.

Jeanne looked after her son with a faint smile. "The snake was more frightened than the children, I think; it escaped at the first opportunity. My Henri must have glimpsed it coiled beneath the rock."

"Monsieur de Nostredame," I said. "What did he say?"

"What?" She blinked. "Oh, is that his name?" Her tone grew amused.

"He fancies himself a soothsayer. I was offended at first by his forwardness, but he was pleasant enough."

"Yes," I said, impatient, "but what did he tell you?"

She gave a little laugh. "He made the somber pronouncement that I had given birth to a king. And I said, 'But Monsieur, I am Queen of Navarre—so of course my son shall one day be King.' It was all rather funny. What a silly little man."

"Yes," I said. "Yes. What a silly little man."

Monsieur de Nostredame spent one night at Blois. His carriage left at dawn, and when I rose from my bed later that morning, I found that he had left me a quatrain, scrawled in a looping hand:

One skein still runs true
Restore it, and avert the rising tide of evil
Break it, and France herself will perish
Drowned in the blood of her own sons

I was sorely tempted to cast it into the fire; my heart had already been shattered by the deaths of the twins, and Nostredame had dared to pierce it again.

Instead, I refolded it and put it in a compartment hidden in the wainscoting on my cabinet wall.

Those who have never lost a child at or before birth think that the grief would be less than for an older child or an adult, but they fail to account for the peculiar ache of loving someone one has never known. I cloistered myself in the months after the twins' deaths, refusing to hold audiences or ride on the hunt or even to eat with my family. When my husband asked whether he might resume his evening visits to my chamber, I produced excuses until he stopped asking. I endured the regular company of no one but my necessary ladies, and my friend, Jeanne.

I conferred once with Ruggieri, who could not entirely hide his jealousy that I had summoned the famous Nostredame. Even if Monsieur de Nostredame had foreseen my husband's death, Ruggieri said, the future was malleable. The seer was wrong: God indeed heard prayers. I did not have the heart to ask him whether the Devil heard them, too.

Twenty-nine

My husband's longtime nemesis, the old and ailing Emperor Charles, unofficially abdicated in January 1556, leaving his brother Ferdinand to rule the German countries and his son, Philip, to rule Spain, Naples, and the Low Countries. I was happy to hear the news, thinking it would bring peace.

But war came in my husband's thirty-ninth year. One of Philip's viceroys, the Duke of Alba, launched an attack on the entire southern region of Campania in Italy. Alba's army secured the area with startling speed and began marching toward Rome.

The new Pope, Paul IV, remembered the horrors wrought on the Holy City by invading Imperial troops more than two decades earlier. Terrified, he begged my husband for military aid.

Henri acquiesced, and sent François of Guise to Campania in his stead, at the head of a large army. Guise was a brilliant strategist and swore not only to protect Rome but to take Naples for France. We had great hopes that the campaign would go swiftly, but our Italian allies failed to produce either the funds or the men they had guaranteed.

We soon discovered that Alba's attack had been part of a trap: Once we sent Guise and his army to Italy, Philip's Imperial ally, the Duke of Savoy, invaded the region of Picardy, on France's northeastern border with the Empire.

Henri sent his old friend Montmorency to lead the fight against Savoy's invaders. Montmorency took with him his nephew, the brilliant but arrogant Admiral Gaspard de Coligny. Before leaving for Picardy, they conferred with the King and decided upon a strategy that Coligny swore could not fail.

In the final, brutal days of August, Montmorency and his men met the Imperial invaders at the French stronghold of Saint-Quentin, near the banks of the river Somme. My husband was a day's ride away; in spite of my protests, he had insisted on being close enough to the battlefield to stay in constant touch with Montmorency. I served as the King's regent in Paris, only two days' ride from the front, a fact that made the citizens apprehensive.

I was at supper with Jeanne and the children when a messenger appeared at the door. Haggard and gasping from his long ride, the young officer wore an expression of total despair; before he could utter a word, I excused myself and stepped out into the hall, closing the door behind us.

"What news?" I demanded, rigid with dread.

"I come from His Majesty," the young man gasped, and I went limp with relief.

"The King is well?" I asked.

"The King is well," he confirmed. "But our army has suffered a terrible loss at Saint-Quentin. A third of our men were killed . . . and Constable Montmorency and his top officers have been captured and are on their way to a Spanish prison."

I closed my eyes at the news. I grieved for the dead, but at least their suffering was over: I mourned more for Montmorency and the humiliation and torture he would now endure.

"The King," I said. "Tell me that he does not plan to rally the troops, to lead them himself in the fight against the Duke of Savoy."

"His Majesty is returning to Paris to confer with advisers. He has sworn to avenge this defeat."

My legs threatened to give way; I pressed a hand to the wall and leaned heavily against it. "Thank you," I whispered. "Thank you . . ."

I heard only that Henri was coming home to Paris—to me. Tears of relief stung my eyes; I believed, foolishly, that my husband would never return to the battlefield and would be spared.

I did not know, then, that Montmorency's imprisonment would bring about the very thing I most feared.

King Philip of Spain was not the brilliant strategist his father had been. He should have ordered his troops to march directly to Paris, which they could easily have captured; instead, he ordered his men to take several small northern towns—a waste of time that worked to our advantage. Winter loomed, forcing Philip's men to retreat.

In the interim, my Henri returned home. I scarcely saw him: He spent the entire day closeted with his advisers, discussing plans too secret to share with his wife. Henri aged quickly during those bitter months: shocks of white appeared at his temples, lines beneath his eyes. His smile, which had once come so easily, now was infrequent and haggard.

I worried at a distance. The nursery was my only distraction—and even that joy was tempered by disappointment. François was almost fourteen, the age his father and I had been when we had married—but my son was still mentally and physically a child. His sister Elisabeth, almost thirteen, seemed years older, and his fiancée, Mary, was at fifteen a brilliant, capable young woman; I did not doubt that, when François inherited the throne, Mary would rule. My second son, Charles, suffered from abscesses and other infections, but physical weakness did not stop him from exhibiting signs of madness: He had to be restrained from biting the other children viciously enough to draw blood—and, during a momentary lapse of the governess's attention, had managed to break the neck of the children's little spaniel with his bare hands. My husband replaced the dog with a puppy, with the caveat that it was to be locked away whenever Charles was present. Only Edouard, then six, grew to be strong and tall and kind, like his constant companion, little Navarre.

On a cold winter's day in Paris, with iron clouds that in any other northern city might have indicated snow, I sat with Edouard and Mary and the little spaniel in my antechamber, whose tall windows looked beyond the dull, muddy trickle that was the Seine River, to the twin towers of Notre-Dame. Mary had learned to be civil to me—she had resigned herself, I think, to the fact that I was healthy and disinclined to die soon—and began to come to my chambers to practice the art of embroidery. Edouard accompanied her that day and played nicely with the little dog, whose antics made us laugh.

On that morning, Mary and I were at work on her bridal gown—a sumptuous creation of shining silk satin in her favourite color, white. It was an odd choice for a wedding gown, especially in France, where white was the color of mourning for queens. Yet Mary stubbornly insisted on it, and I must admit that it flattered her. We were busily stitching white fleurs-de-lis on the bodice when Madame Gondi appeared in the doorway, grinning broadly.

"Madame la Reine!" she called. "Forgive me, but you have a visitor who will not give me leave to announce him! He says that you will be overjoyed to see him."

I frowned, unable to fathom who might be so rude. "Send him in."

Madame Gondi stepped aside. A man strode confidently over the threshold, dramatically dressed in a blue velvet doublet cut in the Italian style, with huge sleeves of gold brocade. His head was small for his body, which perhaps explained the large plumed hat covering his riotous curls. He sported a very long black mustache—curling, like his hair—and when he saw me, he beamed broadly.

"Cat!" he cried. "Oh, Cat, how grand you look! How magnificent, Your Majesty!" He doffed his hat and swept it to one side as he bowed low. Then he rose and, spreading his arms wide, approached with the clear intention of embracing me.

I stared at him stupidly for an instant, until something in his eyes, in the curls that recalled childish ringlets, made me drop Mary's gown and spring to my feet. "Piero! My Piero!"

We embraced, laughing and weeping, while Edouard and Mary watched, astonished. When I pulled back, I pressed my hand to his face. It was no longer plump but manly and weathered from many battles.

"Piero," I said, in French for the children's sake. "You were fighting in Italy, with the Duke of Guise. What brings you to Paris?"

"Your husband," he answered, his arms still about my waist. "He has called me and Monsieur Guise to France. Things were not going so well in Italy, and so he has other plans for us." He stopped to smile politely at

Edouard and Mary. "Are these your son and daughter? What beautiful children!"

"This is Mary, Queen of Scots," I said, "soon to be the Dauphine."

Piero's hand still clutched his huge hat; he swept it dramatically across his body as he bowed very low, his head almost even with his knees. "Your Majesty," he said. "Please forgive me for failing to be properly announced. I thought only one queen was present. Truly, you are as beautiful as everyone says you are."

Mary, who was inclined to be sour toward strangers, giggled and tossed her head.

"And this is my son Edouard," I said.

Edouard scrambled to his feet and executed a polite bow. The excited little dog began to bark at Piero; Edouard picked it up and shushed it.

"Ah, Your Highness," Piero told him. "You are quite the young man now; you must make your mother very proud."

I called for Madame Gondi to return the children to the nursery, then linked arms with my cousin and led him on a tour of the Louvre.

After we had wandered about for a bit, and our excitement abated, I asked Piero, "Has the King spoken to you yet of his military plans?"

"I've only just arrived," my cousin said. "I don't know the precise strategy, but I do know our aim."

"And that would be?" I pressed.

Piero looked about to make sure we were alone, then said softly, "Why, to seize Calais, of course."

"Calais!" I exclaimed, then at his shushing, quickly lowered my voice. "Piero, you're joking!" The northern city of Calais had long been an English stronghold. It was considered impregnable, so much so that a well-known verse said

Then the Frenchman Calais shall win
When iron and lead like cork will swim

I could understand why my husband would want to take Calais: It was beloved by Queen Mary of England, Philip's wife—Bloody Mary, the people called her now, because of her eagerness to see Protestants killed for their faith. Invading Calais would be a personal affront to her—and thus, to Philip and the Empire. I was terrified at the thought that Henri would provoke the combined wrath of England and Spain; besides, taking Calais was, simply, impossible.

"Not in the least," Piero countered, a bit indignantly. "Think about it, Cat: No one will ever expect the attack, so the element of surprise will be with us. His Majesty has drawn every last one of his troops from Italy. All of us—along with some mercenaries—will take part in the invasion. We can't lose."

"That is what Henri said about Saint-Quentin," I said witheringly. "Please, Piero . . . Talk my husband out of this. He wants revenge, because of Montmorency's capture. But this is insanity. Fighting Spain is one thing; fighting Spain *and* England is quite another."

"With all respect, Your Majesty," Piero said, his swagger replaced by calm determination. "It is not insanity but brilliance. And we will win."

We went on to discuss other, happier things. I said nothing to the King, who would have been livid to learn that Piero had divulged a state secret. But with each day, my anxiety grew, along with my fear that France would find herself in the midst of war—during the King's fortieth year.

François, Duke of Guise, arrived at the Louvre later that afternoon to great fanfare. In front of the entire Court, Guise knelt before my husband, who hurried to raise the Duke to his feet and embrace him like a brother. The assembled crowd burst into hurrahs, as though Guise had not failed in Italy.

For weeks, I feigned ignorance of Henri's plan to storm Calais in the dead of winter, when the intemperate climate discouraged anyone but the greatest of fools from waging war. And when my husband came at last to my bedchamber, late on the night of the first of January 1558, it was not in search of love but rather to confess that he had sent an army to Calais under the command of Guise, with my cousin Piero as his second.

I wanted to chide Henri severely for such a foolhardy venture—but the die was cast. I held my curses and instead told my husband I prayed for success. There was nothing left to do.

I was entirely unprepared when, only a fortnight later, Henri burst into my apartment at midday. I was embroidering with Elisabeth when the wooden door banged against the stone wall like a shot, startling me so badly that I pricked myself. I looked up from my bleeding finger to see my husband, wearing a madman's grin.

"We have taken Calais!" he cried. "Guise has done it!"

Elisabeth screamed with happiness and dropped her sewing. I flung my arms around him and buried my face in his chest, thinking that my husband would be safe from the danger of the battlefield at last.

Peace came. Stung by the loss of Calais, Philip of Spain agreed to negotiate with Henri for Montmorency's release; in the meantime, all hostilities ceased.

This time, when François of Guise returned from battle and knelt before the throne, Henri asked him to make whatever request he wished of the Crown and it would be granted—"in celebration of your stunning victory for France."

By then, Guise was thirty-nine years old—my age, and my husband's. The privations of warfare had left him looking much older, however; he was now almost completely bald, with skin pitted by the pox and scarred by the bite of swords.

"I have only one desire," he proclaimed, in a ringing voice, "and that is to see my niece married to your son before God takes me from this life."

"It is done," Henri announced, to the courtiers' roars of approval. "I hereby put you in charge of all arrangements, Your Grace. Do as you please."

It pleased the Duke of Guise for his niece Mary to wed the Dauphin on the twenty-fourth of April.

First, however, came the issue of the marriage contract. The Scottish Parliament agreed quickly that François would become King of Scotland rather than a mere royal consort; however, if François were to die first, they wanted Mary to rule France as Queen—in violation of Salic law, which barred women from the French throne.

Normally I would have remained silent and left all negotiations to my husband, but the thought of Mary taking precedence over my own sons made me livid. I went to Henri and spoke stridently of the need to protect the Crown for our heirs. He listened silently and patiently, and when I had given thorough vent to my feelings, he smiled gently and took my hand.

"I will not see our sons slighted, Catherine. Mary will never rule France alone."

"I would prefer she not rule it at all," I said with asperity. I was so agitated I nearly withdrew my hand.

Henri knew, of course, that Mary and I shared little love for each other, and he wished sincerely that we felt otherwise. But in this case, he agreed with me: In the end, the contract specified that, upon François's death, Mary's right to the French throne would be forfeit. It was a condition that sorely disappointed the Guises, but Henri would not be moved.

The twenty-fourth of April dawned red and warm. I had slept little, having spent a good deal of the night comforting my weeping son François, who was terrified of humiliating himself by stuttering or fainting. Morning found me still sitting beside my drowsy son. His eyelids were swollen almost shut, his face was blotched and puffy. I ordered cold compresses and applied them tenderly to his eyes and cheeks.

By noon, all of us in the royal wedding party were dressed—Henri and I sedately, in shades of black and dull gold, so that Mary and our son might shine brightly. The rest of the royal children were there, all wearing their best; Elisabeth, now thirteen and a striking young woman in pale blue velvet—surely next to be married, as Henri was already considering suitors for her hand—made sure the younger ones behaved themselves as princes and princesses ought. With the exception of Mary, who waited out of sight in an alcove, we assembled at the main entrance of the palace. The bride's uncles were outfitted grandly. The Cardinal of Lorraine wore scarlet satin and a large cross covered in rubies. The architect of the celebrations, the Duke of Guise, had dressed from head to toe in silver and diamonds, as if he were the bridegroom.

The sight of my François in his fine gold doublet was pathetically touching. His height matched that of his nearly eight-year-old brother, Charles; his head was too large for his body; and his high-pitched voice was still a boy's.

Even so, he had managed to effect an air of regal dignity. When Elisabeth bent down to kiss her older brother's cheek and pronounced him "as handsome a man as I have ever seen," Henri's eyes filmed with tears, and he reached for my hand and squeezed it.

Several coaches festooned with white satin and lilies awaited us in the courtyard. Henri and François climbed into the first carriage; when they had rolled out of sight, Mary emerged from inside the palace.

She was a dazzling, dark-haired angel in white satin and sparkling diamonds, with a jewel-encrusted golden coronet upon her head; we all gasped at the sight of her. She smiled, knowing the impression she made; her massive train sighed upon the cobblestones as she made her way toward the waiting carriage, despite the two demoiselles who struggled valiantly to hold it aloft. Once she was settled inside with her two young attendants, I climbed in. We crossed the Seine to the Island of the City, the Ile-de-la-Cité. Our destination was the palace of the Cardinal de Bourbon, next to Notre-Dame.

There, our wedding party began its slow public procession. Guise had overseen the construction of a wooden gallery leading from the steps of the Archbishop's palace to the steps of the cathedral. It was covered in purple velvet, from floor to ceiling, and decorated with Mary's white lilies and silver ribbons; inside stood foreign dignitaries, ambassadors, princes, and courtiers, all eager to get a close look at the bride. The Cardinal led the procession with François. Mary followed a good distance behind, arm in arm with the King. I came next, at the head of my children, followed by Diane and my ladies. François of Guise and his brother came last.

The smell of fresh timber evoked memories of the day, long ago, when I was a frightened, vulnerable bride. The crowd gasped appreciatively as Mary passed them while jubilant Parisians roared outside. I smiled to see my cousin Piero, dashing in a uniform of dark blue, and was taken aback when my gaze caught Cosimo Ruggieri's. He looked exceptionally fine—if one could say such a thing of an ugly man—in a new doublet of dark red brocade edged in black velvet. Red and black, reminders of blood and death, of what had been required to reach this place, this moment.

He was smiling brightly—an incongruous expression on such a pale, ghostly visage. I grinned back at him with a sudden welling of affection, knowing that, without him, I would not have survived, would not have seen my son born. Our glance held more intimacy than any I had ever shared with my husband.

Our party emerged from the gallery and ascended the steps of Notre-Dame in full view of the wooden amphitheater holding thousands of joyfully noisy citizens, contained by Scottish guards and fences. Guise had decided that Mary should be wed not inside the cathedral but outside, for the sake of the crowd. The Cardinal halted at the great central entrance, the Portal of Judgment, beneath the magnificent Rose West window, a medallion of stained glass and stone. François stopped an arm's length from the Archbishop, then turned toward the crowd and waited for his bride.

When Mary arrived to stand between my son and the King, the people fell silent. The ceremony was brief. When the Cardinal demanded of the groom and bride a vow, the Dauphin miraculously answered without a single stammer; Mary's reply was strong and assured. The King produced the ring—a simple gold band—and handed it to the Cardinal, who slipped it onto Mary's finger. The Cardinal paused—the cue for the Dauphin to kiss his lovely new bride.

But Mary cried loudly, unexpectedly, "All hail François, King of Scots!" She knelt and bowed low, her white skirts pooling about her.

It was a brilliant bit of theater. The citizens, already dazzled by Mary's poise and beauty, thundered their approval of such humble deference toward their future king.

I glanced over my shoulder at the nobles who had congregated behind us on the cathedral stairs. Every face radiated appreciation for Mary's lovely gesture—save one. Cosimo Ruggieri stood unfooled and unsmiling. In his black eyes, on his white face, was the same dark intensity he had worn thirty years ago in Florence, when he had uttered an ugly word.

Betrayal . . .

After the ceremony, we returned to the Cardinal's palace for the traditional feast, followed by a ball. I was standing beside Mary when her uncle François of Guise came to lead her to the dance floor. He was already inebriated and whispered far too loudly in her ear:

"You are Queen of two countries now."

Mary seemed amused and directed a sly, feline smile at me as Guise escorted her away.

The sun was setting when we returned over the bridge to the Louvre, Mary borne upon a litter, the dying light painting her skin and dress a brilliant coral. We were exhausted when we returned to the palace, but Guise was not done with his lavish spectacle. We were ushered to the Louvre's grand ballroom. The King made his appearance in a clever little mechanical boat decorated with lilies and white satin, and equipped with silver sails. Accompanied by nautical music, the boat glided across the marble floor as if floating upon the sea; it made its way over to Mary. My grinning husband helped her into the little boat, then the two of them slowly circled the ballroom, to the marvel of the guests.

As they sailed away from me, a second boat appeared, with my son aboard. I did not relax my public smile as I settled beside him on the velvet cushion, but I let go a weary sigh as I kissed his cheek.

"Are you very tired, *Maman*?" he asked. His eyes were drooping from exhaustion, but he was in good spirits and obviously greatly relieved that he had survived the ceremony.

"A little," I said and patted his knee to reassure him. "But not so tired as you are."

He nodded in grave agreement. "Isn't Mary beautiful?" he asked suddenly.

"She is," I replied and hesitated. "François . . . You know that Mary is a very opinionated young woman."

"Yes," he said, with blithe innocence. "She can be very stubborn."

"Which is why you must learn to exert your will forcefully with her; otherwise, when you are King, she will try to rule in your stead."

He dropped his gaze at once. "Mary loves me. She would never do anything bad."

"I know," I said patiently. "But when your father and I are gone, and you are King, you must remember that you alone can make decisions."

Even as I spoke, François spied his bride riding alongside Henri and waved frantically until he caught her attention. She blew him a kiss, and he grinned stupidly at her until her little boat moved out of view.

"François," I said, "I will ask you to make only one promise to me, ever."

He looked up at me, his eyes wide and ingenuous; he had already forgotten what we had been discussing. "Of course, *Maman!*"

I drew in a long breath. "Promise me that, when you are King, you will not let Mary make the decisions. Promise me that you will listen to your advisers instead."

"The Guises will be my advisers, won't they? And Mary always agrees with them. So of course, I will promise you." He leaned forward and kissed my cheek.

"Thank you," I said tenderly. "You are a good son." And with a sinking heart, I realized that I could not afford to die so long as my eldest son lived.

Thirty

The wedding celebrations continued for five days, with pageantry and circus; they concluded with the customary jousting tournament. Tradition required that the bridegroom take part in the last joust of the day, but François's ill health made his participation impossible; he sat with Mary, Diane, and me in the stands to cheer his athletic father on.

I suffered through another banquet hosted by François de Guise, then retired to my chambers. To my surprise, Henri arrived not long afterward.

He bent down as I stood on tiptoe to kiss him. His face was still flushed and his cheek warm from the joust; his skin smelled of soap. I scrutinized him carefully: He had come with no amorous intent; indeed, he sagged back in the chair and sighed with exhaustion. A tired man would simply have gone to his own bed.

"What is troubling you, husband?" I asked bluntly. We were both too fatigued by the recent celebrations to waste time with formalities.

His feigned smile fled. He turned his face toward the hearth, empty now in late spring, and sighed again.

"It's François," he said finally. "And Mary . . ."

I had not asked about the wedding night; I had been too afraid. My eldest son had miraculously survived the marriage ceremony, but I dared not hope he could survive the marriage.

"You know I was required to be a witness," Henri began. "If it had been another boy, a healthy, normal boy, perhaps it would not have been difficult. But given that it was our François . . .

"It was terrible." His voice was a low monotone as he stared dully into the blackened, empty hearth, where the chambermaid had set a large crystal bowl of white lilies in honor of the wedding couple. "I had explained things about . . . you know, about the marriage bed, to François. And I thought he understood well enough. But when I arrived, and he and Mary were underneath the sheets together . . . Well, he just *lay* there. I had to whisper to him that he was supposed to take her, but he answered that he was far too tired.

"I was so ashamed," Henri continued. "I seized his shoulder and said in his ear that I was not the only one waiting; there was the Cardinal, too, who had to report to the Pope. Then he grew upset, and had one of his fainting spells, there in the bed. I had to call for the physician, who advised that we wait until morning."

"Poor Henri," I said, shaking my head. "Poor François . . . Could anything be done?"

"The next morning, François declared himself indisposed," my husband said unhappily. "But there were other affairs to attend, and Mary wouldn't tolerate his missing any of them. I endured endless jokes about the newlyweds' first night together. . . . But how could I tell anyone the truth of it? How can I ever?"

I put my hand gently on Henri's forearm. "Did anything . . ."

"Did anything ever happen?" he finished for me, without humor. "Yes, something, on the second night. Let us just say that François made the attempt but lacked the determination to finish what he had started. He was frightened, poor boy, and unwell, and I left him sobbing in Mary's arms. So I lied to them all—lied to the Cardinal, who came in after me and found them in what he assumed to be a nuptial embrace. I will swear before God to anyone who asks that the marriage was consummated. But I fear Mary might have said something to Diane. And if *she* knows . . ." He shook his head at the thought.

"Oh, Henri, how awful for all of you."

"It *is* awful." He turned toward me at last; yellow lamplight glinted off the silver strands in his hair and beard. "I've said everything I can say to the boy. So I've come to you— He loves you so, Catherine, and you've always been better at explaining things to him. Could you . . . ?"

"I'll go to him," I said quickly. "He must understand how critical it is to produce an heir." I put my hand upon his and smiled. "After all, I still remember what it's like to soothe a nervous young man in the bridal chamber." My tone grew serious again. "But you must set the Guise brothers straight on the issue of succession. They think to make themselves kings. If word gets out of the Dauphin's behavior, the question of succession might arise. If it does, it must be clear to everyone that the Bourbons are next in line to the throne. The Guises must be put in their place. Otherwise, there will be unrest—perhaps even war."

My husband's expression subtly hardened. "They've been too full of themselves. I can scarcely bear François of Guise's preening anymore; I do so only for Mary's sake."

"Mary must know," I said smoothly, "and her uncles must know, that if there is ever a question, the Bourbons take precedence over them. If you die, if I die, how would François ever stop the two families from killing each other?"

Henri nodded thoughtfully. "What you say has merit. I will think on it, Catherine."

I looked at him, at the faltering resolve in his eyes, and knew he would do little. Still, I had planted the seed, and could only hope that time would water it.

I rose and laid a hand upon my husband's shoulder. "I'll talk to our son," I said softly. "Don't worry. He and Mary will have sons, many sons, and this palace will be filled with our grandchildren. That I promise you."

Henri smiled up at me. "Of course," he murmured. "Of course."

But when I looked into his eyes, I saw the truth that was surely reflected in my own: There would be no children.

My words about trouble with the Bourbons quickly proved prophetic: On the fourteenth of May, the First Prince of the Blood, Antoine de Bourbon, mounted his stallion and led four thousand Protestants on a march through Paris. One afternoon, I stared out the windows of the Louvre and saw what appeared to be an army of hymn-singing civilians marching over the bridge from the Ile-de-la-Cité. Henri was outraged—as were the good Catholic Guise brothers.

I summoned my friend Jeanne, Antoine's wife, and told her I felt betrayed to think that someone in the Court knew of such plans and had failed to warn the King. Jeanne was, like me, a queen and did not take kindly to my insinuation. She had not known, she claimed, and with a burst of temper added:

"Surely you, of all people, understand that a wife cannot always control her husband's public actions, nor can she be privy to all his secrets."

Her remark stung. Though we parted with polite words, we became distant from that moment on.

Shortly after Henri's visit to my chambers, I summoned Ruggieri.

"Once again, the question of producing an heir has arisen," I told him, annoyed at my own embarrassment. "The Dauphin requires . . . help. To instill lust."

The morning light was unkind to the magician, showing all too harshly his sickly pallor, his scarred cheeks, the shadows beneath his eyes. "A simple talisman, perhaps?" he asked.

"That would be suitable, yes," I answered. The room seemed suddenly close and warm.

He nodded; a stranger would have thought his expression ingenuous, innocent. "Might it also be salutary to have two talismans: one for health, one for fertility?"

"That would be fine," I said, a bit irritably. "So long as—"

"Yes, *Madame la Reine*," he said with consummate courtesy and a nod. "So long as no one is harmed. I understand."

"Very good," I said. "You may go."

Tall and still thin, in a black silk doublet that fit too loosely, he rose and bowed, but as his fingers touched the door, he turned to face me.

"Forgive me, *Madame la Reine*," he said. "Forgive me, but should the talismans fail to produce a child . . . ?"

My voice grew cold. "They will not fail."

He cast aside his courtly manners and said bluntly, "Without blood, there can be no guarantee. The talismans of which we speak will bring mild improvement to the Dauphin's health, and to his sexual desire. Beyond that, the rest is chance." He did not wilt beneath my withering gaze but added, "I want only to be clear."

I rose from my desk. "*Never again.* That is what I told you fifteen years ago. Do not make me repeat it."

He bowed low and left quickly, closing the door behind him. I stood listening to the sound of his rapid steps dying in the hall.

Within a fortnight, Madame Gondi delivered a small bundle to me, wrapped tightly with ribbon. I opened it: Upon the black silk, two talismans—one of ruby, one of copper—hung from a single cord.

François accepted the necklace without question and swore that he would neither speak of it nor show it to anyone, including Mary.

The next morning, I was urgently summoned to the King's chamber. It was early—I had not yet finished dressing and hurried my ladies in order to respond promptly.

Henri's antechamber was decidedly masculine, paneled in wood and furnished in brown velvet and gold brocade. Over the mantel was the gilded relief of a salamander, the emblem of Henri's father, François I. In front of the cold hearth, Henri stood waiting, silent and motionless, until the valet departed.

His lips were taut with contained rage, his eyes narrowed with fury. He was a very tall man, and I a very small woman; I sank into a low curtsy and stayed there. "Your Majesty."

Such a long silence followed that I at last dared to lift my gaze.

Henri was holding out his hand. In his open palm lay the necklace with the ruby and copper talismans I had given François.

"What is this, Madame?"

"A simple charm, Your Majesty," I answered smoothly. "For the Dauphin's good health."

"I will not have my son involved with this—this filth!" He flung it into the empty fireplace. "I will have it burned!"

"Henri," I said quickly, rising, "it is a harmless thing. It is a *good* thing, made according to a science based on astronomy and mathematics."

"It is a heinous thing," he retorted. "You know how I feel about such things. For you to give this to our *son* . . . !"

I bristled. "How can you believe that I would give my own child something harmful?"

"It's that magician of yours. He's poisoned your mind, made you believe that you need him. Let me warn you now, Catherine, that things will go more easily for you if you dismiss him today, now, rather than later!"

"I have no intention of doing so," I said, indignant. "Do you threaten me, Your Majesty?"

He let go a long, unsteady breath and calmed himself; dark earnestness replaced his anger. "Two months ago, I petitioned the Pope so that I might organize a French Inquisition."

I froze.

"Last week, His Holiness granted my petition. I appointed Charles of Guise as head. Can you imagine, Madame, how I felt when the good Cardinal dropped that *thing*"—he gestured in disgust at the fireplace—"into my hand? How *he* must have felt when his frightened niece Mary brought it to him?"

Mary, crafty Mary; I should have known that François could hide nothing from her. "So what will you do, Henri? Will you bring your wife before a tribunal for questioning?"

"No," he said. "But if you were wise, you would tell your magician that the King's Court is no longer a safe place for him."

Heat rose to my cheeks. "Were you to arrest him, would that not bring ugly attention to me? Would it not start rumors that would only harm the Crown?"

"There are ways to do it without implicating you," he replied coldly. "You have been advised, Madame."

I called Ruggieri to my cabinet that afternoon. I did not give him leave to sit—there was no time—but held out a velvet purse filled with gold ecus.

"The King has organized an inquisition; you will be one of its first victims.

For my sake, take these," I said. "Ride far from Paris and remain a stranger wherever you go. There is a carriage waiting at the side entrance. The driver will help you gather your belongings."

Ruggieri clasped his hands behind his back and turned his face from me. There were no windows in my tiny office, but he seemed to find one, and looked far beyond it at a distant scene.

"For your sake, I cannot go," he said, then settled his arresting gaze back on me. "Matters grow dangerous, *Madame la Reine.* The King's fortieth year is upon us."

"There is no war," I said lightly. I set the velvet purse upon my desk, midway between us. "And if war comes, I will not let Henri go. You know this, Monsieur. Do not test me."

"I would never do so," he replied. "But consider this: There can be battle even when there is no war."

"What are you saying?" I demanded. "Do you tell me now that your magic was worthless?"

He remained maddeningly calm. "Every spell—no matter how powerful—has its limits."

A thrill coursed down my spine. "Why do you hurt me?" I whispered. "I'm trying to help you."

"And I you. For that reason, I will not leave until the very moment my life is threatened."

I made my eyes, my voice, my bearing hard and imperious. "I am your Queen," I said. "And I command you to go."

With unspeakable rudeness, he turned his back on me and strode to the door, then paused to glance over his shoulder. I caught a flash of wildness in his eye, of the Devil I had seen more than thirty years before, when someone in a hostile crowd had grazed me with a stone.

"And I am Cosimo Ruggieri. Devoted to you, Caterina de' Medici. I will not desert you until forced to do so."

He left, closing the door softly behind him.

I did not speak to Ruggieri for days; his words and his insolence rankled me at the same time that they provoked my worry, for him and for Henri. In the interim, I was not without my spies, who kept close watch over the King and the Cardinal of Lorraine.

Late one summer night, my sleep was disturbed by a knock at my chamber door and the movement of a flickering lamp. I murmured drowsily and turned my face away from the light.

At the feel of fingertips upon my arm, I opened my eyes to see Madame Gondi, her face golden in the lamp glow, still in her nightgown, a shawl thrown over her shoulders.

"Madame la Reine," she hissed. "You must wake up! They are coming for him!"

My body woke instantly; I swung my legs over the edge of the bed and sat, my bare feet dangling. My mind did not respond quite as quickly.

"What is it?" I murmured. "What has happened?"

"The officers of the Inquisition. They are sending men to seize Monsieur Ruggieri—at dawn, if not sooner!"

I willed myself to consciousness. "I must go to him myself and warn him," I said. I knew Ruggieri would listen to no one else.

Madame Gondi's eyes widened in horror. "But, Madame . . ."

"A carriage," I said quickly. "One without the royal crest. Have it brought to the rear of the palace, then come help me dress."

The light cast by the carriage's dual lamps was too feeble to dispel much of the darkness on that moonless night; the street was silent save for the clatter of our horses' hooves against stone. Madame Gondi rode with me, at her insistence. Like me, she had dressed all in black and veiled her face; it hovered above her body, indistinct and ghostly behind the gauze.

We did not ride far; Ruggieri lived on the street hemming the western side of the Louvre. Our carriage came to rest along a row of three-story narrow houses, crammed side by side. After a moment of stealthy exploration, the coachman found the correct number, 83, then fetched me from the carriage. I stood beside him at the entrance as he knocked, persistently but discreetly.

After a time, the door cracked open, and a wizened old woman, her uncovered hair in a long white braid, scowled through the slit above the flame of a candle.

"For love of Jesus and the weeping Virgin," she hissed. "What breed of mannerless bastard dares disturb decent folk at such an hour?"

"I wish to see Monsieur Ruggieri." I stepped into the wavering arc of light cast by the flame and lifted my veil.

"Your Majesty!" Her mouth gaped, revealing a dozen jagged brown teeth. The door swung wide.

I turned to the coachman. "Stay here," I said.

I passed over the threshold. The old woman was still kneeling, in such a state of shock that she crossed herself repeatedly with one skeletal hand while carelessly clutching the candle in the other, far too close to the disheveled braid that fell onto her bosom. I leaned forward and gently pushed the braid out of harm's way, causing her to start.

"Is Monsieur Ruggieri still abed?" I asked softly.

She nodded, stricken.

"Do not wake him, then," I said, "but lead me to his door."

The sweep of candlelight revealed nothing to indicate a magician's lair—only sparsely furnished, unremarkable rooms, punctuated randomly by stacks of leather-bound books, some open. The smells of mutton, raw onions, and charred wood emanated from the kitchen.

The old woman halted in front of a closed door. "Shall I knock, Your Majesty?"

"No," I said. "I'll wake him." I shot her a pointed look. "We shall require privacy."

I refused the candle and waited until she retreated down the hallway, then entered the bedchamber and closed the door behind me.

The curtains had been drawn, leaving the room utterly dark. Disoriented, I paused, drawing in the scents of male flesh, rosemary, and frankincense, my imagination manufacturing a thousand hideous things that might be lurking here, in a magician's bedchamber. In the stillness, I heard not the deep, restful breath of slumber but quick, muffled gasps. I sensed movement, the sudden looming of a figure toward me.

"Ser Cosimo," I whispered.

"Catherine?" The figure halted its approach. Quick footsteps followed, muffled by the carpeted floor, and a match flared as Ruggieri lit the lamp at his bedside.

His black hair fell tangled about his face; his nightshirt revealed a sprig of dark hair at the neck. His trembling left hand gripped the hilt of a double-edged long knife, the shorter version of a knight's sword.

"Catherine," he repeated, gasping. "My God, I might have killed you!" He laid the knife down on his mattress.

My words tumbled out in Tuscan, our native tongue. "Cosimo, must I explain why I have come?" And when he, still overwhelmed, did not answer, I added, "They're coming for you before daybreak."

He bowed his head and studied the carpet as though it contained an unutterably poignant message. His mouth worked but could not find the proper words. At last he said, "You will need me."

"If you stay, it will only hurt us both," I said. "What would happen to me if you were imprisoned? Or burned alive?"

He looked up at me and, for the first time, had no answer.

I fumbled for the pocket sewn into the folds of my skirt and produced the velvet purse, heavier now than it had first been. "Take this," I said. "A horse awaits you on the street. Tell no one where you are going."

He reached for it. I loosened my grasp, thinking he would take it—but he let it drop and instead closed his hand over mine, and pulled me to him.

"Caterina," he murmured in my ear. "You think yourself evil. I tell you, you are better than them all. Only the strongest, most loving heart is willing to face darkness for the sake of those she loves."

"Then you and I are kindred souls," I said. On tiptoe, I pressed my lips to his scarred cheek and was astonished to find the skin there soft and warm.

He brushed the backs of his fingers against my face. "We will meet again," he said. "Soon. Too soon."

He bent down to retrieve the purse. I turned and did not look back.

As the old woman with the candle approached, I covered my face with the veil so that she could not see me weeping.

If Henri noticed Ruggieri's disappearance, he said nothing of it to me. I suspect he was relieved that I had been spared seeing the magician brought before the Inquisition.

Once François of Guise saw his niece safely married to the Dauphin, he returned to battle in the north and snatched the town of Thionville from King Philip's grasp. My cousin Piero rode at his side—and fell during the attack, his chest shattered by lead shot from an arquebus. He lay bleeding to death in Guise's arms, and as Guise, ever the good Catholic, begged him to pray that Jesus would receive him into Heaven, Piero answered irritably:

"Jesus? What Jesus? Don't try to convert me at this late hour! I am only going where all those who have ever died go."

I wept as Guise, heartbroken by Piero's heresy, relayed the story of my adored cousin's death. I felt at that moment that I had lost everyone I had ever loved in my old life: Aunt Clarice, and now Piero; even Ruggieri had vanished.

But the victory brought good news as well. Grieving over the recent death of his wife, Queen Mary—whose attempt to revive Catholicism in England was being swiftly overturned by her half sister and successor, Elizabeth—and financially exhausted by constant wars, King Philip of Spain was at long last ready to make peace. This brought Henri great hope, for he was eager to free his old mentor, Montmorency, from Spanish prison.

Philip offered this: If Henri agreed never to launch another war to seize Italian properties, France could keep Calais and the other northern towns, and Montmorency would be freed. To secure the treaty, our thirteen-year-old daughter, Elisabeth, would marry Philip. After months of deliberation, Henri at last agreed.

I rejoiced that our greatest enemy should now be our friend, and that all cause for war was extinguished—for His Majesty, King Henri II, had entered his fortieth year.

Thirty-one

Elisabeth was married on the twenty-second of June, 1559, at Notre-Dame Cathedral. King Philip chose not to appear for the wedding. "The Kings of Spain," he wrote my husband, "do not go to their wives; their wives are brought to them." Instead, he sent a proxy, the dour and elderly Duke of Alba, Fernando Alvarez de Toledo. Don Fernando and his entourage arrived without pomp, in such plain black clothing that Henri was at first affronted, until the ambassador convinced him that this was simply Spanish custom.

We politely ignored the Spaniards' austerity and proceeded with a ceremony almost as lavish as that of the Dauphin and Mary, Queen of Scots. Grand Master Montmorency was given a prominent place in the procession. He was white-haired now, stiff with age and gaunt in the wake of his imprisonment, but bright with joy to be home in the presence of his King.

On the wedding night, my ladies and I undressed my nervous daughter. She lay down upon the great bed, and I drew silk indigo sheets over her naked body. We ladies retreated; as I stepped out into the antechamber, I passed the Duke of Alba, Don Fernando, clothed in a black doublet, with one legging rolled up to expose a thin white calf.

The King appeared in order to watch an ancient ritual: Don Fernando lay down beside our daughter, rubbed his bare leg against hers, then got up and left the room. The marriage between Elisabeth and King Philip had just been legally consummated.

A week of celebrations followed: parades and spectacles, banquets and masked balls. Through them all, my husband and Montmorency rarely left each other's side. Finally, the tournaments began. For the jousting lists—the lanes for the horses—workmen had lifted the paving stones from the rue Saint-Antoine in front of the Château des Tournelles, a palace in the heart of the city. They had also built tall wooden stands on both sides of the street for the nobler spectators and draped them in banners bearing the royal arms of France and Spain.

Henri was invigorated by the return of his old friend and relished the thought of participating in the joust, perhaps eager to dispel the notion that, at forty, he was no longer the athlete he had been in his youth. Many a warm day before the wedding, he spent hours engaging in mock tourneys astride his new, magnificent stallion named Le Malheur, Disaster, a wedding gift from his former enemy, the Duke of Savoy.

I, too, had recently turned forty, and the festivities left me exhausted. I did not appear at the first two days of jousting but waited until the third day, when His Majesty was to enter the lists.

The afternoon before, the day turned abysmally humid, and evening brought violent rains, ending all outdoor revels. My bedchamber was hot, and I, strangely anxious; despite my weariness, I resisted sleep. The chambermaid opened the drapes, and and I stood staring out at the dark courtyard, listening to water crash against stone.

When the rain finally eased, I fell into an uneasy dream: I stood again on the scorched battlefield, gazing at the setting sun. In the near distance stood a man, his body dark against an incandescent sky. I saw his silhouette with dazzling clarity—the ridges of armor at his shoulders, the edges of the breastplate covering his heart. His helmet trailed plumes of black and grey.

Catherine, he called.

I ran to him. *How can I help, Monsieur? What am I meant to do?*

Suddenly he lay wounded. As I knelt beside him, shadowy forms hovered over him, invisible hands lifted the helmet from his head. With it came gushing blood; beneath that crimson spring, a man's lips formed a single word.

Catherine, he said and died.

I woke to the sound of my whispered scream, and a grey and sultry dawn.

On that last morning of June, I sent a letter to the King before either of us had dressed. At the same time, I tried to reason with my fear: We had ransomed Henri's life, had we not? But how old had the prostitute been? How many years had we purchased? My mind, normally so swift at mathematical calculation, tried to count them and failed.

If you love me, I wrote my husband, *forgo the lists today. I know you scoff at such things, but God has sent me an evil dream. Perhaps I am foolish; if I am, what harm can it do to set my mind at ease? Do this one thing, and I shall be ever grateful and ask for nothing more.*

I did not mention the astrologer Luca Guorico's warning, or the words of Nostradamus; certainly, I dared not write Ruggieri's name. I sent the letter knowing that Henri would not heed it; he had spent more time in recent days in the Guises' presence than in mine, as they planned the strokes of the new French Inquisition. His reply came within the hour:

> *Have no fear on my account, dear wife. You ask that I withdraw from the tournament for love of you; I beg you, for love of me, to put your fears aside and cheer me on today. Tradition bids me wear a certain lady's colors of black and white, but I will also wear your color, green, next to my heart. This evening, when I return victorious, greet me with a kiss. It will seal our private pact that from this day forth, you will put aside all superstition and trust in God alone.*
>
> *Your loving husband and most devoted servant,*
>
> *Henri*

When I received the message, my first impulse was to surrender to fear. My second was to calm myself, as there was little I could do: I had a responsibility to my daughter Elisabeth and her wedding guests, and there were many more functions that day requiring my attendance. I told myself that the storm had troubled my sleep and given me a bad dream, nothing more.

I repeated this firmly to myself each time panic loomed. I stood calmly while my ladies dressed me in a gown of purple damask with a bodice of gold; I smiled at my reflection in the mirror, and at my attendants, until I could recall the joy I had felt upon hearing of the truce with Philip, until the gesture became faintly genuine.

In that way, I survived the morning, and there were times as I looked at Elisabeth's glowing young face that I forgot my worry and my heart brimmed with love.

In the early afternoon, Elisabeth and the dour, unsmiling Don Fernando made their way to the stands and a special box constructed for the "bridal couple." The rest of us royals headed to the Château des Tournelles. One of its second-floor balconies overlooked the lists where the King would meet his opponents.

As I climbed the stairs to the second floor, anxiety seized me; my heart pounded so rapidly I could not catch my breath. I murmured an excuse to the others and walked across the landing to an open window to take in the warm, heavy air.

While I stood gasping and clutching the windowsill, something moved in the corner of my eye, accompanied by a faint murmur. It drew me, and I stepped away from the window toward it and a tiny alcove hidden from view.

In it stood Gabriel de Montgomery, captain of the King's Scottish guard, twenty-nine years old and in his prime—tall and muscular, his dark auburn hair brushed back and face clean-shaven, the better to show the magnificent angular lines of his cheeks and jaw. His expression was intent as he gazed down at a young woman, dressed all in white, who whispered earnestly to him. As I neared, he jerked up his head and met my gaze with the wide, guilty eyes of a conspirator.

Mary broke off in midwhisper and looked over her shoulder at me. Furtiveness glimmered on her features and resolved into a disingenuous smile.

"Madame la Reine!" she exclaimed cheerfully. "I shall join you and the others directly. Captain de Montgomery has agreed most kindly to wear my colors today."

A lovers' tryst, I thought, and felt hurt and sorrow for my son. But I said nothing—only smiled in return, greeted Captain de Montgomery, and returned to the others.

We took our places upon the second-floor balcony to great fanfare, followed by the cheering of thousands. Every roof, every window was swarming with spectators, eager to see the King joust. I sat between Diane and the Dauphin, who was flanked by his duplicitous wife. The air was stifling and still, adance with the constant flutter of the women's fans. François was so red-faced and breathless that Mary and I angled our fans discreetly to send him the breeze.

The lesser nobles had finished their jousting the day before. This day, Friday, was reserved for the highest-born and the King. We cheered on dukes and counts as the trumpets blared and the riders bellowed *Monjoie!*—the French soldier's victory cry—when they galloped down the narrow lists, separated only by a low fence designed to keep the horses from colliding. We sat so close to the combatants that the noise of the crowd failed to drown out the pounding of hooves and the crash of wooden lances against steel armor. Clods of flying dirt struck our skirts and slippers.

Hours later, the heralds announced the King. He rode out from his pavilion on his gleaming chestnut charger, caparisoned in white and gold, and raised his lance to the roaring crowd. The sight of him, straight and strong in his gilded armor, made my heart swell; with the others, I rose and clapped and shouted my approval.

Henri broke his first lance with his old enemy the Duke of Savoy, and unseated him on the first run. On the second, Savoy's lance struck the King square in the chest, lifting him from the saddle into the air. Henri clattered to the ground and for an instant lay so motionless that I moved to rise. Diane lightly touched my forearm in a gesture of reassurance—and indeed, in the next breath, Henri rose and waved to the applauding onlookers. The third run ended with both men still mounted. The match was a draw—the perfect outcome, given that my competitive husband did not stomach defeat well but had no wish to endanger his reconciliation with Savoy.

Henri's second opponent was the Duke of Guise. Out of three runs, Henri was unseated once and managed to unseat Guise once, giving His Majesty another draw.

By then it was late afternoon. The sun had slipped low and heated our west-facing balcony to a beastly degree; even Diane, who rarely perspired, was forced to mop her brow with her kerchief. I raised a hand to shield my eyes from the dazzling light and focused on the men below.

The King's last match that day was with Gabriel de Montgomery, Captain of the Scottish Guard. As it was the final run of the day, the crowd thinned, and several of the noble spectators in the galleries began to leave, hastened by the relentless heat.

Diane was elegantly appointed in black velvet and white satin—the colors of the plumes upon my husband's helmet and horse.

"Let us hope His Majesty scores a win," she said pleasantly into my ear. "Captain de Montgomery taunted him when he replied to the King's invitation. He was eager to break a lance with His Majesty, he said, to see whether he jousted as well in his forty-first year as in his twenty-ninth."

I glanced at Mary, her fan pumping rapidly as she gazed down at Montgomery riding out onto field. The plumes upon his helmet were scarlet, his sleeves black, his lance striped in the same alternating shades. If he wore Mary's color, white, I could not see it.

The red of Mars, the black of Saturn.

There can be battle, Ruggieri had said, *even when there is no war.*

At that instant the Duke of Nemours, who had finished jousting for the day, joined us on the balcony to pay his respects to the Dauphin and his bride. Before he could bow to me, I took his hand and drew him close.

"His Majesty has been unwell of late," I said into his ear, "and this heat has surely undone him. Please, go to him. Tell him—no, *beg* him, for love of his wife, to forgo the last match and come to me."

Nemours, a gracious man two years older than my husband, bowed deeply and kissed my hand. "*Madame la Reine,* I shall not return without him."

I waited, breathless, until Nemours emerged from the Château des Tournelles to make his way across the field to the King's pavilion, at whose entrance my mounted husband was just emerging. At Nemours's signal, Henri bent low and listened; when the Duke had finished speaking, the King gave his swift reply.

Nemours paused for the beat of a heart, then bowed and crossed the field alone. My husband reined in his handsome steed, Disaster, and guided him into the lists, opposite Montgomery.

I sat frozen as the heralds announced the riders and the trumpets gave the signal for the charge.

"Monjoie!" my husband roared, and Montgomery echoed him. The horses thundered down the lists, and when the wooden lances thudded against steel breastplates, the animals reared, shrieking. Both riders fell. Silent, I kept my hand pressed hard to my heart until Henri pushed himself to his knees. He returned to his horse, wobbling so badly at one point that a groom rushed out of the pavilion to aid him, but my proud husband pushed him away. Montgomery had risen quickly and already remounted.

"Forgive me," a voice said, and I glanced up to see the Duke of Nemours. "Forgive me, *Madame la Reine,*" he repeated. "I could not keep my promise. His Majesty bade me tell you: *It is precisely for love of you that I fight.*"

I could not answer; I was too alarmed by the sight of Montgomery's weapon: Its dull metal tip, designed to keep the lance from piercing armor or splintering into deadly shards, had fallen off. Surely Montgomery had noticed, too—but rather than return to his pavilion for a replacement, he guided his charger back to the lists and faced the King. Behind him, his armor bearer noted the loss and called to him, but Montgomery seemed oblivious.

By then, my husband had climbed back upon Disaster. So intent was he on victory that he unlatched and raised his visor and, wiping the sweat from his brow, shouted at Montgomery to come at him again.

I stared spellbound, a dreamer unable to move my limbs, to find my voice. Henri lowered his visor but failed to heed the call of his armor bearer to latch it; Montgomery did not hear—or ignored—the hoarse cries of his own.

The crowd, too, had marked the unshod lance, as had the trumpeters, who, despite the King's shouts, were too distracted to sound the call. Diane again put her hand upon my forearm—in alarm now, not reassurance—but, like the spectators, grew hushed. In the dying light, the white of her gown bled to grey.

The King, too impatient to wait for the trumpets, charged.

I rose. The world was silent save for the battle yell *Monjoie!* and the drumming of hooves. Montgomery and Henri hurtled at each other, two projectiles, and collided.

Separated by the low fence, the mounts collided at the shoulder and screamed. There came a loud crack like lightning: Montgomery's lance dissolved in a firework spray of shards.

But Henri did not fall.

He reeled drunkenly and pitched forward, losing the reins, and feebly clutched Disaster's neck. The horse carried him down the list until the King's grooms ran out to catch the reins and guide the mount to an open area, where the earth had been torn by the lifting of paving stones and the pounding of hooves. Alongside François of Guise, white-haired Montmorency ran from the King's pavilion. He cradled my husband's shoulders and, with Guise's aid, lowered Henri from the saddle to the ground.

The young lion will overcome the old, in
A field of combat in a single fight. He will
Pierce his eyes in a golden cage, two
Wounds in one, he then dies a cruel death.

He was no royal lion, the Scotsman Gabriel de Montgomery, but he rode that day for young Mary, his Queen.

Colors failed in the waning light. Against the reddening sky, dark figures worked to relieve my motionless husband of his armor. With the help of a valet, Guise pulled off the King's gilded helmet: with it came a rush of blood. Captain de Montgomery staggered onto the scene and dropped to his knees.

Shrill screams pained my ears: They belonged to Diane, to François, to hundreds of noblemen, thousands of commoners. Beside me the Dauphin swooned and pitched forward in his chair. Mary caught him, her face a mask as white as the gown she wore, but I could not stop to accuse her, or even to help my son. I ran from the balcony down the stairs to the palace entry and out onto the paved driveway.

The black iron gate that led to the rue Saint-Antoine swung open. From the center of a swarm of onlookers, a small, grim procession emerged: Henri, bloodied and still, lay on a litter borne by Scottish guardsmen and flanked by old Montmorency and François, Duke of Guise. I pushed my way to my husband's side and drew in a sharp breath.

One end of a jagged wooden shard—thick as two fingers, and almost twice as long—protruded from King's right eye socket; the other end had shattered his skull at the temple and forced its way through the skin just in front of his right ear. The globe of the eye had been punctured, leaving nothing of the white or iris visible, only a dark, congealing mass of blood. A second, smaller splinter emerged from his throat just beneath the jaw, and miraculously had bled little.

I pressed my husband's hand to my lips. He stirred at my touch and murmured faintly. My numbness fled, replaced by overwhelming horror and hope: Henri's wound was grievous, his suffering unspeakable, yet Ruggieri's magic had held. The King was still alive. As he came to himself, he waved for the litter to stop and demanded to be set upon his feet. Montmorency held him fast beneath the shoulders, and François of Guise held up his head; in this manner, my husband staggered over the threshold, a paragon of bravery.

The Dauphin followed on a second litter, still in a faint from which he could not be roused. Mary walked beside him, a vision in white—the color of a queen in mourning—and started as the iron gate clanged shut behind her.

Our sad party made its way up the stairs, to long-unused royal apartments; François was carried to a separate chamber, and his young Queen went with him. Henri was laid carefully upon the bed and his bloodied tunic cut away.

Upon his chest, soaked with sweat and blood, was pressed an emerald kerchief, embroidered with gold fleurs-de-lis by my own hand. At the sight of it, I cried out, then took it and put it next to my heart.

The next few hours were evil ones. The King's doctor, Monsieur Chapelain, appeared and removed the smaller splinter from Henri's throat, then probed the wounded eye to see whether he could dislodge the large shard. My husband would not cry out but could not keep from retching during the worst moments. The doctor afterward announced that the shard was fast situated and could not be removed.

Afternoon faded to night. I hovered at the King's bedside, watching as Henri's face purpled and swelled, as his blackened eye began to bulge with trapped blood. Pain left him senseless most of the time, but there were a few moments where he came to himself and spoke sweetly to me. I was only vaguely aware that Montmorency and François of Guise disappeared, replaced by the Chief Inquisitor, Charles of Guise, and the Duke of Savoy.

At dawn, the aging Montmorency, grey-lipped and haggard, came to fetch me. He caught my arms gently and tried to coax me away, saying that I needed rest. I pulled free, stating loudly that I would never leave my husband's bedside. My words drew Henri from his semidelirium; at his whispered insistence, I yielded and let Montmorency take me from the room. Out in the antechamber, I fell into his arms and we wept together, all differences forgotten.

At my apartments, Madame Gondi awaited me, dressed and alert. I directed her to send for Ambroise Paré, the most famed surgeon in all France. I was convinced that Henri could survive with the proper surgery, so long as he did not yield to infection. Afterward, I dozed for an hour, and woke filled with dread.

At midmorning I returned to the King's chamber to find Montmorency and François of Guise with him. The swelling on the right side of Henri's face had reached grotesque proportions, though the eye had been bandaged. Doctor Chapelain had worked throughout the night to keep the wound clean and drained, with some encouraging result: Henri had no fever.

When I sat close at his bedside and called his name, he turned his face toward mine. I thought perhaps he knew me—but his remaining eye, glittering in the lamp glow, wandered.

"The young captain," he breathed, and I knew at once he spoke of the Scotsman who had dealt him the blow. "He must know I forgive him . . ."

"Captain de Montgomery has fled," old Montmorency answered, shooting François of Guise a dark look; the enmity between the two men was palpable. "No one can say where he has gone."

Later I would learn that the Guises publicly blamed the old man for the King's injury, arguing that, as Grand Master, he was ultimately responsible for the King's armor, and thus Henri's unlatched visor. Montmorency, it seemed, was keenly desirous of questioning the now-missing Scotsman.

"Ah!" the King said and closed his good eye; a single tear spilled from its corner and into his ear. "Diane . . . Where is Diane?"

"Madame de Poitiers remains in her apartments," the Grand Master answered. "She is indisposed, Your Majesty, and begs your forbearance."

I reached for Henri's hand; he returned my grip with surprising strength. He would not die, I told myself sternly, looking at his long, well-muscled body beneath the white sheets.

"*I* am here." My voice caught, but I forced it to steady. "It is I, Catherine."

"Catherine!" he murmured. "Oh, Catherine, I thought you foolish, but there is no greater fool than I. Forgive me. Forgive me for it all . . ."

I bent over my husband and leaned my cheek against his chest. The pulse there was the soft, rapid flutter of a bird's wings. Tears spilled from my eyes onto the linen I felt as though I were melting into him, merging until there was nothing left of me—only his singular heart, beating wildly.

"I blame you for nothing," I said, "and so there is nothing to forgive."

"How I love you," he whispered and began to weep silently. He wound his left arm around my shoulders and pressed me fast against him. I would have killed afresh for him then, would gladly have wielded the knife to shed more blood so that he, Henri, would not endure another second of pain.

That was the one moment I try to remember of those terrible days: The rest was only suffering.

The famed surgeon Ambroise Paré arrived the morning after. Even he was intimidated by so grisly a wound. By that time it had grown pustulant, and my husband feverish. The surgeon was frank: The shard was so firmly wedged into my husband's skull that any attempt to remove it would be instantly fatal. Not removing it would inevitably lead to infection and death: In short, nothing could be done to save the King.

I sent for the Dauphin, to ensure that he saw his father one last time. Montmorency returned, shaking his grizzled head: François had refused to come. I went to get him myself. Mary sat stone-faced in the Dauphin's antechamber while my son sat cross-legged upon his bed, moaning and rocking and striking the wall with the back of his head. I pulled him to his feet and led him to his father.

As the King turned his face toward our approach, François let go a wail: the right side of Henri's face was so grotesquely swollen that the cheek had pressed against the side of his nose, pushing it to the left. His wounded eye—bandaged to permit the jagged shard to protrude two fingers' width beyond his profile—stunk of rotting meat.

The Dauphin's eyelids fluttered and his head lolled upon his shoulders;

Montmorency and I caught him as he fell. The Grand Master laid him gently in his father's arms and told Henri that his son had come. At the sound of his old friend's voice, Henri opened his good eye, then reached out blindly to embrace François. When the boy stirred, Henri whispered: "God bless you, my son, and give you strength. You shall need it, to be King."

At that, François let go another low wail and fainted again; Montmorency and a valet carried him from the room. Henri's eyelid closed as he returned to his unhappy rest. I remained on my feet at the King's side—but, overwhelmed, pressed my hands against the mattress in an effort to hold myself up.

"Catherine," my husband whispered, his eye still closed. He fumbled for my hand, his touch hot.

I gripped his hand and kissed it. "I am here," I said. "I will not leave you."

He let go a groan that was also a sigh. "Promise me," he said.

"Anything." My voice sounded deceptively strong.

"Promise me you will protect and guide my sons. Promise me an heir of Valois will always sit upon the throne."

"I swear it." Ignoring the reek of pustulance, I kissed his grey lips—lightly, gently, to avoid causing him further pain.

Afterward, he sank into a deep slumber, from which he could not be roused. I kept my promise: I did not leave him but stayed at his side, still dressed in the purple gown I had worn to the tournament. For seven days, he lay blind and speechless, unable to give voice to his agony.

In the early afternoon of the tenth of July, His Most Christian Majesty King Henri II died in Paris at the Château des Tournelles. Once the doctor had pronounced him gone, a gentleman of the chamber ran to part the heavy brocade drapes and push open the window, releasing the stench of rotting flesh. Outside, the air smelled of rain.

The living move swiftly to dispose of the dying: As I lay grieving, my cheek pressed to Henri's silent chest, Doctor Paré pulled all the bed curtains open with blunt finality. Those who had sat vigil with me that day—François of Guise and the Cardinal of Lorraine, the Dukes of Savoy and Nemours—left at once to spread the grim news. The corridor filled with murmurs and footfall. I heard the gentle sloshing of water and looked up: Two serving women had arrived, basins in hand, to wash the King's body.

"Go away," I snarled and turned from them, only to start at a gentle touch upon my shoulder.

Madame Gondi stood over me, her lovely face swollen from too many tears. *"Madame la Reine,"* she said softly. "You must come. Please. You will make yourself ill."

"A few more minutes," I told her. "Do not take me from him so very soon."

Her lips trembled. "Madame," she said, "you have lain here for six hours."

I planted a kiss upon Henri's cooling cheek and ran my fingers tenderly over his wiry beard; only then did I let myself be led away toward my apartments. On the staircase, I balked, panicked.

"The children," I said. "They must be told. The Dauphin must know at once."

"They already know," Madame Gondi said gently. "Some hours ago, the Duke of Guise and his brother went to inform them."

"It's not right," I said. "They should have heard it from my lips, not another's."

"Come up to your room now, and lie down," she soothed. "I will have you brought something to eat."

I had refused food for days and drunk little; when I began to climb the staircase again, the walls started slowly to spin. I gasped and turned to Madame Gondi, but there was only darkness.

I woke to find myself undressed to my chemise, lying in my own bed. The window was open to the midsummer heat and encroaching dusk. Nearby, Madame Gondi stood next to the silver-bearded, portly Doctor Chapelain. On the bedside table was a platter of mutton and boiled eggs, and a flask of wine.

"You must eat and drink, *Madame la Reine,*" he said, wagging a plump forefinger in my direction. "And then you will sleep until morning."

I said nothing. The doctor left, and I took the plate Madame Gondi proffered. I chewed and swallowed the mutton and drank the wine, but tasted nothing: Food was an offense, a bitter reminder that Henri was dead and I was alive, that I should have to eat and drink from that moment forth without him.

It would have been easy, then, to lie down and let sorrow blot out all else. Yet one small ray pierced the growing gloom: the thought of my children. For their sake, I rose from my bed, suddenly desperate to tell them gently of their father's last hours and to offer what comfort I could. I demanded fresh clothing, so emphatically that my ladies quickly obliged me.

They produced a new dress of white silk damask studded with pearls, with a high ruffed collar of starched white lace. It was a pristine creation, an exquisite mourning gown for a French queen, with a matching hood and a veil of white gossamer. The seamstresses had no doubt worked long, feverish days since Henri's mishap to complete it.

I spat on it and ordered them to take it away. I called for my gown of plain black silk, the one I had worn when the twins died. But before I could put on my slippers or lower the dark veil, I heard a high-pitched, anxious call in the antechamber.

"*Maman . . . ? Maman,* hurry, you must come at once!"

Barefoot, I moved as quickly as shock allowed into the next room, where my darling eight-year-old Edouard stood in the doorway leading to the corridor. He was slender, with the Valoises' long torso and limbs, and his father's shining black eyes. His expression was one of pure panic.

"My precious eyes," I said. "My sweet child, what is it?"

"The Duke of Guise and the Cardinal," he said, his cheeks stained with tears. "They have told François to meet them downstairs. He is to bring Mary, Charles, Margot, and me. They are going to take us all away. They said not to tell you, that they must speak to François alone now that he is King." His eyes narrowed; he was capable even then of understanding intrigue. "I don't trust them, *Maman.* They are friends with that wicked Madame de Poitiers."

My fingers dug into the sides of his shoulders. "When? When are you to meet them?"

"Now," he replied. "At the entrance leading to the western gate."

I gripped his hand. Together, we dashed from my apartments, down the spiraling staircase leading to the ground floor. On the landing, I almost collided with Montmorency. The old man was so stricken by his master's death that he did not react at all to the fact that I had been running at full tilt down the stairs.

In a voice as dull as his bloodshot eyes, he said, "I came to inform you, Madame, that the vigil in the King's chamber will commence tomorrow, at nine o'clock. You must rest well tonight, for the coming days will be long ones for you."

He referred to the mourning vigil kept by all French queens: Tradition bound me to spend the next forty days at the Château des Tournelles, secluded in a darkened room beside my husband's embalmed body.

But I had vowed to protect Henri's sons. "I cannot stay," I answered quickly. "The Guises are taking François away. I must go to him."

He drew back, for love of Henri offended, but I had no time to explain. I squeezed Edouard's hand, and my son and I ran down the stairs, through the vast, echoing reception halls to the chateau's western entrance.

Outside, a carriage waited at the edge of the driveway. The sinister-eyed Cardinal of Lorraine, Charles of Guise, was holding the Dauphin's elbow as my son ventured the high step into the carriage. The Duke of Guise, Mary, and my two younger children were waiting to follow them in.

Thunder rolled in the distance. François, skittish at storms, jerked and almost hit his head upon the carriage ceiling as he climbed inside. A cold drop of rain stung my cheek, then another.

"François!" I cried—sharply, but as the others turned to face me, I forced the muscles in my face to ease. "Here is the missing Edouard," I called calmly, as if the Guises themselves had sent me to look for him. "And I shall come, too."

The Guise brothers' eyes widened with shock, but they dared say nothing. For an instant, Mary looked at me as though I were an asp that had just stung her, then composed herself and nodded a somber greeting. She was lovely and fresh despite the heat, a glittering vision in her white wedding gown.

"Madame la Reine," she said. "Should you not remain with the King?"

She referred, of course, to my dead husband, but I pretended not to understand.

"That is precisely what I intend," I answered, with a nod at François. "As I promised his father I would do."

She said nothing more but stood silently as the Duke of Guise moved to one side of the carriage door and his brother the Cardinal moved to the other. They held out their hands to me.

"Please, *Madame la Reine,*" the Duke said and bowed.

"I am no longer Queen," I told him. "That lot falls to Mary now."

I stood my ground, holding Edouard's hand, and waited until the Guises helped their niece—Mary, Queen of France and Scotland—into the coach, to sit beside her husband the King. At last the Guises turned to me.

By then the rain had begun to fall in earnest, slicking the pavement and bringing an abrupt chill to the summer air. I thought of Aunt Clarice—ragged and trembling, yet utterly determined on that frantic ride from the Palazzo Medici—as I set my bare foot down on the wet cobblestone and took the short walk away from the Château des Tournelles, away from Henri and my heart, away from everything past.

PART VII

Queen Mother

July 1559–August 1572

Thirty-two

The Guises' carriage took my children and me to the Palace of the Louvre. François, Duke of Guise, and his brother Charles, Cardinal of Lorraine, wanted desperately to separate me from my son—now François II, King of France—so that he would refuse my advice and listen only to them and to Mary, whom he adored. But I would not leave François, and when he asked sweetly whether he might speak privately with the Cardinal and the Duke, I surrendered myself to such earnest—if calculated—paroxysms of weeping that he was too frightened to desert me.

I feared for him on more than one account. The strain of his father's suffering and death had left François physically debilitated: even in the carriage, he laid his head upon Mary's shoulder and moaned feebly at every lurch. He was dizzy, he said, and his ear had begun to pain him.

Nevertheless, François tried his best to understand my words about the necessity of a smooth transfer of power. By nightfall, I had convinced my son to establish a regency council whose decisions bore a weight equal to those of His Majesty. I was to share power with the Guises, who had moved into Diane's and Montmorency's apartments after throwing the former occupants' belongings out onto the Louvre's paved courtyard.

Old Montmorency—too late realizing that it honored Henri more to save his kingdom than to sit with his dead body—came to the Louvre the following day, and offered his services to François. My son thanked him stiffly, then haltingly recited a cruel speech written by the Guises: Montmorency was too old to be of use, and his position of Grand Master now belonged to François, Duke of Guise. The new King suggested Montmorency retire to his country estate.

In the days after my husband's death, many faces changed at Court: old Montmorency, a reliable fixture, was gone; the young Scotsman, Captain de Montgomery, could not be found. Diane de Poitiers retreated to her home at Anet. At my request, she promptly returned the Crown Jewels my husband had given her in his smitten youth, along with a letter asking my forgiveness for any pain she had ever caused me.

When the jewels arrived, in a beautifully sculpted crystal casket—a wedding gift to me from Pope Clement—I took Mary to see them. I treated her politely in public, but I had not forgotten her conspiratorial conversation with the man who had killed my husband, nor François of Guise's stray comment, at her wedding, that she was already Queen of France.

"These are yours now," I told her. And when she brightened at the sight of them, I sidled next to her and whispered, "Regicide is the worst crime before God. Those who commit it are doomed to the worst circle of Hell."

She glanced sharply at me, her eyes wide and perhaps frightened as her hand went to the diamond-studded crucifix at her breast.

Easily, I looked away from her, down at the glistening casket filled with rubies and emeralds and pearls. "You are a very lucky girl," I murmured. "Fortunate that my son loves you so dearly. Fortunate that Captain de Montgomery cannot be found."

She stared at me, her eyes owlish, her lips so tightly pursed as to be in danger of disappearing. I left her thus, pale and pinched and silent.

I don't understand how, in those early days, I managed to do what was necessary to protect my son. They say that after a soldier loses an arm or a leg, the body insists the limb is still there, moving, touching, feeling. Perhaps that is how I survived the horror of losing my husband; I breathed and spoke and moved, thanks to a phantom heart.

In the moments I was not needed, I succumbed. I swathed my cramped apartments at the Louvre in black crepe and sat alone on the floor, clutching my skull. There are no words to describe grief: the howling madness, the bitter ache in the chest and throat, the terror caused by loss of meaning. It came in waves less predictable than those of labor but infinitely fiercer. One instant I would be issuing orders to Madame Gondi; the next, clutching her skirts as I collapsed, sobbing.

Nor are there words to describe the endless feverish workings of my mind as it sought to understand how I had failed Henri, how—despite everything—I had let him die. Why had the sacrifice of the harlot not been enough? Why had I not insisted more vehemently that he avoid the joust?

Summer turned relentless: Black waves writhed in the air above the pavement and turned to steam in the wake of afternoon showers that gave no respite. Night brought sudden storms: I woke often to the crack of lightning, hearing instead the shattering of the Scotsman's lance.

A month to the day after the King died, Ruggieri returned to Paris. Before I hurried to meet him, I peered into my mirror and saw a haggard woman there, with a new shock of white hair at one temple and a pronounced pallor from lack of outdoor exercise. Grief did not flatter me.

Ruggieri looked better than I had ever seen him. He had grown a black beard to cover his pitted cheeks and put on a bit of weight, which suited him. He had even seen a bit of sun. The instant Madame Gondi closed the door on us, Ser Cosimo went down on one knee.

"Madame la Reine," he said, his tone formal but heartfelt. "Words fail to express the sorrow I felt upon hearing of His Majesty's death."

"We meet again, too soon," I responded.

"Too soon," he answered, his voice and eyes sad.

I walked around my desk to where he knelt. "Rise, Monsieur Ruggieri," I said and caught his hand.

He rose. When he stood looking down at me, expectant yet somber, I lifted my arm and, with all my strength, struck him. The gesture loosed a storm of rage: I curled my fists and pounded his chest, his stomach, his arms.

"Bastard!" I screamed. "Bastard! You made me kill a woman and her children, but it was not enough, and Henri died!"

He averted his face patiently until I was breathless and spent.

"You *lied*," I gasped. "You said that Henri was safe."

"We gave him years," Ruggieri answered. Misery glimmered in his eyes. "I did not know how many. The stars, you understand, can be cheated only so long."

"Why did you not *tell* me?" I wailed and struck out again. My fingernails caught the tender skin beneath his eye and left three bloody marks; he made no sound as I drew back, aghast.

"Would you have preferred to live those years already grieving?" he asked. "Counting the days and dreading what must come?"

"I murdered innocents for naught! How do I know the pearl isn't useless? How do I know it keeps my children safe?"

"We purchased your husband almost two decades," he countered. "Half a lifetime. Or would you have had Henri perish as the young Dauphin, in his father's wars? Would you prefer that your children had never been born? The pearl has bought them time—I know not how long—that they would never have had."

I fell silent and stared, disconsolate, at the floor. I am not certain what followed: I felt giddy and thought that the lamp upon my desk had suddenly dimmed.

When I came to myself, I was propped up on many pillows in a chair in my antechamber, my legs resting on an ottoman. Madame Gondi was fanning the air in front of my face.

"*Madame la Reine*, thank God!" she said, with a small smile of relief. "You have returned to us at last." She made me sip from a goblet of wine.

I put a hand to my brow. "Where is Monsieur Ruggieri?"

"Out in the corridor. I did not think him capable of being so thoroughly frightened."

I handed her the goblet. "Bring him in."

She knew me well enough not to argue. She admitted Ruggieri, then stepped just outside the door. Too dizzy to risk standing, I remained seated.

At the sight of me, the magician brightened; I motioned for silence. I was too weak and ragged to waste energy on a meaningless conversation about my health.

"You did not tell me everything about my husband," I said, "but you will tell me everything about my sons. François's health is poor. I must know whether it will improve, whether . . ." I let the words hang unspoken between us.

"If you are sure that you can bear to know the truth," Ruggieri said, "I will present to you the future, more clearly than any nativity can display it. Give me a week, perhaps two. But we will need privacy. It is not something that can be easily accomplished here in the city, where there are too many eyes." He paused. "And if the truth is not to your liking . . . ?"

"No more blood," I whispered.

"I shall speak to you again soon, *Madame la Reine,*" he promised with a bow.

As he left, Madame Gondi remained in the doorway, watching curiously while he made his way down the corridor.

"He is a strange man, I know," I sighed.

"Perhaps," she said thoughtfully. "But he carried you here in his arms; he was so undone by worry, I thought that he would faint himself. I believe, *Madame la Reine,* that he is in love with you."

I gave her a sharp glance: My heart was raw over Henri; I could not bear to think of Ruggieri's odd affliction. Madame Gondi changed the subject to what I had failed to eat and drink over the course of the day, and we spoke no more of the magician.

The Château de Chaumont rests on a promontory overlooking the Loire River. A clean, new structure, it features round whitewashed towers capped with dark grey slate and views of the forested valley. I had begun to negotiate its purchase in the days before Henri's death, thinking to turn it into a haven for my overweary husband: Now, I wanted to hide there because it held no memories of him.

Ruggieri awaited me at Chaumont. He had ridden on his own horse and arrived some days before, the better to avoid rumors. He did not greet me upon our arrival but remained closeted away, preparing for our latest crime.

I spent the remaining daylight hours restlessly inspecting my new property, wandering through empty rooms. When dusk came, a sliver of moon rose over the dark river. I stood upon my balcony, watching the light play on the rippling water.

Within a few hours, Madame Gondi's knock came at the door. I followed her through a gallery that led outdoors to the building that housed the chapel. She took me inside, to the foot of a winding staircase leading up to the bell tower. I refused the lamp and left her there to climb the high, narrow stairs in the dark. The tall door at the top was closed, its edges limned with pale, feeble light. I pushed it open.

The room was vast, high-ceilinged, and empty, all of which conspired to give the sense of infinite, uncharted darkness. At its center, Ruggieri waited in the heart of a large circle. Candles flickered faintly at each of the four cardinal directions—one of them just behind a low, silk-draped altar, which held a small wooden birdcage and a human skull, its crown sawed away to admit a censer. Smoke streamed from its eye sockets, perfuming the air with the resinous, sacred smell of frankincense.

He moved to the edge of the pentagram but no further; a double-edged dagger glinted in his left hand.

"The circle has already been cast. Come." He pointed at a spot just outside the black perimeter. "Stand there and do as I tell you."

I went to it and watched as the magician wielded the dagger, touching the tip to floor at the circle's edge and lifting it up to carve an invisible archway just wide enough to permit me passage.

"Enter now," he whispered. "Quickly!"

I hurried through, and he performed the reverse motion swiftly, sealing the gap.

Inside the circle, the darkness was dancing, alive. Ruggieri sheathed his dagger and returned its center. The pale blur of his hand moved swiftly, and I found myself suddenly staring at an apparition: a tiny woman, dressed and veiled in black, her white face haggard with grief.

I reached toward her; my fingers brushed cold metal and recoiled. It was a large oval mirror upon a stand, draped in black until that instant. Ruggieri set aside the cloth and pulled a stool in front of the steel mirror.

"Sit," he commanded, and I obeyed.

He moved to the altar and took a white pigeon from the cage. It sat trustingly in his hand until he reached out to wrest its neck suddenly, savagely. The dagger flashed; the pigeon's head fell to the floor as blood gushed onto white feathers. Ruggieri lifted a quill from the altar and, dipping it into the bloody stump, painstakingly formed strange, barbarous letters upon the steel. Red sigils soon covered my reflection, until the mirror was almost filled; he set down his gruesome inkwell and quill to stand behind me.

"Catherine," he said. "Catherine . . ." It was a chant, musical and strangely sensual. "You wish to know your sons' fates," he sang. "Let the mirror now reveal the future kings of France."

Bitterly weary from grief, I closed my eyes and leaned back against him, passive and on the verge of slumber. My breathing grew deep and languorous; I wanted never to stir.

"Catherine," he hissed.

I opened my eyes with a start. I was sitting unsupported on the stool, and Ruggieri had vanished. I called his name, but no answer came—only the gentle trill of the surviving bird. The slab of polished steel revealed two shining candles at the circle's edge, nothing more.

The mirror suddenly filmed as if censed with smoke. As I stared into it, a countenance formed in the mists. I thought at first that the magician had come to stand behind me again, but the face was not his. The features were blurred and translucent, the specter of a dark-haired boy with dark eyes.

"François?" I whispered. The features, the cant of the head and shoulders, could well have been those of my eldest son.

The face gave no answer but grew slowly incandescent. It pulsed once, dazzling as fireworks, then quickly dimmed.

The mirror darkened and began to swirl. As the mists cleared a second time, a face appeared, this one in profile but again blurred and indistinct. It, too, was of a boy, round-cheeked and sullen, with an ugly red mark on his upper lip: my second son, Charles.

Let the mirror now reveal the future kings of France.

François, my poor frail boy, was doomed. I pressed my hands to my eyes in an effort to hold back tears. Ruggieri had been right; I had not wanted to know.

When I parted my fingers, Charles's countenance was pulsating with light. Bright and dark, bright and dark alternated until I began to count the fluctuations: four, five, six . . . Were these increments of time? Years? If so, how many had I missed?

A black tear trickled down Charles's ghostly cheek; I pressed my fingertips to the mirror's cold surface. Dark liquid rushed from the top of the mirror downward, spilling like a black curtain to blot out the sight of my son. I pulled my hand away and spread my fingers—sticky, red, smelling of iron.

At once, the bloody curtain vanished. I let go a sob at the realization that Charles's face had also disappeared; within the mirror, clouds roiled. A third face formed, one bearded and handsome, very like my husband's.

"My precious eyes," I gasped. Of all my children, Edouard was most suited to be King. I began to count the oscillations but did not get far: The bloody veil soon fell again.

The steel flashed as if reflecting the sun. Dazzled, I cried out and covered my eyes.

When I looked again, the mirror was clear, unclouded—a mirror, nothing more. I peered into it and saw my own reflection clearly.

Above my right shoulder hung the sun-browned face of a little boy, perhaps six years old. It was solid, not ghostly, with close-cropped chestnut curls and large eyes—green, like those of his grandmother Marguerite of Navarre, like those of his mother, Jeanne.

I whirled about, the stool skittering beneath me as I struggled to my feet. The boy stood near the door—a real boy, flesh and blood, mouth gaping at the sight of me.

"You there!" I shouted and started as a strong hand gripped my arm above the elbow. The boy dashed out the door and disappeared.

"Don't go after him," Ruggieri warned. "Don't break the circle."

"But I know him!" I said. "Henri of Navarre, Jeanne's son. What is he doing here? He should be in Paris!"

"It's only a groom," Ruggieri countered, "from the stables. A curious boy who needs a beating, nothing more. Let him go. We must close the circle properly."

"*No,*" I said. "Not yet. I must ask the King what this means. My husband—I know that you can summon him."

Ruggieri sighed wearily and stared at the candle flame behind the altar and the smoke that streamed up from the skull.

"All right then," he said at last. He took the second pigeon from the cage and wrung its neck, then wiped the mirror clean with his sleeve.

"Give me your hand," he said. I balked until he added, "He knows you, Catherine. Your blood will draw him the fastest."

I surrendered my hand and did not flinch when the blade stung the tip of my finger. The magician milked it a bit, then pressed it to the mirror's cold surface.

Ruggieri sat upon the stool and began to breathe rhythmically. Soon his head lolled, and his eyelids trembled.

"Henri," he whispered hoarsely. It was an invitation, a plea. "Henri de Valois . . ."

His eyes closed, and his body sagged upon the stool; his limbs began to twitch. Abruptly he straightened, though his head lolled forward, as though he were sleeping. The dagger flashed again: The pigeon's severed head softly struck the floor as the magician's left hand fumbled for the quill.

I watched, transfixed, as Ruggieri dipped the nib into the pigeon's bloody stump and wrote across the mirror's gleaming surface. The script was my husband's.

Catherine

For love of you I do this for love of you this time I come

Ruggieri's hand ceased its spasmodic efforts and hovered above the steel—waiting for a question.

"Our sons," I whispered. "Will they all die without heirs?"

A pause; Ruggieri's fingers trembled.

My one true heir will rule

"One heir?" I pressed. "François alone will rule?"

The quill steadied and did not move. François was sickly; if he was the only Valois heir, what was to become of his brothers?

"Why the blood?" I demanded. "Why was there blood on Charles's face, on Edouard's? Why did Navarre appear? Is it because he will kill them?"

Destroy what is closest to your heart

"Should I kill Navarre first?" I whispered. "Before he takes their throne?"

Destroy what is closest to your heart

"No!" I said. "I cannot . . ." I cradled my face in my hands and did not look up until Ruggieri gripped my shoulders and shook them.

"Catherine!" His voice was harsh. "I have undone the circle. We must go."

"I can't do it," I sobbed. "I cannot kill Navarre, too. A sweet, innocent boy . . ."

"Navarre never appeared." Ruggieri was adamant. "I saw no one but a stableboy, a black Ethiopian, with straw in his hair."

"I thought that I was strong enough," I moaned. "But I am not strong enough for this."

"The future is not fixed," the magician said urgently. "It's fluid, like the ocean, and you, Catherine, control the tide."

I stared up at him. "A tide of blood. Tell me how to stop it, Cosimo. Tell me how to save my sons."

My plea disarmed him. For an instant, his composure fled, revealing infinite tenderness, helplessness, pain. Stricken, he reached unsteady fingers toward my cheek, then withdrew them and gathered himself.

"Come, *Madame la Reine,*" he said softly and took my hand.

Thirty-three

I returned to Paris in time to see my daughter Elisabeth off on her long journey to the welcoming arms of her new husband, King Philip of Spain. I wept as I kissed her farewell, knowing what awaited her: the loneliness of finding oneself surrounded by strangers, the frustration of wrestling with a foreign tongue. As her carriage rode away, I wrote her the first of many letters, so that she should not have to wait long before receiving a reminder of home.

During my absence, Charles of Guise, Cardinal of Lorraine, had been busy trying to put France's financial affairs in order. The recent wars had left the country near bankruptcy—and the Cardinal, arrogant fool, decided that the best solution was to refuse to pay the French soldiers returning at last from battle. That, combined with his energetic persecution of Protestants, left him and his brother despised by the common folk.

Protestant leaders had gathered near the port of Hugues and birthed a plot to overthrow the Guises and replace them with the flighty Antoine de Bourbon. The Cardinal's face was livid as he relayed this to me. "Those damnable Huguenots," he said, "will not stop until they have overthrown the Crown itself."

Worst of all, François's health had failed in my absence. The young king's ear pained him constantly now and exuded an evil smell; his mottled cheeks were covered with boils. Terrified, I consulted with his doctors and agreed to whisk him from the city's oppressive heat to the Château at Blois.

By the time we boarded the coach, François was so miserable that he laid his head in my lap and groaned pitifully the entire way—pausing three times, when we signaled the driver to stop, to lean out the window and retch.

When we arrived at Blois, the Guises carried François to his bed while I sent for the doctors. I sat at my stricken son's bedside next to Mary—she still in a queen's white mourning, her regal composure stripped away to reveal a frightened young woman. Her affection for her young husband was not entirely feigned; she clung to his limp hand and murmured reassurances. He was fifteen years old—an age at which his father had been a man—yet the body that lay prostrate upon the bed was a child's, narrow-shouldered and spindly, with cheeks that bore no trace of a beard.

"François!" she begged. "Speak to me, please . . ."

He opened his eyes a slit. "D-don't m-make me," he stammered. "It hurts . . ." And he closed them again.

Charles and Edouard entered the room, their eyes wide with uncertainty as they solemnly studied their eldest brother.

Homely and hot-tempered, with a wheezing cough that had plagued him from infancy, Charles turned to me and asked, in a loud, heartless tone: "Will he die, then? And will I be King?"

François's eyelids flickered. Mary let go her husband's hand and leaned past me to slap Charles's childishly plump cheek.

"Horrid boy!" she exclaimed. "What a dreadful, ugly thing to say!"

Charles's face contorted with rage. "It's Edouard's fault!" he bellowed at his younger brother, who was handsome, intelligent, tall, and endearing—everything Charles was not. "He told me what to say!" He whirled on Edouard, who cringed in my arms. "You want François to die. And me, too. You can't wait until we are both dead, so that you can have your way in everything!"

"It's a lie," Edouard whispered. "François, forgive him . . ." He began weeping softly.

I handed the boys over to their governess, with strict instructions that they were not to come back until I sent for them.

Mary and I spent the rest of the day and night with François. Each of us gripped one of his hands and held it tightly while the doctor poured warm oil of lavender into his ear; François thrashed and howled piteously.

Hours later, he sat upright and shrieked; a foul-smelling yellow discharge trickled from his affected ear. Mary and I were horrified, but the doctor was pleased: The abscess had burst. If the patient could be strengthened with tonics, he might still overcome the infection.

With the swelling and pain reduced, François fell asleep at last. Relieved, I took the doctor's advice to go to my bed, where I dropped into fitful slumber.

I dreamt: Again I stood staring out at a field—the torn lists in front of the Château des Tournelles, I thought at first, but there was no palace, no stands, no spectators—no one, save myself and the black, silent form of the man at my feet. The barren ground stretched to the horizon and the fading sky.

My Henri lay dying. I did not call to him or ask how I might help: This time I knew there was nothing I could do save hear him whisper, *Catherine,* and watch him die.

When his final breath was free, blood bubbled up from his wounded eye and flowed forth onto the earth. Farther and farther it spread, streaming outward, until the ground was covered and a thousand separate pools appeared.

From each pool grew a man, in his final anguished throes. And from each man, a fresh spring gushed forth, to form more and more soldiers, each one mortally wounded. A groan slowly rose in strength until it became a roar, until I pressed my palms against my temples to crush the noise echoing in my skull:

Madame la Reine, aidez-nous

Help us, help us, help us . . .

Tell me what I must do, I demanded. *Only tell me what I must do!*

My voice was drowned out by the rising crescendo. I began to shout, more loudly, more insistently, until I woke in my own bed, to a crushing realization.

My sons were not the only ones endangered. Henri's death had marked not the end of the bloodshed but, rather, the beginning.

I saw the future keenly in the moment after waking: How François would soon die, how his brother ten-year-old Charles would replace him. But

Charles was too young to wear the crown; French law required that a regent rule the country until the King reached his majority at the age of fourteen.

By law, an assembly of nobles chose the regent, and given the growing resentment over the Guises' ascendancy, there was little doubt the assembly would hand the regency to the First Prince of the Blood, Antoine de Bourbon.

François's death would strip Mary of her French crown and the Guises' connection to it. They would not permit Bourbon to claim his rightful place, as he would surely cast them from power. Bourbon, in turn, would lead a Huguenot army against them—and the Guises would call upon all good Catholics to fight the heretics. France would be torn apart by civil war.

I rose and called for Madame Gondi, and directed her to send for Bourbon at once.

The days before Antoine de Bourbon's arrival were colored by tentative hope. François's fever abated somewhat; he sat up briefly and ate a bit of barley gruel. Relieved, I went outside alone to take the cold autumn air. I covered the courtyard lawn in good time, came upon the enclosed tennis gallery, echoing with the shouts of boys and the ball's report as it struck the walls, and remembered the hours I had spent watching my young husband and his brother playing tennis.

Another shout came: *Tenez!* At the same instant, a ball sailed past me, prompting me to turn and look behind me at the sprawling lawn. A surge of nausea seized me; I put my hand to my eyes, and when I drew them away, a mass of naked, mutilated bodies lay piled upon the grass.

I was too stunned to do anything but stare at them. They wavered in the light, then vanished in the wake of running footsteps coming from the direction of the gallery.

I turned to see six-year-old Henri of Navarre, a racquet in his hand. He had stopped several arms' lengths away, to stare, his eyes stark with fear, at the very spot where I had seen the corpses.

I motioned to him, and he began to run away.

"Henri, wait!" I cried.

He paused, allowing me to draw close enough to speak to him.

"You saw them, too, didn't you?" I asked, amazed. "You *saw* them . . ."

He looked over his shoulder at me; his face abruptly crumpled, and he ran back into the gallery.

The minute I returned to the palace, I called for Ruggieri.

When the magician sat before me, pale and ageless, I said, "Henri's death was not the end of it. My dreams brought me to France not only for his sake: There are more who will die, thousands more, unless I take action. We must discover what I am to do."

Ruggieri's gaze did not meet mine. He stared beyond me and said, "The lives of your sons were bought with the blood of others. Surely you do not mean to slay a thousand men so that a thousand more might not die."

"Of course not," I snapped. "But I am already doing everything that I can, on a practical level, to prevent war between the Catholics and the Huguenots. You are the magician, the astrologer; you are my adviser. Surely you know of something more that can be done—short of shedding blood."

"I told you before that talismans avail little in the face of overwhelming catastrophe. Eventually, the stars will have their way." He inclined his face gently downward, strangely diffident. "I have studied those stars recently; they have changed since the day I gave you the pearl. I had thought that . . ." An emotion I had never seen in him—guilt—rippled over his features. "Your husband's death should have put an end to your dreams, Madame. It should have put an end to the blood. The impact of one child upon the future was, I thought, safe, but three . . ."

The words of the prophet echoed in my memory:

The tapestry of history is woven of many threads. Let even one be exchanged for another that is weak and flawed, and the veil will tear—and blood be loosed, more blood than you have seen in any dream.

Madame la Reine, *these children should not be . . .*

"No," I whispered. "I am a mother who loves her children. What are you saying? That I should blame my sons? That I should lift my hand against them? Surely you are not, Monsieur, for if you were, I would lift my hand against *you.*"

His head was bowed; in the cant of his shoulders, I read sorrow and defeat.

"You want me to kill them, don't you?" I whispered. "You're asking a mother to destroy her own children . . . *Damn* you. Damn you to Hell!"

Ruggieri drew in a long breath and leveled his gaze at me, his expression mournful, urgently tender. "The time *will* come, Catherine. And if you fail to do what is necessary, there will be unspeakable carnage. It may already be too late."

"How dare you speak so vilely to me," I said, my voice trembling as I got to my feet. "How dare you speak so of my children. If you will not help me in the manner I desire, perhaps the time has come for you to leave my employ."

He rose. The sadness left his features, replaced by the elegantly composed mask. He bowed, the consummate courtier.

"As you wish, *Madame la Reine,*" he said.

By the following morning, I had convinced myself that my memory of our conversation was faulty, that Ruggieri was not capable of saying such awful things. I had misunderstood him, certainly. When I sent for him again, my courier returned to say that his apartments were already vacant, and his serving woman did not know where he had gone.

I blotted Ruggieri's impossible words from my mind and turned it to more practical concerns. I worried that rumors of the young King's poor health might have circulated and alerted Bourbon that the moment had come for him to rally his followers and march upon the palace. Happily, he arrived only three days after my summons—in the company of his valet and two lesser nobles, no more.

On the threshold to my cabinet, Bourbon balked when the guards there informed him that his friends would have to remain outside. I sat behind my closed door and listened to his vehement curses: Subtlety and self-possession were traits he lacked.

Yet when he calmed—and the door to my office was opened—he smiled brightly at me and bowed with an unctuousness verging on the comical. He doffed his velvet cap, revealing a goodly number of white hairs and his fluffy grey hairpiece. He wore more jewelry than I: a gold earring studded with diamonds, a ruby pendant, and several glittering rings.

"Madame la Reine!" he said. "I stand ready to be of service. What shall I do to please you?"

I held out my hands to him. He was the husband of Henri's cousin Jeanne and the father of little Navarre, though—involved with scurrilous politics and women—he rarely saw them. On the occasions we met, we treated each other as family.

"Come," I said, "and sit with me. It has been so long since we have spoken."

He took my hands eagerly and kissed the back of each one, then settled happily into his chair. I smiled also, but it faded quickly. I was too hollow after Henri's death to waste time with pleasantries. My tone turned serious.

"I have heard, Monsieur, that the Protestants have grown disaffected. That there was a meeting at the port of Hugues, and that the overthrow of the Guise brothers was discussed."

His eyebrows lifted in surprise; the fine skin of his brow wrinkled easily into a dozen shallow creases. For a moment he stared, quite speechless, at me, then stammered, "Ah, *Madame la Reine* . . . Ah. It is nothing personal, you see. It is only that my rights, as First Prince of the Blood, must be protected." He paused and, in a pitiful attempt to switch the subject, said, "On my arrival here, I inquired after His Majesty and was told he is indisposed. I am sorry to hear this; is he unwell?"

"He is troubled," I said, "by the actions of the Huguenots. By the thought that men would conspire to take up arms against him—"

"Not him!" Bourbon waved his hands as if to ward off the very idea. "No, *Madame la Reine*! I would rather die than act against the King!"

"But you would lift your sword against Grand Master Guise, whom my son himself appointed, and against his brother, the Cardinal of Lorraine, whom my husband named Grand Inquisitor. Is that not treason, Monsieur?"

Bourbon's eyes widened in dismay; whatever he had expected from me, it was not this. "No! Madame, I beg you, it is not!"

"*How* is it not?" I demanded.

"We do not take up arms against the King. But we wish to show, most emphatically, that the Guises have overstepped their bounds."

"You would show His Majesty," I said, my voice growing lower and ever more dangerous, "with arquebuses. With swords and cannon. You would shed blood, to force him to oust the ministers he and his father chose. That is not loyalty, Monsieur de Bourbon. That is treason." I rose, forcing him to rise with me.

"No! I swear before God!" He wailed and wrung his hands. "*Madame la Reine,* please listen to me—"

"I have heard enough," I said coldly. "Step aside so that I can call the guards."

At that, he fell to his knees—blocking my path—and quivered, a weak, disgusting thing.

"For the love of God!" he shrieked. "What must I do to convince you? I will order them all to disband. I will disavow them. Only tell me what His Majesty wishes, and I shall do it, to prove that I am loyal only unto him."

I sat down. I slid open my desk drawer and drew out a piece of parchment covered in a copyist's perfect script. Bourbon could disavow the Huguenots all he wished—but he was only a figurehead. The rebellion could easily continue without him.

"Get up," I told him, "and sign this."

He pushed himself to his feet and peered uncertainly at the paper. "Of course, *Madame la Reine*. Only what is it?"

"A legal document surrendering your rights to the regency in the event of King François's death," I said, "and transferring them to me."

Revelation dawned in his eyes as he stared down at the writing; the color returned to his cheeks and increased to a full-out flush. He had been played, and he knew it. "The regency?" he whispered, then more loudly said, "Do not tell me our young King is seriously ill."

I answered nothing. I did not want to call for the guards to haul him to prison—but I would, if necessary, and Bourbon sensed it. Beneath my ruthless gaze, he began to fidget. *Wretched creature,* I thought. *God help France if you ever become King.* I found it hard to believe he had produced such a fine son.

I dipped a fresh quill in the inkwell and proffered it across the desk.

He stared at it as though it were a scorpion. Yet after a long moment, he took it, and asked, "Where shall I sign?"

I pushed the parchment toward him and pointed to the spot.

He leaned over and scribbled rapidly: the *A* and *B* were huge, dramatic, looping. Afterward, he sat back with a long sigh of self-loathing.

I took the document and waved it a few times to dry the ink before setting it back into the drawer. Then I stood, prompting him to do the same.

"Your Highness," I said, as though finally remembering that I was speaking to a prince. "Your heroic act of self-sacrifice shall not go unmarked. When the time comes, I shall tell everyone how you have put the good of France far above your own."

We both knew, of course, that neither of us would mention this again—I, out of the need for secrecy; Bourbon, out of a sense of shame.

Even so, I continued warmly: "Please stay with us awhile at Blois. You are among family here, and ever welcome."

He murmured barely coherent phrases about his gratefulness for my hospitality, about his pressing need to return to Paris. I offered him my hand and repressed a shudder when his lips touched my flesh.

I did not need Cosimo Ruggieri, I told myself. I had just averted a potential war using my wits, and nothing else. Yet after Bourbon had sidled out the door and closed it behind him, I lowered my face to the cool, smooth surface of my desk and sobbed.

After my meeting with Bourbon, I made my way down the winding staircase that led to the King's apartments. The Duke of Guise was bounding up the steps and was so distracted that we nearly collided. He was gasping, his native arrogance overcome by blind panic; in his eyes, I saw the death of dreams.

Abandoning protocol, he seized my arm. "*Madame la Reine!* We have been searching everywhere for you! Doctor Paré needs you to come to the King's bedchamber at once!"

We flew. I kept pace with Guise on the stairs and pushed past the solemn assembly in the corridor to enter the royal antechamber. I was met by Doctor Paré's bleak, weathered face. Mary stood beside him, a wide-eyed wraith with a twisted kerchief in her restless hands—waiting, all this time, for me and for her uncle the Duke of Guise, who put his arm about her shoulder.

Doctor Paré did not waste time with pleasantries; he was a man unimpressed by titles and, certainly, by Mary, Queen of France. He understood that a mother's love trumped that of a political wife and so addressed himself to me.

"His Majesty has worsened, Madame," he said. "Within the last two hours, his fever has risen sharply. The infection has spread to his blood."

I closed my eyes. I had heard the same words from Doctor Paré before, when they had sealed my husband's doom.

"What does it mean?" Mary demanded. "What must be done now?"

"There is nothing more I can do," the doctor told her. "It is a matter of hours now, at most a day or two."

She lunged at him; the motion caused me to open my eyes just as she was raising her hands to claw the doctor's face. The Duke of Guise struggled to hold her back as she screamed, "He cannot die! You must not let him!"

While the Duke and Doctor Paré did their best to calm her, I went into the sickroom to sit vigil beside my son. François lay with his eyes tightly shut and crusted, his cheeks flushed an unhealthy violet hue. A heavy fur throw had been drawn all the way up to his chin; even so, his teeth chattered. I crawled into bed beside him and wrapped my arms around him, pressing my body against his in an effort to warm him. I remained there even after a calmer Mary entered and sat nearby. Her face hung over us, a wan and anxious moon.

There is little more to tell. François never came to himself, though at times he groaned with pain. At the end, his body convulsed pitifully, again and again. He fell still to the sounds of Mary's whispered recitations of the *Ave Maria* and *Pater Noster,* and when he let go his last rattling breath, citrine pus streamed from his nostrils.

Only then did I open my arms and climb slowly from the bed. Mary had given up praying to gape with horror at her husband's body; she remained limp and unresisting as I embraced her, only long enough to whisper in her ear: "Go home to Scotland now. I promise you, it will be safer for you there than here."

I left François to Mary and the Guises' hysterical ministrations and went off to find my surviving children. The prescient governesses had dressed the children in black and assembled them in the nursery. Charles was sitting impassively watching Edouard, Margot, and little Navarre throw a tennis ball for the spaniel, who fetched it, safely beyond Charles's reach. At the sight of me, Charles glanced up, scowling.

"Is he dead, then? Is François dead, and am I King?"

I could only nod. Edouard threw his arms around Margot as she and little Henri began to cry, while Charles's lips curved in a self-satisfied smirk.

"You see?" he told Edouard. "I am King, after all, and now you shall have to do everything I tell you!"

At the sight of the children's tears, I had been on the verge of loosing my own, but Charles's words drew me up short.

"No, he doesn't," I corrected him. "You are King in name only, Charles. It is I who rule France now."

Thirty-four

After François's death, Mary wisely sailed home to Edinburgh. In an effort to tighten their loosening grip on the Crown, the Guises formed an ultra-Catholic group dedicated to eradicating the Huguenots. Because of Antoine de Bourbon's reconversion to Catholicism, his wife, Jeanne—Queen of the now-Protestant kingdom of Navarre—separated from him. Although she remained at Court, the growing political tension caused her to avoid my company.

Bourbon's younger brother Louis, the Prince of Condé—a man of more impressive constancy—took his place and proved an able leader alongside Admiral Coligny. Protestantism continued to spread. Many intellectuals at Court—all sincere, rational people—were drawn to it; I therefore failed to sense the enmity growing beyond the palace walls.

The Guises threw themselves wholeheartedly into their zealous anti-Huguenot campaign. One Sunday the Duke of Guise was riding through the countryside when he heard the distant singing of psalms. With his entourage of armed guards, he discovered the source: a barn, packed with Huguenots worshiping in secret.

Under French law, heresy was punishable by death—a technicality that my husband and his father had often chosen to overlook. But Guise loosed his guards upon the singers, slaughtering seventy-four innocents and leaving a hundred more savaged but alive.

The Huguenots took revenge swiftly. Catholic Paris remained at peace, but battles were fought in the countryside. Condé and Coligny led the Huguenots, Guise and the inconstant Bourbon the Catholic royalists.

For a year, fighting was fierce. I argued in favor of negotiation, but Guise, a popular war hero, argued strenuously against it and garnered enormous support. Resigned, I went to rally the troops; when I walked the ramparts, old Montmorency scolded me: Did I not realize the terrible danger I had put myself in? I laughed, not knowing that, just outside the walls, Antoine de Bourbon had taken an arquebus shot to the shoulder while relieving himself beneath a tree. He died shortly thereafter, leaving his nine-year-old son, Henri, King of Navarre.

His widow decided that it was time for her and her son to return permanently to the tiny country Henri now ruled.

"No tears," Jeanne warned sternly, as I embraced her in the instant before she boarded the coach.

I obeyed and kissed her solemnly, and put my arms around little Henri.

"Whatever frightening things you see," I whispered into his ear, "you mustn't be afraid. They appear in order to guide you. Write to me about them if you wish, and I will try to help."

As I pulled back, he nodded shyly. I put a copy of Italian poetry into his hands—Tasso's *Rinaldo,* a fine adventurous romance for a precocious boy—then stepped back as the Queen and her son boarded the carriage.

Bourbon was not the only loss suffered by the royalists. The Duke of Guise once again distinguished himself in war by capturing the Huguenot leader Condé in battle—only to die a few months later outside Orléans, shot in the back by Gaspard de Coligny's spy.

I used the opportunity to prevent further bloodshed. Over the protests of Guise's family, who craved revenge, I negotiated with the rebels. In exchange for Condé's release and a limited right to worship, the Huguenots laid down their arms. I appointed Guise's son Henri to his late father's position of Grand Master and welcomed the Huguenots back to Court. During those years of peace, my children grew.

Margot became a high-spirited creature with dark, glossy ringlets and expressive features. When she smiled, her dark eyes came alive and made otherwise sensible men swoon. Supremely healthy, she adored riding and dancing, and proved herself a prodigy at mathematics.

Edouard—now the Duke of Anjou—grew to be tall, with his father's long, handsome face and black eyes. He also showed a Medicean taste for elegant clothing and favored jewelry, the more glittering, the better. With Edouard, I shared all that I knew about governing, and he proved himself an apt pupil, quick to understand intrigue and the more delicate nuances of diplomacy.

Charles grew, but I cannot say that he ever became a man. His chin was weak, his eyes and forehead too large; this unfortunate combination of features was not improved by the glaring birthmark beneath his nose. The slightest exertion left him pale and gasping. He was angered by his poor health and slow-wittedness, and deeply jealous of his brother's good looks and brains, and often flew into incoherent rages.

I thought that he would outgrow his fits of angry mania, but over time the frequency and intensity of them worsened. When His Majesty reached fourteen—the age of majority—he continued to rely on me to govern the country; I passed a law requiring him to have the approval of his Privy Council before issuing a command. In public, Charles did a fine job of parroting the speeches I wrote for him. But he made a show of rebelling against me in every other way, and on his fourteenth birthday he insisted, against my wishes and those of his physicians, on joining the hunt.

Edouard, almost thirteen, and his younger sister, Margot, rode alongside the King and me. It was late June, and the Loire Valley rolled out before us, lush and alive. Even white-haired Montmorency had accepted our invitation to the hunt, adding to the feel that it was just like old times.

It was difficult for me not to cast a thousand nervous glances in Charles's direction, or to call for a halt when his breath grew wheezing. But the chase filled him with such excitement that he spurred his mount to go faster and burst into unrestrained laughter, his eyes wide and bright.

I had told the Master of the Hunt to make the chase short and the prey easily taken. In half an hour, the hounds trapped our target in a thicket: a wild hare, the least threatening victim for a sickly boy.

"I have it!" Charles crowed, as the Master called the hounds off. My son dismounted and began to thrust a spear savagely into the thicket. When the hare emerged, Charles skewered the creature through its stomach, pinning it to the ground. By then, Edouard and Margot and I had dismounted and approached, in order to congratulate Charles on his first kill—but the odd light in my son's eyes silenced us.

The hare struggled to free itself, legs scrambling, yellow teeth bared. Laughing, Charles crouched down to touch the animal's wound and the hare bit him.

He let go a terrible howl and feverishly worked his fingers into the creature's wound, then pulled outward until the hare screamed; its skin tore, revealing glistening red muscle beneath. This excited Charles even more; he reached inside the dying animal and pulled out its entrails. With a maniacal grin, he held them up—intestines trailing from his fingers—for the world to see.

As the other riders arrived behind us, Charles lowered his face to his hands. Against a backdrop of alder leaves and evergreen, he looked up, his eyes bright, his teeth bared in a ferocious grin. From between them, the entrails—sinister red, like the birthmark above his lips—dangled.

He growled and tossed his head like a dog snapping the neck of its prey. I stepped in front of him, vainly trying to shield the others from the sight.

"My God," Edouard whispered.

He strode up to Charles and, with a hard blow, sent the King reeling. Charles roared and choked on the gore, then spat it out.

"Damn you to Hell!" the King bellowed. "How dare you strike my person!" He lunged at Edouard.

I tried to position myself between them: Charles struck out blindly, forcing me away, while Edouard tried to grab his brother's arms. Old Montmorency appeared in the middle of the melee; in the scuffle, Charles was knocked down and Edouard pulled off.

The King shouted incoherently. Tufts of sod flew as his fingers and teeth tore spastically at the grass, as if he meant to murder the innocent ground.

The other hunters left quietly. In the end, Charles exhausted himself and had to be carried away on a litter. He coughed so long and so hard that his kerchief grew soaked with blood.

I sat at his bedside that night, his only attendant besides Doctor Paré, who could not entirely mask his alarm at the sight of the blood. Fortunately, Charles developed no fever and, during breaks in the coughing, became his usual sour self.

"I shall die young," he announced gloomily, "and everyone will be glad."

"Don't speak so!" I chided. "You know very well that, if you were ever to die, it would break my heart."

He lifted a thin brow. "Surely you would rather Edouard be king."

"What a horrible thing to say! I love all my children equally."

"No, you don't," he said wearily. "You love Edouard best. And that is sad, *Maman,* because when I am dead, he will show himself as the monster he really is."

None of my well-reasoned arguments could convince him otherwise; soon, I gave up trying altogether.

When the King reached his seventeenth year, and the Duke of Anjou his sixteenth, trouble developed in the Netherlands and Flanders, ruled by Philip of Spain. The inhabitants were Protestants—Huguenots, as we called them all—and they rebelled at the harsh repression of their religion. Philip sent hundreds of Spanish troops to quell the uprising, but they were not enough to stop what had become a war.

On a cold winter morning in Paris, the Spanish ambassador, Alava, announced that Philip was sending twenty thousand troops to the Netherlands: Would I permit them to march through France?

I would not. Our relations with French Huguenots were strained enough without putting twenty thousand Catholic soldiers in their midst. As a precaution, I hired six thousand Swiss mercenaries to guard the border. I did not for an instant think that Philip intended to invade France, but I did not trust his army.

I never expected that the Huguenots would be alarmed by the Swiss soldiers at the border, nor did I consider that they would launch a rumor: While Philip quashed the rebellion in the Low Countries, I would send the Swiss to slaughter the Huguenots.

Indeed, with the Swiss watching over our borders, I felt confident—enough to take His Majesty, whose health was still poor, to the village of Monceaux, southeast of Paris.

On a cool September day just before noon, Margot, Charles, and I were sitting on the balcony looking out at the little carp-filled pond in the courtyard below. Beyond, the forests spread out in shades of crimson, rust, and saffron.

Edouard appeared suddenly on the balcony, sweating and flushed.

"They're massing," he gasped, "in the very next town. We have to leave at once!"

"It's only rumor," I chided. There had been talk earlier that the Huguenots were planning an attack, but I judged it unfounded. "Calm down and sit with us."

"I was off riding, *Maman.* I saw them myself!"

"Who?" Charles asked, but I was on my feet before Edouard finished talking.

"Where are they?" I demanded. "And how many?"

"Two villages away, to the west—hundreds of infantrymen. I've already sent scouts. If we're lucky, they'll report within the hour."

I drew in a steadying breath and reminded myself that an army moved with a fraction of the speed as a rider on horseback.

Charles thumped his fist on his chair's armrest. "I am the *King.* Will no one answer my question?"

Although Margot's features were slack with fear, she put a soothing hand upon her brother's arm. "The Huguenots, Your Majesty. We might need to take precautions."

Charles got up from his chair. "You're dreaming," he said to Edouard. "Surely you misunderstood—"

"They were carrying swords and pikes," Edouard retorted, "and the cavaliers had arquebuses. They spoke French, and there are no royal armies nearby. Who else would they be?"

I turned to Charles. "If there are indeed Huguenots on the march, we must protect your person. There is a fortress half an hour's ride from here, at the town of Meaux. We should go there at once."

"Edouard lies," Charles grumbled. "If anyone at this Court loves to start rumors, it's he."

But I was adamant. Within an hour, we boarded a coach and left behind all but our most valuable possessions to head straight for Meaux.

Encircled by a long-dry moat, the keep at Meaux was an intimidating bulwark topped by jagged battlements. We rode inside its gaping jaws and flinched at the earsplitting squeal of the ancient iron gate as it was lowered behind us.

The castle rooms were dank and bare, the gatekeeper deaf and unwelcoming. For the next several hours, Edouard paced the battlements with our Scottish bodyguards, while Margot and I sat with Charles. In between fits of coughing, he insisted that this was all a cruel practical joke of his brother's.

Night fell. His Majesty fell asleep with his head in Margot's lap. I wandered up and down long, dank corridors, blaming myself for my family's peril, wondering how I should ever get them safely back to the Catholic stronghold of Paris. Well past midnight, a figure hurried toward me, a lamp in his hand.

"Maman!" Edouard hissed. "They are coming!"

"Who?" I asked.

"The Swiss," he said, "or the rebels. Either way, we shall know the answer soon."

He led me up to the battlements. The wind at the top of the tower was strong and cold; I pressed my hand against the stone to steady myself and my flapping skirts, and gazed down.

Beyond the grassy meadow in front of the castle stood a forest; steadily approaching lights twinkled between the black limbs of its trees. The bearers of a hundred blazing torches emerged onto the meadow below; the wind in my ears swallowed their footfall. The lights slowly moved up to the edge of the dry moat and assembled themselves into a perfect square.

Far beneath us, one of our Scotsmen bellowed at the gate. "Who goes there?"

I seized Edouard's arm. The answer was garbled by the wind, but I understood the gist. The Swiss army had arrived, to serve at the pleasure of the King.

The immaculately courteous commander, Captain Bergun, wore the same uniform as his men, a plain brown tunic with a square white cross upon the breast. He and his mounted officers flanked the infantry that had come to our rescue. Bergun politely ordered us back into the coach and instructed our driver how to proceed to Paris.

Our carriage was situated at the center of a formation of one hundred men. A row five men deep marched ahead of us and behind us, and a row five men deep marched on either side of us, each holding a pike. I peered out the carriage window at a sea of gleaming steel blades moving to a rhythmical chant in Swiss German.

For a quarter hour, we rumbled along slowly; I fell into an uneasy reverie, which was interrupted by the crack of an arquebus. One of our horses reared; the drivers' curses were drowned out by Captain Bergun's shouts. Torchlight swept wildly over the dark landscape as another arquebus fired. The ball struck our carriage door, prompting Margot to pull the terrified King's head into her lap.

Outside, a blond, downy-cheeked pikeman stumbled and struck the wheel with his shoulder, his cheek and upper lip blown away. He fell, trampled by the others as they hurried to close the gap.

From the darkness came the battle cry: *Monjoie!*

Margot crossed herself while Charles wailed in her lap; Edouard and I stared out at the play of torchlight on the pikemen's backs as they lowered their blades in unison. An arquebus sounded again; our driver fell sideways to the ground as our horses screamed. The carriage tilted backward, slamming my shoulders against the interior wall; Margot fell on top of me. Charles and Edouard became a tangle of limbs until the carriage righted itself with a jerk.

I scrambled to the window and stared out at the dancing pikes. The wounded screamed: One Swiss fell, then another, and I began planning how to convince the rebels to spare my children.

Lead shot whizzed past my ear, and Edouard yelped. He pressed a hand to his shoulder and drew it away, bright with blood. I rose, thinking to shield him with my body, but he caught my arm and yanked me hard against the seat.

"For God's sake, *Maman,* sit down before they blow your head off!"

The Swiss closed ranks about us again; an officer abandoned his mount to take the reins of our coach. We rolled on for a bit, then stopped as Captain Bergun rode up alongside.

Leaning low in his saddle, he called, "It was a Huguenot scouting expedition; two escaped and will return to tell their superiors of our location. We cannot continue at this pace. They will send more cavalrymen with arquebuses." He peered beyond me at Edouard. "*Monsieur le Duc,* you are injured!"

"Only grazed," Edouard called back.

I craned my head out the window. "How far are we from Paris, Captain?"

"An hour, if we move swiftly," he replied. "My officers and I will ride with you, though we cannot offer as much protection as the pikemen."

"Thank you," I said. "Tell the driver not to spare the horses."

We rode so fast and hard that the carriage shuddered mercilessly, forcing us to cling desperately to our seats.

"God damn every Huguenot ever born!" Charles gasped. The effort to hold on left him ashen and breathless, but no less furious. "We must hunt them down to the last man—and I will draw and quarter the wretch who ordered this attack myself!"

Like Edouard, I remained darkly silent on that frenzied ride, my hand pressed to his shallow wound as I nursed my growing hatred. Before that night, my life had been devoted to keep the peace at all costs, but this attack on the persons of Anjou and the King was beyond forgiving. I stared past Charles and Margot toward the future, and the war that was surely coming.

We arrived at the Louvre forty-five minutes later, an hour before dawn. Montmorency awaited us: I had sent a message saying that he was needed to head an army. When I saw him—white-bearded but still square and resolute—with Doctor Paré in the driveway, I felt gratitude. I had never much cared for Montmorency, nor he for me, but he had led my husband to victory in battle.

He and Doctor Paré were alarmed to see the blood on Edouard's upper sleeve and were not easily convinced that the Duke of Anjou was not seriously injured. As the doctor herded my sons off, I took Montmorency's huge hands in mine.

"You were right, Monsieur, and I wrong," I said. "The rebels were ready to kill the King and Anjou. If I learn who is behind this—"

"The Prince of Condé," he answered at once. "My spies say that my nephew"—by whom he meant Admiral Coligny, a name he uttered only with great shame—"disapproved and did not lend his support."

"But Condé is a traitor," I said, "and I will not rest until he meets a traitor's end."

I never saw my bed that night but summoned my generals and advisers. Montmorency's scouts had determined that Condé's army was marching from the northeast toward Paris.

Over the next month, we rallied an army sixteen thousand strong while Condé's men camped on the banks of the Seine just outside the city, effectively cutting off our supplies. I swallowed my hatred and sent emissaries to Condé—whom he returned with the message that the good people of France were "tired of paying taxes to support the lavish lifestyles of foreigners, especially Italians."

Oh a drab November day, The Battle of Paris began. In the Louvre's courtyard, Montmorency and his commanders mounted their horses to salute the King before riding off to the front. Impetuous Charles, eager to spill blood, ran to one of the saddled steeds, but Montmorency hurried over and seized the bridle. "Your Majesty," he said, "your person is too dear to us, and the Huguenots have demonstrated their desire to capture you. Do not tax us; we would need at least ten thousand more men to protect you properly."

Even Charles could not argue with such logic. We royals remained inside the Louvre; never before was I so grateful for its reinforced walls and iron gates. I climbed up to the roof and looked northeast, though buildings blocked my view of the battle. Edouard—who had casually dismissed the gouge left in his shoulder—soon discovered me; together we watched as storm clouds converged overhead, driven by cold winds.

The armies engaged each other at three o'clock in the afternoon. Condé had amassed ten thousand men against our sixteen thousand; our victory seemed assured. After an hour, scouts brought word that the rebels had taken heavy losses; the second hour brought news that we had suffered equally. My mood darkened with the clouds, which now blotted out the sun.

The third hour brought cold rains, and a messenger soaked to the bone. "Constable Montmorency is at the western gate!"

I frowned, confused: Were we so lost that Montmorency had abandoned his troops? I hurried down to the gate, where an exhausted rider and horse trotted up, dragging a litter in the rain.

Montmorency was strapped to the litter; the blanket beneath him was covered with blood, though I saw no wound. His helmet had been removed, and his white hair was slicked to his scalp; the rain was falling earnestly, and I leaned down to shield him.

"Montmorency," I said. "Dear Constable . . ." I put my hand upon his filthy one, and his eyelids fluttered.

"Madame la Reine," he croaked. "I have failed you."

"No, Constable, did you not hear?" I forced a great smile. "Our troops are victorious! You have routed the enemy; you have saved France."

"Is it true?" he whispered.

"Yes," I answered, "yes!"

At that, he let go a long sigh and closed his eyes. Edouard had followed and was already shouting for Doctor Paré. I took the old man's hand as others carried the litter inside and had him laid in my bed.

He died there the next day, without coming to himself again. I had him entombed near Henri, the King he had so loved.

Thirty-Five

Within four days, our army forced Condé to retreat. The rebel forces marched southwest into the countryside and were joined by those of Montmorency's heretic nephew, Admiral Coligny. Our spies reported that the Huguenots were hiring German mercenaries to increase their ranks.

We had no choice but to recruit mercenaries of our own. But I faced an even greater dilemma: Montmorency's death had left a critical vacuum—that of Lieutenant General, head of the French army—yet none of the candidates for the position filled me with confidence.

At the end of a long day spent with my advisers, Edouard came calling at my chamber door.

"Make me Lieutenant General," he said.

I laughed. He was only sixteen, dressed in a scarlet velvet doublet and a ruffed collar of spidery ecru lace; large pearls hung from his ears. The thought of him smeared with grime on the battlefield was ludicrous.

"You're mad," I said.

His manner was intensely serious. "I'm not. Look at me, look at Charles—we're spoiled and cosseted, living in splendor while the people suffer the brunt of this war. Yet we ask them to die for us. Charles, with his evil temper, is hardly the sort to inspire loyalty, and I waste my days fencing and playing the fop.

"Let me give the people a Valois worth fighting for, *Maman,* one who will inspire devotion. I'll give up my pretty clothes to play the heroic soldier. I'm not afraid to fight. And I will win this war for you."

"You have no military experience," I said flatly. "You cannot lead an army."

"True. But if you give me someone experienced as my second, I'll listen to him—just as Father listened to Montmorency."

"Where will I find such a person?"

He answered very quickly. "In Marshal Tavannes."

I lifted an eyebrow, impressed by Edouard's choice. A man of unquestionable loyalty, Tavannes had begun his career as a page to old King François, defending his master at Pavia even as enemy Spanish troops surrounded and captured them. Tavannes then served Henri and played a large role in the victory at Calais. Although nearing his seventh decade, and blind in one eye, Tavannes was as sharp-witted as ever.

But the thought of sending my much-loved son to war caused an old, familiar fear to well up within me. Edouard read my thoughts in a glance.

"Make me Lieutenant General," he said lightly, "and I shall make you a promise."

"What is that?" I asked cautiously, and he replied: "I won't die."

He spat into his palm and held it out to me.

Slowly, reluctantly, I spat into my own, and clasped his hand.

Months passed, during which time Edouard educated himself in the art of war. On the day he left for the front, I smiled bravely as I kissed him good-bye—but afterward, I fled to my chambers and loosed a torrent of tears.

For more than a year, the fighting was fierce. Edoward's confident letters failed to ease my maternal fear; the strain soon left me feeling exhausted and unwell.

On a Monday afternoon, I sat with the Cardinal of Lorraine and other members of the war council discussing the upcoming battle: The Huguenots were massing outside the town of Jarnac, and my son and Marshal Tavannes were leading ten thousand troops to intercept them. In two days, the fighting would begin. My throat and head throbbed so badly that I had difficulty following what the other councillors were saying.

I was listening to one of the Cardinal's tirades against the Protestant heretics—closing my burning eyes from time to time, for the light pained them—when Madame Gondi appeared at the door and announced that the Spanish ambassador, Alava, wished to see me privately. I did not trust my son-in-law, Philip, or his ambassador and sent a pointed message back: If Alava wished to speak to me, he must do so in the presence of the other Council members.

Shortly afterward, Alava—a short, rotund man with fingers like sausages—entered, a letter in his plump hands. From my daughter Elisabeth, I thought, for one bright instant hopeful before I looked again at the ambassador's sorrowful eyes.

"*Madame la Reine,* forgive me for being the bearer of terrible news."

I pushed myself to my feet and stared at the letter in his grip, addressed in Philip's own hand.

"I am so sorry, Your Majesty," Alava said, "so very sorry." He proceeded to tell a hideous tale about a young woman giving birth to a stillborn daughter and bleeding so much afterward that she grew white as chalk and died.

I forgot about the hushed Council members and the ambassador. I saw only the evil letter, written in a foreign tongue, in a King's bold script; I walked around the table and snatched it from Alava's hand.

I did not open it. I pressed it to the pearl at my heart as though it were Elisabeth herself and sank to my knees, moaning.

I do not remember fainting; I only remember staring up at the ceiling in my bedchamber and hearing Madame Gondi's distant, incomprehensible murmurs. My body and emotions melted and mingled, resolving into one agonizing, singular ache.

I was out of my head with grief, with fever: I clenched my teeth in a futile effort to stop their chattering. Margot's and Charles's voices floated above my bed, but I had no strength to parse their words.

The shadows on the ceiling blurred and shifted, taking on the shapes of soldiers, swords, and cannon; women's whispers took on the cadence of battle cries and screams. For hours, I endured scenes of men slaying and slain, of armies defeated and victorious, of blood spilling and congealing and drying to ash.

When I finally woke, Margot sat at my bedside; nearby, Madame Gondi sprawled in a chair, snoring.

"*Maman!* Thank God you are with us at last!" Margot caught my hand.

"Is it already morning?" I whispered.

"Morning of the fifth day, *Maman*. We thought you would die, but your fever has broken. Doctor Paré says you will recover quickly now."

"Five days!" I said. "Then what of the battle at Jarnac?"

A curious look crossed her features. "You were talking, *Maman,* as you dreamed. You saw a great battle in which many men died. Suddenly, you cried out, 'Look! The Prince of Condé has fallen—and they have killed him!' And then you said, 'God, no, Edouard has fallen . . .' Then, 'Look! He has gotten back to his feet! Look, my son is victorious! The enemy flees!' "

I reached for her arm. "Damn my dreams! What news of Jarnac? Have we engaged the enemy?"

Margot stared at me, her eyes wide. "It's all just as you said, *Maman.* The Prince of Condé is dead, and Edouard is victorious."

Despite the loss of their commander, Condé, the Huguenots refused to surrender. The surviving leader, Gaspard de Coligny, took his followers to the southern kingdom of Navarre, where they were welcomed by Jeanne and her son, Henri, now a young man. Navarre was enormously personable and well-liked; the Huguenots looked to him to replace his fallen uncle Condé.

With Condé gone, my desire for revenge evaporated: It had been he, and not Coligny, who had ordered the attack at Meaux; Coligny wrote me saying that he and his followers denounced the attack on the King and wished only to practice their religion in peace.

Half a year passed. In August, my beloved Edouard returned victorious from the wars. I climbed to the roof of the Louvre, hot and shimmering in the later summer heat, and at the sight of the cadre of soldiers winding through the streets, I ran down to the palace gate.

Unjeweled and unshaven, Edouard rode with masculine grace at the head of his troops. His shoulders had grown muscular and his face sun-browned; his eyes were hardened, the result of seeing many men die. But his grin, upon spotting me, was still brilliant. He dismounted and ran to me, and I to him.

"I did not forget my promise, *Maman,*" he said.

We embraced tightly; I drew in the scent of sun and aged sweat.

"You stink," I said, laughing.

The following evening, I held a reception for him at Montceaux. Every corner of the château's ballroom sparkled with jeweled men and women; to slake their collective thirst, three fountains flowed with champagne. I hired singers, musicians, dancers, and a hundred nubile girls dressed as fairies. Lest the King grow too jealous, I arranged for Charles to make a grand entrance announced by heralds and trumpets; he was hailed as "the great victor, who has brought peace to France" by a well-known poet, who then offered up an ode that credited all our current fortune to King's wisdom.

Charles listened, sighing with faint disgust. When the poet had finished, the King sneered, "Save your pretty words for my brother."

Soon after, the heralds announced *Monsieur le Duc,* Lieutenant General of France. Edouard appeared—no longer the weary soldier, but a courtly confection in pale blue velvet spangled with lace. His hair had been carefully curled, the fat ringlets brushed back to reveal heavy clusters of diamonds at his ears.

Beside me, Margot—herself a jewel, in a gown of sapphire—sighed dreamily at the sight of him. When he had gone off to war, Margot had written her brother almost every day; through their correspondence, they grew closer than ever. When he appeared, she hurried to embrace him.

As Margot was speaking excitedly to Edouard, the Cardinal of Lorraine and his young nephew Henri approached to pay their respects. I watched, unable to hear their conversation over the gurgling fountains.

At twenty, Henri, Duke of Guise, possessed the easy confidence of a man used to power. He was not handsome: his pointed goatee emphasized his sharp chin; his tiny eyes held the same arrogant ambition I had seen in his father's. Yet Guise was very witty, and as he spoke, Margot giggled and lifted her fan to hide her nervous smile. Twice Guise leaned over her hand and kissed it—then held on to it, as though reluctant to let it go. At times, when Guise leaned close enough to kiss her, Margot, crimson-faced, wound her arm around her brother's, unconsciously seeking protection.

Charles came up beside me and said hotly, "If he moves a fraction closer to her, I'll knock him to the ground."

My tone was light. "I think he means to court her, Your Majesty, and if he does, I'll help you knock him down myself."

He let go a snort. "Not Guise! It's Edouard . . . Look how he fawns over her."

I clicked my tongue in exasperation. "For God's sake, Charles, he misses his sister only because he has been so long at war! As for the Duke of Guise, you must understand that your sister is of marriageable age now; I have been studying prospective matches for her. And for you."

Charles let go a groan. "I'm miserable enough already, *Maman.*"

"You must think of the throne," I said. "There must be heirs."

He looked sourly at his brother, who was laughing with Margot and the young duke. "Let *him* give you heirs," he said and turned on his heel.

I returned to watching Edouard. He was joined by two young men—one called Robert-Louis, the other Lignerolles, both recently appointed gentlemen of the chamber to the Duke of Anjou. Margot's eyes flashed with carnal appreciation as she studied Lignerolles. He was clean-shaven, the better to show off his fine, high cheekbones, flawless complexion, and the handsome cleft in his chin. He genuflected to Edouard and Margot in a manner as spare and elegant as his dress.

The same could not be said for Robert-Louis, whose blond hair was almost white. His nose was small and round, his lips coarse; he wore a white satin doublet with a rose velvet mantle. His bow was swift and cursory, and he grabbed Anjou's arm and told some joke that made the Cardinal of Lorraine lift his grey eyebrows in disapproval. But Edouard laughed and slapped Robert-Louis on the back. The latter smiled at the others with smugness that verged on mockery.

After hours of socializing, I encountered Edouard alone near one of the fountains. I sidled next to him and was nearly overpowered by the fragrance of orange blossom.

"You smell better, thank God," I teased.

He smiled at me, preoccupied as he stared at Charles and Margot, who paraded through the chamber arm in arm. "It seems my sister has her hands full these days."

"Charles says he will not marry," I said softly. "He says I must rely on you for heirs." I paused. "I've thought a great deal about the right woman for you. I've written Elizabeth of England, and she's responded with interest."

He emerged from his reverie with a start. "That cow? If it's heirs you want, you'll have to do better than a balding hag with a bad leg."

"Edouard," I admonished, "you would be King of England."

He let go a long sigh. "I would do anything for you, and for France, *Maman*—except that."

I scowled. "If not Elizabeth, then who?"

"No one at all," he said quickly and returned to Guise and Lignerolles, both of whom were still fawning over Margot.

I dismissed Edouard's refusal as impudence and resolved to speak to him again that night, but guests interrupted me at every turn. It grew late, and revelers—including Edouard—still lingered. So did I, for I wanted him to hear me out.

Our victory at Jarnac had eventually led to promising negotiations with the Huguenots. I had welcomed the détente joyfully, believing that the war was truly over.

Yet the night before, I had fallen into a dream filled with thousands of innocent screams. I woke terrified and spent the rest of the night in feverish thought: How was I to avert more war between Huguenots and Catholics?

Reason brought the solution: My daughter Elisabeth's marriage to Philip of Spain had ended a war lasting two generations. Marriages of diplomacy were often used to make friends of former enemies. But Charles, with his surly temperament, was likely to insult or even harm a Protestant bride. Edouard had the mental suppleness to woo such a woman and win her. And Elizabeth of England seemed the only candidate worthy of him.

Henri and I had married when we were both fourteen: Charles was now twenty, and Edouard nearly nineteen. As a mother and a queen, I had been patient, but I could wait no longer.

I wandered out onto the balcony. Below, the courtyard was dappled by fireflies and a hundred lamps nestled in the boxwood mazes; moonlight glinted off the spray from the fountain. I closed my eyes and thought suddenly of my husband—how handsome he had looked when he had stood beside that very fountain, a young soldier returned from war.

A rustle below prompted me to open my eyes. In front of a low hedge, two dark masculine forms moved stealthily toward each other. Their fingers touched, and one man pulled the other into a hard embrace. Their faces merged for a lingering kiss. The smaller man pushed himself free and began to whisper—too faintly for me to hear, but the cadence held shame and sorrow.

The other listened, then spoke his piece, low, reasonable, yearning. He fell silent, and the pair stood still as statues—only to lunge at each other in the next instant.

The tall man led his fellow to a low hedge and swung him about so they faced the same direction. The smaller looked over his shoulder to protest but, at his lover's touch, bent forward at the waist, his cap tumbling onto the lawn as he rested his elbows upon the clipped hedge.

The tall man slipped behind him and fumbled with clothing. A thrust of the hips, and the shadowed forms merged again into a single, many-limbed silhouette. The bent man let go a sharp sensual cry of pain; his partner clapped a hand over his mouth. As the bent man clawed at the hedge, the taller rode him.

I should have left them to their passion, but I was frankly curious. Viewed from the outside, their encounter seemed no different from that between a man and a woman. The rhythm of the act was the same: a trot, then a canter, then full gallop. At the end, the rider gripped his mount's hips and reared back, his face inclined toward the moon, and let go a ragged gasp.

The tall rider staggered backward; his paramour straightened and covered his face with his hands.

The tall man took him in his arms and spoke gently until the shorter had composed himself. They parted with a kiss before walking briskly back toward the building.

I retreated into the shadows as the smaller man neared. The torchlight by the entrance glinted off his face—his fine, smooth, clean-shaven face with its dimpled chin. Lignerolles put a hand to his dark hair, realized that he had forgotten his cap, and sprinted back toward the hedge to fetch it.

The taller man continued on. As he passed by the torches, I saw his face quite clearly, with its long, straight nose and black eyes that glittered like the diamond pendants hanging from his ears.

My Edouard, my precious eyes. I was not scandalized, only sad to know that the royal House of Valois was in danger of dying.

Hours before dawn, a guttural roar expelled me from my bed. Madame Gondi heard it, too, and came rushing out from the closet. The shouting grew closer, and soon I recognized the King's voice.

"Bitch! Whore! How could you have betrayed me?"

A thud and a woman's incoherent screams followed. By the time I peered out my antechamber door, Charles was in the corridor, dressed in silk leggings and an undershirt. He clutched Margot's arm, and when I opened the door wider, he flung her at me.

"Go to your mother, whore!" he screamed. "Tell her how you have shamed us!"

Margot fell to her knees and grabbed my hands. She wore only her cotton nightgown, her hair falling down her back in unfettered waves. "He has finally gone crazy, *Maman*! Help me!"

I smoothed back a dark, errant lock at her cheek and saw that the shoulder of her gown had been torn. Beneath, the red, swelling skin bore marks in the shape of my son's upper jaw.

I glared at Charles. "You have hurt her!"

"Tell her why!" he commanded her, and when she remained silent, he struck the back of her skull. *"Tell her why!"*

She let go a wail; I put an arresting palm in the King's face. *"Stop!"*

Margot wept into her hands, utterly undone. "He spies on me, *Maman*. He watches me in my bed!"

"Because you are a whore!" Charles roared. "Because there was a man in your bed, and you were fucking him!"

He grabbed the hair at the nape of Margot's neck and pulled her head backward to expose her throat. Lightning fast, he reached for a slender, gleaming object at his waist. His eyes shone with the same inhuman light I had seen at the hunt, when the entrails of the hare had dangled from his teeth.

"You don't understand—I love her." He waved the dagger a finger's breadth above Margot's tender skin. "At least, I did—until she betrayed me! Was it your first time with a cock between your legs, my sister? Did it hurt? Or did you revel in it, like a whore? Tell the truth! It was Henri of Guise, wasn't it?"

"It was no one," Margot sobbed.

As Charles lifted the dagger, I shielded Margot with my body and struck his arm. The dagger clattered to the marble floor and skittered toward the doorway.

He twisted Margot's hair tightly and jerked her backward; she screamed and hit the floor. Charles raised the long, thick ribbon of hair in his fist like a trophy.

Margot pressed a palm to the back of her head; it returned covered in blood. I tried to push her brother away.

Swift as an asp, he struck out; the blow landed on my jaw and sent me reeling. I fell, my skull striking hard marble. For a moment, I was winded, paralyzed—yet aware of someone coughing hoarsely, uncontrollably.

I sat up. Margot was pressing both hands to the back of her bleeding head; Charles was hunched over, retching blood-speckled phlegm onto the floor even as he staggered toward the fallen dagger.

I stumbled toward my son; he reached the dagger first and shot me a gloating glance before bending down to retrieve it.

At the instant his fingers closed around the hilt, a bootheel slammed his wrist to the floor. I looked up to see Edouard, still in the clothes he had worn to the reception.

"*Maman,* Margot—my God, he has hurt you!" Edouard spotted the long, dark hank of hair—one end sticky with blood—on the floor and winced as though it had come from his own head.

"I found a man in her bed!" Charles shouted. "She was fucking him, I know it!" He began again to cough.

Edouard stared down at the dagger with dawning horror. "You meant to kill them . . ."

"Get off my damned hand!" Charles wheezed. "I command you, as your King!"

Edouard abruptly reined in his emotions. "I'll lift my foot when *you* let go of the dagger, Charles."

"But there was a man in Margot's bed! Guise, I know it was Guise! Now get off my hand!"

Edouard folded his arms resolutely and remained still until Charles's fingers slowly uncurled and let the dagger drop.

Edouard bent down and picked up the weapon, then lifted his foot; Charles crawled away to sit on the floor.

"I'll have your head for this," he croaked.

I hurried to Margot's side and pressed a kerchief to her scalp; her shoulders and hair were soaked with blood. She had stopped trembling, and her tone was challenging. "There was no man in my room!"

"Lie all you wish," Charles said, "but I know what I saw."

"What *did* you see?" Edouard asked softly.

"Margot, in her nightgown," Charles said. "And beside her, a naked man crawling out the window."

"You didn't see his face?" I asked. "How do you know it was Guise?"

"I . . ." Charles grew flustered, then defensive. "*Maman,* you saw the way he was flirting with her last night!"

"And you didn't look out the window to see where he went?" Edouard pressed. "Or were you too busy jumping to conclusions?"

Charles huffed indignantly. "Margot blocked me from seeing who it was!"

"Charles," I said reasonably, "if Guise despoiled a royal princess, it would cost him his head. However besotted he might be with Margot, he wouldn't be so stupid."

"For God's sake," Margot added irritably, "I detest the man!"

"Tell all the lies you want," Charles hissed. "I'll uncover the truth soon enough." He glowered up at Edouard. "As for you . . . Before God, one day, I *will* kill you." With that, he turned his back and strode off.

I let go an exhausted sigh. When Margot and Edouard believed my gaze to be focused on their departing brother, they shared a look: hers, grateful; his, comforting.

In that fleeting instant before their expressions grew fraternal, there was something else on their faces, something calculating and unmistakably conspiratorial.

Thirty-Six

I told myself that I had been mistaken about Edouard and Margot plotting together. Margot's ladies insisted that nothing untoward had happened in her bedchamber, but the single complicitous glance between brother and sister haunted me: I could not risk Margot becoming pregnant, and certainly could not risk her marrying a radical anti-Huguenot like Guise.

There was one obvious solution, for the good of my daughter and a united France. After the ugly encounter with Charles, I wrote a letter to my friend Jeanne, Queen of Navarre.

Why must we fight? Please come visit us, knowing that you are loved as family. I pray you are well, and happy; please reply quickly.

Her answer arrived several days later.

We are well, and as happy as those can be who are denied the freedom to worship God. Henri is a man now, as brave in battle as his namesake, your husband. He is morally strong and honest—traits that are sadly uncommon at the French Court—and devoted to the Protestant cause. He greets you and says that he hopes to see you again someday.

But he also says that such a day will not come until Protestants enjoy total freedom of worship.

I also penned a letter to Gaspard de Coligny, the Huguenot leader and nephew of old Montmorency. I was not surprised by Jeanne's refusal, but I was delighted by Coligny's reply:

We have no choice but to trust each other. Let me be the first to foster goodwill by putting my life in your hands.

No doubt you have formed an opinion of me based upon the reports of others; you will find that the reality is very different. I yearn to prove to you that His Majesty has no more devoted servant than I.

Admiral Gaspard de Coligny came to the Château at Blois in mid-September, when the oaks and poplars had just begun to turn, giving the valleys a golden cast. The morning his carriage arrived, I was sick with fever. I had tried several times to stand and be dressed, but my legs kept giving way.

A messenger from Edouard brought news that the Duke of Anjou, too, was unwell. The thought that Charles might receive the Huguenot leader alone unnerved me. The day before, the King had thrown a tantrum upon learning of Coligny's visit.

I pointed out that the late Prince of Condé had attempted to capture us—Gaspard de Coligny had openly disapproved of the act. The King would not be jollied, however.

When I received Edouard's message that he was ill, I changed our careful plans. A chaise longue and two chairs were placed beside my bed, and I settled, chattering with fever, beneath my blankets.

Edouard appeared early, in a dressing gown of lavender velvet and accompanied by a little dog with an opal collar. He was so weak that two attendants half carried him to my apartment. We rehearsed what we could say to reconcile Coligny and the King.

After a few hours, the Admiral was announced, and I sent for the King. Charles returned a message that he would not come, but I replied with another saying if he did not want Coligny under his roof, he should be brave enough to tell the Admiral so in person.

My strategy worked. Charles appeared soon afterward, lower lip thrust out in a pout, arms folded. Once he was settled into his chair, I gave the signal for our guest to be admitted.

Gaspard de Coligny entered. He was a short man, lean but thick of bone, with a swordsman's powerful shoulders. Half a century of soldiering had weathered his handsome face. His pale hair was cropped short; his chin beard had been brushed out to give it a downy appearance. He sported no jewelry; his worn black doublet was better suited to a country priest than a nobleman, and his square cap was of plain brushed cotton. Yet his manner and movements were those of a man who expected the world to grant his every desire.

His first act was impressive: Ignoring the growling dog in Edouard's lap and the King's threatening glare, Coligny walked up to Charles, sank to his knees, cap in hand, and bowed his head, revealing a balding, sunburned crown.

"Your Majesty," he said, "there are no words to express my gratitude at your invitation. Your generosity, forgiveness, and trust overwhelm me. Thank you for the opportunity to show you that I, and those who share my faith, revere you as our sovereign lord."

Coligny delivered his pretty speech with such apparent genuineness and humility that Charles was mollified: His scowl was replaced by an expression of hesitant curiosity.

"Welcome to Blois," he muttered and gestured impatiently. "Get up, get up."

Graceful and strong, Coligny rose without using his hands to steady himself. His blond eyelashes were barely visible, giving the impression of a naked, guileless gaze. I shared a surreptitious glance with Edouard that relayed our favorable impressions and our skepticism.

The Admiral's attention was so thoroughly fixed on Charles that Edouard and I might as well have been absent. "I firmly believe, Your Majesty, that God directed you to send for me, so that peace could be restored to France. As your former enemy, let me congratulate you on your military acumen. You have proven, time and again, which of us is the better commander."

Charles's lip curled faintly. "Don't patronize me, Monsieur. You know very well that my brother won the battles."

"Yes," Coligny allowed, "but it is a wise king who surrounds himself with talented men. Ultimately, you are responsible for every victory."

At this, the muscles in Charles's face and body softened. "Admiral," he said, gesturing, "this is my brother, the Duke of Anjou."

For the first time, Coligny's gaze acknowledged Anjou. The little dog on Edouard's lap bared its teeth, but the Admiral seemed not to see it. He bowed very low, and when he straightened, he said, "*Monsieur le Duc.* His Majesty was indeed wise to appoint you Lieutenant General. What a pleasure to meet the worthy adversary who made my life so miserable for so very long."

Despite Coligny's flattery, a subtle ripple of disapproval emanated from him as he—so strong, square, and plain—stared down at my bejeweled son in lavender velvet, with his glittering little dog.

If Edouard realized he was being judged, he did not show it; he laughed easily. "I could well say the same to you, Admiral. I'm glad to finally have you on our side."

"And this," the King announced, "is our beloved mother."

Coligny stepped to my bedside and kissed my hand. His beard was soft against my skin.

"Madame la Reine," he said solemnly. "Only a great mother could raise such great men. May God grant you and the Duke a swift return to health."

"Admiral," I said, smiling despite my feverishness. "I'm pleased to call you friend. I look forward to discussing how we might strengthen the Treaty of Amboise."

Coligny faced my elder son. "Your Majesty, I would like nothing better, but such negotiations are best limited to two people. I look forward to discussing it with you man to man."

Smoothly, Edouard interjected, "Being the wise sovereign, my brother relies heavily upon our mother's advice. She was pivotal in negotiating the treaty."

Again, Coligny turned to Charles. "Should you wish to appoint your mother as your emissary, I shall speak to her. Only give me direction, Your Majesty."

Charles bloomed. "Tonight we shall dine privately and will speak of the Treaty." He patted the seat beside him. "Come, sit and take some refreshment." He snapped his fingers at a chambermaid, who hurried to fill a goblet with wine.

"I am honored, Your Majesty," the Admiral replied. "But I drink no wine, lest it interfere with my ability to serve my God and my king."

I marked the pious pride in that announcement. Coligny's words were calculated to give the impression of humble honesty, which made me trust him not at all. He sat down beside Charles, who seized his arm and quipped: "We have you now, *mon père,* and we shall not let you go so easily!" He laughed at his own wit.

Coligny laughed, too, without a shadow of the unease such words might have inspired in a less confident man. We chatted about his journey, the loveliness of the Loire Valley, and his new young wife.

Within the first quarter hour, Coligny became the King's fast friend. The two left together, as Charles was eager to show the Admiral the palace. Edouard and I stared after them.

"There goes trouble," Edouard murmured, once they were well out of earshot.

"I believe I have made a terrible mistake," I answered softly, "by asking him to come."

Once Edouard and I had recovered, we held a formal reception in Coligny's honor, inviting three hundred dukes, cardinals, and ambassadors. Charles was pleased by the fuss.

The festivities began shortly before dusk. The massive outdoor spiral staircase overlooking the courtyard was festooned with silver brocade and gilded leaves. As our guests watched from the steps, a bevy of young women, scantily draped in gossamer, waved tall plumed fans in the air, then gathered in a circle to touch the tips of the plumes together. These were lowered dramatically to reveal the newborn Venus, standing upon a large "shell" of painted wood.

The nymphets spun away. Venus performed a short dance, after which Mars—Edouard's Lignerolles, in a white toga and scarlet mantle—appeared, brandishing a sword. After a threatening display, Mars pursued the frightened Venus. When he captured her, she kissed him, rendering him a docile creature. The pair promenaded happily, to much applause.

The reception moved inside, where swaths of sheer silk hung from the ceiling; from time to time, the nymphets stirred the fabric to recall the undulating sea. Amid this oceanic backdrop, the King and his family were formally announced, followed by the guest of honor.

As he walked into the hall, Coligny's composure was formidable, his appearance less so: He wore a new doublet of black silk but no ruff, as fashion required, only a plain white collar. It was a brilliant strategy: Against the satins, velvets, and gems, drab Coligny stood out dramatically. He knelt at Charles's throne and, eschewing His Majesty's proffered hand, instead kissed his slippered foot.

Not only was the hostile Catholic crowd impressed, but Charles was giddy at such a show of loyalty. Grinning, he drew Coligny to his feet and kissed his cheeks.

"We are convinced of Admiral Coligny's fealty and goodwill," the King announced, his arm around the Huguenot's shoulder. "We love him as a faithful subject and a friend; whosoever lifts a hand against him, lifts it against us."

Coligny bowed to the Duke of Anjou. For the Admiral's reception, Edouard wore rose damask studded with pearls and a huge ruffed collar of pink lace; his white lapdog wore a matching pink ruff. To my amusement, sly Edouard took the Admiral's hands and kissed him on the mouth like a blood relative; only someone paying careful attention would have noticed how eagerly Coligny disengaged from the embrace.

At a nod from Charles, the lutists and violists began to play. The King was as cheerful and garrulous as I had ever seen him; he took Coligny's arm and marched off to display his new prize.

Margot, Edouard, and I also left our thrones. I hurried over to the Guises—the young Duke, Henri, and his uncle the Cardinal of Lorraine, who had the most cause to be offended by the honors heaped upon the Admiral, because Coligny's spy had murdered Henri's father, the elder Duke of Guise.

The Cardinal took my proffered hand; his own was cool and weightless, and his lips kissed the air just above my cheek.

His nephew the Duke of Guise wore a white ruff collar larger than his head; the stiff lace scraped my skin as he kissed my hand. He smiled, but the gesture was far from genuine; his posture was coiled and tense.

"Gentlemen," I said warmly, "I am so grateful to you both; the circumstances are not easy for either of you, but you put the good of France ahead of any personal considerations. I will remember your graciousness."

"You are too kind," the young Guise said, but his tone was distracted; he was watching Charles's and Coligny's gradual approach.

I opened my mouth to say something further, but the King's loud, jovial voice interrupted.

"Ah, the Messieurs Guise! Here he is, gentlemen: your worst enemy in all the world, Admiral Gaspard de Coligny!"

I turned. There was grinning Charles, arm in arm with the Admiral, oblivious to the others' discomfort.

The Cardinal and the Duke froze. Coligny stood a full head shorter than the young Guise, who stared down his aristocratic nose at the Admiral.

"I must tell you," Charles announced, "that the Admiral swears he had nothing to do with François of Guise's death. His spy was not acting under his orders when he murdered François."

The Cardinal of Lorraine turned to stone. A muscle in young Guise's jaw spasmed as he said, "Since you are such a good friend of the King, Admiral, I must welcome you to Court."

"I fought beside your father on many occasions," Coligny said softly. "There was never a finer man and soldier. When I heard of his death, I wept."

Guise's eyes flared. He lurched toward Coligny, but his uncle put a warning hand on his shoulder, and he stilled again. In the pregnant silence, Charles began to speak again, loudly, carelessly.

"So what is this I hear about our cousin the Queen of Scots? Mary has been scheming again, and gotten herself into trouble. . . . Is it true?"

"She is being held in England," the Cardinal answered stiffly. "Elizabeth is convinced that Mary and the Duke of Norfolk were plotting to assassinate her."

"But it's true, isn't it?" Charles demanded. "Mary always felt the English Crown belonged to her."

"And well so, Your Majesty," the young Guise countered darkly. "Elizabeth is a *heretic*"—he glanced at Coligny—"and a bastard, and therefore has no rights to any throne in Christendom."

"Well, Mary certainly is pressing her luck, isn't she?" Charles asked blithely. "Plot after plot . . . and all of them discovered. I tell you, she'll wind up losing her head."

With that, he walked off with the Admiral. I remained with the Guises for a few more minutes, trying vainly to undo the damage.

The affair lasted well into the night. At one point, I spied Coligny taking the air on the balcony overlooking the courtyard, and went to him.

The balcony was blessedly cool, quiet, and deserted. Coligny leaned against the railing, his expression faintly troubled as he stared out at the dark horizon. At the sound of my footsteps, he turned and forced a smile.

"So serious, Admiral," I said cheerfully. "I had hoped that this evening would be a relaxing one for you."

He laughed. "Old soldiers can never completely relax, *Madame la Reine*. It is one of the costs of battle."

"A pity," I said, "for you are truly safe among us here."

His tone grew wry. "One would not think so, looking at the Duke of Guise."

"He will learn to call you friend. I am determined to reconcile your followers and ours—so much so, that I have come to ask a favor."

He lifted his golden brows, pleasantly expectant.

"Contact Jeanne of Navarre," I said. "Tell her that I must see her here at Court to discuss the marriage of my daughter Margot to her son, Henri."

His expression resolved into one of mild surprise. "Are you serious, Madame?"

"Quite."

"You must understand," he countered, "that my followers warned me against coming to Court. The Queen of Navarre has even more reason to be cautious. Were she killed, she would leave behind a country and a young son."

I let go an honest sigh. "Jeanne has less reason to fear for her safety than you do. I wouldn't marry Margot to her son in order to harm her."

"An excellent point," he allowed. "But do I, *Madame la Reine,* have reason to be concerned for myself?"

"No," I answered emphatically. "The Duke of Anjou has arranged for fifty bodyguards to attend you and transferred a sizable sum to your bank accounts. I hope it reassures you that I am serious about peace."

He tilted his head. "Does His Majesty know about the marriage plans?"

"Marital arrangements are women's work. But nothing will be finalized without the King's approval."

"I see." He looked back out at the night; when he turned to me, his expression was resolute. "If you wish to be a friend to us, consider this: the Spanish are murdering our fellow Protestants in the Netherlands. I need five thousand soldiers to show Philip that France will not permit the slaughter of innocents."

If I sent French soldiers to the Netherlands, King Philip would consider it an act of war. His army was larger and stronger than ours; we would be quickly defeated. But I kept my features bland, my expression agreeable.

"I should like to discuss it more with you once Margot and Henri are married," I said easily. "First, however, I need you to send a message to Jeanne."

"Very well, *Madame la Reine*," he said. "I am your servant."

We returned to the reception, I resting my fingers lightly on his solid forearm. He had aged well, save for his balding crown. Although I didn't trust him, I appreciated his intelligence and poise.

As soon as we walked inside, Charles hurried toward us.

"There you are, *mon père!*" he exclaimed. "The Florentine ambassador is eager to meet you. Come!" He took Coligny's hand and drew him into the crowd.

I proceeded to lose myself in a dozen conversations with as many luminaries. The hour was late by the time I found myself chatting with the Spanish ambassador, Alava, a potbellied, unctuous soul. He was in the midst of relaying an anecdote about my former son-in-law, Philip, when we heard a sudden furious shout.

"Liar! *Liar!*"

I turned. Beside the gurgling fountain, Henri of Guise stood, his body shuddering with barely contained anger. Coligny, an arm's length away, uttered a measured, inaudible reply.

Whatever he said inflamed Guise, who struck out with the back of his hand; Coligny staggered. Guise would have struck him again, but Edouard saw the attack and caught Guise's arm. The young Duke struggled as Edouard held him fast.

"Poltrot de Mére was your spy!" Guise shouted, his face flushed with rage and drink. "Do you expect us to believe you didn't order him to kill my father? I demand satisfaction!"

Charles arrived, red-faced and angry; he would have lunged at Guise himself, but the Admiral waved him away.

"I do not duel." Coligny's breath was coming quickly, but his voice and expression were tightly controlled. "God frowns on gambling, whether it be with lucre or with lives."

"Coward!" Guise roared. "Hide behind your piety, if you wish, but you will pay for your crime!"

"If I die too soon," Coligny answered coolly, "it will be defending the right of men to worship God—not defending myself from scurrilous charges."

His Majesty seized the huge ruff at Guise's neck. "You would be wise, Monsieur," Charles snarled, "to be a friend to the King's friend . . . lest I label you my enemy."

Guise's eyes went wide. Charles pushed him back into the arms of his uncle, the Cardinal. As he marched past Guise with Coligny in tow, Charles hissed:

"And if you come near my sister again, I shall kill you with my bare hands."

Thirty-Seven

The next morning, I went early to the King's chambers, expecting to find him abed; to my surprise, Charles was in his cabinet. I would have gone in unannounced, but the guard stopped me at the door.

"Forgive me, *Madame la Reine,* but His Majesty gave orders he was not to be disturbed. Admiral Coligny is with him."

"Tell the King I am here," I commanded, "and that I must speak to him at once, privately."

The young Scot reluctantly knocked upon the door. Charles cursed the poor man roundly and would have sent me away, but I heard Coligny reasoning with the King. Eventually the Admiral emerged from the cabinet and—after bowing to me—strode away.

My irate son sat at his desk, its surface cleared save for a document that had been overturned to hide it from curious eyes. Charles rested his fist on it and glowered across his desk at me.

"This had best be urgent, *Maman.*"

"It is, Your Majesty," I said. "I came to tell you that the Admiral is going to ask Jeanne of Navarre to visit us."

"Ah," he said, bored. "Well, that's no reason to interrupt our meeting."

"No," I allowed. "I'm inviting Jeanne in order to arrange a marriage between her son and Margot." I was confessing my plan to Charles now because he was infatuated with Coligny and his Huguenot friends and thus, for the first time, likely to approve it.

"Well, I suppose it's a good match," he said, with surprising mildness. "Henri is after all a king."

"Wonderful!" I hesitated. "I've also come for another reason, Charles. I must warn you about Coligny."

He clapped his hands over his ears. "I will not hear it! He is a good man!"

"He's also a persuasive man," I said loudly. "And I've discovered the reason he came to us: He wants soldiers to fight the Spanish in the Netherlands."

As I spoke, Charles put his palm upon the mysterious document, firmly, as though he feared I might take it from him.

I looked down at it. "May I inquire as to the contents of that document?"

"I am a man now, *Maman*. I don't have to tell you everything."

"But you do," I retorted. "I'm your senior councillor—and you can take no formal action without your Council's approval."

I snatched the document from him. It was a royal order authorizing the deployment of five thousand troops to the Netherlands under the command of Admiral Coligny. I should have known within the first few minutes of meeting Gaspard de Coligny that he was determined to drive a wedge between me and my son—yet I was surprised and furious, and lost my temper.

"Fool!" I brandished the document at Charles. "This is tantamount to a direct attack on Spain! Do you know what will happen if Philip retaliates?"

"We will defeat him at last," Charles said; his eyes held a madman's gleam.

"No!" I shouted. "*We* will be the ones defeated. Spain's navy is unmatched; she has more soldiers at her command than we do."

"But the Admiral—" Charles began to protest.

"The Admiral *wants* to see us trapped in a losing war—because if our soldiers are busy fighting the Spanish, there will be no one left to protect *you* from the Huguenots. They could destroy us. They could set their own leader on the throne!"

Charles's features hardened into a sullen mask. "Coligny loves me as a son. He would never do such a thing."

I rolled up the incriminating decree and leaned forward.

"If you value Coligny's word over mine, then I am no longer of any use to you. Send troops to the Netherlands, and I will retire from the government. I will not stay to see the House of Valois fall!"

Fear flashed in Charles's eyes. If I abandoned him, the truth—that he was incapable of governing—would become resoundingly obvious to all.

"Don't leave, *Maman!*" he said, suddenly penitent. "I won't send the troops."

"Indeed you won't," I said, straightening, and tore the paper to pieces. The shreds fluttered into a pile on the King's desk.

I walked out, still furious with Coligny but pleased with the way I had played Charles. Foolish woman: I was happy over winning the battle. I did not realize that I had already lost the war.

The old year passed, and a new one, 1572, took its place. I was happy, in those days before the maelstrom, because I thought I had convinced Charles not to trust Coligny, because I thought my daughter's marriage to Navarre would bring peace to France. I was happy, too, because early spring brought Jeanne to Blois.

An hour after her arrival, I went to her guest apartments; when the attendant answered the door, I lifted a finger to my lips and slipped inside the antechamber. As I stole toward the inner room, Jeanne called out: "Who knocked?"

I hurried to the threshold. "No one at all, Madame."

She was standing over a basin, frowning into a mirror as she patted her cheeks dry with a towel. Her French hood and ruff collar had been removed, leaving her in the unstylish black gown favored by Huguenot women. When I spoke, she glanced up, startled, then broke into a broad smile.

Almost ten years had passed since we had set eyes on each other. Jeanne's hair was frankly grey, and deep lines had insinuated themselves into her brow and around her mouth. More ominously, she had lost so much weight that her features were skeletal; the effect was not helped by her consumptive pallor.

But her green eyes were still full of life. They brightened at the sight of me, and she set down the towel and genuflected. *"Madame la Reine,"* she said graciously.

I bowed, low and humble. *"Madame la Reine."*

We held our poses an instant, then rose laughing and embraced. She was frail and feather-light in my arms.

"Catherine!" she said. "I thought I might be uncomfortable seeing you again, but it is as though the last decade never happened."

"I am so glad that you've come," I answered honestly.

"All of your reassurances that I would be safe made me smile," she said. "I've never believed the rumors that you eat little children."

"You haven't dined with me yet," I countered, with mock darkness, and we laughed again.

Supper was as cordial as I dared hope. Charles called Jeanne Cousin; Edouard kissed her on the lips. Her eyes widened at her first glimpse of his sartorial excess, and she pulled away from the embrace coughing—partly from consumption but also from the overwhelming scent of orange blossom, which Edouard had applied liberally that night.

Fortunately, it was Jeanne's opinion of Margot I most cared about, and my daughter did not disappoint me. She appeared in a gray gown of smart but modest cut and had forgone face paint, with the effect that she looked freshly scrubbed.

"Margot!" Jeanne exclaimed, as my daughter curtsied respectfully. "What a beautiful woman you have become!"

Margot lowered her lashes as though embarrassed by the compliment. "We're so honored by your visit, *Madame la Reine*! I'm glad for the chance to see you again—I was so young when you left that I should like to know you better, as my mother speaks of you so fondly."

The meeting continued in convivial fashion. Jeanne presented Margot with a present from Henri: a modest-size diamond pendant. My daughter displayed delight at the humble gift, and Edouard rushed to fasten it around her neck.

Over the course of the evening, Margot showed herself to be demure and well-versed in the poetry written by Jeanne's mother, the late Marguerite. Only one sour note was struck: When Jeanne inquired what Margot knew of the Huguenot faith, my daughter grew somber.

"Enough to know that I am at heart a Catholic," she answered, "and will remain so until I die."

Jeanne fell silent, and the conversation lagged until I asked how Henri most preferred to spend his time.

"I can answer you in three words," Jeanne said. "Riding, riding, and riding. He doesn't like anything that he can't do astride a horse."

We all laughed politely, and Jeanne smiled, but a crease had appeared between her eyebrows and remained there for the rest of the evening. She retired early, begging exhaustion. At the first chance after supper, I took Margot aside.

"What possessed you to become, overnight, an ardent supporter of the Church?"

"You never asked," she said, with sudden heat. "You never ask me anything, *Maman,* because it doesn't matter what I think! I won't go to Navarre! I won't live among oxen and dress like a crow!"

Tears filled her eyes. There was more she wanted to say, but she could not bring herself to give it voice. *Guise,* I thought with amazement, *she is in love with him.* Why else would she have displayed such uncharacteristic enthusiasm for her faith?

I moved to put a hand upon her shoulder, but her face crumpled and she lifted her skirts and ran away.

I did not follow. Only time—and Henri, perhaps, if he was as kind a man as he had been a boy—could help her.

I spent the rest of the evening with Charles in his downstairs study, trying to undo the damage wrought by Coligny. It grew late, and I left for my chambers.

I climbed the spiraling outdoor staircase, shivering at the March chill. On the landing I stopped to catch my breath and stared out at the courtyard, remembering an instant, decades past, when I had paused on the first floor of the same palace to see the Duchess d'Etampes cavorting naked with King François. I was recalling my terror of repudiation when muted voices brought me back to the present.

I looked up. The staircase was hemmed by ornately carved railings; through them, I glimpsed the arms and averted faces of two figures, indistinct in the darkness, on the landing above. Their voices floated down, the words incomprehensible, though the emotions—the woman's tearful rage, the man's determined calm—carried easily.

Unpleasant scenes between romantically entangled courtiers were common, but I had no patience for them. I was on the verge of clearing my throat and pressing onward when something—the timbre of the young woman's voice, perhaps, or the man's placating gesture—held me fast.

I watched as the woman loosed a stream of heated words, her fingers spread in hopeless anger. The man—tall, composed—grasped her hand and, curling it in his own, pressed it to his lips. She stopped to listen as he spoke, softly, reasonably—but when he finished, she pulled something from her neck and cast it from her.

It fell, softly striking the landing below her—an arm's length from my feet. The man pulled her to him, and they kissed fiercely. I leaned down, grateful for their distraction, and picked up the glittering object from the stone.

It was the diamond necklace Jeanne had given Margot.

I closed my fist over the gem and looked up, riveted; by then, the embrace was over. Margot hurried inside to her chambers; the man began to descend the stairs. Panicked, I slipped from the landing inside the square archway and drew back into the shadows.

The man made his way rapidly down to the very place I had been standing and paused there. At the instant he arrived in full view on the landing, I closed my eyes.

I remained motionless and sightless for the long minutes he slowly walked the course of the landing, looking for the missing gift. At last he muttered a curse and proceeded farther down the stairs.

Only then did I open my eyes, but it had not been enough to shield me from what I could not bear to know. In the cold air lingered, unmistakable and cloying, the fragrance of orange blossom.

For hours I grappled with what I had witnessed. My mind, I decided, had tricked me: I had been so certain I looked upon quarreling lovers that I had injected passion into a kiss that had been only fraternal. Edouard, after all, was far too taken with his gentlemen to fall in love with a woman, least of all his sister.

But I grew more devoted than ever to seeing Margot married off to Henri—and I didn't care if she spent the rest of her life in backward Navarre.

The negotiations began early the next morning. The fire had already warmed the council room, and the open curtains admitted the feeble sun. Jeanne wore the same plain dress of Huguenot black. Her smile was not so bright as when I first saw it; she settled into the chair with a sigh, already exhausted.

I suggested that we begin by writing down the points we deemed important. When it was done, we exchanged papers. Jeanne's contained no surprises: Henri was to hold fast to his faith, and Margot was to convert so that they could be married in a Protestant ceremony in Navarre. The couple would spend most of the year there.

I, of course, wanted Henri to convert to Catholicism and marry Margot in Notre-Dame. Given that Henri was King of Navarre, I was willing to let the couple spend half the year in that tiny country.

As Jeanne read my list, her expression grew cold and regal.

"He will not convert," she said flatly. "This is not Catholicism; he was not born into his faith. He came to it through self-examination and God's grace."

"And Margot," I said, "would be excommunicated if she renounced her faith. She would lose her royal status."

"He will not convert," Jeanne repeated. From the set of her jaw and the hardness in her eyes, I saw she was serious and so moved on to a different issue: where the couple should live.

"Henri will spend as little time as possible at the French Court," Jeanne said, with the same air of finality.

"Being First Prince of the Blood and heir to the throne, Henri has a responsibility to the French people," I argued. "He will wind up spending half the year in Paris anyway, so it hardly seems reasonable—"

Jeanne cut me off. "There is too much moral laxity here in Paris. God does not smile on ostentation, adultery, and drunkenness."

"You cannot tell me, Jeanne, that every single soul at your court in Navarre is pure and devoted to God."

She was silent for so long that I took offense. "Margot seems to be a fine young woman. Let her come live with us, then decide for herself whether our ways suit her."

"Margot has already told me that she prefers to remain in Paris," I said. "She is used to a sophisticated lifestyle. It isn't fair to make her spend her days in a place so . . . provincial."

She lifted her chin, haughty. "Provincial, perhaps, but not corrupt."

"Have we forgotten so quickly that we are friends?" I asked. "Henri and Margot have known each other since they were children. They were born in the same year; she is Taurus, and he Sagittarius, so they are compatible."

"Please do not inflict your astrology on me," she said. "Deuteronomy, chapter eighteen: Witchcraft, sorcery, spells, and necromancy—all are an abomination to the Lord." There was no sanctimony in her; she seemed tormented, on the verge of crying.

Ma fille, m'amie, ma chère, je t'adore

For love of you I do this, for love of you this time I come

The hairs on the back of my neck lifted; I put a hand to the pearl at my heart. She had remembered, after all these years, what I had confessed in the agony of childbirth: that I had bought my children with the darkest magic.

We stared across the table at each other. "So you consider me damned," I said hoarsely. "Jeanne, I was mad with pain when I cried out those things about Ruggieri . . ."

"I thought that you were raving—until I learned you had corrupted my own son." Her features twisted with the effort to hold back tears. "I intercepted letters he tried to send to you, Catherine. You made him believe that both of you saw secret visions, of horrible, bloody things. I made him beg God for forgiveness and forbade him to speak of them again."

I felt sickened, exposed. "If you look on me with such horror, why are you here?"

"I am here because I must protect my son's rights as First Prince of the Blood."

She spoke the truth: If she balked, I had only to petition the Pope to excommunicate her son. As a result, Henri would lose his right to the succession, which would fall to the Duke of Guise.

"And so you cut me to the quick," I said. "You demonize me. You do not ask me what the truth is; you judge and send me straight to Hell."

She wavered. "I've told no one what you said to me. And I never will." She opened her mouth again, but I rose and silenced her with a gesture.

"I will hear no more," I said heavily. "And I want no more of these deliberations."

Thirty-eight

I left Jeanne and went straightaway to my chambers. Her accusations had shaken me deeply, but I had been shaken before and was determined to distract myself with pressing business. I sat at the desk in my antechamber and reviewed my correspondence—reports from diplomats, requests for the King's favor.

But anxiety gnawed at me until I could no longer sit still. I was filled with dread, convinced that something terrible was about to pass. The letter in my hand began to quake; I closed my eyes and was abruptly transported to the Palazzo Medici in Florence, many years past. I heard the clatter of stones against glass, and a workman's shout:

Abaso le palle! Death to the Medici!

Troubled, I sent for an astrologer in my employ, Guillermo Perelli. I had assigned him the task of choosing an auspicious day for Margot's wedding.

Perelli was a nervous young man, with bulging eyes and a neck so long that it extended far beyond his ruffed collar. He was not a genius, but he was capable enough, and quick.

"Tell me," I asked him, "what evil alignment of the stars is coming? Is there an aspect that bodes ill for the royal family?"

"No time soon," he said, then hesitated. "Perhaps . . . in August, I believe, Mars will enter Scorpio, enhancing the possibility for violence. I would be happy to prepare a charm for the King or for Your Majesty, which would offset any ill effects."

"Please do so," I said. "And look at our stars in light of the coming transit, to see what August holds. This must be done at once. I . . . had a dream that something awful is going to occur."

It was no secret among the courtiers that I had foreseen my husband's death and Edouard's victory at Jarnac. At my words, Monsieur Perelli leaned forward, intrigued.

"You must help me, Monsieur," I said. "Something terrible is coming, I know it . . ." I realized, to my embarrassment, that I was on the verge of tears.

Perelli sensed it. "I am completely at your service, *Madame la Reine,* to do whatever I can to protect your family. Let me set to work at once."

"Thank you," I said. I sat at my desk and watched, without confidence, without hope, as the door closed behind him.

I lost myself in work. By late afternoon, I was calmer and asked one of the ladies to fetch my embroidery and invite Margot to join me in my antechamber. I waited for her by the fire, until a knock came at the door. It was Jeanne; her head was slightly bowed, her voice low and humble.

"May I speak to you privately, Catherine?"

"Of course." I gestured at the chair beside mine.

"Thank you," Jeanne said and sat; after an uncomfortable pause, she said, "I've come to beg your forgiveness."

My cautious smile did not waver. "You mustn't blame yourself," I replied smoothly. "You're tired from travel. I can see that you've been ill."

"I *have* been ill," she allowed. "But that doesn't excuse my harsh words. I've spent the hours since our encounter in prayer. I see now that I've wronged you." She drew in a breath. "I've been afraid of how the French Court would influence my son because I myself was corrupted."

I laughed. "Jeanne, if anyone was corrupted by our decadent ways, it surely wasn't you."

She colored. "I was wicked. You cannot imagine, Catherine—you, who were always faithful to your husband, always honest with your friends. . . . I think sometimes you're too good-hearted to see the evil that surrounds you."

"But I deal with sorcerers," I said softly. "I read the stars."

She looked down at her hands, folded primly in her lap. "I know that if you became entangled in such things, it was for good reason. That is why"—her voice broke—"that is why I must ask your forgiveness. It was wrong of me to judge you."

She began to cry. She wanted to say more, and tried to wave me away, but I embraced her and let her sob in my arms.

She dined with us that night, and in the morning, the marriage negotiations began afresh. I could not call them cordial, but they were civil; the memory of them remains a small, bright spot of hope before the descent into madness.

Jeanne stayed with us at Blois well over a month and remained steadfast in her demands: Henri would not reconvert to Catholicism, nor would he be wed at Notre-Dame. Weeks passed without progress, and we grew irritable with each other.

One afternoon, the young astrologer, Perelli, came to inform me that Mars would move into the constellation of the Scorpion in the latter half of August, and form a square with Saturn on the twenty-third and twenty-fourth. This could lead to arguments with diplomats and foreign powers. He had cast four protective rings, one for me and one for each of my children.

I thanked him and directed Madame Gondi to pay him but had no faith in his feeble charms. Nevertheless, I gave the rings to my sons and daughter to wear; my own went into a drawer.

The first week of April passed without event. I remained determined that Margot should be married at Notre-Dame, while Jeanne was just as determined to see the couple wed in a Protestant ceremony. My nerves grew frayed, for with each passing night, my dreams of bloodshed grew more intense. I felt that the only way to avert war was to see Margot and Henri wed quickly.

After one particularly frustrating session with Jeanne, I visited Edouard, hoping for fresh insight to break the impasse. I went to his quarters, knowing that no one would search for me there, and settled into a chair. At Edouard's invitation, I began to speak of my difficulties with the wedding negotiations, and Jeanne's stubbornness.

As we were conversing in his bedchamber, a knock came on the door in the room beyond us. I heard Robert-Louis's unctuous response and Madame Gondi's muffled, anxious reply.

Shortly after, an apologetic Madame Gondi entered and curtsied. "*Madame la Reine,* forgive me, but an urgent message has come for you."

She handed me a small package wrapped in a letter. I excused myself and hurried to my bedchamber, where I sat down and removed the letter; beneath, wrapped in black silk, was an iron ring with a clouded yellow diamond. I set the ring in my lap and broke the letter's seal.

Most esteemed Madame la Reine,

Given the placement of your natal Mars and your skill at reading the sky, I suspect you are already aware of the approach of catastrophe.

Herewith is a talisman named the Head of the Gorgon, called by the ancient Greeks Medusa. In the skies, she is represented by the star Algol, which the Arabs call ra's al-Ghul, *the Demon's Head, and the Chinese call the Piled-Up Corpses. No star in the heavens is more powerfully evil. Algol brings death by decapitation, mutilation, and strangulation—not to one victim but to multitudes.*

Two hours before dawn on the twenty-fourth of August, the star Algol will rise in the sign of Taurus—your ascendant, Madame la Reine*—and precisely oppose warlike Mars while the former is strengthened in the sign of the Scorpion. France has never been in greater danger; nor have you.*

Long ago, I gave you the Wing of Corvus, which served you well; with similar hope, I give you now the Gorgon's Head. When carefully channeled, the Demon Star provides courage and bodily protection.

On that distant day at the Palazzo Medici, I said that your stars revealed a betrayal that threatened your life. I see betrayal coming again, Madame la Reine, *and warn you to take extreme care, even among those you most trust.*

As for what might be done to prevent the coming calamity: My opinion on the subject has not changed since we last spoke. I doubt you would want me to reiterate it here.

Ever your humble servant,

Cosimo Ruggieri

I put my hand to the pearl beneath my bodice and closed my eyes. My memory traveled to the moment, a dozen years past, when Ruggieri had last sat with me in my cabinet.

The stars have changed since the day I gave you the pearl.

The time will *come, Catherine. And if you fail to do what is necessary, there will be unspeakable carnage.*

The letter bore no return address. I slipped the ring on the middle finger of my left hand and stared out at the courtyard, at the future ghosts of Piled-Up Corpses. Intuition told me Ruggieri was not far away. He was lurking, waiting, watching to see if I had the courage to avert the coming bloody tide.

The next morning, I asked Jeanne to join me in my antechamber. When she arrived, I invited her to sit by the fire. Tense and wary, flushed from a recent coughing spell, she settled stiffly in the chair next to mine and looked askance at my smile. During her visit, she had lost even more weight; her eyes were fever-bright.

"These negotiations have grown too unpleasant," I said kindly. "They've made us forget we are, despite everything, friends. Let us dispense with them."

"Dispense with them?" Her brows lifted in dismay. Was I quashing the marriage?

"The King asks for only two things," I said. "One, that Margot remain a Catholic, and two, that Henri come to Paris to be wed *outside* Notre-Dame. Your son need never set foot inside a cathedral; a proxy will accompany Margot inside for the Catholic ceremony."

She frowned, unable to entirely believe what I was saying. "And the couple will spend several months of the year in Navarre?"

"As many as you like. If you wish, the couple can be wed afterward in a Protestant ceremony."

Her features softened, revealing a glimpse of her old sense of humor. "You're too sly, Catherine. There's something you're hiding."

"There is," I admitted. "The wedding must take place on the eighteenth of August." I did not want the ceremony to fall even a day closer to Algol's influence. Before the evil star rose, I wanted to solidify the peace between Huguenot and Catholic.

"August? But it will be beastly hot in Paris then. May is a much better month for a wedding, or June."

"We haven't time," I said softly.

"*This* August?" She gasped so hard that she fell into a fit of coughing. When she could speak again, she said, "It would be impossible to make all the arrangements! A royal wedding—with only four months to prepare?"

"I'll take care of everything. You need only bring yourself and your son to Paris."

"Why such haste?" Jeanne pressed.

"Because I fear another war between your people and mine. Because I believe this marriage will bring an end to bloodshed, and therefore cannot take place quickly enough."

The deal was struck. We stood and kissed each other on the lips to seal the bargain; I prayed she did not sense my desperation.

Thirty-nine

Soon after the marriage contract was signed, Jeanne left Blois. Although she spoke eagerly of buying wedding gifts, she looked desperately ill. By the time she reached the Paris château of her Bourbon relative, her health was failing. Nonetheless, she persisted in preparing for the upcoming wedding throughout the month of May. The overexertion proved fatal; she took to her bed the first week of June and never rose from it again.

I expected her son to ask that the wedding be delayed. To my surprise, Henri never made the request; he attended his mother's funeral on the first of July and appeared in Paris on the eighth with an entourage of almost three hundred Huguenots, among them the Prince of Condé, his young cousin.

The King privately welcomed Henri of Navarre to the Louvre on the tenth of July. Charles sat flanked by me on his left hand and Edouard on his right as Navarre, accompanied by his cousin, entered. At eighteen, Henri sported powerful shoulders, a narrow waist, and the muscular legs of horseman. His curls had been tamed into dark waves about his face, and he wore a goatee and thin mustache after the current fashion. Though he dressed in the drab black doublet of the Huguenot and wore no jewelry, his grin was dazzling and his expression relaxed, as if he had been separated from us by mere days, not years of enmity and blood.

In stark contrast to his cousin's genuine warmth, young Condé's manner exuded distrust. He was slighter than Navarre, with a blandly attractive face, but his smile was reserved and faintly sour.

"Monsieur le Roi," Henri proclaimed cheerfully; he did not bow, as he was himself a king. "I'm overjoyed to see you and your family again, and to enter the Louvre as a friend."

Charles did not smile. "So you've come, Cousin. You'd best treat our sister well; we have methods for dealing with heretics who test us too sorely."

Navarre laughed graciously. "I'll treat her like the princess she is, and the queen she'll soon become. I'm aware that I stand on enemy soil—and, more frighteningly, that I stand before my intended bride's brothers—and that my every act must prove my honorable intent."

Charles grunted, satisfied. Admiral Coligny had the highest regard for Navarre and had spent the past several weeks regaling the King with stories of his intelligence, courage, and honesty.

Edouard rose and greeted his cousin with a proper kiss. Navarre, half a head shorter, robust, and plain, was no match for the willowy Duke of Anjou, who had swathed himself in emerald Chinese silk embroidered with dozens of tiny, glittering gold carp.

"Welcome, Cousin," Edouard said, smiling.

"I hear you are a formidable foe at tennis," Navarre said. "I would far prefer opposing you in the gallery than on the battlefield."

"Perhaps a match can be arranged." Edouard put a hand upon Navarre's shoulder, directing him to face me. "My mother, the Queen."

Navarre turned his warm, open gaze on me. *"Madame la Reine."* I hurried to him and threw my arms about him.

"I am so very sorry about the death of your mother," I murmured into his ear. "She was a dear friend to me."

He tightened the embrace at my words, and when he drew back, his eyes were shining. "My mother always loved you, *Madame la Reine.*"

"*Tante* Catherine," I corrected him and kissed his lips.

He laughed, dispelling our shared grief. "*Tante* Catherine, I never had the chance to thank you properly for the copy of *Rinaldo.* I loved it so much that I must have read it a hundred times."

"After all this time," I marveled, "you remembered." I took his arm and gently turned his attention to the double doors. "But you didn't come all this way simply to talk to your old aunt."

Margot entered, a dark-haired, dark-eyed vision in deep blue satin overlaid by gossamer *cangiante* silk, which shimmered first blue, then violet. A talented coquette, she lifted her chin to make her neck as long as a swan's, then tilted her head and gazed at Henri with a playful smile. He was honestly transfixed before looking down, a bit abashed to be caught leering.

"Monsieur le Roi," Margot said, with a small curtsy, and extended a hand as white and velvety as milk.

Navarre pressed his lips to it. As he rose, his composure regained, he said, "Your Royal Highness. Can you still run faster than I?"

She laughed. "Most likely, Your Majesty. Unfortunately, I am now impeded by these trappings." She gestured at her heavy skirts.

"Ah." He feigned disappointment. "I had so hoped for a contest after supper."

She laughed and drew him to her for a chaste kiss upon the lips, as befitted cousins. We then welcomed the Prince of Condé; the greetings were more restrained on both sides. Afterward, we proceeded to the dining room.

Henri's company was a delight; the conversation grew increasingly punctuated by laughter. After the meal, I led him to the balcony overlooking the Seine. In the last week, summer had descended upon the city with a vengeance, and the muddy river offered no breeze, only the faint odor of decay. Nonetheless, Henri leaned against the railing and looked out at the Seine and the city, with the yearning of a long-unrequited lover.

After a time, I spoke quietly. "Your mother said that you wrote me letters, but she would not send them."

Henri's expression did not change, but I sensed a sudden caution in him. He shrugged. "I suppose my . . . youthful imagination frightened her. I had questions about things she didn't understand."

"That day you were chasing a tennis ball," I said, "it seemed you and I were possessed of that same imagination. Was I wrong?"

He didn't answer for a time. "My mother was obsessed with God and sin.

But unlike my fellow Huguenots, I'm not a religious man; I fought beside them because I believe in their cause. As for me, I believe in what I see: the earth, the sky, men and beasts . . ."

"And visions of blood?" I asked.

He turned his face away. "And visions of my comrades dying horribly."

"I don't see their faces, but my dreams and visions have grown worse of late. I've always taken them to represent a warning, a glimpse of a future that can be averted. But if you don't believe in God, perhaps you believe them to be without meaning."

He met my gaze soberly. "I believe, *Madame la Reine,* that this marriage presents us with an opportunity—to ruin France, or to save her."

"How startling," I said, "that we should both have come to the same conclusion."

His stare grew unsettlingly intense. "I came here against the advice of my advisers and friends, who fear this wedding is an elaborate trap meant to destroy us. I have come because I trust you, *Tante* Catherine—because I believe, most irrationally, that we have seen the same evil coming and intend to avert it."

I lifted my hand, heavy with the iron Head of the Gorgon, and set it upon his shoulder.

"Together, we will stop it," I said and turned at the footfall of the Prince of Condé and his attendant, who had come to fetch their king.

The first days of August were stifling; beyond the ancient walls of the Louvre, heat hung like black, writhing specters above the pavement. The door to my windowless cabinet was always open, not only in the hope of catching the breeze but also to admit a constant stream of guests, advisers, seamstresses, and others. One morning found me sitting at my desk across from the Cardinal de Bourbon—the groom's uncle and brother of the spineless Antoine de Bourbon, whom the Cardinal had long ago disavowed. The Cardinal's disposition was admirably steady and his health sound: At the age of fifty, he had not a single grey hair.

We were discussing the steps involved in the wedding ritual—both inside and outside the cathedral—when a guard knocked on the lintel.

"Madame la Reine," he said. "The Spanish ambassador waits outside. He requests a private audience immediately."

I frowned. I didn't know the new ambasssador, Diego de Zuñiga, well, but his predecessor had been given to overly dramatic proclamations. Perhaps Don Diego was similarly inclined.

I rose and went out into the corridor, where Zuñiga waited, cap in hand, at the entrance to my apartments. He was a small man, middle-aged and severe. His hair, slicked back with pomade, was very black and thin at the temples.

I faced him without smiling. "What matter, Don Diego, is so dire that it requires me to abandon the Cardinal de Bourbon?"

He responded with the most cursory of bows; his manner was outraged, as if he were the offended party. "Only a deliberate act of war, *Madame la Reine,* committed by France against Spain."

I stared at him; he stared back, combative. Beyond the entrance to my apartments, the Louvre's narrow corridor bustled with servants, courtiers, and Navarre's guests.

I put a hand on Zuñiga's forearm. "Come."

I led him to the council chamber and settled into the King's chair at the head of the long oval table.

"Speak, Don Diego," I said. "How has Charles offended his former brother-in-law?"

Zuñiga's brows lifted in surprise as he realized I truly did not know what event he referred to.

He drew a long breath. "On the seventeenth of July, five thousand French soldiers—Huguenots—trespassed onto the soil of the Spanish Netherlands. Their commander was your Lord of Genlis. Fortunately, King Philip's commanders learned of the coming attack and intercepted your forces. Only a handful survived, among them Genlis.

"Forgive my candor, but I suggest you have a frank discussion with His Majesty, considering that his action was a violation of his treaty with Spain, and an act of war."

I pressed my hand to my lips in an effort contain the invective that threatened to spill from them. Coligny: The deceitful, arrogant bastard had overreached himself, had dared to send troops to the Netherlands in secret, hoping for a victory that might convince Charles to support an insane war.

"This is the work of a traitor," I said, my voice shaking. "France would never encroach on the sovereignty of Spain. I assure you, Don Diego, that Charles neither knew of this incursion nor approved it. We shall see that the responsible party—"

Zuñiga risked the extraordinary act of interrupting a queen. "The responsible party is outside the King's chamber now, awaiting an audience. No doubt the meeting will be cordial; it is said Genlis bears upon his person a letter of support from Charles."

I rose. "That is not possible," I whispered.

"*Madame la Reine,* it is so."

I left the chamber and pushed my way down the stiflingly hot corridor, past sweating, genuflecting bodies and the black-and-white blurs of startled Huguenots. I stopped at the closed doors to the King's private apartments, where a small group of men had gathered.

Coligny was among them, his hand on the shoulder of a weathered Huguenot nobleman with a pockmarked face and thick red hair; a black silk sling cradled his injured arm. With them was the young Prince of Condé, for once wearing a genuine smile.

Henri of Navarre had just joined them. As I watched, he threw his arms around Coligny and kissed the Admiral affectionately upon each cheek. Coligny then presented Navarre to the stranger, who attempted to kneel until Navarre stepped forward and raised him to his feet. The two shared an embrace—a cautious one, owing to the stranger's injury—after which Navarre and the stranger kissed, then launched at once into an animated conversation.

I see betrayal coming, Ruggieri whispered.

I stepped forward into the men's line of sight and ignored their bows. I did not acknowledge Navarre or the others; I had eyes only for the stranger.

"Tell me, sir," I asked, "do I have the honor of addressing the Lord of Genlis?"

The other men grew still as the stranger's mouth worked. After a time, words emerged: "You do, Your Majesty."

"Ah!" I reached toward the black sling and let my hand hover just above it. "Your wound . . . Is it so very terrible, Monsieur?"

Genlis's cheeks and neck were scarlet. "Not at all, *Madame la Reine;* it is almost healed. I wear this"—he nodded at the sling—"only at my doctor's insistence."

"Thank God you did not suffer the harsh fate of so many of your fellows." I summoned the foolish smile of a superstitious woman and confided, "No doubt it is due to the lucky talisman you wear." I had heard, in more diplomatic terms from Madame Gondi, that the Huguenots regarded me as a witch who consorted with the Devil.

"Talisman?" He cast about, perplexed.

"The letter of support for your enterprise from His Majesty," I said. "Do you have it with you, even now?"

He glanced desperately at Coligny, but the Admiral's eyes revealed nothing. Perhaps Genlis sensed my determination, or perhaps he suffered an astounding lapse of stupidity.

"I do," he said.

I held my hand out expectantly as he struggled with the sling and fished the letter from a pocket.

I snatched it. The wax, impressed with the royal seal, had been broken; the creased paper was limp and stained, as though Genlis had anointed it with his sweat.

The barrier that housed my burning fury fell away as I opened the letter, read it, and saw my son's signature there. Without a word I abandoned the men and, clutching the letter, advanced on the pair of guards who barred entry to the King's chambers.

"Stand aside," I commanded.

When they did not obey, I forced myself between them and pushed the happily unlocked doors apart. I stormed past servants and nobles into the royal bedchamber, where His Majesty Charles IX sat upon his chamber pot as one of his gentlemen read poetry aloud. One glance from me and the gentleman closed his little book and vacated the room. I slammed the door after him and, waving the letter, advanced on Charles.

"You fool," I hissed. "You magnificent, impossibly witless fool!"

Charles clumsily pulled up his leggings with his right hand while sliding the cover over the chamber pot with his left. He was accustomed to inflicting anger upon the world but had so rarely witnessed it in others—least of all, his mother—that he raised his arm defensively and cringed.

"Five thousand French soldiers, dead in service to sheer stupidity!" I shouted. "And the Spanish King knew of them before I did! His ambassador came to warn me today that Philip considers this . . . this madness in the Netherlands an act of war!"

"What of it?" Charles challenged weakly.

"What of it?" I echoed, aghast. "Are you so mad as to think we could win a war with Spain?"

"The Admiral says we can," he ventured. "Do not hurl insults at me, Madame."

I lowered my voice. "You dream of military glory—but you will not find it in an ill-conceived war. You will find defeat and shame. The people will rise against you and put a Huguenot on the throne."

"Coligny loves me," Charles said, "as he loves France. War against a common foe will unify the country."

"I have lived a long time, my son, and I have seen what war with Spain brought this country. Your grandfather suffered a horrible defeat, and your father spent over four years as a prisoner. Philip's army is too strong. Do you not see how Coligny plays you? How he tries to turn you against me?"

Charles's jaw grew set, and his eyes rolled upward in a madman's gaze. "The Admiral said that you would say this. It is unnatural for a woman to command such power as you have; you have usurped me for too long."

I clenched my jaw and swallowed the bile that rose in me at Coligny's words, so obligingly parroted by my son.

"If you're so convinced that France's best interests would be served by war with Spain," I said quietly, "then Admiral Coligny must present his proposal to the Privy Council so that it can reject or approve it. If the Admiral's reasoning is sound, then the other members will be swayed to his point of view. Why not speak openly to all? It would be impossible to wage a successful war in secret."

Charles nodded as the idea took root. "I will tell the Admiral. We will prepare a presentation."

My tone lightened at once. "Good. There's only one thing you must bear in mind."

He frowned quizzically at me.

"You must abide by the Council members' vote. If they agree with the Admiral, you can wage your war in public. If they don't, the idea must be put to rest—permanently."

He pondered this, then said, "Very well."

"Excellent! I will notify the members and set a date for the meeting, and I will rely on you to tell Admiral Coligny to prepare his argument."

I left Charles's bedchamber wearing the falsest of smiles. It was still on my lips when I passed into the corridor, where Coligny and Genlis remained conversing with Navarre.

Coligny was first to turn and acknowledge my appearance with a bow. We smiled, though surely he had overheard my shouting. In his eyes I saw smug challenge: He was waiting for my departure, at which point he would go in and speak to the King.

As I passed by, Navarre also smiled. I turned away, unable to bear the sight of his eyes.

Forty

Eight days before the wedding, the King's Privy Council convened. It had rained steadily the previous night, and Sunday morning brought no respite from the storm. Despite the downpour, the windows had been opened a hand's breadth to let in the sweltering air, which steamed the windowpanes and turned the stack of papers at my right hand limp.

I sat at the head of the long oval conference table, flanked by Edouard and Marshal Tavannes—now sixty-three years old, completely bald and almost toothless. Tavannes had fought beside François I at Pavia and had been taken prisoner with his king. The battle had cost him the sight in his left eye; the clouded eye now roamed constantly, always at odds with the right. I loved Tavannes because he had once offered to kill Diane de Poitiers for her arrogance; I loved him more because he had led Edouard to victory at Jarnac.

Beside Tavannes sat his peer and fellow soldier Marshal Cossé, who had served during the wars as my envoy to Jeanne. In contrast to Tavannes, Cossé was still meticulous, with a neatly trimmed white beard.

Across from Cossé sat the dashing Duke of Nevers, a diplomat by the name of Louis Gonzaga, born in Tuscany but educated in Paris. As a youth, Gonzaga had fought with Montmorency at Saint-Quentin. The final member of the Council was the gouty, aging Duke of Montpensier, whose wife had long ago been part of King François's little band of women.

Admiral Coligny entered several minutes late with the cheery comment that God demanded rest upon the Sabbath—but perhaps the Almighty would forgive him when "it is, I hope, God's work we do here today." His pious pronouncement met with silence and a roll of distant thunder.

A gust caused the lamps to quiver as I said, "Gentlemen. Admiral Coligny shall present his case for war, after which there will be a vote."

I nodded at the Admiral; Coligny rose and, resting his fingertips lightly upon the table, began to speak.

"Five years ago," he began, "King Philip sent his general, the Duke of Alba, to occupy the Netherlands and to inflict upon its people a reign of terror. Since that time, ten thousand have been slaughtered for nothing more than their desire to worship God as they see fit." He turned toward me. "You, *Madame la Reine,* have always been for France the voice of tolerance. Let France stand against tyranny and for freedom.

"Save, now, the innocents to our north; for if we fail, the blood of tens of thousands more shall be spilt. Stop, I beg you, this swelling tide of blood."

I was speechless: Coligny had appealed so brilliantly to my beliefs that I had been moved. Even more, he had played on my darkest fears, as though he knew of my terrible visions. Impossible, I thought—until I remembered Navarre, leaning against the railing to stare out at the Ile-de-la-Cité. *And visions of my comrades dying horribly . . .*

I stared down at the table's dully gleaming surface in an effort to contain the bitterness that welled up in me. When I had regained my composure, I lifted my face to the Admiral.

"Would that I could help them," I said, "save for the inescapable fact that France lacks the means to displace Alba. Both the Huguenots and the royal army have taken heavy losses and left the country nearly bankrupt after years of civil war. We simply do not have the men or arms or money to take on so great a foe. Even if we tried to help them, those innocents of yours would perish—along with thousands of Frenchmen."

"That would not happen," Coligny countered swiftly, "because we would not fight alone. The Prince of Orange will fight alongside us, and he has recently secured aid from Germany and England."

"But it has already happened," I said. "Five thousand of our soldiers died. French blood has already been spilt."

"I submit," the Admiral said, "that war with Spain is inevitable. We can face her now, in the Netherlands, or later, upon our own soil, when Philip finally yields to the craving to expand his empire by straying over our border. That is why we must strike now—while we have the support of Orange, England, and the German princes."

Tavannes spoke in a low growl. "I have seen two kings make the error of starting foreign wars with hopes of conquest. They, too, were given promises of support. In the end, we retreated after heavy losses, only to return to a country in financial ruin. A foreign war will claim more lives and gold than we have to spend."

"I fought beside Montmorency at Saint-Quentin when I was a callow youth," Gonzaga, the Duke of Nevers, added passionately. "I went into battle filled with dreams of an easy victory. I came to my senses when the Constable and others—including myself—were captured by the Spanish."

"I was there at Saint-Quentin," Coligny muttered, indignant.

Gonzaga's tone was deprecating. "Yes, you were there—responsible for the city's defense, as I recall. Why, then, should we trust you to take more of our soldiers to war, when five thousand have already died as a result of stupidity?"

All the other men in the room began speaking at once. Gonzaga offered the Admiral another insult, while the Duke of Montpensier railed about the damage another war would inflict upon the economy. In the end, old Tavannes shouted them down and, when the room was silent, asked:

"Admiral Coligny, have you anything else to offer?"

"Yes," Coligny said. "When His Majesty King Henri II listened to the advice of his privy councillors, he was obliged to consider it carefully—but he was not required to obey it. Such is not the case with King Charles; he is obliged by law to follow this Council's bidding.

"This was understandable when the King ascended the throne as a boy of ten, but he is a man now, twenty-two years old. It is an insult to him to force him to accept the rule of his elders, even when it goes against his judgment."

Coligny continued. "I am a Huguenot, speaking before a group of Catholics. Yet I know every one of us would agree that Charles is King because God set him on the throne. Is that not so, gentlemen?"

Tavannes and Montpensier allowed that it was; Edouard and I exchanged dark glances, while Gonzaga refused to reply to a question whose answer was known.

"If Charles's will is thwarted by this Council," Coligny said, "then God's will is thwarted. And it is Charles's will to go to war with Spain."

I gasped at the man's audacity, at his wild reasoning.

Coligny directed a pointed look at me. "Her Majesty gasps. Yet I tell you now that government is the business of men, not women; such is the rule of Salic law. And I ask you: Who rules France? Who rules this Council? And who rules Charles?

"Each man sitting here must look into his own heart for the truth: Listen to the small, still voice of God within you. Is it right that the will of our King should be foiled by a womanish fear of war?"

My face burned. Beside me, Edouard muttered a barely audible curse.

"By God, you are a lunatic," Tavannes said, "and a mannerless cur to speak so of our Queen."

I did not look at him, or my fellow councillors; I could only stare at the bright piety in Coligny's eyes, at the beatific self-righteousness that glowed upon his face, stoked by the internal fires of madness.

"It is a holy war," the Admiral said; his voice paled to a whisper. "A war to free men who wish to worship in freedom. I tell you, it is God's own war; only the Devil would bid you not to wage it."

The room was silent until I gathered myself and asked coldly: "Is that all, Admiral? Have you finished your presentation?"

"I have," he said, with an air that said he was most pleased with it, and with himself.

The Duke of Montpensier interjected, "Your Highness, Your Majesty, I should like to move that we dispense with any further discussion. Admiral Coligny has presented his viewpoint sufficiently and heard the major objections to it. I see little point in revisiting these in an exchange that is likely to grow heated. I suggest a vote be taken immediately."

"Point well taken," I said. "Gentlemen, are there any objections?"

There were not. Coligny—confident that his appeal had swayed hearts—was asked to wait in the corridor. He went happily, though he paused on the threshold to direct a smug, triumphant look at me.

What followed did not take long. The members were in such obvious agreement that the paper ballots went unused and a voice vote was taken.

I rose and put a hand up to stay my fellow councillors from their impulse to spring to their feet with me. "I should like to tell Admiral Coligny myself."

I went alone into the corridor. Aside from a pair of bodyguards, there was no one within earshot. Coligny leaned against the opposite wall, hands folded, head bowed in prayer; at the sound of the door opening, he looked up eagerly.

At the sight of my face, his own went slack with surprise, then slowly hardened.

"So," he said. "I should have realized their ears were closed. After all, you chose them because they were loyal."

"I chose them because they were wise," I retaliated, "and loyal to my son—who was born without the temperament needed to rule. Should you persist in taking advantage of this fact, Admiral, I will banish you from Court."

His eyes—starkly blue inside a fringe of golden lashes—narrowed with the same sullen, bitter obstinacy I had so often seen in Charles. He took a menacing step closer, to remind me that he was a large man and I a small woman.

With the slow, emphatic delivery of a bully, he said, "Madame, I cannot oppose what you have done, but I can assure you that you will regret it. For if His Majesty decides against this war, he will soon find himself in another from which he will not be able to escape."

Though he loomed in my face, I refused to take a single step backward. Imperious, unafraid, I scowled up at him.

"We welcomed you as a guest. And you dare threaten us—under the King's own roof—with another civil war?"

"You would not be fighting me," he said, "but God."

He turned his back to me without taking his leave and strode away. When he had moved out of view, I closed my eyes and let go a sigh as I leaned back against the wall.

Under the jaw, like this, Aunt Clarice whispered and closed her hand over mine, around the hilt of the stiletto.

Forty-one

I charged the fearless Tavannes with reporting the results of the Privy Council's vote to the King. I then took Edouard aside to tell him of the Admiral's threat.

I convinced the Duke of Anjou to accompany me to our estate at Montceaux, a day's hard ride from Paris. We left immediately without informing the King, so that he would be surprised by our departure and assume I had made good on my threat to abandon him. I prayed that Charles would rush to Montceaux to beg me to return—thus allowing me to keep him out of Coligny's clutches, at least until the wedding celebrations commenced.

Within three hours of the Council meeting, Edouard and I were in a carriage moving south out of the crowded city. The rain had ended, and the wind chased slate clouds away to reveal a scalding August sun; the streets were once again crowded with merchants, nobles, clerics, beggars, and the black-and-white garb of Huguenots, strangers to this Catholic city, come to celebrate the marriage of their leader, Navarre.

I leaned back against the wall of the carriage and stared out the window, too pensive to acknowledge Edouard's lengthy diatribe against the Admiral or the whining of his dog, a spaniel perched in a jeweled basket that hung from the Duke of Anjou's neck by a long velvet cord. I remained silent as the air grew sweeter, and the clatter of the wheels was muted by the mud of country roads. Stone buildings gave way to the dark green, trembling leaves of late summer; mist rose from the road ahead like vaporous souls streaming heavenward.

I could not yet digest my final conversation with Coligny. As the carriage rocked, I closed my eyes and imagined Aunt Clarice beside me, shaken to the core yet fearless, in her tattered, glorious gown.

"Such hubris!" Edouard railed; the little dog in his lap cringed, and he began to stroke it carelessly. "He thinks he is Moses, and we Pharaoh!"

I opened my eyes. "He thinks he is Jesus," I said, then fell silent at the implications of my own analogy.

My son stared across the carriage at me. "He will not stop, *Maman*. You saw his eyes: He is a lunatic. *We* must stop *him*."

I shook my head. "What can we do? We cannot arrest him now, before the wedding. Think of the outcry: He is an honored member of the wedding party. Think of the embarrassment to Navarre, to us . . ."

I had not permitted myself to reflect on Navarre for days. I had loved him as a son; I was going to marry my daughter to him. Now I looked on him with distrust. Had he come here knowing what Coligny was planning?

"Coligny is sincere in his desire to see our troops sent to the Netherlands," I added, as though trying to convince myself. "He has spent a great deal of time ingratiating himself with the King. It would not make sense for him to attack us now."

"Attack us?" Edouard leaned forward abruptly. "Are you saying that everything he has done is simply a distraction? That he means us harm?"

I stared out at the changing countryside and thought of Paris's streets, flooded with Huguenots, and of the Louvre, its corridors brimming with black-and-white crows.

"No," I answered. "No, of course not, unless . . ."

. . . you will regret it. For if His Majesty decides against this war, he will soon find himself in another.

"Unless this is part of a greater plot," Edouard finished. "Unless Coligny and Navarre and the rest of them came here with the thought of capturing the Crown. Henri brought an entourage of hundreds, and thousands of his followers have descended on the city. Every inn in Paris is overflowing with Huguenots; they have even opened the churches to house them all."

My fingers found the heavy iron ring of the Gorgon's Head and began to worry it. "They could not be so foolish," I murmured.

"We are speaking of Coligny, who is fool enough to admit he thinks God has sent him here," Edouard reminded me, a look of sickened distrust settling over his long, handsome features. "And he will do whatever 'God' bids him. Even if he is not guilty of plotting a revolution—even if he means us no real harm—he will continue to manipulate Charles. We must do something."

"If we do something now, in a city crowded with Huguenots and their resentful Catholic hosts," I said slowly, "there will be a full-scale riot."

"Maman"—Edouard clicked his tongue in exasperation—"we cannot sit back and let a madman drag us into war."

"We will discuss it at Monteceaux," I said. "I don't want to think about it now."

I closed my eyes again, lulled by the rocking carriage, and saw the prophet's round full-moon face.

Beware of tenderness, he said. *Beware of mercy.*

Charles arrived at Monteceaux in the middle of the night. I feigned mute, sulking anger when I was summoned from my bed by a desperate King, but I could scarcely hide my gratification when Charles fell to his knees and, wrapping his arms about my legs, swore to abide by the Privy Council's vote and begged me to return with him to Paris.

I insisted Charles stay with us at Monteceaux for four full days. During that time, Edouard and I spent endless hours trying to convince the King that Coligny had coldheartedly manipulated him. At many points, Charles sobbed like a child or let loose venomous, spittle-laced rage, but by the third day, he was spent and began to listen to our point of view. I made him agree to avoid Coligny until after the celebrations.

Only then did we return to the city—on the fifteenth of August, the day before the betrothal ceremony. Since the tenth, the withering sun had hung unobscured in a faded blue sky; our carriage kicked up clouds of dust on the return journey.

I climbed from the carriage exhausted. At Monteceaux, I had spent long days with Charles and long evenings discussing Coligny with Edouard; we had resolved nothing, only that we should wait to take action until after the wedding.

As I climbed the stairs to my apartments, I spied Madame Gondi—still beautiful, but worn and in failing health—waiting for me at the top of the landing. She did not smile when she caught my gaze but tightened her grip on something in her hands: a letter.

When I arrived at the landing, I held out my hand for the letter. Once I had it, I broke the seal, unfolded it, and, walking alongside Madame Gondi and her lamp, began to read.

The handwriting was masculine but not Zuñiga's. It belonged to the Duke of Alba, that dastardly persecutor of Huguenots, and it was dated the thirteenth of August.

To the most highly esteemed Queen Catherine of France
Your Royal Majesty,

I understand that King Philip's ambassador to France, Don Diego de Zuñiga, has informed you of the incursion of French soldiers into the Netherlands under the command of one of your Huguenot generals, and that this said Huguenot general is a confidant of your son, King Charles.

You might wish to ask your son whether he or his Huguenot friend has any knowledge of the three thousand armed French troops who arrived at our shared border early this morning. And you would do well to consider the fact that my own sources—who are very knowledgeable about this Admiral Coligny and his activities—informed me within the last hour that he is actively mustering an army of no fewer than fourteen thousand troops.

It is said that most of these heretics are now in Paris to attend the wedding of their leader to your daughter, King Charles's sister, and they have brought with them arms so that they might leave immediately afterward for the Netherlands.

Don Diego also reports that you claim to be entirely unaware of this situation—that in fact, Charles's own Council has voted against Admiral Coligny's invasion. If that is true, then your family is in no small amount of danger; perhaps I should lend Your Majesty a few of my own reliable spies, who say that the metalsmiths in Paris are working day and night to produce swords and armor for the Huguenots and that, shortly after the Council vote, Monsieur Coligny publicly bragged that he does not recognize its authority and that he will come to the Netherlands, with or without his King's approval, and defeat me with his army of fourteen thousand Frenchmen.

My King would say that this is Your Majesty's reward for allowing heretics to dine at her table.

I have not retaliated because Don Diego is certain that King Charles will wish to deal with this matter internally, and has urged me not to take up arms against France but to advise Your Majesty of this grievous offense against Spain.

I have sent this by my fastest messenger, who is with you now, awaiting your reply.

Your servant, by God's grace,
Fernando Alvarez de Toledo
Duke of Alba
Governor of the Netherlands

I had reached my antechamber by the time I finished reading Alba's letter; I sank into the chair at my desk and glanced up as Madame Gondi set the lamp down beside me.

"Please," I said, "invite the Duke of Anjou to visit me at once, in my chambers. Tell him it is a matter of pressing urgency."

When she had left, I laid my head wearily upon the desk, my cheek resting against the cool wood. The lamp flickered, casting my leaping shadow against the far wall; I thought suddenly of my aunt at her desk, writing letters late into the night despite her injured wrist, on the day we had fled Florence.

No more blood, I had told Ruggieri. *No more blood,* but the House of Valois—my blood—was now at risk.

I thought of the stableboy's eyes, wide with shock and mute reproach, and hardened.

The next morning, a Saturday, the betrothal ceremony took place in the Louvre's great ballroom, officiated by the groom's uncle, the Cardinal de Bourbon. In full view of some three hundred guests, Navarre and Margot prepared to sign the thick marriage contract.

As Margot hovered over the final page of the contract, quill in hand, she let go a wrenching sob, then threw down the quill and covered her face with her hands. I moved forward and put my arms about her, then smiled up at the Cardinal.

"Nerves," I said to him, then whispered in Margot's ear: "Do not think—simply do it. Now."

I placed the quill in her fingers and closed my hand over hers. Her shoulders shook with repressed tears, but she lowered her hand and scrawled her signature.

Navarre kept his pleasant, dignified gaze focused on the Cardinal, politely ignoring the incident. Like the reluctant bride, I could not bear to look at him: At the same time, I reminded myself I had no real evidence that he was abetting the Admiral and his war. If I called off the wedding, I would quash any real hope for lasting peace, and signal my intent to act against Coligny.

Instead, I wrapped my arm around Margot and stood beside her as the Cardinal made the sign of the cross over the couple and intoned a blessing. When it was done, I kissed my daughter, then Henri, and welcomed him into the family.

"You are my son now," I told him.

During the reception afterward, I caught the arm of the Duchess of Nemours, an old friend. "Will you come to see me tonight, in my cabinet?" I whispered into her ear.

She bowed graciously in assent. She had spent her entire adulthood at the French Court and was known for her scrupulous discretion—a quality on which I planned to rely heavily.

Night found us alone in my cabinet, with the door closed and barred, despite the stifling heat; I had not invited Edouard, for if the conversation went awry, I did not want him implicated.

The Duchess sat smiling placidly across the desk from me, fanning herself. She was forty-one years old, soft and plump, a woman who possessed no natural beauty and therefore appeared to change little as she aged. Her eyes were large and her nose and lips small; folds gathered easily beneath her receding chin, a gift from her grandmother, Lucrezia Borgia. Her eyebrows were so heavily plucked as to be invisible.

She had been born Anna d'Este and raised in her native Ferrara until she was married at the age of sixteen to François, Duke of Guise. She quickly mastered the subtleties of courtly life and proved an able helpmeet to her ambitious husband. When François was assassinated by Coligny's spy, the Duchess did not retire quietly into widowhood. Seething with outrage, she demanded that Coligny be prosecuted for the murder and brought so many petitions before the King that an exasperated Charles declared the Admiral innocent and forbade her to bring up the matter again. But like her son Henri of Guise, who had inherited the title of Duke from his late father, she continued to despise Coligny and to denounce him vehemently whenever she could. Six years ago, she had married Jacques de Savoie, the Duke of Nemours, a staunch Catholic who had fought bravely against the Huguenots.

"Anna," I said, speaking to her in Tuscan to indicate the intimate, delicate nature of our conversation, "I know that it must be difficult for you to smile so graciously in the company of Huguenots. On behalf of the King, I thank you for your civility in Admiral Coligny's presence."

"He is no less a murderer, Your Majesty; today I felt as though I had fallen into a nest of vipers." She said this softly and with complete composure, as if we were discussing the most mundane of subjects. "I can only pray that His Majesty and France suffer no harm as a result of your association with him."

"This is precisely what I wish to speak to you about," I said, "for I have come to realize that the Admiral does indeed wish His Majesty harm."

Her composure did not waver. "I am not surprised to hear this."

"Then perhaps you will not be surprised to hear that Admiral Coligny has violated the King's order forbidding the deployment of troops to the Netherlands."

She snapped her fan shut. "The Admiral boasts to everyone that he is leaving for the Netherlands as soon as the wedding celebrations end, and that he will be taking many troops with him. Troops who are here in Paris, armed for war. I fear, Your Majesty, for the safety of the King."

"As do I." I drew in a long breath, then said, "His Majesty will no longer protect the Admiral from the justice that is due him." I leaned back in my chair and studied her intently.

She was still as a portrait for several seconds before she finally glanced down at her hands, one of which held the fan. When she looked up again, her eyes held tears. "I have waited many years. I made a vow to my dead husband's soul that I would avenge him."

"It must happen on the twenty-second," I said, "the day after the celebrations end. There will be a Council meeting that morning, which Admiral Coligny will certainly attend." I paused. "It must be done in such a way that the King and the royal family are not implicated."

"Of course," she answered softly. "That would be disastrous for the Crown."

With that, she indicated that the House of Guise would take full blame for the assassination. It would be seen as the result of a blood feud, an isolated incident for which the King could not be blamed.

"I will see you and your family protected from any backlash, though your son would do well to quit the city when it happens. I will send for you tomorrow morning to discuss the details. Tonight, speak to no one save your son; you and he must consider how our aim might be skillfully accomplished."

I dismissed her and went out to my antechamber to find Madame Gondi.

"Will you please invite the Duke of Anjou to visit me in my cabinet?" I asked her.

When Madame had left, I returned to the tiny, airless room and sat at my desk, leaving the door open behind me. I stared down at the backs of my hands and marveled at their steadiness. Unlike Anna d'Este, I shed no tears.

The night brought no breezes, only a suffocating dampness that settled over me as I lay on my bed, the sheets kicked away. When the darkness finally eased, I rose and directed Madame Gondi to invite Anna d'Este and her son the Duke of Guise to visit me as soon as possible that day.

Wedding preparations followed. I visited Margot's apartments with Edouard—who had an artist's unerring eye—to oversee the final placement of jewels on the wedding gown and its dazzling blue cloak and train. My daughter's eyes were red-rimmed and puffy, though I pretended not to notice. When the last diamonds had been carefully sewn in place, Margot stood before a full-length mirror and studied herself with awe.

Unable to contain himself, Edouard jumped up from his chair. "How stunning you are! You will be the most beautiful queen in all the world!" He took both her hands and kissed her on the mouth—lingering, I thought, a bit longer than a brother ought. Margot flushed and giggled, just as she had when Henri of Guise had flirted audaciously with her.

Once the cloak was prepared, three princesses—one Guise, two Bourbons—were ushered into the room to practice holding the train, which was so long that one girl stood holding its end in Margot's bedchamber, while two stood out in the antechamber to lift the middle and Margot herself laughingly walked out of her apartment and down the corridor before the train was taut enough to lift off the ground.

I left my daughter laughing with the three young princesses and took Edouard to my apartments, where Henri of Guise and his mother waited in my cabinet.

Our efficient conversation lasted less than a quarter hour. The Guises owned property on the rue de Béthizy—a house that Anna d'Este herself had once occupied. As chance would have it, Gaspard de Coligny had rented a hostel on the same street, only a short walk from the Louvre.

The Duke of Guise's eyes burned with a cold, bitter light as he said, "Coligny walks past our property every morning when he goes to meet with the King, and returns every afternoon the same way."

Chance smiles on you, Catherine.

"There is a window," Anna added, "from which a shot could be fired."

"And the shooter?" I asked.

"Maurevert," the Duke replied.

"I know him," Edouard said. "During the war, he infiltrated the Huguenots"—he turned to explain to me—"in order to assassinate Coligny. He was not able to reach the Admiral, so instead he shot one of his closest comrades, a man named de Mouy. De Mouy had been Maurevert's tutor at one point; they had known each other for many years, but Maurevert pulled the trigger without a second thought."

"Cold-blooded," I said, nodding. "He will be perfect. There remains the matter of timing: This must not mar the wedding celebrations, which end on the twenty-first. I will arrange a Council meeting the next morning requiring Coligny's attendance. I will send a messenger to you with the time. Tell Monsieur Maurevert to be ready, for we may not have another opportunity."

"Very good," young Guise replied. "Before it is done, however, I would humbly request one thing of His Majesty . . ."

"You will have royal protection," I said. "Secretly, of course. You would be well advised to quit Paris immediately afterward, if not sooner."

When the Duke and his mother had been escorted out, Edouard signaled for us to remain behind.

"The situation in Paris has grown volatile," he said. "I have ordered the deployment of a few troops to keep the peace, but I believe our good friends the Guises are fomenting trouble. Most of the priests in the city are denouncing the Huguenots and stirring up the Catholics against them. Let us hope that the wedding distracts the people from their hatred."

I unfurled my fan and fluttered it rapidly; the room felt as close as an oven. "It will," I said shortly. "It must."

At dusk, I accompanied Margot to Cardinal de Bourbon's palace, where she was to spend the night. As our carriage rolled over the ancient, creaking bridge to the Ile-de-la-Cité, Margot looked behind us at the Louvre palace and burst into tears.

"My darling," I said kindly, "you will sleep at home tomorrow night. Very little will change."

"Except that I will be the wife of a Huguenot," she said, "and if there is another war . . . Neither my husband nor my family will trust me."

She was right, of course, and the realization broke my heart. I put my arm around her and smoothed the tears from her cheeks.

"Sweet girl," I said and kissed her. "Sweet girl, there will never be another war, thanks to you." I paused to lighten my tone. "Did you know that the day I married your father, I despised him?"

She stopped crying long enough to frown at me. "Now you are teasing me, *Maman.*"

"But it is true. I was in love with my cousin, Ippolito." I smiled, remembering. "He was so tall, so handsome—older than your father and far more sophisticated. And he said that he loved me."

Margot dabbed at her nose with her kerchief. "Why didn't you marry him?"

I sighed. "Because my uncle Pope Clement had different plans. He delivered me to France in exchange for prestige and political backing. And so I married your father. He was only fourteen, shy and awkward, and he resented me, a stranger from a foreign land. We had not yet learned how to love each other.

"I am glad now that I never married Ippolito. He was brash, foolish... and a liar. He didn't really love me; he meant only to use me as a pawn in his political schemes."

Margot was listening, wide-eyed. "How awful, *Maman!*"

I nodded. "It was terrible. You must understand, Margot, that there are men willing to use you only to further their aims. Luckily, Henri of Navarre is not such a man. Things are not always what they seem; and although you might not appreciate Henri now, in time, you will come to love him if you open your heart."

Margot leaned back against her seat, her expression thoughtful. We were both exhausted, and the rocking of the carriage lulled us into a drowsy silence.

With feigned offhandedness, I said, "I am concerned about your brother Edouard. He and Charles despise each other so; when the King learns that his younger brother favors something, he immediately opposes it. Edouard has often confessed to me that he wished he had a useful spy, one to whom the King opened his heart.

"You are so very close to them both, my daughter; does Edouard ever speak of such things to you?"

Margot's cheeks flamed; she turned and looked out the window with eyes so full of guilt that I closed my own, unwilling to see more.

She had been a gift to me, a child not bought by blood. A child who, I hoped, had been heaven-sent, to undo the evil wrought by the purchase of her brothers' lives.

Sweet Margot, they have corrupted you.

We rode the rest of the way in silence.

Forty-two

On Monday I woke to a joyous cascade of church bells exhorting the citizens of Paris to rise and ready themselves for this most festive day. I went to the open window in the hope of a hint of morning coolness. But the sky was already bleached by a harsh, fast-rising sun. The Louvre's courtyard was filled with grooms fastening bright carapaces to the horses that would pull the royal carriages; the palace itself was alive with voices and footfall.

The ritual of dressing soon began: My nightgown was pulled over my head and replaced by a chemise of sheer lawn, which was followed by two voluminous crinoline petticoats and a corset with wooden stays laced cruelly tight. I stepped into my aubergine gown and held out my arms as huge sleeves were laced to it. My hair was brushed out, then braided and wound into a thick coil at the base of my neck; the whole was covered with a French hood, its band of purple damask edged with dozens of tiny seed pearls. I was already melting by the time the corset was laced; by the time the hood was set in place, I was drenched.

After a dozen long strands of pearls were hung round my neck, and diamonds affixed to my ears, Madame Gondi pronounced me ready. I went down to the courtyard, where Edouard and Charles stood watching Navarre's beribboned carriage roll out the gate.

My sons wore matching doublets made from pale green silk heavily embroidered with silver thread. Edouard had added a toque adorned with peacock feathers and pearls the size of raspberries. The Duke of Anjou was of good cheer, the King dismal and distracted.

We climbed into our carriage and rode over the bridge through the pressing, curious crowds, punctuated by black flocks of Huguenots; the Duke of Anjou and I leaned out the windows and waved to them while Charles sat back, sulking.

We arrived shortly at the episcopal palace next to Notre-Dame, where the Cardinal de Bourbon greeted us, already accompanied by Henri, who wore the same pale green with silver embroidery as my sons. The King of Navarre was accompanied by his mentor, Coligny, and his cousin Condé. The Admiral wore finery that matched Condé's: a doublet of dark blue silk damask with gold velvet piping and breeches of blue satin striped with red. Coligny was giddy, one moment laughing and cuffing Navarre upon the shoulder, the next, wiping away tears. He seemed not to notice the King's reticence, or the way Charles averted his eyes every time the Admiral glanced at him.

"I am as proud of him as I would be of my own son," Coligny said, referring to Henri. "Proud of his bravery as a lad, prouder still of the man he has become. He is an inspiration today to all Huguenots." He impulsively wrapped his arm around the young king's neck and kissed the side of his face.

Navarre responded with a queasy smile and silence. He looked grand in his silver costume and ruby-encrusted crown, but nerves had bested him: He kept wiping his hands on the sides of his doublet and responding to questions or comments with monosyllables. He returned Edouard's enthusiastic embrace mindlessly, and did not notice when the King failed to greet him.

At last we took our places before the massive wooden doors at the front entrance of the palace. Trumpets blared as the doors opened to reveal the crowds, cheering and jubilant despite the heat.

The youngest relatives of the bride and groom—two grinning girl twins and a trio of timid boys—went first, scattering rose petals. They were followed by the Cardinal and at some remove Navarre, flanked by Condé and Coligny.

Once Henri and his party had begun to descend the palace stairs, Margot emerged from her hiding place with her attendants bearing the long, rustling train. A thousand diamonds glittered on her cloak and gown; a hundred encircled her long throat. Her eyes were so swollen and red that I knew she had spent the night weeping. I told myself it did not matter: Few would be able to see her as closely as I could; they would notice only the gown, the cloak, the jewels, and her regal manner, and deem her a proper queen.

With her brothers flanking her and her three attendants in tow, my daughter slowly walked down the steps of the palace. After several paces I followed her; the remaining princes and princesses of the blood from the Houses of Bourbon and Guise came after me.

At the base of the palace steps stood the entrance to the gallery, which stretched from the Cardinal's palace to a small, roped-off opening in front of a high platform. This platform had been built atop the steps at Notre-Dame's western façade so that it was level with the cathedral doors and extended fifty paces outward, rendering it entirely visible to the throngs filling the plaza. The gallery was constructed of tall wooden posts—carpenters' families ate well the year of a royal wedding—set upright into the ground, connected by crossbeams, and covered with a canvas roof. It was draped inside and out with garlands of red roses and swags of billowing pale blue silk to match the bride's attire.

I forced a dignified smile as I processed behind Margot, past the rows of lesser nobles who stood inside the gallery. The canvas roof provided shade from the fierce midmorning sun, though the air inside was a cloying mix of the essences of rose, sweat, and fresh-cut timber. Sunlight streamed in the gallery's eastern side and fell on the glorious train of moiré silk. I stared at it, entranced by the way the blue fabric shifted in the dappled light like an undulant, shimmering ocean; tiny diamonds, sewn a finger's width apart, flashed in the sun.

The noise of the crowd suddenly dulled, as if I had been submerged in water; its cheers became muted shrieks of terror, its cries of encouragement faint mortal groans. I looked out of the gallery into the ruthless sun and saw not joy upon the thousands of faces but grimaces of fear and pain.

A torrent of blood gushed out from under Margot's glorious blue train, past the ankles of the girls who held it aloft. It swept past me, soaking my slippers and the hem of my gown, rushing out to fill the width of the gallery. I stared at the nobles who stood inside the gallery, watching. Their self-conscious grins were unchanged. They did not see the blood; they did not hear the screaming.

I looked down at the fierce red current and thought, *It will stop the instant Margot says yes. It will stop the instant they are married.*

I set my slippered foot down and watched it disappear beneath the dark stream. I could see the blood but not feel it: My heel struck dry cobblestone. I lifted my gaze and forced my lips to curve in a parody of a smile. I did not look down again.

I survived the long procession through the gallery and emerged into daylight and an open space that led to the platform in front of Notre-Dame. The area was cordoned off, heavily guarded, and blessedly unbloodied; Henri and his men awaited us there. Two sets of steps led up to the platform; Navarre's group ascended the northern stairs, Margot's the southern. Both groups met at the center of the platform, where the Cardinal de Bourbon stood waiting behind a prayer bench. A row of chairs had been placed nearby so that the wedding party could sit and watch the proceedings; we filed in front of them and sat at the Cardinal's signal. Margot and Henri knelt at the bench, and the ceremony began.

The ritual had been stripped to the bone, and the Cardinal was efficient. He carried no breviary, but recited from memory from Paul's first letter to the Corinthians:

"If I speak in the tongues of men and angels, but have not love, I am as a ringing brass or clanging cymbal. If I have the gift of prophecy and can fathom all mysteries and knowledge, but have not love, I am nothing.... Love does not delight in evil, but rejoices in the truth."

The full sun was brutal: Beneath swaths of damask and layers of petticoats, I melted. Perspiration trickled down my forehead; I quashed the urge to wipe it away. My eyelids fluttered as the Cardinal's face began to shift, growing rounder, fuller, paler.

What was done out of fear must now be done out of love. Madame la Reine, *these children should not be.*

I shook off my dizziness and refocused my gaze until I saw the Cardinal's features again. He was addressing Navarre.

"Do you take this woman to be your lawfully wedded wife? To love her, and cherish her, so long as you both shall live?"

Navarre's strong voice carried over the hushed, breathless city. "Yes."

The Cardinal looked to my daughter. "And do you, Marguerite, take this man to be your lawfully wedded husband? To honor and obey him, so long as you both shall live?"

The crowd waited. Margot bowed her head and answered nothing. After a torturously long pause, the Cardinal—assuming that heat or emotion had overwhelmed the bride—repeated the question.

Margot did not reply. Her lips were pressed together tightly, her face flushed from something other than the heat. Her groom resolutely fastened his gaze on the Cardinal.

"God be damned," Charles muttered beside me. "God be damned, haven't I endured enough?" He leaped from his seat; beside me, Edouard tensed as the King marched up to Margot. He put his hand firmly upon her jeweled crown and began to pump it up and down, forcing her to perform a parody of an affirmative nod.

Margot's features crumpled with humiliation and fury—but the relieved Cardinal took it as an answer and pronounced the couple man and wife. The crowd's response was thunderous. The couple rose, and the Cardinal presented them to the assembly—Henri de Bourbon, King of Navarre and Prince of France, and his wife, Marguerite de Valois, Queen of Navarre and Princess of France.

I rose to embrace my daughter and her husband. But as I stood up, daylight suddenly flickered. I looked down at my feet and saw there a dark, spreading stain. It traveled quickly until the entire platform bled crimson.

Margot had married the Huguenot king, but it was not enough.

Something prompted me to look over my shoulder and down. On the northern edge of the platform, an arm's breadth from the halberd-bearing Swiss, was Cosimo Ruggieri.

He stood near a group of black-clad Huguenots and might well have been mistaken for one of them were it not for the red satin stripes on his black sleeves and breeches. The past thirteen years had taken their toll: His blue-black hair was streaked with silver, his shoulders markedly stooped. In the midst of the jubilant revelers, he alone did not smile. He stared somberly, intently, directly at me.

I wanted to run to him, to ask him if he, too, saw the river of blood. But I could only stare fixedly at him until Edouard hissed at me: The time had come to go into the cathedral for the proxy ceremony. While Navarre and his party waited outside, I reluctantly entered the church with the others.

When the ritual was over and we came back out onto the platform, accompanied by the deafening chorus of Notre-Dame's five bells, I turned my searching, anxious gaze to the crowd, but Ruggieri had vanished.

A banquet followed at the Cardinal's palace; afterward, the sated diners headed for the Louvre's ballroom. I ate and danced and kept an anxious eye on my daughter, who had apparently resigned herself to her fate; she danced and smiled with apparent sincerity, though she scrupulously avoided meeting the admiring gaze of her husband.

I had unwisely joined in a vigorous *saltarello* and was returning to my chair, fan pumping madly, when Ambassador Zuñiga caught my eye and motioned me aside. He, too, had just performed the jumps and twists of the challenging dance; his face was streaked with rivulets of perspiration.

"*Madame la Reine,* forgive me," he gasped. "I do not mean to dampen the joy of this celebration, but I must lodge a protest."

I looked at him from behind my frantically gyrating fan. "What now, Don Diego?"

"It is that ill-bred boor Coligny. Go and listen to him now: He is bragging openly that he will return victorious from the Netherlands and present Charles with the captured banner of Spain. How can I listen idly to this blatant affront to my King?"

My fan stilled. "He is a traitor," I said softly, "and he will soon pay for his crimes against our King, and yours. But not today, Don Diego. Today, we will celebrate my daughter's wedding."

The intrigued tilt of the ambassador's head indicated that he could guess very well what I had *not* said, and that it would be to his benefit to forget our conversation.

"Thank you, *Madame la Reine,*" he said and kissed my hand. "In that case, I must apologize for interrupting your joyful day."

I was tempted to go and hear Coligny's boasts for myself but decided against it: I did not want to be seen reacting to his arrogance. I sat in my chair listening to the music for the rest of the evening, until most of the guests had left.

Near the end of the revels, an exhausted Navarre approached me. "*Tante* Catherine," he asked, "might I have a private word?"

"Of course." I patted the empty chair beside me. "You are my son now."

He sat down and handed me a small velvet box and a letter. "These are from my mother. She asked me to give them to you after the wedding."

I took them from him. The sealed letter was addressed to me in Jeanne's careful hand; I knew it well, from all the many lists of demands we had shared with each other during the marriage negotiations.

"I will read this later, in private," I said and slipped it inside my sleeve.

I opened the dusty little box. Nestled inside, against white silk that had yellowed with age, was a brooch made from a large, perfect emerald surrounded by clusters of diamonds.

"This is exquisite," I murmured. "And it must be worth a small fortune. But I never saw your mother wear it."

"Nor did I," he admitted. "I don't know how she came by it, but she wanted you to have it. Her gentlewoman told me she wrote the letter on her deathbed."

"Thank you," I said, touched, and kissed him upon the cheek. He flushed with charming shyness; I took advantage of the moment to speak frankly.

"So," I said, closing the box, "will you be going with the Admiral to the Netherlands after the celebrations?"

His eyes widened before he caught hold of himself and frowned. "No," he said firmly. "I must apologize for him, *Madame la Reine*. He has overstepped his bounds. I have made my opinion known to him, yet he ignores me."

"What would that opinion be?" I asked.

Henri's expression hardened. "It is mad to bait Spain; it can bring only disaster. We are just recovering from years of war. Now is the time to recover and rebuild, not tear down."

"Well put," I said, though I did not believe he had meant any of it.

The smiling Cardinal de Bourbon, with Margot and Charles in tow, approached us and leaned down to speak into my ear.

"The time has come, *Madame la Reine*."

I led Margot upstairs to her own chamber, outfitted as a bridal suite, with satin indigo sheets and pale blue velvet hangings. With my ladies, I dutifully scattered handfuls of walnuts over the antechamber floor. Then I helped my daughter undress and settle beneath the silk sheets. As she pulled the top sheet over her breasts, tears slid down the sides of her face. I embraced her tightly.

"My darling," I whispered, "you will be happy, and this marriage will bring us peace."

She was too overcome with emotion to answer. I went out to the antechamber to find the Cardinal and Edouard looking troubled.

"His Majesty refuses to come witness the consummation," Edouard said irritably. "He insists I do so in his stead."

The Cardinal was shaking his head. "This is unheard of," he said. "The King must sign the contract as a witness, to verify that the act took place."

"And he will," I told the Cardinal and turned to Edouard. "Tell him that he *must* come!"

"I did, *Maman,*" Edouard said. "He refuses to listen."

I let go a sound of pure exasperation. "Where is he?"

"In his bedchamber. I tell you, he will not come," Edouard said.

I was already out the door. I found His Majesty huddled in his bed with the sheet pulled up, fully dressed in his wedding garb.

"Get up, Charles," I said.

"I won't do it," he whined. "You don't understand, *Maman.* No one understands me . . . no one, except Margot. And now this—this Huguenot bastard means to take her from me."

"Don't be a child," I said. "Get up. The Cardinal is waiting."

Tears came to his eyes. "Everyone is trying to take her away from me. Edouard, Henri . . . and now you. Don't you see, *Maman*? I love her . . ."

I slapped him so hard that his skull struck the headboard.

"How dare you!" he snarled. "How dare you touch the person of the King!"

I moved to strike him again, but he raised an arm defensively.

The words tumbled out of me. "We all must do things we despise, my son—but I would remind you that your sister is not your wife. She belongs to another man—rightly so—and you will now behave as a good brother ought, and do what tradition demands."

A spasm of grief contorted Charles's face; he let go a wracking sob. "I want to die," he gasped. "No one else can abide me . . . no one else is kind to me, because I am so wretched. What will I do without her?"

"Your Majesty," I said, "you speak as though she is lost forever. You forget that she is, even now, under your roof—and she will likely remain here for years to come. Now that Henri's mother is dead, he will spend little time in Navarre."

Charles looked up at me, his face damp; mucus had collected on his dark mustache. "You are not lying to me?"

"I am not lying," I said, without trying to hide my irritation. "Charles, if you ever speak of her again as though she were anything more than your sister . . . I will do worse than strike you. Now get up, and perform the duty all French kings have performed before you."

In the end, he came with me to the antechamber and went, trembling, to sit beside the Cardinal while Henri and his bride performed the nuptial act. The Cardinal later confessed to me that Charles had spent the entire time with his hands over his eyes.

When the King emerged from Margot's bedchamber, he looked down at me with red, swollen eyes. "By God, I will kill him," he whispered. "I will kill him, too . . ."

Three days of nonstop festivities followed—although the more vigorous entertainments, including the joust, were canceled after too many of the participants fainted in the merciless heat. On the last day, the twenty-first, Edouard reported to me that he had witnessed a confrontation between Coligny and the King outside the tennis gallery. Coligny had demanded an audience; Charles had stalled him, saying, "Give me a few more days of celebration, *mon père*—I cannot think with all these parties going on."

"If you will not see me sooner, then I shall be obliged to leave Paris," Coligny reportedly responded. "And if I do, you will find yourself embroiled in a civil war rather than a foreign one."

The comment prompted Edouard, as Lieutenant General, to station troops at strategic points around the city, ostensibly to keep the peace between the Guises and Coligny. It also worried me that our victim might quit the city too soon—but the Admiral had responded with an emphatic affirmative when I asked him later that day whether he would attend the Council meeting on the following morning. Poor fool; he actually believed he still could sway us.

Late in the evening, against the backdrop of distant music and laughter coming from the final masked ball, Edouard and I met with Marshal Tavannes, whom we had entrusted with the news of the coming assassination, as well as Anna d'Este, her husband, and her son the Duke of Guise. Anna's husband, the Duke of Nemours, reported that the arquebusier, Maurevert, had already arrived on the rue de Béthizy property and was busily determining which location gave him best access the street.

The conspirators' expressions displayed grim exhilaration and the occasional pang of conscience. I felt nothing, only the sense that everything around me—the conversation, the faces, the music and voices of the gay revelers in the distant ballroom—was unreal.

That night I lay abed in a pool of sweat and struggled to relax my limbs, my quickened breath, my curiously throbbing heart. A sickness settled over me, the same burning chill I had often experienced during pregnancy just before a bout of retching. This time, I could not expel what troubled me; this time, I was not giving birth to life.

I did not dream because I did not sleep. I did not sleep because I feared the dreams that had dogged me for so long. I stared up into the darkness, praying that the stifling air above me would not suddenly transform itself into blood and spill down on me like mortal rain, drowning me in my bed.

I wish now that it had.

Forty-three

Friday, August twenty-second—the day the government resumed its business—dawned the hottest of them all. There had been no rain since the previous Sunday; in the streets, carriage wheels and horses' hooves kicked up clouds of dust. The air was heavy with unspent moisture: I traded my soggy nightgown for a chemise and petticoats that immediately clung to my shining, damp skin.

Edouard and I had agreed that the best course of action on that fateful day was to make as many public appearances as possible, so that it was clear we royals were consumed by far happier things than an assassination. I went to early Mass at the nearby cathedral of Saint-Germain-l'Auxerrois with Anjou and Margot—who was exhausted but remarkably cheerful—as well as all the Catholic members of the wedding party.

Edouard and I returned for the Privy Council meeting scheduled for nine o'clock; we arrived early, and the Duke of Anjou took the King's place at the head of the long oval table. I sat beside him. I had already warned His Majesty that Coligny would be present and would again press Charles to support his Netherlands war, more vehemently now that he realized he was in danger of losing the King's tacit blessing. As a result, Charles decided to linger cowardly in his bed that morning and left the running of the meeting to his brother.

Coligny arrived at the stroke of nine, just after the white-haired Duke of Montpensier, and before the dashing young Gonzaga, the Duke of Nevers, and the aging soldier Marshal Cossé. Last to enter was the bald, near-toothless Marshal Tavannes, whose years of service had earned him the right to keep royals waiting.

I studied Coligny, knowing this would be the last time I should see him. His once sun-browned skin had faded after his prolonged absence from the battlefield, and he had gained a bit of weight on the Court's fine fare. Despite his talent for duplicity, he had been unable to fully mask his disappointment at the King's absence. I felt no anxiety at the sight of him, only a curious relief at the knowledge that he would be dead on the morrow. If I hated him, it was only as a mother might hate a viper that threatened her children; there was no personal animosity, only a desire to protect my own.

After giving the assembled a chance to share complaints about the abysmal heat, the Duke of Anjou called the meeting to order. Coligny asked to present his argument for war in the Low Countries again. Just beyond our northern border, he claimed, fresh atrocities were being committed in Flanders. Given the location, we could deploy troops quickly there, and the victory would give us the needed momentum to move farther, into the Netherlands.

Edouard listened to his request with exquisite composure, then said, "The matter of war with Spain has already been discussed, and a vote taken. There is no need to revisit the issue. Are my fellow councillors agreed?"

We were.

Fury flickered brightly in Coligny's eyes and was replaced by hard determination. He had prepared for this probability; his decision had already been made. The meeting continued another two hours. During that time, the Admiral sat with his fist against his chin and stared out the window as he plotted war. Upon adjournment, he left quickly, without a word.

Afterward, the Duke of Anjou and I made our way to a public lunch. The shutters had been opened and the curtains drawn in order to light the vast, high-ceilinged chamber. Dust hung in the air and glittered in shafts of harsh sunlight.

Edouard and I sat at one end of the long dining table. Guards hovered discreetly at intervals between us and the standing crowd of nobles. While

Edouard and I were served the first course, an octet performed a pair of songs that spun witty tales of love peppered with misunderstandings, double entendres, and jokes, all of which led to happy endings. The crowd applauded them enthusiastically.

As the music died, cathedral bells throughout the city marked the time: eleven in the morning, the hour of Coligny's death. In the Guises' château on the rue de Béthizy, Maurevert was lifting his arquebus and taking careful aim.

I looked to my son. As we directed our attention to our bowls, Edouard seemed lighthearted and at ease. If Lorenzo, the wise-eyed boy from the mural on the Medici chapel walls, could have seen us, I wondered, would he have approved?

We began our meal in silence. I was keenly aware of every sight, sound, touch: of the clang of my spoon against the porcelain bowl, of its handle, quickly heated in my hand, of the ripples in the broth when the edge of the spoon broke its surface. Edouard's black eyes were very bright, his hands steady.

"I should like to take Henri to the château at Blois," I said languidly. "It would be much cooler there than in the city. I hope to go as soon as business allows."

"An excellent idea," my son replied. "I would enjoy taking Henri on the hunt."

We soon finished the first course. Given the weather, I had little appetite and sent it back to the kitchen half-eaten. The second course—one of my favorites, eels in red wine—was delivered piping hot, and the steam from it prompted me to draw back in my chair and wave my fan. As it cooled, Edouard and I exchanged a few more inanities.

My Edouard, I thought. *My precious eyes . . . I could not bear this without you.*

How could Ruggieri have been such a monster? How could he ever have suggested that I harm my beloved child?

A plate of cold pickled beef had just been set before me when I saw the Duke of Anjou glance up sharply; I followed his gaze.

Marshal Tavannes was moving urgently through the crowd of waiting nobles. Of all those assembled, he alone did not smile, but was discreet enough to contain his shock so as to avoid catching the attention of those around him. I caught sight of his eyes—guarded, intense—and I knew.

I forced myself to smile as he neared. He could not bring himself to respond in kind but bowed and asked permission to approach.

He came to me first and leaned down to speak in my ear, so quietly that even Edouard could not hear him.

Admiral Coligny had been shot in the arm. His men—some of them guards Edouard had given him upon his arrival at Court—had carried him to the safety of his lodgings at the Hôtel de Béthizy.

The smile was still on my lips, frozen there by shock. "Is the wound fatal?" I whispered to Tavannes.

"They think not, *Madame la Reine.*"

"Who else knows?"

"The Admiral sent two of his captains to inform the King immediately. I understand that Henri of Navarre is speaking to the King this very moment."

Tavannes said more, surely, but his words were muffled by an insistent, growing drumming in my ears, like that made by the hooves of approaching horses. I put a hand upon my son's forearm.

"Edouard," I said softly. I rose and indicated that I wished Tavannes to accompany us.

As we walked sedately through the great reception hall, nobles parted to let us pass. I lifted my skirts and did not look down; I did not have to. This time, I could feel the blood.

Here is the story, pieced together from Marshal Tavannes's report, as well as those of witnesses:

Immediately after the Council meeting, Admiral Coligny went in search of the King. To his chagrin, Charles was in the tennis gallery, playing a set with Coligny's brother-in-law, Teligny and—as luck would have it—the young Duke of Guise. Charles was embarrassed; Coligny, put out, since the King had promised to hear Coligny out as soon as the wedding celebrations were over. The Admiral demanded a private audience on the spot; when the King refused, Coligny grew outraged and strode off.

He left by the Louvre's guarded northern gate and made his way to the rue de Béthizy. Following him were four Huguenot captains and ten Scottish guards. As he neared the property owned by the Guises, he took from his pocket a pair of spectacles and a letter written by his young wife, who had recently given birth. He was reading it when he walked into the assassin's sights. At that instant, he stopped in his tracks upon realizing that an inner binding in one of his shoes had come loose.

Unaware of the binding, Maurevert fired.

Simultaneously, the Admiral bent down to inspect his shoe.

The ball tore through Coligny's left arm and very nearly severed his right index finger, which hung, dangling, from a flap of flesh. The Admiral promptly fainted.

His men closed ranks around him. All of them had heard the shot and agreed it came from the nearby property owned by the Guises. Three of them forced their way inside and discovered the smoking arquebus. By then, Maurevert had escaped.

I was prepared to deal with the outcry following Coligny's assassination, but I had never considered the possibility that he might survive the attempt.

Edouard and I entered Charles's antechamber to discover a dozen outraged Huguenots, clustered so tightly together that I could not at first see the King. At the sound of our step, the black-clad nobles turned and, upon seeing us, glared in disapproval even as they grudgingly made way to reveal Charles sitting at his desk, with Henri and Condé standing beside him.

At the sight of us, Condé recoiled; Navarre was so preoccupied with the King that he appeared not to notice our arrival. Charles huddled in the chair, clutching his skull. Tears of rage ran down his cheeks, flushed scarlet after his vigorous tennis game.

"Leave me!" he howled. "Leave me, I cannot think! Why does God torment me so?" He began to beat his forehead against the surface of his desk.

Navarre glanced up and caught my gaze. He had too much self-possession to recoil as Condé had, but I saw mistrust and veiled fury in his eyes.

"Madame la Reine," he said, with distant formality. *"Monsieur le Duc.* You must help us. Admiral Coligny has been shot, and His Majesty has lost himself. But justice must be done! Now, before violence erupts!"

"I *am* lost," Charles agreed with a groan. "Too much trouble . . ." He squeezed his eyes shut and began to rock slowly back and forth in the chair. “I can bear no more!”

“It is only the heat,” I said protectively. “The heat and the terrible shock.” I flicked open my fan and directed the breeze onto his face. “Dear Charles,” I said, “you must listen to me.”

His eyes snapped open; he looked up at me with utter desperation.

“Why do they torment me?” he moaned. “Please make them stop, *Maman.* Make them go away and die!”

“I can make it stop,” I soothed, “if you will help Admiral Coligny.”

“ “But what must be done?”

“You must denounce the criminal who has committed this heinous act,” I said, glad to have Huguenot witnesses, “and make it clear that the Crown will not rest until he is brought to justice. There must be a full investigation.”

Edouard sidled closer to us. “Coligny’s surroundings must be secured,” he said briskly. “I will clear all Catholics from the neighborhood surrounding the rue de Béthizy, to reduce the risk to the Admiral and his men. And I will send fifty of my best arquebusiers to surround the Admiral’s hotel.”

“Yes,” Charles said, with a gusting sigh of relief, though his eyes were still wild. “Yes, see that it is done.”

“Is there anything else, Sire?” I asked gently.

“Yes.” Charles put his heels on the edge of the chair, knees bent, arms wrapped about his shins, and slowly rocked. “Doctor Paré . . .” The surgeon who had tried, and failed, to save my husband’s life now served as the King’s personal physician. “Send Paré to the Hôtel de Béthizy.”

“It is done,” I said.

Charles suddenly stilled and looked up at me. “I must see the Admiral, and beg his forgiveness for failing to protect him. I must let him know that I have not deserted him. Let us go now, *Maman.*”

“I would ask only one thing, Your Majesty,” I said.

He scowled up at me.

“Permit the Duke of Anjou and me to accompany you.”

It was of course too soon to hurry to Coligny’s side; Doctor Paré had yet to perform surgery on the wound. But by midafternoon, a party—Navarre,

Condé, ten bodyguards, Anjou, the King, and I—had assembled near the Louvre's northern gate. I also invited old Tavannes, who had heartily approved the assassination plot, yet possessed the nerve to accompany me and feign sympathy for Coligny in the midst of a crowd of Huguenots. Navarre was politely distant, Condé still too angry to say a word to us.

I had suggested that we make the short walk to Coligny's surroundings, as it would be good for the people to see our concern for the Admiral. In addition to Navarre's guards, our group was accompanied by a dozen Swiss soldiers to protect the King.

After two guards lifted the thick iron bar from the latch, a trio of grooms swung open the heavy gate. The soldiers surrounding the palace parted for us as we headed into the street.

We soon left the Louvre behind and passed on to the overheated cobblestones of the rue de Béthizy, where scattered flocks of black-clad pedestrians caught sight of us and coalesced into a single wave, which surged toward us. Tavannes and Edouard instinctively flanked me, while Condé and Navarre did the same for the King.

"There goes the Italian woman!" a man shouted, no more than five paces away. "She greets her friends in Florentine fashion: with a smile on her face and a dagger in her hand!"

The mob roared in affirmation. A jumble of black linen and pale flesh loomed abruptly. On my left, old Marshal Tavannes staggered; his shoulder struck mine and threw me off balance, against Edouard. The Swiss troops seized their halberds and leveled the shining blades at the onrush of angry spectators.

"Do not harm them! Let them be!" I shouted; a fatal incident could easily provoke a full-scale riot.

The King, Navarre, and Condé paused to look over their shoulders at us: The crowd had not touched them.

"Let them pass!" Navarre shouted, and the black swarm receded.

We began to move again, at a quickened pace, and arrived at the Hôtel de Béthizy without further trouble, though the crowd dogged us the entire way, their murmured curses forming a single ominous rumble.

The outer perimeter of the hotel was patrolled by more than fifty restless men in black—some of them hard-bitten troops with unshaven faces, others well-groomed nobles. All of them greeted Navarre with courteous bows but had only sullen, stony glances for the Duke of Anjou and me. Ambassador Zuñiga had been right: They were all armed for war, some with long swords, others with arquebuses. The four men standing watch on the front steps sweated beneath heavy chest armor. Navarre ascended the steps alone and spoke to them; they moved aside to let us pass.

Inside, a score of guards and noblemen choked a sunny, stuffy vestibule, some weeping, others ranting, all outraged. At the overpowering smell of unwashed flesh and of sausage scorched upon a nearby cookstove, I pressed my scented kerchief to my nose. The Huguenots reacted to Navarre with expressions of hope, gratitude, and respect; at the sight of Anjou and me, their faces turned away, lips twisted with disgust, as if they had just looked on something vomitous.

We proceeded up the creaking wooden stairs to the second floor, the whole of which served as the Admiral's vast, open bedchamber. Although the room was larger than my own bedchamber in the old, crumbling Louvre, its low ceiling gave the impression of more cramped quarters; the effect was enhanced by some fifty men who had congregated around their wounded leader's bedside.

Navarre led the way. His fellows parted willingly for him, with murmurs of gratitude, yet were it not for Navarre's warning gaze, they would have hissed at me. We made our way to Coligny, in a bed of ornately carved cherrywood.

The Admiral was markedly pale as he lay propped up by pillows. His right hand, cradled carefully in his lap, was heavily swathed in bandages; Doctor Paré had been obliged to cut away the dangling index finger while the patient was fully conscious, and Coligny was exhausted from pain and blood loss. His blond hair, dark with sweat, clung to his scalp; his eyes, narrowed with misery, did not brighten as we approached. Paré stood at the head of the bed, white-haired and leonine, his yellowed gaze protective. The windows had been shut for fear a breeze might bring a chill and hasten infection; the room was stifling. I could smell the blood.

"Your Majesty," the Admiral murmured at the sight of Navarre; when Charles stepped forward, Coligny repeated the phrase.

"My father," Navarre said softly and bent down to kiss the top of the

Admiral's head. "I have not ceased praying since I heard the news. Is the pain bearable? Is there anything the doctors can do to ease it?"

"It is not so bad," Coligny whispered, but his grey lips trembled. I had wanted only to kill him; I had not meant for him to suffer.

"I have sent fifty bodyguards to you," Navarre said, "so that you will be safe and can spare your own men to find and punish whoever has done this."

"Mon père!" Charles exclaimed. "May God himself strike me dead if I do not find the bastard who has done this to you, and see him drawn and quartered! Forgive me! If I had only listened to you this morning, this would not have happened. . . ." He began to sob.

Coligny held out his left hand, the fingers spread and trembling; Charles clasped it.

"There is nothing to forgive," the Admiral whispered. "It is God's will." Relishing his role as martyr, he directed a feeble, beatific smile at my son.

"I swear to you, *mon père,*" the King gasped, "I will not rest until you are avenged."

We have lost him, I thought as I stared at Charles; it had all turned upside down. Had Coligny been killed, the King would have grieved but ultimately accepted the death. Wounded, Coligny could play upon the King's sympathy; the situation had grown more dangerous than ever.

"My heart breaks to see you suffer, Admiral," I said loudly as I stepped closer to the bedside. "His Majesty is right—a full investigation will be launched and the perpetrator brought to justice. I, too, have been praying all morning for your protection and recovery."

Coligny's face lolled toward mine. "Have you?" he whispered.

Though dulled by pain, his gaze bore through me. He knew, I realized. He knew and was determined to exact revenge, but I kept my head high and did not flinch beneath his scrutiny.

Edouard sidled closer to the bed. "The perpetrator will be found quickly," he said. "I, too, have sent men to help you—fifty of my finest arquebusiers. The street has been cleared of Catholics; you are surrounded by friends. Already we have launched our inquiry: As you know, the shot was fired from a property owned by the Guise family. We are attempting to locate the Duke for questioning."

Charles unclenched the Admiral's hand. "Guise? Impossible! I was playing tennis with him this morning."

"We must not rush to conclusions," Edouard replied calmly, "but we must examine all the possibilities."

"Admiral," I asked, "what of your hand?"

"Ah," he said. "The finger . . . I wish the doctor's scissors had been sharper. It took three attempts, but the finger is gone." He paused as Charles, Edouard, and I groaned at the thought. "Forgive me, but I must request permission to speak to His Majesty in private."

Coligny, damn him, knew that we had no choice. I turned to Charles, floundering about for the right words to make him refuse the Admiral without revealing my guilt. There were none.

Charles waved dismissively at Edouard, at me. "I'll call for you when we are done."

I could do nothing save take Tavannes's proffered arm and, with Edouard flanking me on the other side, turn my back to Coligny.

We took three steps away from the bed and were obliged to stop. A giant with an arquebus slung by a strap over his shoulder stepped into my path and stared down at me, his tiny eyes full of loathing.

"Make way for Her Majesty," Tavannes snapped.

When the giant did not yield, the old Marshal shoved him. Edouard immediately filled the gap, and we managed to push our way forward a few more steps—men in wrinkled black linen encircled us and began to close in. They did not genuflect to us royals; their glares revealed hatred, and their hands rested upon the hilts of their swords.

One of them—a haggard man of thirty—approached us. He, too, had his hand upon the hilt of his long sword, and as he neared, Edouard tensed beside me. I touched the Dauphin's arm in warning, lest he draw out a hidden dagger: We were outmanned and would quickly lose any fight.

The Huguenot's face was thin and sharp as a hatchet; when he spoke, his red chin beard wagged.

"There will be Hell to pay for what you have done," he hissed. His breath was so fetid, I turned from it.

Someone behind him added, "God punishes murders."

A different man, with a goiter the size of a tennis ball on his neck, stepped forward to stand beside the red-bearded soldier. "We don't need God." His eyes were blue, like Coligny's, and just as mad. "*We* will strike them down."

He swung an arquebus from his shoulder and nestled the stock against his chest. He took a step closer and touched the elbow of my sleeve with the barrel.

Now they will kill us, I thought. I was furious with myself for not realizing how dangerous the situation had become.

"Mannerless bastard!" Edouard shouted. "Touch the Queen's person again, and I will kill you!"

"Do you want war?" the red-bearded soldier hissed. "We will give you war!"

The owner of the arquebus cried out, "You lure us to your Catholic city, so you can slaughter us like swine! But we will kill you first!"

"I married my daughter to one of your own," I countered haughtily. "How dare you suggest that we would harm the Admiral! The King loves him as a father!"

My voice must have carried. I heard Navarre's shout; the men dropped their hostile gazes to the floor and withdrew as he hurried to my side.

"Madame la Reine," he asked, with disturbing formality, "did they harm you?"

Edouard pointed. "*He* touched her with the barrel of his arquebus!"

Navarre turned to the implicated man and drew his arm back to slap him; I caught his upraised arm.

"Don't punish him," I said. "Feelings are running high enough." I looked back in Coligny's direction. "Please," I said to Navarre, "will you escort me back to the Admiral?"

When I arrived, Charles was sitting on the edge of the bed, his jaw set, his brows knit in a formidable frown. He looked up at me, his eyes narrowed with mistrust.

"Your Majesty," I said softly, "Admiral Coligny is surely exhausted. We must let him rest."

Charles was ready to contradict me, but Doctor Paré, who had been standing at the head of the bed, spoke up suddenly.

"Yes," he said. He caught my gaze and immediately looked away, as if afraid his own might be too revealing. "It is difficult enough for him, with all his men here. It would be best, Your Majesty, if he were able to be quiet for a time."

"Very well," Charles said, with sullen reluctance, then turned to Coligny. "But I shall return soon, *mon père*. God keep you in the interim. You have all my prayers and my love."

"As you have mine," I said to the Admiral.

Coligny gazed up at me. He was trembling, his brow beaded with sweat, but I saw triumph in his eyes.

Given the hostility in the streets, Edouard sent one of our guards to fetch a carriage. Navarre and Condé remained at the Hôtel de Béthizy, while the King, Anjou, Tavannes, and I rode back to the Louvre at a slow pace, our carriage surrounded by the guards who had accompanied us on our walk to Coligny's lodgings.

Charles remained darkly silent, refusing to look at his brother or me, though we tried several times to draw him into our conversation.

Exasperated, I finally demanded, "What, precisely, did Admiral Coligny say to you that has upset you so?"

He lowered his face, taut with rage. "Only that I cannot trust either of you. Only that you wish to subvert my will, to use me as it suits your purposes."

Edouard flared. "Have you considered, my brother, that he says such things because *he* cannot be trusted? Because *he* means to subvert your will, by using you to further his insane war? He speaks ill of us because he knows we want to protect you from his cold-blooded manipulation."

"Enough!" Charles shouted. "Enough lies, lies, lies!" He clapped his hands over his ears.

By then we were slowing on our approach to the palace. Suddenly, one of the horses shrieked; I heard the drivers' curses, followed by a furious, deafening clatter of hail on the carriage walls and roof.

Outside the window, a hundred black-clad protesters stood at the northern gate, some pelting rocks at us, others waving swords and screaming at the Swiss soldiers who now stood, two men deep and armed with arquebuses, around the Louvre's walls. A fresh contingent of Swiss had marched into the street to form a human barricade. Just beyond them, a few dozen peasants—ragged, starving men with pitchforks, shovels, stones—had gathered.

Death to heretics! the distant peasants screamed, while the Huguenots at the gate cried out:

Murderers! Assassins!

We are striking back, and will kill!

Another volley of rocks struck the carriage; one sailed in through the window like a shot and buried itself in the padded seat beside Charles, abruptly checking his anger.

"Jesus," he whispered.

"So it begins," I said, staring out at the raging crowds, remembering Ruggieri's final words to me.

It may already be too late.

Forty-four

Under a hail of projectiles—stones, bricks, rotting garbage—our carriage dashed inside the palace gates, thanks to the guards who held back the onrush of angry Huguenots. We were met immediately by one of Edouard's commanders, who reported that "disturbances" had erupted in several neighborhoods, provoked not only by outraged Huguenots but by fearful Catholics convinced that they must rid themselves of a growing threat. Edouard responded by deploying more troops to key locations throughout the city, ostensibly to keep peace.

I was shaking when I returned to my apartments but insisted on going down that evening for a public supper an hour after the sun had set. The Duke of Anjou was preoccupied with his commanders, and Charles so distraught he took to his bed; Margot had joined her husband at Coligny's bedside. I went to dine alone.

It was a tense affair. In light of the Admiral's misfortune, no entertainment was offered that evening; the dozen nobles who had gathered were intense, brooding, silent. In the absence of conversation, the clatter of the spoon and knife, the clink of the glass, echoed in the still chamber. I forced myself to chew, to swallow, to appear as though I enjoyed a meal grown bitter.

As I stared down hopelessly at a pair of freshly delivered roasted doves, a shout shattered the silence.

"Madame la Reine!"

A noble I had often seen at Court but whose name I could not recall—he was a baron, I believe, and a Huguenot—stood three arms' lengths away from my table. My solitary guard had caught his elbow, but the baron—a giant, tall and broad as an oak, with a great long face framed by a streaming cloud of white hair—would not be moved. He did not genuflect; he did not bow. His large yellow teeth were bared, but not in a smile. He shouted my name as though it were an accusation.

"We will not rest, do you understand?" His face was very red against his white hair. "We will not rest until the murderers are brought to justice. We will not rest until they hang!"

My guard tried vainly to push him back. "Show the Queen respect, you cur!"

"I do not bow," the baron announced, "to a bloodstained Crown! Enjoy your supper while you can, Madame!"

He shook off the guard's grip at last and, turning his back rudely to me, stalked out of the dining chamber. No one followed him; no one rushed to my defense or offered apologies. The few nobles standing in attendance murmured among themselves, then turned their eyes to me.

I stared down at the little corpses on my plate and pushed them away. I rose and left the chamber slowly, regally, on unsteady legs.

Instinctively I went in search of Edouard. He was just leaving the war room, on the ground floor beneath the King's apartments, after a meeting with Marshals Tavannes and Cossé, and the city's Provost of Marchands. As my son crossed the threshold, our gazes met; his expression was as mine must have been—stricken—and I knew at that instant that we had finally arrived at the same conclusion.

He stopped in the doorway and, when I approached, took my hand and guided me inside the chamber, then closed the door softly behind us. The lamp had been snuffed; he gestured in the darkness for me to take a chair at the long conference table. I sat and watched as he struck the match and held it to the wick, which caught with a flare.

"It is worse than I thought," I said huskily. "I have been called a murderess to my face, here, in the palace. We aren't safe, Edouard."

"Maman," he said. He was trying to gather himself, to voice difficult words. *"Maman . . ."*

In the end, he could not utter them but set a piece of paper in my hands—a missive penned in an unfamiliar masculine script.

Strike at dawn Monday, it began, *when Notre-Dame first marks the hour. We will strike inside the palace at the same instant, sparing Charles—as a public abdication would serve us—but not his mother and brother, as they are a danger to—*

I let go a soft cry and pressed my fingertips to my lips. The letter fluttered to the table and stayed there. I turned my face from it; I wanted suddenly to retch.

Edouard brought his face close to mine. "Written by Navarre, *Maman,* to his commander in the field. The provost intercepted it at the city gate. Our scouts say that five thousand Huguenots are on the march toward Paris and will encamp outside her city walls on Sunday night."

"No," I said and closed my eyes.

He said nothing more, only hovered next me; like the lamp, his unseen face emanated warmth. In the room's heat, the smell of orange blossoms grew suffocating. Reason abandoned me. I had loved Navarre since his birth, and trusted him as I would a son; now, he had betrayed me. Whose blood had he seen in his visions? Had it been my children's, and my own?

I opened my eyes to stare down at my hands, at the ring infused with the power of the Gorgon's Head. *The star Algol, which the Arabs call* ra's al-Ghul, *the Demon's Head, and the Chinese call the Piled-Up Corpses.*

Two hours before dawn on the twenty-fourth of August, the star Algol will rise in the sign of Taurus . . . and precisely oppose warlike Mars. . . . France has never been in greater danger; nor have you.

This was Friday night, the twenty-second.

I thought of the huge entourage Navarre had brought with him to the wedding—most of them housed here, at the Louvre. Military commanders, captains, generals, all of his former comrades-in-arms—three hundred men.

"I welcomed him into my home," I whispered, "and he brought his army with him, in open daylight. Coligny may truly want his war in the Spanish Netherlands, but Navarre sent him here only to distract us. They are lying in wait for us. They mean to kill us in our beds."

"We must stop them," my son said softly.

I looked up at him. Edouard's eyes, infinitely black, glittered in the lamplight. I had worked so hard for peace, not knowing that we were already at war.

"We must strike first," I said.

I spent the next few hours with Edouard in the Council chamber, planning the attack. I recruited him to send a discreet messenger to the young Duke of Guise, directing him to gather men for an attack on Coligny's lodgings at the Hôtel de Béthizy. Coligny must be assassinated, and every one of his commanders killed. With my guidance, Edouard wrote the secret orders for the Swiss troops who protected the palace and the Scots who guarded the King: At the same instant that Guise moved against Coligny, our soldiers would attack the Huguenots sleeping at the Louvre.

To avoid mass slaughter, Edouard and I wrote down the names of those fated to die, all of them military commanders or strategists. I wanted no revenge, only the swift, if ruthless, execution of those who could bring war. With their leaders gone, the Huguenots would be crippled, unable to threaten the Crown or the city.

It was all to begin before dawn's light on Sunday, the twenty-fourth of August, when Saint-Germain's cathedral bell struck the third hour after midnight—one hour before the demon star, Algol, moved into precise opposition to warlike Mars.

When the list of the victims had been written, I looked somberly up at Edouard. "We must tell Charles," I said. Without the king's signature upon such a gruesome order, the guards would not obey it; and once the killing began, it would no longer be secret.

Edouard nodded. "It will be safer for him. We will have to reconcile him to our viewpoint."

"But not tonight," I said, sighing, and fell silent as Saint-Germain's bell signaled midnight and the first seconds of the Eve of Saint Bartholomew.

We parted then. Both of us were exhausted by the strain and retired to our separate apartments.

I did not dream that night; my long nightmare had grown waking now. I abandoned my bed and pulled a chair to the window to stare out at the brooding darkness and listen to the occasional faint shouts of angry men in Paris streets. I thought of Aunt Clarice's strength in those awful hours before we escaped the Palazzo Medici; I thought of Ruggieri's cruel words during our final conversation, and my response:

The impact of one child upon the future was, I thought, safe, but three . . .

What are you saying? That I should blame my sons? That I should lift my hand against them?

The veil will tear, Nostradamus had whispered, *and blood be loosed . . .*

I answered them silently with Clarice's words. *Sometimes, to protect one's own blood, it is necessary to let the blood of others.* The House of Valois must survive at all costs.

I had made my choice; I would not sacrifice my own.

Outside the Louvre's gates, the shouting began in earnest at sunrise and grew steadily in volume throughout the day. As soon as it was light, I dressed and went to find Edouard. He was in the Council room with Marshals Tavannes and Cossé, commanders of the Paris militia, and the city provost; the guards at the door insisted they were not to be disturbed. I left word for the Duke of Anjou to come to my chambers after his meeting and went to my cabinet to write a message to Anna d'Este about the specifics of our plan. I did not dare write her son the Duke of Guise directly but instead trusted Anna to relay the information to him; she would no doubt be delighted to tell her son that he had been chosen to lead the strike against Coligny. I instructed her to send his confirmation as soon as possible.

Edouard arrived an hour later in my antechamber looking haggard. He had not slept at all either but had roused Tavannes and Cossé and read them Navarre's letter. Both men heartily approved of our decision to strike first. At dawn, Edouard was visited by the provost and militia commanders, who revealed that street fighting had increased. Gangs of armed Huguenots were roving the city, alarming citizens. Merchants had boarded up their shops, innkeepers their taverns. Members of the militia were quietly distributing arms to Catholics eager to protect themselves from the growing threat.

We agreed that Charles should be told that evening, after supper. The King was fond of crusty old Tavannes and, of all our confidants, trusted him best; I insisted that Tavannes be the one to tell Charles the truth. Once he had time to recover from the shock, Edouard and I would appear with the fateful royal order and its list of victims, for the King's signature.

At midday, when Navarre and his cousin Condé returned from their vigil at Coligny's bedside, a scuffle broke out between his Huguenot bodyguards and the King's Scotsmen, fueled by incendiary comments on both sides. I did not witness the fighting, which quickly broke up—though not before one of Charles's senior guards lost an ear.

I saw Charles briefly after lunch. His conversation with Navarre and Condé had left him elated; he revealed eagerly that Doctor Paré was very pleased with the patient's progress. Coligny's wound showed no signs of infection and was already beginning to heal.

"As soon as he is well enough," Charles said cheerfully, "I will move him to the Louvre and care for him myself." His features suddenly went cold with anger. "Did they tell you, *Maman,* that they found the man who led the assassin onto the Guise's property? He has confessed that the shooter was Maurevert. It's only a matter of time before we apprehend him.

"But it was Guise after all who ordered the killing—what nerve, playing tennis with me that very morning and smiling at the Admiral!"

I shook my head and feigned shock but said nothing.

By late afternoon, my nerves were utterly frayed. For appearances' sake, Edouard and I were required to separate and attend to our usual business—he to discuss the matter of military pensions with his advisers and treasurers, I to hear petitions and, afterward, to take Margot to my chambers for an hour of embroidery. Despite the palpable tension at the Louvre, my daughter was obliviously cheerful. At my mild statement that she appeared in good spirits, Margot blushed and smiled primly.

"Henri is very kind," she said. "You were right, *Maman*—it is not so terrible after all."

Had we been speaking about any other man, my smile would have been genuine. I waited until the subject shifted, then put my hand upon my daughter's arm.

"I'm troubled," I said, "by the violence in the streets. Ever since the Admiral was shot, I worry that something else terrible will happen. It might be wise . . ." I paused. "Perhaps it would be better, Margot, if you slept in your own room tonight."

She looked up from her embroidery with a start. "You don't really think Henri is in danger, do you?"

I looked away quickly, casting about for words that warned but did not frighten. "Not that anyone is in danger, but that we should be cautious. Perhaps you heard that there was a fight between your husband's guards and your brother's today. I'm merely saying . . ." Anxiety stole my words, my breath. I stared down at my sewing, suddenly terrified for my daughter, and aware that I had no idea how to protect her. I dared not take her into my confidence; she would have been aghast, disgusted, she would have gone directly to Navarre.

She saw my panic and dropped her sewing in midstitch. "*Maman!* Did you have a dream? Is something dreadful going to happen to Henri?"

I looked up at her, for an instant speechless; then habit overcame me, and I managed a feeble smile. "Of course not," I said. "Nothing bad is going to happen. I'm simply worried, as any mother would be, with all that has happened. Indulge me, Margot. Retire early tonight, to your own bed."

"All right, *Maman,*" she said, but her eyes were narrowed; she saw through my false cheer, with the result that I dared say nothing else to her about the matter.

After supper, Edouard, Tavannes, and I went in search of Charles. Outside the guarded, half-ajar door of the King's apartments, we stopped, and the Duke of Anjou handed Navarre's incriminating letter to the Marshal. We had agreed that Tavannes would lead Charles to his office; after allowing time for the Marshal to break the news to the King, Edouard and I would present the list of those to be executed.

Tavannes went inside while Edouard and I drew back, carefully out of the

King's sight; I glimpsed Charles as he and Tavannes passed through the corridor. As the old Marshal held open the door to the cabinet, I heard him murmur something to Charles, who stopped on the threshold and let go a panicked cry.

"Dear God! Don't tell me he is dead!"

Tavannes murmured reassurances; the King went inside, and the Marshal closed the door behind them. Edouard and I scurried inside the apartment and—ignoring the King's bodyguard who stood watch—lingered just outside the door, like the guilty conspirators we were. I strained my ears but heard little save for the calm, steady rumble of Tavannes's voice.

It was interrupted suddenly by a shrill howl, then an angry curse. Edouard abruptly dismissed the guard. As he did, something hard and heavy thudded loudly against the cabinet's interior wall. Edouard moved to open the door, but I stayed his hand; I had thought that Charles would not dare strike old Tavannes, but I also knew the Marshal was rugged enough to handle the King's physical outbursts.

I knew the precise passage in Navarre's letter that had prompted the violent reaction:

> *Coligny's injury complicates matters, but I, too, have earned the King's trust and can guide him easily into our clutches and, once there, convince him to abdicate. Without his mother and brother, he will be quite helpless.*

There followed wracking sobs, and coughing, and finally, gentle weeping. At the last, I nodded to Edouard, and we entered quietly.

Tavannes stood in front of the King's desk, a dark, liquid slash across the breast and shoulder of his dull gold doublet. He was wiping his face with a handkerchief, and when he looked up at me, his blind, clouded eye roving wildly, he lowered the cloth to reveal a brown stain on his clean-shaven chin. Behind him, the far wall held a large, irregular splatter of the same dark brown liquid; on the floor just below, a silver inkwell lay on its side, bleeding onto the carpet.

Charles was nowhere to be seen, but soft whimpers emanated from behind the desk. I hurried round to find my son huddled beneath it, rocking; I pushed the chair aside and knelt beside him.

"Lies," he moaned, his baleful gaze rolling up at me; tears coursed steadily down his cheeks. "You mean to break my heart with lies."

"Your Majesty," I began calmly—but at the sight of his suffering, and at the sheer horror of what I had to do, I broke, put my face in my hands, and wept myself. For several breaths, I failed to master my emotions; Edouard and Tavannes watched, hushed.

I caught my breath finally and looked up at poor Charles.

"It is awful, Your Majesty," I admitted, with complete sincerity. "And it wounds me to bring such horrible news. But we could not spare you such ugliness; too much is at stake."

"It isn't true," he countered fiercely, but his features crumpled at once and he cried with renewed fervor. "How could he betray me so? He loves me, *Maman,* as the son he never had. He told me so . . ."

I leaned forward to take his hand and was gratified when he did not pull away. "Charles, my darling, this is a hard truth, a terrible truth, but you must be brave now. You are our King; we look to you to save us."

He cringed. "But what can I do? I cannot believe this, *Maman!* I don't know whom to believe anymore! Coligny warned me—"

"He warned you," I said smoothly, "that Edouard and I wished him ill—precisely because he knew that, if we uncovered his plot, this moment would come."

He shuddered from another ragged sob. "But I don't know what to do!"

"That is why we are here." I reached into my sleeve and pulled out the fatal document, then glanced up at Tavannes. "Marshal, if you would be so kind . . ." I nodded in the direction of the overturned inkwell; the old man hurried off in search of a fresh one.

"There is a way to prevent this, and the war that would certainly follow," I crooned, unscrolling the paper. "You can stop it with your signature. We must finish, Your Majesty, what Maurevert began."

He blinked suspiciously at my own flawed, irregular scrawl on the white page and recoiled faintly.

"An order, Your Majesty," I said, "striking at the Huguenots before they strike at us. The names of the conspirators are listed here. We must do more than cut off the Hydra's head; we must remove all those who would bring war against us in Paris."

He snatched the list from me and squinted down at it for a long moment. I feared he would quail at the stark reality it represented, but the skin beneath his eye began to twitch rapidly as he passed easily from tortured sorrow to incandescent rage.

"They would lock me in prison," he muttered bitterly, "and steal my crown. They would murder my family . . ."

"Yes," I whispered. "Do you remember now, Charles, what you said to me in the carriage on our dreadful escape from Meaux? They would have killed us all then. They have been waiting all this time for another opportunity. . . . And I gave them one. I trusted them." I paused. "What sort of man is Gaspard de Coligny—daring to threaten you if you do not yield to *his* will? Daring to violate an order forbidding the movement of troops to the Netherlands—an order signed by your own hand? He has never shown the proper respect to you, Your Majesty. He has laughed at you privately all this time."

Charles grimaced with fury. "Then kill them all," he whispered, his voice raw and ugly. "Why spare any of them, *Maman*?" His voice rose to an impassioned roar. "Kill the bastards! Kill them all! Kill them all!"

At that moment, Tavannes reappeared with the inkwell; I glimpsed the troubled face of the dismissed guard, who had also reappeared. He had heard the King's cries but remained outside as the Marshal closed the door on him.

I motioned for Tavannes to set the inkwell on the floor beside me as Edouard handed me the quill.

"Let us show ourselves to be better than our enemies," I told Charles. "We will not, as they would, kill the innocent."

He calmed a bit to study the order. "When will it happen?"

"Tonight," Edouard answered. "In the hours just before dawn. You would do well to keep to your bedchamber. I have arranged for extra security; we will not let you come to harm."

Breathing heavily, Charles looked up at him, then back down at the list in his hand. "May they all die miserably," he said, "and their souls go straight to Hell."

Solemnly, I handed him the pen.

Forty-five

Edouard and I remained with Charles for a few hours to calm him, and to ensure that he did not leave his apartments. By eleven o'clock, my younger son and I went to our separate apartments; it would be best, we decided, to retire as usual to avoid stirring anyone's suspicions. I struggled to hide my growing anxiety as my ladies dressed me for bed; I dismissed them before my nervousness grew too apparent.

I climbed into my bed but was not able to hold still, much less sleep; my window overlooked the Louvre's courtyard, and I was terrified of what I might soon see. After two hours of fidgeting, I lit the lamp, slipped into my dressing gown, and made my way through my darkened apartments to my closet.

The windowless little room was hot and stale, but it offered a sense of security; in it, I could not see or be seen. I locked the door and resolutely began to leaf through a stack of correspondence—some letters from our diplomats abroad, others from petitioners—then settled down to read. The attempt was futile: I stared at one letter from our ambassador to Venice for almost an hour without making much sense of it; foolishly, I attempted to write a reply, but words eluded me and I dropped the quill. The heat left me light-headed. I leaned back in the chair, closed my eyes, and almost dozed, but instead of dreaming, I drifted off into memory.

I thought of Margot in her beautiful wedding dress, and of how she had bewitched Navarre with her smile. I remembered Ruggieri, standing at the edge of the crowd at the wedding—how his hair had grown streaked with silver, how he had not smiled at the sight of me; I wondered whether he was still inhabiting Paris's dangerous streets.

I thought of Henri of Navarre: how, as a little boy, he had run out from the tennis gallery onto the courtyard lawn and seen, with me, the piled-up corpses of Algol; I wondered whether he saw them now.

The bell of Saint-Germain tolled twice, for each hour past midnight, and my pulse quickened. In an hour, the killing would begin.

I forced myself to breathe, forced my limbs to relax in the chair, and summoned the past again. I thought of all my children when they were young: my poor, sweet Elizabeth, feeble François; and Charles—even then surly and cruel; my darling Edouard, my little Margot, and even Mary, Queen of Scots, with her sour, disdainful smile. They moved and laughed and spoke in my memory, and I smiled and wept and sighed with them. I thought of my husband, Henri, how he had loved them all, and gathered them into his arms.

Rivulets of sweat, mingled with tears, trickled down my cheeks.

I saw Navarre, leaning against the railing looking out toward the Ile-de-la-Cité. *I have come because I trust you,* Tante *Catherine—because I believe, most irrationally, that we have seen the same evil coming and intend to avert it.*

I saw Jeanne, standing on the lawn beside three-year-old Henri, staring after Nostradamus with a curious smile. *What a silly little man.*

I opened my eyes to the lamp's flickering yellow glow. In the furious preparations for Margot's wedding, I had never read the letter that Jeanne had written me on her deathbed, as I had not wanted grief to interfere with the joyful celebrations; but even grief would be a welcome distraction from intolerable dread.

I took a key from the top drawer of my desk and turned to the carved wainscoting near my elbow. Down the span of a hand, and another span to the left, almost hidden by the leg of my desk, was a small keyhole. I unlocked it; the wood panel sprang open, revealing the small secret compartment built into the wall.

Inside were documents I had almost forgotten: the yellowed bit of parchment that bore the words my dead husband had dictated to Ruggieri at Chaumont, and the quatrain in Nostradamus's hand, written shortly before he had left Blois. There were jewels, as well—including a priceless ruby and a pearl and diamond choker that Pope Clement had given me for my wedding; there was also the small velvet box from Jeanne, which held the exquisite emerald brooch.

Beneath it rested her letter, still sealed. I picked it up, broke the wax, and began to read.

I am dying, dear friend, and must now confess my sins to you, although the pain of doing so is so great I can hardly grip the pen.

I told you that I had been tarnished by the decadence of the French Court. Perhaps it is truer to say that I yielded to my own wicked heart. When I said you were faithful but surrounded by evil, it was to myself I referred. I, who called myself your friend, betrayed you.

I loved your husband, Catherine, and after years of resisting each other we fell into sin. Though Henri surrendered to the temptation of the flesh, his every thought and word revealed that he possessed for you a far greater love than that shared by mere paramours. Even now, I cannot say why it was we sought each other out, or why sanity and virtue failed us so. It is the greatest regret of my life, and as I go to meet death, I desire your forgiveness more urgently than I do God's.

My Henri, my only son, was the product of our fall. I know that you love him, and I am glad for it. Please, do not divulge this painful truth to him; let it die with us. His heart will be broken badly enough by my death. I should not want to harm him further from the grave.

My love for the King was not my only transgression. I am guilty of withholding this truth so that my son would be able to marry his half sister, Margot. Perhaps you understand better why I was devoted to protecting Henri's rights as First Prince of the Blood, and eager to see him wed into his father's family. As a Bourbon by name and a Valois by blood, he is doubly entitled to the throne. Your husband, I think, would have approved.

Forgive me, my friend—and if you cannot, at least show kindness to my Henri. He has inherited his father's honesty and tender heart, as well as his sincere affection for you.

I go now to God with prayers for you upon my lips.

Jeanne

The letter fell into my lap; I raised my hands to my face and let go bitter, wracking sobs, strangely unaccompanied by tears. I felt deep, poignant sadness—not because of the betrayal but because of the suffering the three of us had endured in our efforts to find happiness. For some time I sat, overwhelmed by sorrow, before a stark and dreadful revelation brought me to my feet.

In my memory, the Duchess d'Etampes's laughter tinkled as she ran nearly naked into the night, with her lover, King François, in close pursuit.

Louise is a lovely girl, don't you think?

And François's irritable reply: *Don't vex me, Anne. . . . Henri's cousin Jeanne—she's of marriageable age, and brings with her the crown of Navarre.*

Had I allowed myself to be repudiated—had I not spilled blood to purchase children—might Jeanne have taken my place? Would her son now be King?

My surroundings fell away: I stood suddenly in the courtyard of the Louvre, my bare feet on warm cobblestones. In the blackness, a man lay prostrate, his face turned from me.

Catherine, he groaned. His head lolled toward me, and I saw him clearly. His face was long, bearded, and handsome—like my late Henri's, like his father's—the very face that had always visited my dark dreams.

I sank beside him and touched his cheek. "How can I help you, Navarre," I whispered, "when you would kill me and my children?"

Venez a moi. Aidez-moi. A spot of black appeared on his brow, between his eyebrows, and spread like a stain. It spilled down the sides of his face and pooled upon the stone.

I came back to my cabinet with a start and at once bent down to reach into the compartment. I pulled out the other papers—the message from my dead husband, the seer's quatrain—unfolded them both and set them side by side on my desk.

Catherine, for love of you I do this for love of you this time I come
My one true heir will rule
Destroy what is closest to your heart
Destroy what is closest to your heart

One skein still runs true
Restore it, and avert the rising tide of evil
Break it, and France herself will perish
Drowned in the blood of her own sons

I looked up from the pages and closed my eyes. In my mind, Navarre still lay groaning at my feet, gripped by the final throes of mortal anguish. His lips trembled as they struggled to form a single word:

Catherine

I bent down and put my fingers on them, to stop him from uttering his last.

"I have come all the way from Florence, Monsieur," I whispered, "too far to let you die."

I lay reason down like a burden and went out into the night.

When I stepped out of my apartments into the corridor, the three royal bodyguards flanking the door turned to regard me with surprise.

"Madame la Reine," the senior of them hissed, as he and his fellows executed cursory bows. He was no more than eighteen, a clean-shaven, gangling youth with russet hair and a face full of freckles to match; the knees beneath the hem of his red kilt were likewise spotted. "The hour is about to strike! Please, it would be safest for you to remain in your chambers."

"Where is your captain? I must speak to him at once!"

"Madame, forgive me," the Scot replied, "but he is intensely occupied at present; it may be some time before we can bring him to you."

"But there *is* no time!" I hesitated and peered down the shadowed corridor. Since the trouble in the streets had begun, the wall sconces had remained lit at night, the better to aid the patrols. "I'll go to him myself. Where is he?"

My challenger hesitated and lowered his voice to a barely audible whisper. "Madame, he awaits the signal outside the lodgings of the King of Navarre."

I frowned, staring down the dim, narrow hallway. Beyond it, out of sight, lay the long gallery that joined the old fortress to the new southwestern wing, where Navarre and his party were housed. If I went at top speed, I could arrive at my destination within minutes; even that might not be soon enough.

I lifted my skirts and began to run. The senior guard followed, whispering furiously.

"*Madame la Reine!* Please! I am bound to keep you safe!"

"Then do so!" I snapped but did not slow.

He outpaced me easily and positioned himself in front of me, his hand upon the hilt of his sword.

"Swear to me," I panted, "that you will help me find Navarre, and keep him safe! It is all a horrible mistake—he must not die!"

"Madame," he said, "I will."

We hurried down the stairs to the second floor, where the King and Anjou were housed, and proceeded west through the old Louvre's cramped, low-ceilinged corridors. They opened finally onto the broader halls of the long gallery leading to the new wing built by my father-in-law.

The gallery was blocked by a barricade of soldiers facing west: four Swiss halberdiers, each wearing the square white cross upon the back and breast of his tunic, all bearing tall pikes topped with razor-keen blades. Four kilted Scots accompanied them—two with arquebuses, two with broadswords.

"Make way for the Queen!" my man gasped as we approached.

Eight men whirled about to regard us with disbelief.

"Jesus," one whispered.

A ripple of rapid, barely perceptible bows followed.

"*Madame la Reine!*" the head bodyguard exclaimed sotto voce. Sweat trickled from beneath his cap and glittered in the light from a hall sconce before he wiped it with the back of his hand; his eyes were bright with nerves. "You cannot come here! Please return to your chambers."

"I must speak to your captain," I said impatiently. "Navarre must be spared. Let me pass!"

The highest-ranking Swiss said, "The hour is upon us, *Madame la Reine.* We dare not let you through."

I began to push past them, taking advantage of their reluctance to touch my royal person, but the halberdier stepped into my path.

"I cannot argue!" I said, not bothering to lower my voice. "It is a matter of life or death! If you love your own neck, you will step aside *now*."

"Let me relay a message then, to the captain of the guards," the halberdier said, "for your own safety, Madame."

His manner was unctuous, his gaze insincere. If I trusted him, Navarre would die. I took a step to my right, and he matched it, polite but determined.

"Get me through!" I demanded of my freckled young guard.

He put a hand on the hilt of his sheathed sword.

A sound penetrated the palace walls, causing the men to freeze: the low, dolorous toll of Saint-Germain's bell. It rang once, twice . . .

On a nearby Paris street, the Duke of Guise and his men were breaking down the doors of the Hôtel de Béthizy.

In my mind, Ruggieri whispered, *It may already be too late.*

On the third chime, I propelled myself past the guards; my young Scot came to himself and followed. The others dared not desert their posts; we ignored their muted calls and dashed into the gallery.

It was a long, arduous run, past paintings, statues, dazzling murals framed by Cellini's gilded molding. To our right, tall windows looked onto the paved courtyard, where Swiss halberdiers and crossbowmen waited beneath a great marble statue of the god Vulcan reclining on his anvil, his freshly forged spear lifted heavenward. The raised windows admitted a sultry breeze, which stirred the sconce flames, casting looming shadows on the walls. My side pained me; my breathing grew ragged, but I dared not slow. As we neared the southwestern wing, I heard shouting: The attack had already begun.

The gallery ended abruptly at a corridor that also served as a staircase landing. As I passed, two men in nightshirts hurtled screaming down the steps from the floor above.

Aidez-nous! "Help us!"

They almost collided with my young Scot, who drew his sword and bellowed, "Make way for the Queen!"

The wild-eyed victims seemed not to hear him, or to see me at all; they fled shrieking down the stairs that led out of the palace to the courtyard.

Ignoring the frantic footfall behind us as others fled down the stairs, we continued on, and made our way into the hallways of the new wing. Soon we were at the entrance to Navarre's antechamber. Across its open threshold, a naked man lay on his side—pale-haired, with the handsome, sculpted muscles of youth and a bloody gash at the juncture of his neck and shoulder; dark rivulets coursed across his hairless chest and ribs onto the marble floor. From beyond him, in the antechamber, came the shouts and groans of the battlefield.

"Madame la Reine!" my young Scot ordered. "Put your hands upon my hips, and cling to me! Do not lift your head!"

I obeyed without a blush, pressing myself against his sweat-soaked back. We took two staggering steps forward into the chamber, dark save for lamplight coming from the open door of the bedchamber beyond. I glimpsed movement in the dimness, the flailing of limbs, the whistling sweep of swords, the lurching of torsos, all accompanied by grunts, screams, curses. The room had becoming a writhing mass of bodies, but I did not try to interpret them. I ducked my head and held fast to the thick leather belt encircling my savior's narrow hips. The muscles in his back bunched as he hefted his weapon; I winced as it crashed against another's sword.

Death to the Huguenots! a man cried out, and was answered hoarsely:

Death to Catholic assassins!

"Navarre!" I cried, my words swallowed by the young Scot's flesh. "Navarre, it is Catherine!"

"We come in peace!" my Scot bellowed, as he struck out, again and again. "Make way for the Queen!"

A horrid gurgling came from in front of us; my man's muscles suddenly relaxed as he lowered his sword and we advanced two steps. On the second, I nearly stumbled over a body and was forced to let go of the leather belt for an instant in order to lift my tangled skirts and hop clear.

Everywhere around us, innocents screamed for help. The Scot collided with one of his own and spoke frantically in Gaelic; I made out the word *Navarre*. The leather belt pulled me along as he turned toward the door to the bedchamber. I stumbled again over a sprawling limb and lost my grip. My man quickly turned to offer me his hand.

As he did, I glimpsed up. Limned by the window, a man's black form stood; a tiny flame, smaller than that of a lamp, floated in front of his shoulder. I caught the smell of burning match cord just as my Scot cried out.

A deafening boom followed, accompanied by the tang of gunpowder. My guardian fell backward onto me, knocking me to my knees. I struggled from underneath his limp weight; in the dimness, I made out his open eyes and reached for his chest. My fingers fumbled, searching for the rise and fall of breath, for a beat, and found neither; they slipped into a warm, hot chasm near his heart and recoiled instantly.

I pushed myself up just as the arquebusier was reloading his weapon and staggered into the bedchamber. It was brighter there, given the bedside lamp, but no less chaotic: a dozen bodies—of Huguenots, naked or in thin nightshirts, of Swiss soldiers, of Scottish royal guards—sprawled on the floor, while the survivors fought on.

On the far side of the bed, the captain of the guards, his sword wielded in battle against a bald, cursing Huguenot, caught sight of me.

"*Madame la Reine!* My God!"

He dared not disengage to rush to me but returned his attention to his combatant. Nearby, at the foot of the bed—five fighting men away—stood Navarre.

He was still in his white undershirt and black leggings, as though he had not dared to undress completely. His damp shirt clung to his chest and back, his hair to his scalp. He was grimacing, his eyes ablaze, his face gleaming with perspiration as he wielded his sword against that of an equally fierce Swiss soldier. At the captain's cry, he glanced up quickly at me, and his face went slack with shock.

I ducked my head at the whizzing blades. "Navarre!" I scrabbled past another pair of fighting men, and another. I held my hand out to him, not knowing whether he would grasp it or cut it off. As I did, a figure stepped into my path.

It was the white-haired giant of a Huguenot who had threatened me two nights before, at my public supper; he gripped a short sword at the level of his waist. He leered down at me, baring his great yellow teeth, and drew it back, the better to plunge it forward and run me through. I staggered backward; my foot caught on a prone body, and I went down, arms flailing.

The grinning giant bent over me, then just as suddenly toppled sideways, encouraged by the flat of a sword against his skull. Navarre appeared beside me, his eyes wild with rage, confusion, and despair. I looked on him with infinite hope: He had not killed me.

"Catherine!" His voice was barely audible over the roar.

"I've come to help! Follow me to safety," I shouted, but he shook his head, unable to hear, and gave me his hand.

As he pulled me to my feet, I glanced over the slope of his shoulder to see a white equal-armed cross looming; as the Swiss swordsman lunged toward him, I cried out. Navarre turned swiftly to him and reared backward from the waist in an effort to avoid the oncoming blade. He failed; the tip split his brow with a thud and he dropped to the floor.

I fell to my knees beside him as his eyelids fluttered.

"Help us," he whispered and fell still.

Bright blood welled up from his forehead and spilled onto the carpet. Gasping, I unfastened my dressing gown, gathered up what I could of the hem, and pressed it hard against the wound. Above us, the Swiss soldier bent his elbow and pulled his weapon back, ready to deliver the final blow.

I crawled atop Navarre and lay my body atop his.

"Kill him," I shouted, "and you kill the Queen!"

Beneath me, Navarre stirred and groaned. The stunned soldier lowered his weapon and stepped back. He, too, fell suddenly away, and I looked up to see the young Prince of Condé, his features slack, his eyes very wide. At the sight of Navarre bloodied, he let go a short cry, then pulled off his nightshirt and flung it at me. I pulled my sodden dressing gown away; the wound was still bleeding, and the victim's brow swelling, but the skull had not been split. I tied the shirt around Navarre's head and looked up at Condé, who leaned his ear toward me.

"Help me get him to safety!" I cried.

Condé did not hesitate. He pulled me up, and together we dragged Henri to his feet. Navarre was dazed, unsteady, but he understood enough to wrap his arms about my shoulder and stagger with me behind Condé, who raised his sword and slashed his way past the Swiss and Scots—some of whom drew back, chastened and confused, at the sight of me.

"Why?" Henri sobbed as we lurched into the antechamber, where the fighting had abruptly stopped. A score of his comrades lay slaughtered on the marble. "Why?"

I did not answer as we headed into the corridor but addressed Condé, whose eyes were guarded but free from the rancor that I had always encountered before. "This way." I pointed east.

We passed the staircase—quiet now—and entered the deserted gallery. A humid breeze had found the drapes and softly stirred them. Two floors below us, out in the courtyard, victims cringed in Vulcan's colossal shadow. Henri let go a wail and stopped to stare through the window, his eyes stark with horror.

More than a hundred terrified Huguenots had fled from the palace into the courtyard, only to discover the Swiss waiting with their crossbows and halberds. Mounds of bodies were heaped along the western wall; in the glare of torches, a dozen screaming men huddled together as the crossbowmen forced them, step by step, back over the blood-slicked cobblestones onto the waiting blades of the halberdiers. I pressed a fist to my lips, to stifle bitter nausea and grief. I had ordered this because I feared war, because I had not wanted men to die.

Condé watched darkly, too stricken for words.

"Why?" Henri moaned again; he turned to me. "Why do you do this to us?"

"We must not stop here like this," I said. "If we do, they will find us and kill both of you. Come."

I stole a lamp from its sconce and guided them to a small door at the midpoint at the gallery, which hid a narrow, spiraling staircase—an escape route known only to the royal family. The stale air inside was wilting, and Navarre swaying, but we managed to make our way down three flights to the blessedly cool cellars. I led them past great, ancient wine barrels to a prison cell and took the rusted key hanging from the wall to open it. Condé helped his cousin to one of the hanging planks that served as a bed; Henri sat down and leaned heavily against the earthen wall while I lingered outside—then closed the bars and locked them. Both men started as the metal clanged shut.

Condé flared. "What do you mean to do with us? A public execution?"

"I mean to keep you here," I said, "until I can determine my next action. It is the one place you will be safe. Before God, I will not harm you."

Henri pulled the blood-soaked undershirt from his head and stared down at it, disbelieving. "Why do you kill our fellows?" His tone was mournful, dazed.

"Because you meant to kill *us*," I answered fiercely. "Because your army is marching on Paris even now. Because you meant to kill the Dauphin, and me, and steal my son's throne."

He and Condé stared at me as if I had suddenly stripped off my nightgown.

"You're mad," Condé whispered. "There is no army."

Navarre put a hand gingerly to his swelling brow and squinted as though the feeble light of the lamp pained him. "Whose lies are these?"

"I have your letter to your commander in the field," I said, "revealing the plot to make war on Paris and force Charles's abdication."

"You lie!" Condé said. "You lie to make war on us! Pardaillan, Rochefoucauld, all my gentlemen—you have killed them for a lie!" He began suddenly, bitterly, to weep into his hands. Navarre put a hand upon his shoulder and turned to me.

"Bring this letter to me," he said, "and I will show you a forgery. We have committed no crime, save to tolerate Coligny's boorishness on the matter of the Spanish Netherlands. *Madame la Reine,* for the love of God you must stop this. All my men"—his voice broke—"fifty of them came from their own quarters to sleep upon my floor, because they feared for me after the attempt on the Admiral's life. And now they are dead . . ." He let go a gulping sob, and lowered his face.

"What of your army?" I demanded. "Edouard's scouts say that it is on its way and will encamp outside our walls tonight."

"There is no army!" Condé cried out. "Anjou and his scouts lie! Madame, your younger son is as crazy as his brother—but more dangerously so!"

"Don't insult him!" I cried, but my anger was tinged with growing confusion. I gripped the bars separating us. "You came here armed for war. You came here ready to fight."

Henri lifted his face, so contorted by grief that he could not open his eyes to look on me. "We came here afraid for our lives," he said and bowed his head.

Muted by stone and earth, Saint-Germain's bells marked the fourth hour after midnight. Up in the heavens, the star Algol moved opposite Mars: Coligny and some two hundred Huguenots who had patrolled the area around the Hôtel de Béthizy were dead. My grip on the bars loosened; my palms slid against the cool metal as the weight of my actions forced me to my knees. I was the author of this—I, and my fierce love for my misbegotten sons.

"God help me," I whispered. "God help us all."

Forty-six

I found the back stairs leading up from the cellar to the second floor of the south wing and the secret passageway to the Duke of Anjou's apartments; several times, my knees buckled, and I was obliged to lean against the wall and rest. I arrived, trembling, in the closet off Edouard's bedroom. Lignerolles was dozing on the small bed there and sat up with a gasp as I pushed open the creaking door. He lit the lamp at once and, at the sight of Henri's blood on my gown, shrieked.

"Who goes there?" Edouard called from the bedchamber. Dressed in a thin nightshirt, Lignerolles jumped up and took my elbow; by then, I was shaking so much I could hardly stand.

Edouard appeared in the archway, wrapping a silk robe over his bare flesh. I looked on him as if for the first time: His face was not, like mine, drawn and tortured and dazed by guilt, but he gaped at the sight of me and caught my arm. We hurried from the bedroom—where the yellow-headed Robert-Louis sat wide-eyed and naked, the covers pulled up to his chest—to the antechamber, where my son sat me in a chair.

"My God," he cried. "*Maman,* you are bleeding!" He wheeled on Lignerolles, and the guards and valets who suddenly appeared. "For God's sake, get her a doctor! And fetch a basin and linens at once!" He turned back and crouched beside my chair. "Where did they hurt you?"

I rested a violently trembling hand on his forearm. "No doctor," I said. "I'm not hurt."

"But the blood—" He touched my hair; I looked down at the braid falling over my shoulder and saw that it, too, was stained with Henri's blood.

"I was foolish," I said heavily. "I made the mistake of leaving my chambers. There were Huguenots . . . they stained me with their blood."

"But how . . . Where did you come from?" He looked in the direction of the closet; I averted my eyes and did not answer.

Lignerolles arrived with a basin of orange blossom water and a towel; Edouard dabbed the towel in the basin and smoothed it over my face. It came away bloodied.

"Look at your lovely dressing gown," he clucked soothingly. "It's ruined . . . How did you come across so much blood? This is not like you, *Maman,* to be so reckless." He set my dirty hand in the basin and gently washed it. "What in God's name were you doing?"

I looked up at him. "Edouard . . . the letter from Navarre to his commander in the field. I must see it at once."

He paused to wring out the towel. "Why?"

"Because it might be a forgery."

His gaze, which had been so keenly focused on me, retreated subtly inward. "That would be impossible."

"Why? It was the Provost of Marchands, was it not, who gave it to you? Can he be trusted? Can your scouts?"

"If he could not, I would not have him in charge of the city's defenses. Of course he can be trusted—and the scouts, too! What kind of question is that?"

"I would like to see Navarre's letter, please," I said. "Certainly it is still in your possession."

He scowled, incredulous, and loosed an exasperated gasp. "I have no idea where it is. I will ask my secretary to find it in the morning."

"And I should like to speak to your scout," I said. "The one who reported that the Huguenot army is on its way to Paris. I would be curious to learn where it is now."

"You don't believe me," he said. He gave a short, nervous laugh, the way that my cousin Ippolito had when I had asked him about all the other girls.

"I only want to see the proof for myself," I told him.

Just as Ippolito had, he grew abruptly furious. "What is the point of all this? What can be gained now from studying evidence that has already proved damning? They are all dead; nothing will bring them back to life! Even if we have made a terrible mistake, it is for the best—they can never again wage war against us, never!" He narrowed his eyes at me. "You have been talking to someone. Who?" His fingers dug into the tender flesh of my upper arms. "Who tells you these lies?"

I stared into his faithless eyes, and my heart broke; he had played me as easily as he had his innocent sister. I gazed beyond him then, at the windows overlooking the haunted courtyard. He knew, of course, that Charles was sickly and could not live much longer; Navarre and the Huguenots would have been the only real threat to his reign. Coligny had merely presented him with an opportunity to rid himself of his chief rivals.

I should not have been surprised by my son's ruthlessness, knowing what I did of his mother.

"Cosimo Ruggieri," I whispered. "He said that I would be betrayed."

The bodies of the dead lay in the courtyard for more than a day, as the soldiers who had slaughtered them were needed to defend the palace. In the relentless sun, the stink grew intolerable; we shut the windows despite the heat, but the flies found their way inside along with the smell, which clung to our clothes and hair. I pulled the drapes and could not be coaxed outside.

The battle continued on the streets of Paris for five days while we fearful royals huddled inside the reinforced walls of the Louvre, listening to the screams and savage fighting outside the palace gates. The people misunderstood the assault on the rue de Béthizy and the dispensation of arms to Catholics for self-protection. A rumor began that the King had ordered citizens to attack the Huguenots, and it spread with a vengeance.

Over the course of a week, seventy thousand innocents died in Paris and the countryside. Responsibility for the attack was laid, rightfully, at my door: *Madame la Serpente,* they call me now, *the Black Queen.*

I will not stop them from telling the truth. But now my adopted countrymen believe that I had planned the attack from the very beginning, luring first Coligny, then Navarre, as part of my scheme to eradicate the Huguenot movement.

Guise's attack on the Hôtel de Béthizy was a resounding success. Two of his common soldiers kicked down the door to the bedroom where Coligny lay with Doctor Paré at his bedside. When asked to identify himself, Coligny did so freely but looked on the soldiers with disdain, saying, "I should be killed by a gentleman, at least, and not these boors." In answer, one of the boors ran his sword through the Admiral's chest and flung him out the window. The body chanced to land right beside the delighted Duke of Guise.

By then, vengeful Catholics had taken to the streets; they castrated the body, dragged it through the city, and hurled the mutilated corpse into the Seine. Guise proudly delivered the head to me, in a silk pouch that failed to contain its overpowering stench. I turned away in horror and ordered it embalmed.

I managed to keep Henri of Navarre and his cousin the Prince of Condé out of Anjou's clutches. On the day Coligny died, I went secretly to Margot and told her of her brother's deception; together, we went to Charles and presented the evidence of Navarre's innocence. His Majesty was then easily convinced that Navarre and Condé—being Princes of the Blood—must be spared and issued a royal order. Afterward, once the fighting had eased, I went to the Provost of Marchands, who verified that no Huguenot army had ever arrived and that he had not been the one who personally intercepted the letter to Navarre's field commander. Edouard had produced it; the Provost, like Marshal Tavannes and other military leaders, had relied on the Duke of Anjou's word.

Edouard never came up with the incriminating letter supposedly written by Navarre, nor did we ever again confide in each other. I warned Navarre of Anjou's guile; he was grateful, though ravaged by grief at the loss of his companions and coreligionists, and resentful of the fact that, for his own protection, he was required to reconvert to Catholicism and remain at the Louvre under courteous house arrest.

The massacre born on Saint Bartholomew's Day broke Charles. He began—no doubt to Edouard's glee—to spiral down toward death.

September came, bringing with it relief from the heat and the violence. When the palace gates were again opened—a week and a day after Admiral Coligny's assassination—I received my first visitor behind the closed doors of my cabinet.

Cosimo Ruggieri was no longer ageless: The lamplight showed too clearly the silver in his hair and beard, the deep, wrinkled folds under his black eyes, the slackness of age beneath his jaw. He was gaunt, even skeletal, the ugliness of his irregular features enough to send the bravest child running to its mother. He had given up his customary red and now dressed all in black, like a Huguenot.

He entered to find me sitting at my desk as always, as if little time had elapsed since our last encounter, and as he always had, he bowed low. But when he raised his face to mine and the time came for him to utter a greeting, the words died upon his lips. Stricken, he stared at me.

"Cosimo," I said, rising. I came around my desk—perhaps to take his hand, perhaps to embrace him, I cannot say. But before I could reach him, my legs and my nerve at last gave way, and I sank to my knees, senseless with grief.

He knelt beside me. I clung to him, broken, weeping.

When I could speak, I gasped, "They have come again—the evil dreams. The dead are not even all buried, and yet the dreams have come. I will do what I must: I will kill my sons, by my own hand if I must, to make it stop. You warned me, and I would not hear. But I am listening now."

His expression was open and raw, free from the magician's dark glamour; the play of lamplight on his unshed tears dazzled me. "There is no more need of blood," he murmured. "Only set the demon free, and let the stars take their course."

I shook my head, not understanding.

He echoed my husband's words to me: *Destroy what is closest to your heart.*

It was a simple matter, accomplished in Ruggieri's temporary lodgings nearby: the casting of a circle, the placing of the bloodied pearl upon the altar, the invocation of the barbarous name. When the demon appeared—its presence announced by the sudden leaping of the flames and the prickling of gooseflesh on my arms—the magician thanked it and released it from its task. With all supernatural support withdrawn, my sons would meet their ends quickly.

Ruggieri would have disposed of the disempowered pearl himself, but I put my hand on it first. "This falls to me," I said.

My carriage rolled through quiet streets up to the banks of the river Seine, and the nervous driver waited while Ruggieri and I picked our way through scattered refuse down to the muddy shore.

The sky was cloudless that day, the air fresh; the previous day's storm had washed away the dust and the smell of decay that had permeated the city. For a moment, I stood looking south at the twin towers of Notre-Dame and the dainty spires of Sainte-Chapelle—sights that had filled my husband's namesake Henri of Navarre with such longing. And then I lifted my arm and hurled the pearl into the dark waters; it skipped twice and sank beneath the surface without a sound.

I, too, sank silently. Had it not been for Ruggieri's restraining arms, I would have fallen.

"I kept my promise," I whispered. The magician did not reply; he knew I did not speak to him.

"I kept my promise, my love," I repeated, my voice stronger. "A son of Valois will always sit upon the throne. Your one true heir will rule."

My blind selfishness, my unwillingness to step aside and release my husband to find his rightful wife had birthed incomprehensible misery. Beneath its weight I could neither stand nor walk, but Ruggieri nonetheless returned me to the carriage before I dissolved completely, like the spell.

Epilogue

I dreamt again that night.

I dreamt of Charles's imminent death, of the coughing and the fever, of the blood-soaked sheets that were changed almost every hour. Knowing that my own actions had hastened his final agony, I lay sobbing beside him in the bed, my arms around him as he whispered his final words: *Ma mere . . . Eh, ma mere . . .*

I dreamt, too, of Edouard, of the madness, deceit, and cruelty he no longer hid once he ascended the throne and stripped me of all power. I saw the brutality, the executions, the murders, the hatred he provoked until the people turned on him and he met his untimely end disemboweled, fittingly, by an assassin's blade.

I dreamt of Henri, King of France and Navarre, who—for the sake of peace—became a Catholic so that he could be crowned properly in a cathedral, saying, *Paris is well worth a Mass.* I saw Huguenots and Catholics reconciled and a country united, ruled at last by a canny monarch who put the welfare of its citizens before his own, a ruler so beloved by his subjects that they dubbed him Henri the Great. I saw a France at peace and prosperous.

I did not dream of blood. I woke grief-stricken yet relieved, with prayers of contrition on my lips.

I reported this all to Ruggieri the next afternoon, after he had arrived with his paltry belongings to settle into his new apartments at the Louvre. Clad in a plain black doublet and matching ruff, he seemed incongruous with the gilded walls, the delicate, feminine furniture, and the pale blue brocade curtains, pulled back to admit the waning light. Like me, he had slept little since the massacre on Saint Bartholomew's Day; at the sight of his exhaustion, I insisted he sit beside me in the antechamber while his valets thumped about in the bedroom, unpacking his things.

"I have done my best to make amends," I said softly. "But I cannot bring back all the innocents who have perished. And I cannot bear to watch my beloved sons—monsters though they may be—die. I have had more than enough sorrow for one life. Let me die, too, Cosimo."

He tilted his head to regard me somberly. Such an ugly face, yet as a shaft of light from the window penetrated his black eyes, I saw how very beautiful they were.

"Your time has not come, Catherine," he answered. "You have set things aright—and now you and I must live many more years to ensure that they remain so. Navarre still faces many obstacles."

Sickened by the thought, I turned my face from him and closed my eyes. I soon opened them again as something soft and warm brushed against my cheek. Ruggieri had risen from his chair to kneel beside mine; his fingers hovered, tender and unsteady, in the air between us.

"Do not give up hope," he said. "I promised you many years ago that I would see you through all challenges. I will remain always at your side."

"But I am damned, Cosimo," I said sadly.

"Then we are damned together, Caterina Maria Romula de' Medici."

I gazed at him, remembering the words he had uttered on the day the harlot died. His affection and loyalty had been deeper and more constant than those of Aunt Clarice, of my husband, of my own children. Just as I had been willing to risk everything for my Henri, so Cosimo had been willing to risk everything for me. At the thought, my dark, faltering heart opened.

"Only ever out of love," I whispered.

"Only ever out of love," he repeated solemnly, and his hand began again to reach for me.

I caught it in my own, drew him to me, and kissed him.

AFTERWORD

Henri of Navarre—better known to us as Henri IV, or Henri the Great to his countrymen—was the first of the Bourbon monarchs and certainly the most beloved. His marriage to Margot was eventually annulled, and he remarried Maria de' Medici, who gave him several children.

Catherine de' Medici lived to the venerable age of sixty-nine. She was an assiduous astrologer, a mathematical prodigy, and—according to many French historians—the most intelligent individual ever to sit on France's throne. The details of her horoscope as presented here are, to my feeble knowledge, accurate. She met twice with Nostradamus and eventually named him Physician of the Realm, although their conversations were never recorded. Her prophetic dreams are a matter of record; her daughter Margot wrote that her mother dreamt of King Henri's death as well as Edouard's victory at Jarnac.

The young Dauphine Catherine was indeed in danger of repudiation, and for the first ten years of her marriage was childless—after which she gave birth to ten children in as many years. Rumors began that she had relied on the talents of her court magician, Cosimo Ruggieri, to whom she was devoted. Catherine's collection of talismans and interest in magic were legendary; after her husband's death, she gave Diane de Poitiers the property at

Chaumont in exchange for Chenonceaux. When Diane moved to Chaumont, she was alarmed to discover pentacles painted on the floor and abandoned magical implements, with the result that she abandoned the property.

The star Algol—also known as the Head of the Gorgon—is still considered the most evil star by astrologers. It opposed Mars on the twenty-fourth of August, 1572, at roughly 4:00 a.m.—an hour after the Saint Bartholomew's Day Massacre began, as Mars passed through Catherine's ascendant, Taurus. Mars transits through an individual's ascendant augur periods of extreme crisis, possibly resulting in death.